City of Ladies

Praise for
The Cross and the Crown Series

"*The Altarpiece* by Dr. Sarah Kennedy is an imaginative response to a gaping void in our otherwise abundant knowledge of Tudor England. The novel illustrates the enormous challenges faced by England's nuns. Kennedy does an admirable job exposing unpromising choices and extreme difficulties faced by English Reformation era nuns. This book recommends itself first on the basis that it is quite simply a well told mystery story. It also makes Tudor England accessible to a large audience, and will hopefully even encourage scholarly interest in the subject." - *The Sixteenth Century Journal*

"Sarah Kennedy's debut novel, *The Altarpiece*, is not one to be missed. The thoroughly absorbing story, as finely wrought as the missing artwork that sets the plot into motion, is rife with drama, intrigue, and thrilling history[y] . . . while detailing the utter destruction of the Catholic church in England during the Protestant Reformation. Though the mystery of the missing altarpiece makes this novel a page-turner, at the heart of the story lurks something much more vital: a smart young woman's desire to pursue a much greater life than the one offered to her." *Per Contra*

". . . a great many things are happening in *The Altarpiece*: there is mystery, action, and even some romance. Kennedy has managed to create some interesting characters in the sisters of Mount Grace, particularly in Catherine, who is both intelligent and resourceful. She finds herself torn between her vows to the church and her desire for more in life. Although the mystery and search for the missing altarpiece provide the story with needed momentum, it is the more subtle tensions of the tale that are most interesting. It is intriguing how the nuns Christina, Veronica, Ann, and Catherine struggle and come to terms with the fact that their way of life is changing and may never be the same. Kennedy also deserves credit for approaching the period from the refreshing perspective of the devout." *Historical Novel Society*

"The author described the era well, as well as the hopelessness that the nuns felt. I enjoyed Catherine's character the most, because I felt her character showed the most growth....a short, enjoyable tale about faith, struggle and forbidden love during the Tudor period. I would recommend this to anyone who enjoy reading about that time period, or anyone who enjoys historical fiction." *The Book Musings*

"*The Altarpiece* is a powerful depiction of a horrible time in England's history.... Catherine is a very unique character. She is well-read and highly skilled in medicine of her time. While she lived in her convent, she was safe and protected. Without that protection, she may be considered a witch by people she had helped. I admired Catherine courage and her sense of right and wrong.... a very good piece of historical fiction." *Kinx's Book Nook*

"*The Altarpiece* by Sarah Kennedy is the first in *The Cross and The Crown Series* and what a fantastic start!....Of course I knew of the priories and monasteries being taken by force by King Henry's men but I've never read anything that focused on any one house so I found this very interesting. The author very vividly takes you back to this time period and you can practically feel the brutality and hopelessness of the situation being portrayed. For certain I will be anxiously awaiting the next novel in *The Cross and The Crown Series* called *City of Ladies*!" *Peeking Between the Pages*

City of Ladies

Book Two of The Cross and The Crown Series

Sarah Kennedy

KNOX ROBINSON
PUBLISHING
London & New York

KNOX ROBINSON
PUBLISHING

34 New House
67-68 Hatton Garden
London, EC1N 8JY
&
244 5th Avenue, Suite 1861
New York, New York 10001

First published in Great Britain and the United States in 2014 by Knox Robinson Publishing

A CIP catalogue record for this book is available from the British Library.

ISBN HC 978-1-910282-09-0
ISBN PB 978-1-910282-62-5

Typeset in Trump Mediaeval

Printed in the United States of America and the United Kingdom

www.knoxrobinsonpublishing.com

For Rod

City of Ladies

1

Yorkshire, January 1539

"Lady, there's been a corpse found," the soldier announced. He lifted one arm and in the raised hand dangled a veiled head.

Catherine Havens Overton started awake and found herself alone, but for the infant sleeping beside her. She pushed off the covers and wiped the sweat from her face. She'd had the dream three times since her woman went missing, and it was always the same—she a nun again, walking through the convent, her old herb garden, bending to a sprig of sage, the man in armor seizing her habit. He was always somehow familiar and always holding out the head in one hand.

Catherine shook out the sleeves of her nightdress and lifted the heavy cloak of her damp hair from her cheek. She rubbed her arms. It was only a ghost of the mind. She was safe. She was here, at Overton House, a married woman with a new daughter. The lady of the house. Destined for the court, or so her husband insisted. And now that the baby had come, he would press for it. Her missing woman would surely be found before they went. The watchmen would see to it.

The fire had burned down to embers, and Catherine called for her new maid. No answer. Shifting the baby into the crook of her left elbow, she eased her legs from under the thick quilt. The night had been bitter, even for midwinter, and the window showed a low grey sky. More snow coming, no doubt. She struggled from the feather mattress and, thrusting her feet into the waiting slippers, felt the wad between her thighs loosen. She had left a bowl full of lady's mantle nearby before she began her labors, and she packed the herbs against herself before she tightened the bands around her waist to stop the blood.

The infant mewed, and Catherine uncovered the small head. "Hush now," she said, studying her child. A shock of ginger fluff at the crown, fingernails like chips of shell. Her husband would have been happier with a boy. There were already enough females in the household, he would think. He might even say it, after a jug of wine, if his sister had gone yet again through her litany of traditions and the need for a male heir. She would of course let the word "legitimate" fall in Catherine's hearing. Then she would smile. The tiny mouth gapped, and Catherine laid her daughter on the warm feather mattress. "Let me warm us up, child."

Catherine waddled across her wide chamber to the hearth, kneeling to stir the ashes with the iron poker. She had tended fires often enough without the assistance of a maid. A pile of yew sticks lay to hand, and she built a small hutch of them, then bent to blow gently across the spaces underneath. Soon the smoke licked upward, crackling into flame. Opening her shift, Catherine took the infant to the window, rubbing away the frost with the heel of her hand. The great grey stone Overton House sat on a North Yorkshire hill, overlooking the gardens, sweeps of gorse-spiked moor, and the fields their tenants used for sheep. Catherine's was the only bedchamber in use by the family that looked directly down onto the back buildings, and she spotted her maid below, flattened against the back of the stable, her skirts hoisted to her waist. The girl was short-statured, and bosomy, and she was almost lost under the figure of one of the younger groomsmen, his breeches dropped, who was thrusting against her. She looked cold, even in her pleasure, if she could be said to be enjoying herself. Catherine's fingers went to the latch, but a trio of men came riding into the courtyard, calling, and the boy pulled himself free, buttoning up and running off with his cap in his hand. The maid was left panting and pushing her hair into place under her coif. Catherine could see the girl's breath, a white wraith in the cold air. The mistress of Overton House should not be shouting from the upper windows anyway.

Catherine's husband William rode in behind the others, and he waved when his sister came walking from the stables toward the house, holding her velvet cloak around her shoulders. She did not linger to greet the hunters. The men dismounted and hung a large doe in the largest of the oaks by its hind legs, leaving two others slung across the backs of a couple of sullen ponies. Catherine fancied she could hear the squeaking of the leather thongs as the kill twirled slowly in the wind. The soft, pale belly was slit, and the crimson entrails spilled into a wooden bucket. The hounds circled, snouts in the air, and the groomsman peeled his gloves off to toss them a wad of intestine. He blew on his fingers, then thrust his bare hands into the gut of the steaming carcass. The others laughed, setting up a braying among the bloody-mouthed dogs. "Poor girl," said Catherine, fogging the icy glass.

The heavy door of the bedchamber creaked, and Ann Smith came in, wiping her hands on a coarse cloth. They had been sisters together in the convent, and now they looked after the children together. "What are you doing out of the bed?" Ann said.

"The room was cold," Catherine said.

"Where's that new maid? That Eleanor. I told her to stay with you."

Catherine pointed with her head at the window. "She had business outdoors."

"Christ on a stick," muttered Ann, glancing out. "Do you mean she's got her head turned by one of the young men? You should have left that girl in the country."

"She's not a bad one. Just young. Tell me, Ann. How does my son?"

The other woman yanked the woolen curtain at the window closed. The brass rings clanged. "He will not be coaxed from his room. You cried out fierce at the last. Now, get back under those sheets, or I will carry you there myself. I have told him he could come now."

"He should be acquainted with his sister. Has William said aught about a name?" The women were both tall, and Catherine put her finger on the thin scar across her friend's throat. It blazed in the cold against Ann's white skin. "That has healed nicely."

Ann traced the raised line. "Thanks to you, I can still speak my will. But much good it does me. Now, back to bed with you. We will choose a name ourselves."

Catherine smiled. "Very well." She handed over the infant and slid under the covers. The linen was icy now, and she pulled the blankets to her chin. "You may get in with me. The room is frozen as Satan's nose."

"I haven't washed my feet," said Ann. She rocked the baby. "She's as beautiful as you are. And her eyes will be as green as yours inside a year, mark me." Ann studied the infant's red face and gently rubbed her nose against the baby's. "She will be tall and fair of face. She will be springtime for your old age." The baby's mouth bubbled milk, and Ann laughed.

"The hair is all Overton," said Catherine, leaning over to dab her daughter's lips. "We may thank God for it."

"I don't give a fig whether there is a drop of Overton blood in her," said Ann. "She can be all Catherine, like her brother, and I will love her the more."

"Shh," said Catherine. Her eyes were on the open door.

"He is nowhere within hearing," said Ann. "He just rode in. Just about now he is out kissing his hounds' snouts and cannot be bothered to see his children."

"It's hard for him. Especially in this house."

"Not so hard to make her, was it?" Ann winked at Catherine. "He was not so keen for his dogs that day, was he?"

"Stop your mouth, Ann Smith," said Catherine, but she was smiling for the moment. Only for a moment. "How do the Sisters? Is there any word of our Joan?"

"They say that she was down in the village to teach the day she disappeared. The others are worried, every one. With you down, everyone fears she will not be sought. Everyone except Margaret, as you might expect."

Her sister-in-law's room was on the other side of the hall and Catherine listened for footsteps before she spoke. "Margaret won't be able to speak against me now. This girl has Overton stamped on her head. Tell the other women to search. Tell them to go in pairs."

"They fear the watchmen."

"Tell them to wear Overton colors." Catherine lay back on the pillows. "I have had the dream again."

"Does the man still hold a head?"

"Yes, every time. It is like a visitation from Hell. I can't speak of it to William."

Ann leaned over and stroked the baby's hair. The child opened her mouth and clamped down on the air. "Perhaps its message is meant only for you."

Catherine stroked the infant's cheek with one finger. "I wonder what he will want to call her."

"I will name her myself if her father will not," said Ann. "I say she will be little Veronica. What think you of it?"

"It pleases me. But I favor Mary. Mary Veronica?" Catherine winced and turned onto her side. "I'm sore."

"You labored the better part of the night. I thought you would shatter the stones of the house with your shrieking."

Catherine laughed out loud. But then her mind sobered. "William wanted a boy. And a girl is not safe."

"She's safe if she's an Overton. A confirmed Overton. And your William has a son. One he should love better. Ah, here's our shining star."

A black-haired boy toddled into the room, and when he saw his mother, he inserted a thumb into his mouth, waiting.

"Come here and meet your sister, Robbie," said Catherine. She opened her arms and the child ran on sturdy legs, scrabbling up the side of the tall bed.

"Over on this side, you monkey," said Ann. "Your mother must be handled gently just now."

The child leapt over Catherine's legs and scrutinized the newborn. "Scorch," he said, pushing a chubby thumb against the little cheek. "Have you cooked her in the hearth, Mother?"

"She is red because she has just seen the light and her skin is still fine," said Catherine. "No fire has touched her."

The boy solemnly separated the tiny toes and rubbed each nail. He pulled the blanket away and sat back with a gasp at the stub of cord. "Like a puppy."

Ann roared. "She is no puppy. She is your sister. And that? That is her mortal mark. You had one too." She jabbed the boy in the belly. "Look at where your mother has left her stamp upon you. She held you as tight as she held your sister."

"It is an ugly thing," pronounced the boy. "But I will love it as Aunt Ann instructs me I must."

Catherine and Ann laughed and the boy blushed, ducking his head under his mother's arm.

"What is the jest?" William Overton came in, red-faced from the wind, with his tall manservant behind him. The men brought the scent of snow and fir trees and feathers into the room. William still wore his hunting coat and boots, and Catherine could smell the dog on him, too. His sister Margaret peeked in behind him. She scanned the room, saw Ann Smith, and backed out again.

"Will, come greet your daughter."

Ann placed the sleeping infant into Catherine's arms, took up the boy, and slid around the man. She touched Reg Goodall, the manservant, on the arm as she left the room and he smiled after her.

William Overton settled against the bedside and peered into the blanket. "She seems a hale girl." He lifted a red curl. "An Overtop, I see, like my father." William's hair was brown but it flamed a little when sunlight touched it. He grinned, but when Catherine offered the bundle, he recoiled. "I'm filthy as a pig farmer." He picked a feather from his coat and let it drift to the rushes on the floor.

Catherine's husband had taken up falconing at the same time he had begun to seek a place for her at court. She asked, "Have you had the birds out?"

William nodded. "Ruby. The peregrine. She's the beauty of them all." He spoke to his new daughter. "She's not as red-headed as you, though."

Catherine shifted the child so that her father could see better. "Will we call her after your mother?"

"Mary? A Papist name? The king has given us his permission but we mustn't move him to regret it."

"I would have her Mary. It seems right. Your boy after your father, your girl after your mother."

"My boy." William bent and flicked a scrap of dirt from his boot.

"They should be named after your parents."

"Let me hold this new Mary, then. Shall she have another name?" He turned and saw the open door. "Margaret? Where did she go?"

Catherine said, "I would like Veronica."

"That surprises me. Do you think it wise to recall the convent so intentionally?"

"The woman was like a mother to me. And no one remembers her save Ann and me. Father has not even marked her grave."

"She was good to you. Better than your mother."

"And we could call the child Veronica rather than Mary if it seems better to you."

"That will do. Mary Veronica it will be." William took the girl in his free arm now, and she squirmed at his hold and opened her eyes. Her mouth puckered and she blatted a little wind. "A female, no doubt. She is telling me what she thinks already."

Catherine's arms relaxed and she realized how tight her muscles had been.

William handed the child back and watched as Catherine loosened her shift and put the baby to breast. "There are nurses to do that for you."

"Mm. And their charges die. You have made me a lady, but God made me a woman and I will be one." She slicked back Veronica's hair but it tufted into a curl again.

"Your own charges are gathered below, howling like a pack of wolves. It has been enough to make a man mad. I believe they mean to conjure the constable to our door." He sat gently on the bed. "Catherine, you must disband them now. The time is ripe."

Catherine glanced up. "Joan is still missing. It's been three days. Someone must needs go look for her."

William rubbed his forehead. "Which one is she?"

"Ruth's convent sister. From the North. You know her. She's thin and has a little sharp nose."

"That one. She will be always in the village."

"She's good with the girls. You should see her help them form their letters."

"Letters. People say she teaches them spells. Listen to me, Catherine. You have work enough for your hands with this child. And when others come, you will need your strength to manage me and my household. God's foot, every hag and housewife between here and Durham is down there. They look like disease itself. Turn them out, I beg you, and give me some peace."

"They are only a few. And they instruct the younger maids. What harm do they?"

"Eat my cupboards bare and look like Hell. There is talk, I'm telling you. I cannot be a man whose wife is on the tongue of gossips. They say you keep a herd of starving witches and their familiars in your kitchen. Men laugh at it."

Catherine bit her lower lip. "Men will always find something in women to ridicule."

"And if the king hears of it?"

"What does old Henry care who sits in our kitchen? They are just poor women. You would not have me put them out in dead winter, William, would you? Where would they go?"

"To the devil, for all I care."

"Come, Husband. Show a little heart. They do good. It is what they are called to do. They give me hands to help with the raising of this little Overton." She looked at him. "And with your son."

He jumped up and walked to the hearth. "The fire is almost dead. I will send one of your sorceresses to tend it. Put them to some use for once. Before you rid us of them once and for all." Slapping his thigh, he walked from the room, pulling the door to a booming close behind him.

The infant wailed and Catherine pulled it close. "Poor child. To be born a girl to such a world of men." She lifted her eyes to the window. The snow came down like a quiet reprimand.

2

Catherine could hear the women talking as she came step by step down to the kitchen. At the doorway, she asked, "What news of Joan?"

Two women sat at the big plank table, a jug and pewter cups before them. A third, slight woman poked at a joint of meat over the fire. It sizzled, and drops of fat melted, splashing onto the stones. Catherine moved toward the warmth and took up the basting brush. "Ruth?"

"I didnae want ta wake thee in thy childbed but thou ought ta know. Sister Teresa has sought Joan in the fields all the way up ta her dovecote. She came in like ta die from the cold. She is gone, she is." Ruth reached for the bundle. "Let's see the bairn, now."

Catherine uncovered Veronica's head and the women gathered around her, touching the soft head and cheeks with their fingertips. They passed her from arm to arm, but old Hannah Hoskins refused. "These hands give way. You young ones take the babies. Why isn't she swaddled? Her bones will bend."

Veronica began to cry, and Catherine held her, gently wrapping the cold feet with her shawl. "It seems to me that swaddling stops growth. The Irish do not swaddle their babies, and their daughters are stronger than ours. Now tell me what you know of Joan."

Teresa Trimble sat at the table, coaxing her pet hen into her lap with bits of coarse bread. "She is nowhere to be found, Sister." Teresa burst into tears and buried her face into her hen's feathers, and the bird settled further into her arms, as though awaiting the end of another unforeseen and unavoidable storm.

"You mustn't call me that." Catherine stroked the woman's yellow hair. A few white strands showed, and Catherine was startled to remember that Teresa was twice her own twenty-four years.

"No, you mustn't." Margaret Overton stood like a quill in the doorway. She worked hard to maintain a girlish appearance, but her fair hair and white skin had darkened as she approached thirty years of age to almost the same color of dun. She was tightly corseted and had pulled back her combs so far under her coif that her eyebrows looked raised in alarm. Behind her was the maid Constance, a natural daughter of William's dead older brother, Robert. Connie was a gloomy red-haired girl with a face like a horse and a waistline thicker than her hips, and she stuck close beside her mistress, never daring to call her aunt. Margaret stepped forward as though she meant to take the baby, but she only said, "Tch. A girl. Well, perhaps next time. Catherine, you will do better." She screwed up her lips into a smile. "Come, Con," she said, and spun on the heel of her slipper. The dumpling of a maid minced out behind her.

Catherine clenched her teeth. "We will not forsake Joan, Teresa," she said. "Dry your eyes now lest someone hear you." She went to the big window and scrubbed the leaded panes with her hand. The back courtyard was empty but for the falconer, uncoiling fresh jesses to check their strength, and a skinny hound that worried a striped cat until it swiped out with one paw and sent him howling around the corner of the dairy shed. Snow fell, more lightly now, laying a soft carpet on the flagstones. "Has anyone been down to the village today?"

"I just been this dawn." It was Hannah Hoskins. "I went down to the baker and asked the women but no one will say a word of Joan. Good bread there. I brought a bite for our supper. And I haven't brought it for that bird o' yours." She moved the loaf from Teresa's reach. "I've got no mind to make that walk again to feed a chicken, unless you plan to drown her in a pot."

Teresa tightened her grip on the hen. "She eats hardly anything."

"Ach, you'll have her, I reckon." Hannah turned back to Catherine. "I asked after Joan at the tavern as well but they've not seen her neither."

"Did anyone see Mistress MacIntosh? Talk to her face to face?"

"I walked out that way," Hannah continued. "The woman has a cross to bear. Six of them, the eldest not ten. Five girls. And the husband a drunkard."

"And Joan?"

"She was there. Made the three older girls embroider two lines from the psalms each. The little ones have got a cough, and the noise ended the lessons. Joan left needles for them each and new thread."

"And when was this?"

"Morning three days ago," piped Teresa.

"It's not very long to be gone," said Catherine. "She maybe had another errand and could not be bothered to walk back in the snow." She spoke to Hannah. "Did you step into the church? Maybe she went in to get warm. Maybe to pray. Maybe someone saw her there."

Hannah snorted. "I did not. I never known Joan to darken the door of that place since the king's men went through it. She can't bear to see the empty walls."

"Maybe the anchorhold," said Catherine. "It stands empty, doesn't it? She could get in the side door."

"No one goes nigh there," said Ruth. "They say Moloch keeps his meditations in it. Some say the last anchoress comes through the roof and cries tears of smoke. If you speak to her, she vanishes."

Hannah sliced a sliver from the roast and tasted it. "Your William brings home good meat."

"But Joan is no simpleton. Children's tales of demons would not frighten her."

"But why would she want a cold room when she could come home?" said Hannah. "Nothing in the church would keep her from us."

"Teresa? Has she been down to the goose pens? She loved your geese."

"No, Sister. I been down every morning and every night ta do the feeding. Had three of the young maids with me yesterday ta dress those big ducks for the christening. It took them three hours ta get the pin feathers out. Joan never showed her face."

"Where else? Has she any family left anywhere?"

"Not a soul," said Ruth. She and Joan had been left together at their convent ten years before, two little girls with too many older brothers and sisters. Ruth at twenty still had the look of a tightly groomed novice, and she kept a small bundle of tidy clean underclothes by her cot, along with her hand knife and one silver spoon. "The plague took 'em all years ago. All in the same room, we heard." She slapped down the hearth tools. "She'd've not have gone ta them if they'da been the kings of Yorkshire."

"William says there is talk of us. Have you let anyone see the books?"

The women exchanged glances. "Not a soul," said Hannah. She rose, but Catherine was already at the door to the still room to check on her private

11

library. Hannah said, behind her, "No, Sister Catherine, you must not kneel. You should not be out of the bed. Ach. You see?"

Blood showed at the hem of Catherine's robe, and she lifted it. The pad was still in place. "It's just a trickle. I'll be done before the week gets old. Reach me down the yarrow, will you, Hannah?"

The old woman handed over the herbs. "Let me help you to your bed. Ruth?" The younger woman was already wringing out a rag. "Step back, Sister, or your slippers'll be all ruint."

"No 'Sister,' I say. Sweet heart of Mary," murmured Catherine. She leaned on Hannah and dried her legs with the clout then packed the fresh leaves onto a new pad. "My husband would faint at this sight. Are you certain no one has been at my books?"

The back door of the kitchen swung open, and they all leapt up at the chilly draft, but it was Ann Smith. The snow swirled into the room and Ann, the wind blowing her hair loose from her hood, held out a woolen cloth. It was brown, embroidered around the edges in red, and the other women cried out. Catherine, holding the pad between her legs, ran to her friend.

"That's Joan's, sure enough," said Ruth.

"Where did you find it?" asked Catherine.

"Behind the pig trough. When I went to put out the slops."

"What sign of Joan?"

"Nothing, Catherine. Not a hair of her anywhere." Catherine took the cloak and held it up the light. They could all see the red stain, and Ruth began to wail.

3

"Joan never did harm to any soul," Catherine said to her husband. She tugged her shawl closer. She had never liked this long gallery, with its dark, north-facing windows. "She wouldn't have known how."

William sat in his big oaken chair by the fire, turning the piece of cloak over in his hands, then laying it across the arm. The scrap seemed a sorry thing against the embroidered upholstery. A hairy mastiff lay at William's feet, and he stroked it with the toe of his boot. "She likely dropped it. The cloth is rotted. I can almost pull it apart with my fingers."

"It is perfectly good." Catherine snatched the piece of wool. "And see here? If this is not blood, I am the queen of Sheba." The cloth was smeared along one edge and she held it out for him to see.

"Didn't you say it was in the hog pen? That's probably shite and slobber."

Catherine inhaled the cloth's scent. "No, that it is not."

William shoved himself up and threw a log on the fire so hard the sparks shattered into the air. The mastiff scuttled to a corner, and Catherine pulled her skirts back.

"If you didn't keep them here this wouldn't be your business at all," William said. "Are you my wife? This is not a nunnery. Do I have to remind you?"

Catherine's heart stiffened against him. "They have not the means to obtain the dispensation that we have. And your king is stingy with his pensions."

"He is your king as well."

"Yes, and he has been so very kind to me."

"He gave me permission to marry you. What more do you want?"

Catherine's cheeks stung as though he had slapped her. "Their pensions were almost nothing. They can read and write."

William coughed out a bad-tempered laugh. "That Teresa couldn't make a 'T' with two sticks of wood."

It was true. "She has skills, even if her intellect doesn't follow letters. Have you seen her with her birds? She can almost talk them into jumping onto your falcons' talons. She has shown half the village girls how to raise their own hens and ducks. Some of their mothers, as well. Just yesterday she taught some of our younger maids to dress them for the table. They have knowledge, William, all of them. They could be useful. Even at court."

"Don't talk like a country girl. You and I both know better than that. If we get a summons, it will be you at court and no other. Riding by my side. And that Teresa had better be careful how she talks to her chickens. She will be accused of keeping familiars." William suddenly put his arm around Catherine's waist and, pulling her close, spoke into her hair. "Forgive me. No quarrels, my love. I am wrecked with waking. I have been walking the floors to splinters for worry of you."

Catherine put her head on his shoulder and her anger unwound. "I am well enough. You feel me here. I mean to stay. The worst is past."

"I know it, like enough," he said, straightening. He put his finger under her chin. "My physician. You must rest and heal yourself so that we are ready when the call comes."

"Will you let the women attend the christening? It will break their hearts if they are left out."

"They may sit in the back. And will you let Margaret stand as godmother?" He glanced beyond her and Catherine turned from him. Margaret was standing outside the door, watching.

"Yes." Catherine kept her eyes on Margaret's. "Ann as well."

"Ann as well," said William. "But Margaret stands in the place of priority."

Margaret simpered in triumph. She likely believes her mouth looks like a rosebud, thought Catherine. It looked more like an arsehole. She said to William, "Have Father stay until I can be churched, and Margaret may have the highest place at the christening."

Margaret nodded, said "I thank you, Sister," and went on upstairs.

William whistled softly and the dog came to heel. "By Christ's sweet side, the rites women go through for a child. My brach Lady drops a half-dozen pups before dawn and goes out to the hunt in the afternoon. You women are a breed unto yourselves."

"Oh, you. You, who were saying how wakeful you were for me."

He chuckled and put his arm around her shoulder. "A hit. You have wounded me."

Catherine lifted her hand toward the window. "The winter holds us fast anyway. Look there. It's snowing again."

He moaned at the whirl of white. "When you heal and the weather breaks, I mean to let the court see you. The king's daughters need women. And Veronica will justify our union."

Catherine held up the shred of cloak again. "Will you ride out and seek Joan? I know she was nothing to you, but she was part of our household."

"Still harping on that wench?" William said, a knot in his voice. "She was part of *your* household."

"They teach, William, nothing more. You want the girls of your village to grow up ignorant? We could have a city of learning here. The court could come to the moors and see our castle of knowledge."

"It's no wonder they will not stop calling the village Havenston. Your mother's family still hangs over them like ghosts." William stepped away. "You have the Havens blood. You may teach who you will, but the talk—"

He broke off when little Robert entered the room, clutching a squirming spotted cat. "Mother, Tom has pooped out kitties." The mastiff shoved its big head forward and sniffed wetly.

Catherine loosened the animal from the boy's grip and it streaked away. The dog flopped down with a disappointed sigh. "Then Tom must be called Thomasina," said Catherine. "Where has she put her babies?"

The boy toddled across the room and planted himself before William. "He has put them in the stables beside your Jupiter's stall."

William said, "Then Jupiter will have no mice in his hay. Is that not so, Robert?"

"Tom is a good mother cat," the boy replied solemnly. "I will reward him with a dish of cream if I may, Father."

"You may," said William. The boy remained rooted in front of the man, and William squatted. "Have you sat your pony today, Robert? If you are to ride with me, you must make a horseman."

"William, he is barely three years old," said Catherine. She finger-combed his mass of black curls. "He has barely got his legs."

"He will be four before you can blink. Then five. If he is to be an Overton, he will have horseflesh under him before he needs legs. I'll have Geoff step up his lessons. Two hours. Every day."

"Yes, Father." A maid peered silently around the doorframe and Robert saw her. "May I be excused to my nap now, Father?"

"Yes, boy." William extended his hand, and the child regarded the big fingers before shaking them. His tiny hand vanished into the man's grip.

"He adores you," said Catherine after Robert had run out.

"Where is our daughter?"

Catherine's jaw muscle twisted and she took a breath to loosen it. "Eleanor is watching her. My new maid. The child already sleeps like an angel."

"Thank God for that. Will you have Margaret hold her for the baptism? Since she will hold pride of place?"

"I would prefer Ann."

William cocked his head. "You could hold her yourself."

"No. Not in the chapel."

He cast his eyes down her body. "You look clean enough to me. And I have known you to be unconcerned for rites in the past when they got in your way."

"Don't mock me, William. Breaking from Rome does not mean breaking from God. I want the time." Her breasts ached and she wanted to put her feet up.

"Have it as you will," he said finally.

She was ready to go. "But I would like Ann to hold Veronica, not Margaret."

"Margaret is more fit, and it will anger her to be set aside. There has been enough strife among us. And it should be an Overton."

"Ann held Robert and I heard no complaint. She can hold Veronica just as well." She crossed her arms and hoped the blood was not slipping down her leg. It would stain the floorboards in a place that could not be concealed.

"I will consider it," he said.

Catherine opened her mouth to insist, but Teresa skidded into the room. She had her hen under one arm. "Sister." Her mouth froze and she looked in terror at William. He was staring into the fire and she hurried on. "Madam. Two men at the back door. They have found Joan."

"What?" said William. He grabbed Teresa and shook her by a skinny arm.

"Where?"

"I . . . I don't know," she cried. The hen shrieked and Teresa wrenched herself free and clapped a hand on its white head. "It's horrible, the most worst thing I have ever witnessed."

"Tell me," said Catherine. She dropped the cloth. The dog shot forward and buried his nose in the fabric.

"She's dead. She's all, well, she's all tore up."

"How came she so?" said Catherine, slapping the dog and taking up the cloth. "Where is she?"

"In the kitchen," whispered Teresa.

Ruth's high wailing started up from below, and Catherine and William pushed past Teresa. The narrow back stairs were the quickest route downstairs, but William blocked the top step. "You go to bed. You're pale as the moon. Go have your rest."

"I will have the proof of my eyes first." He gave her a hard look, and she added, "and then I will go to bed."

William relented, and Catherine followed him. The narrow stone stairs wound around the corner of the house and ended beside the wide cooking hearth. A half-dozen men in patched woolen coats and broken-down boots hunkered around the big kitchen table and they dragged the caps from their heads when they saw William. Ruth was lying across the laid-out body, keening and crying, and Hannah leaned against the wall in the far corner, apron over her mouth.

"Get back. Let me see," said William. The men fell away, looking sideways at each other. "Who found her?"

"It were me," said one of the men. He wore a grizzly beard and his eyes squinted as though he were standing in full sun. "I come acrost her whilst I's gatherin' wood. Some pigs or foxes's been at 'er, 'd be my judgment, God rest 'er." He crossed himself, then tried to scrub it out on his chest. "Beggin' yer pardon, Master, I'm reformed as any Englishman."

"You had better be." William pulled at Ruth's sleeve, but she hung over Joan and would not be moved. Catherine gentled her husband aside.

"Ruth, come away and let me look," said Catherine. She bent to speak into the girl's ear. "We must see what has happened here."

Ruth flung herself up. Her apron was spotted with blood and filth and her hair had come loose from her coif. "I will tell you what happened. Some man has got at her. She's ruint and a' has left her like a bitch in the road. She is murdered for bein' what God made her and your king couldnae let her be." She poked her finger at William, her silky yellow hair wild and haloed around her red face. "It 'as one a' the king's rogues, I'll say so right out loud."

The men had gathered backward into a tight band by the back door. William's left eyelid quivered, and Catherine stepped between him and Ruth.

"You speak out of turn, Ruth. This is your grief speaking, not your mind. Leave this place. The sight infects you." She was taller than Ruth by several inches, and she steered the woman toward Hannah. "Will you take her to the chapel? It would do her good."

Hannah, with a swift nod, seized Ruth's arm and marched her away.

William was bent over Joan. "She has fallen along her way, and knocked herself senseless. She has succumbed to the cold."

Joan was frozen, even thinner in death, and her narrow fingers had gone black at the tips. Her nose was ashy, and something had chewed away the end of it, along with a strip of her cheek, so that the jawbone and the roots of two teeth showed through in one place. Catherine pulled the neckline of the dirty shift down. Joan's throat was dark and mottled.

"See there?" Catherine twisted the girl's neck, and the head flopped to the side. Her hair was matted to the back of her skull with blood. She looked up at the knot of men. "Was she against a stone?" There was no answer. The men were staring. "I say, was she found upon a stone?"

The wood-gatherer remained silent, and a tall, sandy-haired young man stepped forward. "I was with Sam here, and I saw no stone. The lady was under some dirt, covered with sticks. We was breakin' 'em up for bundlin' when we seen 'er. Hand layin' right out there, face too. Think somethin' tried ta drag 'er out, but she's too heavy fer it and it leaves 'er. Chawed some, you see, hands black as the dirt she laid in. No, ma'am, no rock, not that I seen. Whatever done that, I wager was movin' faster than a stone."

4

Ruth's screams echoed through the hallways from the chapel on the far side of the house, and Catherine held her hands over her ears. "Fetch the constable," she ordered, but the men remained huddled by the back door. "Go!" she shouted, "or I will saddle up myself."

"Are you deaf?" asked William, and the men stumbled outward, scattering as they hit the courtyard. "I will have to send one of our own men. Those peasants will be in a tavern before they will show themselves to the law."

"Why? Is there a killer among them?" It was Ann, coming down the back stairs. "I will hunt them down and bring them back if you order it."

"It wouldn't surprise me. They are a pack of one-suit villains, as I stand here," said William. "Have you seen this, Ann?"

She nodded. She did not look. "I sought Catherine, but she was not in her bed." Ann cast a glance in Catherine's direction.

Margaret's small heels came clacking down the stone steps from the main hall. "What is it? Is she found?"

"They say she was buried in the woods," said Catherine, "under a pile of sticks."

Margaret took two steps into the room. "She is dead?" She put out one freckled hand, but when Catherine moved aside, she recoiled. "Dead. Dead. I will be sick." She lifted the fingers to her mouth and fled.

Catherine waited until the sound faded up the stairs. "Have you heard of civilized men doing such a thing?"

Ann said, "There is little I set beyond men nowadays. Someone has waylaid her and knocked her in the head." She cast her look on William. "Any of your gossips speak ill of this girl?"

Catherine pulled the shift down to expose Joan's neck to Ann's eyes. "She has been throttled. This is what killed her. Turn your head away, William."

He faced the back wall, and Catherine replaced the collar and lifted Joan's skirt and underskirts. She parted the legs and studied the skin. She settled the clothing back into order and rested her hands on the cloth that covered Joan's legs. "All right."

Ann crossed her arms. "Who has gone for the constable? Besides your pack of villains, I mean to say."

"I will go myself," said William. He kissed Catherine lightly on one cheek. "Back to bed with you, mistress, and I will see to this woman of yours. I swear it." He leapt to the steps and was gone.

Ann now came to the other side of the table. "What did you find?"

"By my troth, it's a rape." Catherine lifted her eyes to the window. "She's bruised all over. I didn't take any of those men who were here for a ravisher. They are no villains, either."

Ann tied up Joan's bodice as close to the bloody jawbone as she could. "Have the king's men been here? Anywhere in the village? I've heard nothing of them."

"If you refer to Cromwell's men, I've heard nothing. Not a one of them for months," said Catherine. She busied herself with Joan's torn stockings. "There is little more they can take, and William doesn't want them around."

"You mean he doesn't want one of them around. Come, you should lie down until the law sees fit to bless us with its presence." Ann helped Catherine up the stairs and into bed. "That Eleanor of yours is a worthless cow. You should send her packing and get you a maid who'll see to you properly."

"I don't want a maid to wait on me at all. You see how well we live. And with prices rising so. Her father is no provider, and her mother is a mouse. Is it any wonder the girl is brooding?"

"Breeding, I think, is the word you want. No laughing, now, you will tear yourself open."

Smiling, Catherine pulled up the blankets to her chin. "I'm healing well enough. I itch this afternoon."

"Oh, Lord, save yourself from that. You'll be with child again before the moon is full."

Catherine lay back on the pillows, and the maid came sliding into the room with the baby in her arms. "Madam, I have brought your daughter. I have cleaned her." She eyed Ann sideways as she came to the bedside.

"Eleanor, have you heard news of our tragedy?" asked Catherine. "Joan has been found dead."

The girl handed the baby to her mother and nodded. "They's been talk of her down at the tavern, Madam. They been sayin' she won't be found living."

Catherine sat up. "Who has been saying such things?"

"What have you been doing in the tavern?" said Ann.

Eleanor went rigid. "I didn't say I was in no tavern. I say they's been talk. Somebody told me."

"Somebody who?" said Catherine. The girl examined her toes, and Catherine added, "You've no need to be afraid. I want to know if the report is reliable."

"I have a friend."

"What friend is that?" said Ann. Her voice was loud and the girl shrank away.

"No one. I can't recall."

"Go to, Eleanor, tell truth," said Catherine. "Your friend is that boy who works in the stable, isn't he? What is his name, the big one. He has thick hair, brown as a squirrel. That one. What is his name? Joseph, isn't it? Joseph Adwolfe. Am I right?"

Eleanor's skin was so fair that it was almost transparent, and her face flushed bright from collarbone to hairline. She stammered, "Oh Madam . . . Madam, I need . . . this . . . my mother is ill . . . my father will kill me outright if I lose this position." She fell to her knees in earnest.

"Stand up." Catherine patted the quilt and the girl's head appeared at the edge of the bed. "I've seen all I need of this Joseph Adwolfe. But what did he say of Joan?"

"Well." Eleanor glanced from Catherine to Ann and bent forward. The women leaned in and she whispered, "They say she murdered newborn babies and fed them to Satan and she wore her old nun's weeds after dark. They say she went stark naked underneath and that she had a swarm of demons to follow her about. They say she could call them by rubbing her old beads against her nipples."

"You don't believe that nonsense, do you?" Ann asked.

Eleanor shrugged, her eyes wide. "I go to the church that's there and don't say a word about it. I been christened in the old way, but I walk in and do things the new way. They'll throw you in the gaol if you say your prayers wrong, but I misremember them so I try to say nothin' atall, just open and close my mouth when the business gets started. What goes on behind closed doors, I don't venture to guess. Magic, some say. Sorcery. Not my business. I keep my nose pointed forward."

"That seems a sensible course," said Catherine.

"But I hear what I hear. They's work to be done whether God's about 'r not." She peered over at Veronica, who nuzzled Catherine's breast. "This one is an Overton, all right. That other one, he's your image, Madam. Like he had no father atall."

"Don't say that," said Ann. Her tone was dark. Eleanor frowned at the older woman. "I'll be takin' your things to the laundry, Madam, if you don't need me here."

"Go on," said Catherine. "Ann will stay with me. Keep that nose pointed forward."

"And your legs pointed down," said Ann. "At least when you're out of doors." Eleanor flopped into a quick curtsey and fled the room.

"What do you think of that?" asked Ann.

"She's a girl. Her mother and father are ignorant as dirt, the father in his cups most of the time. It's a wonder she's not got a child herself by this time. I couldn't find it in my heart to condemn her for it."

Ann sighed. "Nor I, truth be told. But I mean about the talk. You think Joan was killed for a witch?"

"Not for a witch." Catherine gently cleaned the baby's nostrils with her fingertip. "I wager she was killed for a nun."

5

Catherine slept the afternoon away, and by the time she heard William's voice downstairs, the light was slanting far into the west. Veronica dozed beside her, and Eleanor sat dutifully on a three-legged stool by the small fire, sewing.

"I have a fresh shift for you, Madam," the maid said when Catherine stirred. She set the woolen stocking, with a wooden darning egg inside it, into a basket and brought the clean linen. "You will want to change?"

"Yes," said Catherine. She lifted the cover and felt for blood. "You're good to think of that, Eleanor. Lend me your shoulder. I want to burn this poultice before it smells." She heaved herself onto the floor, and the girl helped her peel the used pad of cloth off and replace it. Eleanor folded the old one and threw it to the back of the flames.

"You have done this before," said Catherine.

"My mother lost one last year. She'd like to never stop bleeding. No more coming yet, thank God above."

"And do you not worry for yourself?"

Eleanor opened her mouth but nothing came out. "Madam—" she finally managed.

Catherine smiled. "A woman usually gets the worser part, Eleanor." She gestured to the window. "You should look up now and then. The rooms don't all face the front."

The maid flushed full again. "Please don't send me away."

"I'll not send you anywhere." Catherine put her hand on Eleanor's shoulder again and stepped into her slippers. "I won't have you sticking out to kingdom come either, though. Now help me downstairs if you would."

"Get the baby, Madam, then lean on me. I won't let you fall."

Peter Grubb, the constable, was in the kitchen with William and two watchmen. Ann was leaning against the doorjamb and she took the infant when Catherine came in.

"Beggin' yer pardon, Madam," said the constable, backing toward the door. He looked like a storm approaching, white hair spraying from head and startlingly prominent nose. "You ain't been churched yet, have ye?" He raised one brushy eyebrow at the infant.

"This is my home," said Catherine. "You don't see me out in the road, do you? Where are the other women? They may have information."

Grubb chewed his cheek and looked to William.

"My wife will speak," said William. "As she says, this is her home. We stand upon no superstitions here. Now, Catherine, what do you say?"

"I say it again, where are my other women?"

"Don't want them yet," said the constable. His face was deeply lined, but he was a delicately muscled man, an indoor man, and his fingers now worked nimbly over the wounds in the lifeless form. "Your tenant found her, you say? One of your own men?"

William nodded. "He's never been in a day of trouble. Keeps to himself. Feeds his wife and children well enough. Pays his rent."

"Mm-hm. What's his name?"

"Cobb. Samuel Cobb."

"I know him," said one of the watchmen. "I have a cup with him down at the tavern now and again. Good enough man. Likes his drink. Likes pretty girls." He glanced quickly at the body. "Too good for doings like that."

"Is he a reformed man?" asked Catherine lightly.

Peter Grubb looked up at this, directing his gaze at the watchman.

"Reformed?" said the man. He was taller than the constable by a head, but his dirty hairline suddenly shone with sweat. "Why, yes, as reformed as the next Englishman." He swallowed hard, and his Adam's apple jerked. "As reformed as you, Madam."

"What do you imply by that?" William stepped forward.

The watchman lifted his chin. "Don't mean anything more than what I say. Think a man's word ought to match his mind." One eyebrow jumped. "Woman's too."

"Will you speak this to my face in my own house?"

Now the man backed a step. "I said nothing out of turn. The lady asked a question. I answered it. I don't say as much as some others."

The constable wiped his hands on his handkerchief. "What others?"

A line of sweat rolled down, over the watchman's temple. "No one."

"You've been conversing with no one? It's a wonder they haven't clapped you in chains yet." The constable pocketed the cloth and looked from the watchman to William. "Go to, man, you've come into Master Overton's kitchen and insulted his wife. You seem to hold a demon in your head. Now out with it, or you will shift your place. I'll put you in the gaol myself, watchman or not." The constable barely came to the watchman's chin, but he held his ground.

William and the watchman stared at each other steadily, and the other man finally said, "It's the women. They say the lady here is married against the king's law. They say the women here keep a convent against the king's law. Some say they go to the daughters of the village to turn their minds against the new church. They use bewitchments and potions. It will lead us all to the gallows."

"You are a pack of drunk fools," said Catherine. "My husband has a dispensation from the king himself for our marriage. Did you think all the nuns would be burned up in the fire of the reform and disappear?"

"There were boats," the watchman muttered. "They coulda gone."

"Oh, yes, indeed, a godly solution! Pack the women up and shove them out to sea. Did you not think that some of us are Englishwomen? That some are old? Or without means?" Catherine's chest was hot and tight and she could barely get out the words.

"I have overstayed my welcome," said the watchman. He bowed to William. "Begging your pardon, Master, if I have offended. I have only repeated what is spoken to me, as I was bidden." He pivoted on his heel and pushed through the door.

The constable regarded the second watchman, who was studying a spot high on the wall over William's head. "What do you know about these rumors?"

The man slowly shook his head. "I keep to myself. Keep myself away from drunkards and gossips." His eyes remained locked on the wall. "My occupation is to watch when I am called, not to be talking. I pass my evenings at my own home."

"And what have you seen of this woman in your watches?" said the constable.

The man's blue eyes slowly moved down and over Joan. "I've seen her about. She wears a brown cloak. Teaches the little ones. She can make out her letters right nice. Wrote me out a poem last Christmas that I thought up for my wife. Wouldn't take no pay for it neither."

"Did you see her in the last three days?" Catherine pressed forward, her hands on the table.

The watchman met her gaze. "No, Lady, by my troth."

"Someone did," said Catherine. She touched Joan's leg and it felt thick and soft, like a slab of spitted meat. Tears pooled, hot, behind her eyes and she blinked them back. "Someone who did not keep to himself."

"If you ask it, I will go door to door through Havenston and inquire," said the watchman.

"That will only bring attention to the others here," said William. "Catherine, we should let this woman lie at her peace and be done with it. It may not have been a murder at all. She may have fallen. An animal could have dragged her to where she lay. We don't need to stir up the whole village with talk of a killing."

"Do animals rape?" blurted Catherine.

"You said nothing about a rape, Master Overton," said the constable, coloring around the collar.

"Nor did I know of one," said William. "Are you sure?"

"Yes." Catherine did not like to look in the men's eyes as she spoke about it. "She has all the signs."

"Of a rape or of unchastity?" asked the constable.

The tears burned behind Catherine's eyes again. "I have never heard Joan accused of being unclean in any way."

"Perhaps you didn't know her as well as you thought," William said. He put his hand on her shoulder.

"Had she a suitor?" asked the constable.

"No," said Catherine. She labored to keep her breath steady. The hand felt very heavy.

"You cannot know," said William. "She was off to herself a great deal. Catherine, I know your intent was to help her. But she might have had chapters you could not read."

"Well, that makes it a hard one to prosecute," said the constable. "Who is going to see to the burial? We have enough paupers these days to put in the ground."

"She will go into our tomb," said William. "We will have the priest here for the christening and he will see to her rites. Does that sit comfortably with you, Catherine?"

Catherine could feel his eyes on her. She would not weep. "That is as well as it can be, I suppose."

"Then I will take my leave," said Peter Grubb. "You might keep a closer watch on your womenfolk, Master Overton, if you don't mind my saying it." He slid a cap onto his head and motioned for the remaining watchman to go out ahead. "You don't want any more of this landing on your doorstep."

6

John Bridle, the priest, arrived on his roan gelding from Mount Grace the next afternoon, puffing through light snow into the courtyard. He pushed off his brown woolen hood, and, sitting at her closet window, Catherine was shocked at how bald he had grown. He carried the sparrow hawk he'd come to favor on his right arm and handed it to the trainer before dismounting. The priest had taken to birding since Catherine married William, and now he wore his hawk like a badge of office everywhere. Father John was greeted by Geoffrey White, the master of horse, who took the gelding by the bridle while the clergyman threw his bulk to the ground. Little Robert Overton peered at the men from the door of the stable. His thumb went into his mouth when the priest beckoned to him.

Catherine held her breath until the child walked forward. His footprints were tiny in the wet snow. He allowed himself be lifted into the air, and when the old man swung him high, the boy laughed and pulled his beard, and the priest bellowed with pleasure. "Thank God," Catherine whispered at the glass.

Hannah Hoskins sat by the fire, rocking the sleeping baby. She stopped her soft crooning to mutter, "What is there to thank Him for?"

"Robert has gone to Father without a tear," said Catherine. "I fear sometimes he will grow up to be afraid of his own shadow."

"John Bridle has finally bestirred himself to come? If you had to wait for the men to get anything done, you would still be waiting for both of the children to be christened."

"He's not young, Hannah."

"I have seen him move fast enough to catch a jug of wine."

"Shh," Catherine said, but she was glad enough that Hannah had laid drunkenness at the priest's charge and neglected to mention her own birth in the convent. She pushed the window open and leaned out. "Father! Don't break him!"

The priest looked up, shielding his face with his hand. "This boy is grown a mile! He sprouts like the corn in May." He bobbed Robert in his arm, and the boy grabbed him around the neck.

"I must go down," said Catherine, latching the window tight. "I don't suppose he knows he will have to perform a burial before the christening."

Hannah scooted the chair closer to the fire. "Where will we lay her?"

"The tomb in the chapel. No one can make a grave outside in this cold. And I can't bear to lay her in the hard ground anyway. Come down with me."

Hannah handed the baby to Catherine and eased herself to her feet. "You will have to be the one to convince your man. He would toss her to the pigs if it were left to him."

"No. He surely would not." Catherine shook her head, wishing Hannah had known William before. But before what? The king. The soldiers. Perhaps their marriage. "He's not heartless, you know. It was his idea."

"Hmph. He must be atoning for something. Have you checked his gambling debts?"

"Shh." Catherine checked her paddings and took the main stairs down to meet the priest. Her son had led him around to the front door and he came into the big hall with his arms open.

"Catherine. You shine, Daughter, as always. How do you?" He opened his coat and brought out a large book. "I bring you a gift. This woman is on the lips of every Italian, and you must know of her."

Catherine took the soft, leather-covered volume in one hand. "*City of Ladies*," she read. "What is it?"

"A guide to life," said the priest. He pulled a crock out of the bag on his hip. "Your old friend Elizabeth sends greetings. Here is honey from her own bees."

"And here is a new person who greets you." Catherine offered the baby in exchange.

John Bridle gently held the tiny girl, turning her into the light. "She's an Overton, all right. Look at that hair, straight from the devil."

Catherine slapped him lightly on the arm. "Don't you dare say such a thing."

"Ah, she's a beauty, just like her mother. So, are we going to give her to

God, then?"

Hannah lowered herself to the last step. "There's no giving any of them to God anymore, John Bridle. You and your king should know that as well as anyone."

The priest's face kindled to his earlobes. "Hannah Hoskins, are you still living?"

"So my glass would say. And I see Satan has let you loose into the world for one more day."

Catherine handed the crock of honey to the old nun, who tasted it and nodded. The priest regarded her for a few seconds, then the baby howled. "Our God will have this girl whether there are convents in England or not," he said. He stepped closer to the women and lowered his voice. "And you must watch your tongues when you speak of the king. Walls have ears these days."

"Where are the walls' ears?" said Robert, wedging himself between the priest and Catherine. "Where, Mother?"

"You hear that? Be careful what you say," said the priest. He placed one hand on the boy's head. "It's only a manner of speaking, Robbie."

"She has your eyes," said Catherine. "Look, when she opens them, if you do not see yourself staring back at you, Father."

The priest reddened again, not liking to be reminded out loud that he was Catherine's father in blood as well as spirit, but he grinned at the baby. "When shall we christen her?"

"There is another matter for you. It should be done before the christening. Hannah?"

The old woman took the boy back upstairs, and Catherine led the priest into the front sitting room. She sat gingerly on a hard stool and motioned for him to take William's stuffed chair. He laid the baby on his lap, lifting her hands one at a time to examine the fingers. "You look fine, Daughter. We will have you churched in the month and you will be about before the spring comes. Has William heard aught from the court?" She didn't answer and he rambled on. "We will christen the child well enough. She is strong." Catherine sat silent and her father finally said, "What troubles you, girl?"

"Do you recall Joan? One of the sisters who has come to me?"

"The young one, yes. She had another with her. Little things, not much younger than you. Yes. What has she done?"

"She has done nothing." Catherine lifted one hand toward the back of the house. "She lies in the kitchen below. Murdered, or I am a badger's whelp. Some of the tenants found her in the woods."

The priest stood, pulling the baby to his chest. "My God above. Are you sure? There are dogs in those woods, wild as any wolf."

"She was buried under some sticks and dirt. What animal does that?"

"Bad doings," said the priest. "What does your husband say?"

"Very little. He's convinced it was an accident. But he wants them all turned out to beg. He calls the men who found her villains, then he calls them good tenants. He shifts like the wind."

"Harsh words, Catherine. Consider his position. He was trained to be a younger son, not the master of Overton House. He took a great risk in seeking to marry you. His brother's authority doesn't fall easily on him. Everyone watches to see if he'll lose the fortune. And he hazards the whole enterprise, keeping a gaggle of nuns here." He glanced at the doorway. "As do you."

"What hazard? Are they not women of England now as other women are?"

"They are not as other women, and you know it as well as I. You have a marriage because your husband knew to make his petition when things were . . . well, we need not speak of it. He loved you and made you a lady. Your success will not be repeated for others."

"I know it right well enough," said Catherine, "though Margaret tells me often enough what I truly am."

"If the king of England can make himself the Pope, then the least he could do was to let at least one of his nuns be a lady."

The priest and Catherine faced each other. She was as tall as he was, and when the light outlined the strong curve of his jaw, she couldn't imagine how he had ever thought he could deny her. She wondered briefly if her daughter's face would have the same shape. "You should come and see," she said. "Tell me if I am wrong in the matter of Joan."

He followed her down to the kitchen. Ruth and Ann had washed Joan as well as they were able and had laid a clean linen cloth over her. The body looked almost bridal until Catherine lifted the cloth. The wounded face, without the blood, was a broken death mask, and the priest gasped.

"Mother of God, what has done this?" He pressed the baby to his chest as though to protect her eyes. "This is the work of demons."

"The back of her scalp is scraped nigh off," said Catherine, turning the head slightly. "This is no demon, and no malicious stone risen up to strike her either. This is the work of men and the two-legged animals that follow their dirty business. Am I mistaken?"

"Who knows of this? Have you called up the constable?"

"He has come and gone. He seems to think it was an accident, as well. One of his watchmen said some kind words, but no one wants to cry up a hunt for the killers of a nun."

"Not a nun anymore." The priest seemed to be reminding himself.

"Nor even a woman now," said Catherine bitterly. "The other watchmen said there are mutterings about us down in the village. As though we need to be the word on any man's tongue."

"Men will talk, Catherine. Women as well. When do you want the burial?"

"Tomorrow. I want her laid in the chapel, where the constable may look at her again if need be. We will have the christening the day after. Ann and Margaret will stand as godmothers. Hannah and Ruth and Teresa will attend, Hannah at the front as she midwifed me. We will call her Mary Veronica."

"Veronica?" said the priest. He frowned. "That old woman was a burden to me for fifty years. She was more harpy than nun."

"She was like my second mother. Her scolding taught me my letters."

"Yes, yes." said the priest impatiently. He screwed up his lips, still frowning. Then the baby squirmed and he brightened. "She will be a new Veronica and make all things fresh. We will christen her and the world will turn as it has done before and the sun will shine on her. The past will be put away as though it never happened."

Ann came through the back door with eggs heaped in a basket. She laid them gently on the floor before she pulled off her gloves and scrubbed her hands together to warm them. "Those young hens laying in the dead of winter. I wonder if it means the end times are coming." She greeted the priest with a nod. "You have come to a room of sorrow, John. This should have been a time of joy."

"It will be all happiness," said John Bridle. He lifted one of the eggs. "Teresa's hens are the finest girls in the barnyard and they lay at her bidding." He set the egg back with the others. "We will bury Joan with all fitness, and then we will turn our eyes to the living, as our Lord instructs."

"I'm sure a jug of claret will help you over that threshold," said Ann evenly.

She went to the pantry and removed three pewter goblets.

"It can't hurt us to enjoy the pleasures God grants us," said the priest.

"Where is Teresa?" asked Catherine. "She usually gathers the eggs."

"She has gone to walk Ruth back from her morning lessons," said Ann. "Don't tell her I waited so late to empty the nests." She fetched a jug from the pantry and poured, but they leaned against the walls to drink, no one wanting to sit at the table. They had just finished their first glasses when Teresa came in, shaking the new snow from her cloak. The thick noses of fresh bread loaves showed from the cloth sack on her arm, and she headed to the pantry. She returned with a mug of ale and stomped her feet on the hearth. She warmed her backside and surveyed the room.

"Where is Ruth?" asked Catherine.

Teresa blinked. Her eyelashes were fine, almost white, and they gave her a look of constant surprise. "Is she not here with you? I have just come from the baker, and she said Ruth was on the high road over two hours ago. I thought she had come back early."

"Who did she go to this morning?" asked Catherine.

"The Hills," said Teresa, "but she wasn't there. I went and knocked. They said she had come away. I didn't see her along the road. I thought she had gotten here before me." Her voice lilted upward and her hand went to her throat.

Ann slammed down her goblet and grabbed her cloak. "I will find her. Teresa, you stay here."

"I will go with you," said Hannah, entering from the back steps. "No. No head-shakings from you, Ann Smith. I move slow, but I heard enough. I go with you." She grabbed Teresa for a quick hug and the two women hurried out.

7

The funeral was short, and Ann came up to Catherine's chamber afterward and sat across from the rocking chair on a stool. "Ruth would not have missed laying Joan to rest if she were alive."

Catherine put her face down into the baby's blanket. It smelt of soap and cold wind and she breathed it in to stop herself from weeping. "What does my husband say?"

"Nothing of note," said Ann. "I believe he doesn't know what to think of it. Margaret is worse. She says over and over that Ruth will return 'in good time.' Good time is long since past already."

Catherine's stomach soured and she snapped, "And Margaret knows this how? Because an angel whispered it into her delicate ear? It's a wonder she's not learned to hold her tongue when she has nothing intelligent to say." Catherine sprang to her feet. "It's freezing out and Teresa is desperate with grief. For once in her life, could Margaret not be an idiot?"

"Margaret is my kindred, Catherine." William stood in the doorway, looking at his boots. "She talks out of turn, but she's my sister." He came into the room. "Must you belittle her in that manner?" He leaned on the bedpost and rubbed his face. "I need to lie down. My forehead aches me."

"Lie here," said Catherine. Her anger flattened into guilt, and she pulled back the cover.

Eleanor came in from her little side room. "Shall I carry the baby downstairs, Madam?"

"If she's not fussy. William and I will take an hour of rest."

"Yes, Madam." Eleanor gathered up some dirty linen as she took up Veronica and crept from the room with Ann.

Catherine toed her slippers from her feet, loosened and dropped her skirt, then fell upon the bed in her shift. William threw a log onto the fire and stirred it to flame before he pulled off his boots and breeches and lay beside her. She stroked his arm, then turned onto her side and unbuttoned his shirt. She slid her hand inside, against his skin. He was hot, as he always was, and she let her fingers lie on his chest until his breath came regular and deep. She felt herself drifting into a dream, and she was back in Mount Grace, a young nun in her summer garden. She was picking leaves from a mound of early mint, and the more she clipped, the faster the plant grew. A bee was suddenly at her ear, and when she turned to slap it, the thing had the face of a man, hissing at her. Catherine jarred awake and found the sound was William, snoring at her side. She rolled to her back. At least it wasn't the old nightmare. The canopy was moving gently above them. It must be the force of the fire. If she could only stay like this, quiet and warm. But she could not keep her mind from Ruth, out somewhere in the cold. Alone. She sat up and William's eyes opened.

"What is it?" he murmured. "Lie down with me."

"Nothing." She smiled at him. "You were snoring and I thought I was being stung." But she could not keep back the hot tears. "I dreamed it was high summer, but Ruth is out there in the snow. William, she is dead. I know it."

"Come here. She may have gone back to Scotland. She's not been found, and if something had happened to her, there would be evidence of it." He pulled her into his arms and they lay breast to breast, William combing her hair with his rough fingers. "You are here with me. That is all the matter in the world to me this minute."

"I wish it were so plain as that." Catherine softened, enjoying the feel of his hands. Her skin tingled, and she shuddered with pleasure. "I was every bit as much a nun as they were. And yet I am here and they have nothing."

"They have had your protection. It is more than most will ever get." He leaned back and looked into her eyes. "Would you not consider letting Margaret hold Mary at the christening? You said yourself that she needs calming. Or something to that effect."

Catherine rolled onto her back and stared at the wind-bellied fabric, shifting overhead. "She has acted holier since we left the convent than she ever was during our years inside it, but it has made her no less superior in her attitudes. You know it was she who drove off the rest of the sisters before you and I married. And after she brought them here. With the same promise the king made—to keep them in their old age. And she turned them out and keeps that dreadful little pony-faced Con instead. God knows where they are these days." She tasted the bitterness of the words. "But I know what you'll say, that she's repentant of her behavior. That the times are dangerous."

"They are. And I think she is. We should assist Margaret in her reform. Is it not our duty?"

Catherine sighed. "Oh, sweet heart of Mary, I suppose it must be." She was still seething, though, and the fury brought a picture into her mind. "Con." Catherine rolled to her side. "Her hair is as red as Veronica's."

"So it is," said William.

"And your sister is strangely attached to her. What make you of that?"

William crossed his arms under his head. "I can hear in your voice that you have solved that puzzle long since."

Catherine had never raised the subject directly before. But she had never had a daughter before. "She is your brother's bastard child."

"I'd wager so."

"And who was the mother?"

"That I have never been told." He pulled Catherine into his arms again. "I was gone for too many years. The girl was here before I was home again. She puts me in mind of a talking turnip, but I cannot tear her from Margaret."

"Nor would I ask it, horrible as she is." Catherine chuckled. "Vegetable indeed."

William twirled a lock of Catherine's hair. "And it was my brother who brought me back to Yorkshire, however bad the circumstances were."

Catherine pulled herself free. "He meant to turn me out to beg and to have you stand at his side as he did it." William's face had blanched at the memory, and she added, "But he could not have known what an independent spirit you have. And I will speak to Ann."

William smiled at this. "Ann is solid enough. Her pride will recover."

"Ann is pure gold. She always has been."

"She's not frail, not like those others were. And these women who have come to you—they all seem to be teetering on the threshold. I feel like I'm staring into the past when I behold them. A hole like a grave, the dead past." He flopped onto his back again.

"Dead as three queens," said Catherine.

"Dead as my brother Robert," he answered. "I do not mean to say that I approve of Margaret. Nor did I approve of my brother, as well you know. But we must tread carefully."

"Who will old Harry choose next?"

"That's the great matter of the moment, isn't it?" A tremor of excitement sounded in William's voice. "And there's the daughter. The prince is well petted, of that you can be sure, but the daughter, now. There's an opportunity for someone."

"She's almost my own age. Surely she has women of her own."

"I don't mean the papist one. I mean the little one."

Catherine propped herself on one elbow. "Not the bastard?"

William linked his fingers behind his head and grinned at a spot somewhere above them. "The very one. She's royal, bastard or not, and she needs people about her. Good, sober women. Stable. With those skills you have so much of. She needs someone like you, my love."

"You cannot be serious."

"I'm as serious as a sword, Catherine. Think of it. The king's household is all scattered just now. He's busy seeking something to warm his bed, and the children need tending and teaching. Little girls have ailments. And think how she'd love Veronica, with all that red hair. She'd be a doll to that Elizabeth."

"You would give away your daughter to be a toy for a bastard?"

"Give her away? No, indeed. But let her sharpen her young wits on a princess? I would." William grabbed Catherine's arm and pulled her down for a kiss. "And so will you, my lady, if you know what is good for us all."

He tasted of wine, and Catherine lingered against him. She almost asked *and what of Robbie*? but held her tongue. William was happy, imagining his daughter at court.

Someone rapped, and William called, "Enter." Eleanor's face showed around the corner of the door. His face bent into an annoyed expression. "What is it, girl?"

"The baby wants her mother," said Eleanor without looking into the gap in the bed curtains. "She is hungry."

"Lord, I have married me a fishwife," said William, swinging his legs to the floor. He bent back and kissed Catherine again. "I can't say I blame her, though.

Save something for your husband." He winked and called "Reg!" William's man, tall and rangy as a scarecrow, stalked in behind Eleanor and flapped his master's breeches toward the flames before holding them out.

"Go on, you men," Catherine said. She took Veronica and settled back into the covers.

Eleanor waited until William and his Reginald had gone, then sat on the foot of the bed. "Madam, I think Teresa will run mad. She is sitting in the kitchen crying as though she will burst her heart. Ann and Hannah are taking care of her birds, all but that one she coddles. It has shat upon her best skirt and she doesn't take any notice."

"Who is out looking for Ruth today?"

"Geoff and Joseph rode out after the christening, but they've returned and found nothing. Ann has gone to the village to seek the watch, but only one of the men said he would search."

"One of them who were here to see about Joan?"

"Yes. But no word yet."

Catherine switched the baby to the other breast. "William wonders if she has gone home."

"To Scotland? It's a long way to walk in the snow."

"But where else can she be? Someone should have found her by now."

"I have no answer for it, Madam."

"Nor do I." The baby fell away from Catherine's breast, breathing through her lips in sleep. "We will keep a search out. If Ruth is here, we will find her. Let's pray we find her alive."

8

Ruth was not to be found, however, not that day nor the next. The christening was carried on as planned, the family below in the chapel while Catherine waited, in her bleeding woman's body, up in her chamber. It seemed to go on for hours, and Catherine grew bored, sitting at the open window. The garden was frozen and buried, but to pass the time she began to plan where she might lay out a few rows of apple trees. By the time Veronica could write, they would bear enough fruit for the household. She laid a parchment on the table to sketch the orchard, but the sky had cleared, and her eye was drawn outside, where, under the new sun, the snow in the courtyard had melted into small blue lakes. The young groom Joseph brought out Jupiter for his exercise, and the great black stallion turned a few obedient circles then reared against the halter, striking at empty air. Joseph rapped the horse on the muzzle, and when his sleeve fell back, a plaid ribbon was revealed, knotted on his arm. Catherine squinted, then ran down the stairs and out, stopping only by the back door to throw on a cloak.

"Ho, there, Joseph! Joseph Adwolfe!"

The groomsman turned, and Jupiter snorted out a blast of air. He pawed the ground and nipped at Joseph's shoulder. "Damn you for a devil, Jupiter," said the young man, striking the leathery nostrils. "Get off me." He shortened the lead by wrapping it around his forearm. "Lady, you had best stay back from this demon. He's wanting the road today. He smells spring in the air."

"He's like his master in that." Catherine offered her open palm, and the horse blew hot breath on it, then snuffed with flared nostrils. "He's not a bad animal, Joseph. Just tightly wound. He wants playing to put him in tune."

Joseph laughed, showing his straight white teeth. His arms were hard as oak branches and he held the halter tight while Catherine stroked the horse's neck.

"Careful there, Lady. He likes your touch but he's changeable as the weather. Sunny one second, stormy the next."

"As are we all these days." She stepped back. "Joseph, will you show me the ribbon you wear?"

"What? Oh, this thing?" He pushed back the sleeve. "This what you're on about?"

Catherine touched the end of the fabric. "This belonged to Ruth."

"Your Ruth? How do you know? I never saw it before yesterday."

"And how did you come to have it?"

"Found it. Right there." He lifted a hand toward the stable. "In the straw. I thought someone had cast it off. Works right well for a sleeve garter."

"And how comes it that you found it yesterday? Ruth has been missing for two days. You're in and out of that stable every hour."

"The wind, methinks. There's a mighty strong draft through there. Maybe she dropped it. I don't know, Lady Overton." He pulled the ribbon loose and offered it. "I won't be taken for a thief."

Catherine accepted the strip of cloth. It was woolen, mostly blue, but badly faded. She put it to her face and inhaled but no scent remained save horse sweat and hay. "I believe you, Joseph. You saw no sign of her at all?"

"Not a thing, Madam. We asked at all the public houses when we were in the village. It's as though she dissolved into the very air. Or that is what's said." Jupiter whinnied, and Joseph pivoted, leading the horse at a trot.

"What's that?" Catherine followed the young man as he went. "More talk?"

"Some say she went up like smoke. That's not all. There's soldiers coming this way. They say the constable's summoned 'em to see to the women in the village, to round them up and make them swear to follow the king." He coughed lightly. "That one is coming back this way with them."

Catherine's chest iced over. "Which one?"

Joseph looked back at the stable, then up at the high windows of the house. "That proud one the master's so taken against. That Adam Hastings. He's gathered himself a few men and they ride together. They say he was raised not too far off from here." Joseph spit onto the ground and the horse shied a step sideways. "He claims the king's warrant but they say he's little more than a rich highwayman."

"How do you know he's coming back here?"

Joseph trained his eyes to the dull gorse bristling through the white drifts over the hillside.

"Tell me," Catherine insisted. "How do you come by this knowledge?"

"It wasn't said to me. It was the priest. That John Bridle." Joseph looked her full in the face for a second. "Your father. I heard him tell Geoff. He said to tell the master."

"And what makes you believe your master has any opinion of the man at all?"

"Heard Geoff say it. Might say I've heard the master go on about it a bit with my own ears. Now I've done spread one more tale than I should and I don't want to say another word about it."

Catherine started to go, then turned back. "My Eleanor is a good young woman. She takes care of Veronica. And of me."

Joseph began to work through the tangles in Jupiter's mane with his fingers. "I don't mean her no harm."

"I'll be missed inside." Catherine raised the ribbon and it fluttered in the wind. "Thanks for this."

The groomsman nodded and Catherine hurried back inside. Hannah was in the kitchen, stacking hornbooks and chalk, and Ann poked her head in from the pantry. "What are you doing downstairs?"

Catherine asked, "The christening is concluded?"

"Yes," said Ann, "and your sister has taken your daughter off, your father and your husband with her. They have ordered a meal." She came out when Catherine didn't move. "What is it?"

"This was in the stable." Catherine handed over the ribbon, and Ann held it up to the light at the big window. "It's Ruth's, am I right?"

"Yea, for certain it is," said Hannah, standing. "She told me it was a gift from her father when she was a little girl. It used to be a whole scarf, when she was in the convent."

"It should go to the constable," Ann said. "It may rouse him to a closer search."

"There's other news," said Catherine. "Father was overheard saying that there are soldiers coming to Mount Grace. That the constable has sent for them to investigate women. That means us."

"Where have you been? London? Your man said nothing of it upstairs."

Ann studied the ribbon. She frowned. "Who are these soldiers?"

"Same soldiers as always," said Hannah. "Men with the king's eyes and their own swords. They're all alike."

Ann nodded. "Anyone among them we would recognize?" she asked Catherine without looking at her.

"One, perhaps."

"One what?" said William Overton, coming in behind them.

"Nothing. Women's matters," said Catherine.

"Ah. Of course. And look at you, woman of women, up and about. You look strong enough to travel."

"She is barely out of the childbed," said Hannah. "A month she needs, hale as she may look."

"Not my Catherine." William put his arm around her. "She's off to London, isn't that right?"

9

"William, you cannot think I am able to ride yet." Catherine closed the door to her chamber and lifted Veronica from her cradle. One of the maids had swaddled her tight, and Catherine loosened the bands on the arms and legs. "When will we give up this practice?" The baby waved her hands, and Catherine kneaded the little limbs. "Gerald of Wales says that we should not bind up our children. As though they were criminals at birth."

"And aren't they?" asked William, looking over her shoulder. "They say bears must lick their cubs into shape or they will never stand and fight. Margaret insists that she must needs be swaddled."

So that was the culprit. "Margaret knows nothing of the body. Our daughter is not a bear and she will stand just fine." Catherine backed off to allow him to see. "Her eyes already follow the light and shadows, you see? She will be a philosopher, our Veronica. She is keen for the world."

"Advanced, is she?"

"A female genius. You'll see."

"I mean for the rest of England to see her as well."

"I go nowhere until I am churched."

"That means four weeks."

"I will not go before."

"If you demand it. I'll use the time to send for letters of introduction."

"You had best get to writing, then, Husband." She gave him a sideways smile. "Your gander month will be gone before you can count one hundred."

William slapped his leg. "And you will be tipping a cup for the princess before you see the gooseberry blossoms." He kissed Catherine on the cheek and chucked Veronica under the chin. The baby squawled, and he backed to the door, finger to his lips. When he got into the hall, he whooped and sprinted off.

Catherine lifted the baby and said quietly, "And I will have time to discover who stalks my family."

But the ribbon yielded no new information, and when Ann returned from the village, she flopped down at the table, where Hannah and Catherine were sorting through turnips for rot, and tossed the scrap of wool onto the wood. "No one will say anything about Ruth at all. The constable thinks she has run off to Scotland."

"She has done no such thing," said Hannah. "This is Ruth's home now. She would not have gone without letters. Without her coin. It would be madness."

"That is not the worst of it. Constable Grubb says the Justice will rule that Joan and Ruth quarreled. That perhaps it was Ruth who murdered her friend and has run off from her conscience."

"Ruth would not have touched a hair of Joan's head!" said Catherine. "Ask any huswife in the village. They were fast as kin. Sisters in soul. How can they say so? They would not."

"From the constable's own mouth I heard it," said Ann. "At least he didn't call her a witch."

"Would that I could go down there," said Catherine through her teeth. "If I were churched, I would shove this cloth down his lying throat myself."

"And you think that would convince him that the women of Overton House are not murderesses?" asked Ann.

Catherine put her face into her hands. "God's wounds. We will have to find out the killers ourselves."

But just when the old snow had faded, fresh flakes came one night in a whirl and covered the ground, and there was still no sign of Ruth. At Catherine's order, Hannah left off teaching, and Teresa kept her nose to her poultry yard. Catherine paced her room day after cold day, slapping the fading scrap of plaid against her palm, but she could think of nothing more to do. Joseph and Geoff were sent to search the countryside with dogs day after day, until William finally ordered them to stay home and tend the stables as they were paid to do.

The month crept by, and though the sun shoved the night aside for a few minutes longer each day, the cold would not relent. Finally, four weeks to the day of Veronica's christening, John Bridle rode back for Catherine's churching. She ran downstairs with her daughter to greet him, despite the hard looks from

Margaret and Constance as she dashed outside. "At last the time is over," she said, handing the baby to the priest. "I will run mad in those dark rooms."

"You have more wits than any woman I know," said John Bridle. "Come and walk with me where we cannot be overheard and you may tell me all the news." The baby slept easily in his arms, and they walked a circuit around the house.

"Is there no word from Mount Grace?" asked Catherine. "You have asked everyone who might have sympathy with the women?"

"Nothing, Daughter." John Bridle breathed the winter air in deep. "Your old friend Elizabeth Aden has asked the question of everyone who buys her honey and has come up empty of information, too. If your little Ruth is dead, she is not dead anywhere near there."

"It is a horrible thought. To be dead and alone, flung somewhere savage and wild." Catherine's throat clutched at her own imagination.

"Most hideous to the mind's eye. The only talk in Mount Grace is of soldiers."

Catherine stopped. "Have they come? Do they come this way?"

"Not yet. Too cold. They have harbored in the south, but we have had traders come through the village who say they will come north soon enough." He kept walking, and Catherine caught up to him.

"What more is there for them to take?"

"Men's souls. They punish misspeaking for the pleasure of seeing blood run. Women's souls, too, Catherine. You want to keep your women quiet in these days. They come at the constable's invitation. Everyone must submit to the king in word and deed while they are about the village."

"They are as silent as our tomb, Father. And they stay that way to keep out of men's minds."

"It would be well for them to remember it. And I would not be sorry to see you on a horse to London."

Catherine and her father had come all the way around the house, where William waited in the doorway. "Is my wife ready for her churching?"

"This girl is almost big enough to walk," said John Bridle, handing Veronica to William. "Your wife is an excellent mother. Is the chapel prepared?"

"We are eager to have the rite concluded," said William, standing aside to let them pass.

Catherine went upstairs to dress for the ceremony, and when she came down, Hannah, Ann, and Eleanor were already waiting. "We want more family with us for this happy time," said Catherine to the other women. "It will not be spoken, but I want you all to say your prayers for the souls of Joan and Ruth."

"And for the discovery of their murderers," added Ann.

Catherine set her veil in place and the women made their way to the Overton Chapel. John Bridle performed his role with dispatch, and William lifted Catherine's veil after the priest had anointed her. "No more of these papist garments, Catherine."

John Bridle stepped between them. "Let her keep it. The king leans more to the old rites again these days, I'm told."

"What?" asked William.

John Bridle shrugged. "We race one way, then we run headlong the other. He will still be the head of the church. We just cannot be sure what it will look like from day to day. Best to be safe."

Catherine set the cloth back over her face. "I don't pretend to greater piety than any other wife. But I will not be thought a heretic."

The women said nothing until they had all gathered in Catherine's bedchamber. Eleanor untied the churching gown and sleeves and folded the veil into a neat square, then she joined the others around Catherine's small table. "Now you can come to the village, Madam, and make those cowards say what they know of your sisters."

"No 'sisters,' Eleanor. Our family. That is all. The king hasn't gone that far back toward Rome." Eleanor hung her head, and Catherine stroked her hair. "You speak right, though. I will see to them."

A fist rapped upon the chamber door, and William lifted the latch and put his head in. "Forgive a man for interrupting."

Eleanor folded her hands and stared at her thumbs. Ann took up a piece of sewing from the basket near her feet. Catherine said, "You are welcome in my chambers, as always. Come in, William. We are not plotting the overthrow of marriage."

He laughed and entered the room, the peregrine on his arm. "Not yet. Give you time, ladies, give you time." He held up an envelope. "Time, however, you have none of just now. I have the letters we need, Catherine. We are summoned to make our way to court."

10

"A month or two will surely make no difference," said Catherine. She had followed William downstairs and out the big back door. John Bridle waited with his own bird on his fist, and they all walked into the nearest field. John Bridle set his bird aloft, and Catherine shivered as she watched it dragged earthward again.

"That's a fine little sparrow hawk, John," said William, and the priest beamed like a lord. "I have made arrangements," he added without taking his eyes from the sky. He might have been speaking either to Catherine or to her father. "We will go this week. Eleanor may come and carry the baby." Now William let his eyes fall onto her. "Bring another maid if you like. The things we need will follow us. Spring is coming on, and we want to be in London and secure your position. Now."

"In London? What will I do there? The king's children are in the country, aren't they?"

"We must lay our plans," he said, letting his Ruby fly. "Benjamin Davies keeps a city house where we will lodge. You recall him. He always sells his wool at the highest prices. He taught my brother to excel even our father in trade. I will visit the cloth makers and get their wisdom on making the new draperies here. You will wait until the call comes. From there we will make our way." He whistled and his peregrine circled lower and lower, landing on his upraised arm. "What do you think of converting the convent buildings, John? We will make a pot of money, and you can oversee the works." His voice had gone tight with excitement, and he clutched the bird's claws until his knuckles went white.

The priest, mimicking William's stance, tossed his hawk into the air and they all stood silent until he whistled her down and fumbled a hood over her head. "It seems a wise use of the spaces." He cast a glance over his shoulder at Catherine.

Catherine stepped between the men. "But Ruth is not found, William. Teresa still grieves like she has lost her own sister. Hannah—"

"Hannah and Teresa are grown women. Ann can stay here and mind them if they need a keeper. Let them keep their heads down and act like part of this family and all shall be well."

"Ann will come with me. She must."

"She should stay here for now. It sounds as though she is needed. Perhaps later she may join you. You want her steady head to govern these women, do you not?"

Catherine thought a moment. "So we will go light, is that it? Fly to London?"

"You read my thoughts."

"Where we will sit like fat ducks and do nothing?"

"Being prepared is not nothing. I have already instructed Eleanor to pack your things."

"What?"

William and John handed their birds to the trainer, and Catherine fled up to her chamber and flung open her wooden chests. Her clothes and her stack of books were gone. A cold knot twisted in her stomach. William came in and looked with satisfaction at the empty room.

"And who is to travel with us?" asked Catherine.

"I have said, Eleanor and another maid for you if you want one. I will have a couple or three men for the horses and Reginald for myself. We will lodge with Benjamin Davies. His servants will do for us, as well, at least for a time."

Catherine's hands were shaking, and she gripped the brass handle of the closest chest. "Who will tend to Robbie?"

"The boy will stay at home with Ann. He needs to learn to ride and behave like a gentleman before he leaves his home. We will get you settled into a place first."

"No! He is but three years old, William. He cannot be left alone."

"He will not be alone. Ann is practically his second mother. And Margaret will be here. You mustn't spoil the boy, Catherine."

"Your sister barely knows he exists. I wonder that you would abandon your son."

William's jaw tensed and a muscle under his left eye jumped. "I have not abandoned him. But do not press me on this matter, Catherine. Boys younger than Robert have learned to untie themselves from their mothers' apron strings. The king's son does not cry for his mother. I will see to Robert as I have always done. But just now I mean to show off you and Veronica."

He came to her with his arms opened, but Catherine backed away. "The arrangements have all been made, it seems. You and this Benjamin have been busy indeed." She blinked to clear her eyes. "I have never kept Robbie tied unnaturally to me. It is cruel for you to say so. He is a little boy, William, and I will not stay in London while he grows up here. No, don't touch me, not until you promise me that he will come. Soon. With Ann. Or I will not move a foot from this room."

"Catherine, be reasonable."

"You think dragging a woman from her childbed and throwing her onto a dirty horse reasonable? You think carting a baby barely breathing in the world all the way across England reasonable? You want me to think of the reasons for that?" Catherine stopped, panting. "Well? Your promise?"

"Will you believe me if I promise it?"

"Only if you don't swear it to God. Only to me."

"You're a hard woman, Catherine, for such a young one. You have my word, then. You and I will go with Veronica, and Robert will come with Ann as soon as is practical. That is as much as I can vow. But you and I will go. Tomorrow."

Catherine gasped. "So soon as that?" She stepped away from him again. "Since you have seized my clothes and books, I suppose I have no choice. But I will hold you to that word. Remember it."

"You will not let me forget, I'm sure." He leaned in to kiss her, and she let him have her cheek. He brushed back Veronica's tuft of hair and went from the room.

Ann passed him as she came in. "Are you really going to London? Tomorrow? Eleanor says she has been made to pack up your clothes."

Catherine burst into tears.

11

The road was cold and muddy, and Catherine did not want to get onto it. William was too busy to notice, ordering the pack horses to stand still while the servants loaded the new wool for the London market. Eleanor waited beside the ponies for herself and Catherine while Joseph, whispering, harnessed them, and Catherine held her son against her breast. "You will mind Ann and learn your lessons, do you hear me? And when I send for you, you will come south and perhaps I will introduce you to a princess. How well might you like that?"

Ann, arms crossed, glared over the fields toward the village. "It is unnatural, Catherine, and William knows it. You should be here until you are strong again. Even Eleanor gets to take her young man with her. Let him go see to the new mills for himself and bring you the directions."

"Not so hard, Ann. He has the letters. William's ambition runs before him and he's bound to try and catch it. Joseph comes along because he is good with the horses, not because of Eleanor."

"Men's ambitions. He acts like his dead brother." Ann spit through her teeth onto the gravel. "I notice that his ambition runs off just when that same brother's old companions are rumored to be on their way to Yorkshire."

Catherine looked in the direction of Ann's gaze. "Are they nigh?"

"No, not that I have heard. They are just words on the wind yet. They may be nothing more than that. The terror of serving girls and their gossips."

Robert leaned away from his mother, pushing his hands against her bodice. "Will you bring me a real princess when you return?"

Catherine laughed. "I will have you come and kneel before her yourself. Will you be a courtier, Robbie? You must learn to sit your horse first, you know. And you must practice your bowing and your manners in speech."

"I will practice it, Mother." He squirmed out of her grip and walked over to stand in front of Ann. "Aunt Ann will beat me if I slacken, will you not?"

Ann threw back her head and guffawed. "Listen to the boy. When have I ever beaten you, young Master Robert?"

Robert planted his feet far apart and put his fists on his narrow hips. "My father says to spare the rod is to spoil the child. I will not be spoilt before I am ripe, Aunt Ann."

"You will not rot, Master Robert." She picked him up as William came out, directing his man Reginald with some baskets. "The boy talks like you, Catherine."

"Come kiss me, Son," said Catherine. She hugged Ann and Robert together until the boy pushed the women apart. She saw Ann's eyes stray over her shoulder to Reginald.

"You will strangle me, Mother."

Catherine stroked his hair and leaned to whisper to Ann. "You will see to the matter of these real stranglings?" Ann nodded, and Catherine said to Robert, "You are to be good and say your prayers and feed Thomasina so that she may feed her kittens. Will you do it?"

"I will be sure that he does it," said Margaret, coming up behind them. "I will manage the household as smoothly as my brother has done." She patted Catherine on the shoulder. "You may go with a clear conscience. All here will be just as it should be."

Robert pressed his face against Ann's broad chest, and Catherine placed her hand on the boy's hair. "I thank you, Sister," she said to Margaret.

Then Eleanor squealed behind her. It was time to go. Catherine fixed the baby to her maid's front, then climbed onto her own pony and closed her eyes. "Tell me when we are on the road," she said. "I have said my good-byes."

"But you must turn, Madam," said Eleanor. "They are all out, seeing you off."

Catherine couldn't resist. She looked back at Hannah, Teresa, and Ann holding Robbie. Margaret Overton was behind the other women, one hand raised stiffly. Teresa had her hen under one arm, and she lifted one of its wings to wave goodbye. "She looks like a child, even at her age," whispered Catherine. "I hope God will protect her as one."

12

Four days of travel brought the little group from silent winter to the first whisper of spring. The roads became boggier and boggier, until Catherine's pony could barely drag its hooves through the mud. The saddle bruised her buttocks and thighs, and she shifted from one side to the other, trying to get some relief. The second night's inn had been alive with bedbugs and lice, and Catherine kept picking them from her scalp. Eleanor once tore off her hood with a shriek and scrubbed under her coif with her nails. "Mother of God, do they never clean the linens in that sty? I have never been so infested." She picked something from the baby's face with a little shriek and flung it away with her forefinger.

Catherine itched just watching, and soon she felt a crawling on the back of her neck. She trapped the offender as it entered her hairline. A large flea, which she smashed against her riding boot with the back of her thumb. The baby wailed, and Eleanor opened the band that held her. Catherine could see the red patches on Veronica's fat legs. "I will need to soak the child in lavender water up to her nostrils. You, too, Eleanor."

That evening, they bathed in bowls of hot water and spent the night shaking out their shifts and sifting stavesacre over the clothes in their cases. Eleanor leaned into Catherine's folded skirts and breathed. "What is it made of, Madam?"

Catherine brushed her palms clean. "Larkspur seeds."

"Those purple flowers? They seem like towers of sugar."

"The very ones. Pray the vermin find it less sweet." Her bites still itched and she added dried mint to the stavesacre, but even after the bath and a scrubbing with a rough clout, they lay awake yet again, rubbing at the angry welts while the baby whimpered and tossed.

On the afternoon of the fifth day, when London rose into Catherine's sight, she was so sleepy that the city seemed like a monstrous dragon sunning itself along the southern horizon. The spires of the Tower and St. Paul's lifted along the horizon, spikes on the back of a huge adder, and Catherine shaded her eyes with her hand. "It looks just as I remember. Except that I was eager then. I see poison in its points now."

Eleanor pushed up onto her feet and leaned forward, squinting. "You've been before?"

"Years ago." Catherine stretched toward her maid and pulled the linen over Veronica's face to keep the dust from her nose. "I was fifteen, and my . . . the prioress of my convent thought I would make a maid for the queen."

"The old queen, that one?" Eleanor pulled her pony closer. She whispered, "The first one?"

"The very one," said Catherine softly. "I saw her before she died. Her heart was broken."

"At least she still had her head on her neck." Eleanor sat with a thump but kept her voice low. "She was the real queen, that's what they say in the village."

"Who says that? Do they not know it is heresy? No one should say such a thing aloud."

Eleanor nodded. "They know. No one says it in the public house. Not before the constable. He bends whichever way the king blows."

"Why didn't you tell me this before? I have been accusing the villagers in my mind for the deaths of Ruth and Joan."

"Troth, some would have been glad to see them gone, but not because they hate nuns. It's because they say the king hates nuns. There's others who talk of witches, but not all."

"I wish you had told me this."

"It's just the folk I know, my far kin and such. The king has his people, for sure. There's plenty who'd throw all the old nuns in a fire if they could lay hands on some of their land. I think no one knows what to believe and the confusion makes demons of us all."

"Shh. We shouldn't speak of this here." Catherine glanced over her shoulder to be sure that no one was riding near them.

Eleanor sidestepped her pony closer. "They say that when the king dies, we will have great wars in England."

"We already have wars in England," Catherine said.

"Tell me about the convent," said Eleanor. "Folks say that you were born there. That the village is named after you."

"I suppose I was. Born in the convent, I mean. I don't remember." Catherine closed her eyes and felt her bones rattle in time with the ruts in the road. "My mother was named Havens and I carried her name until I was married. I still carry it within me. What else do you want to know?"

"About you. People say all kinds of things. Some people say I oughtn't work at Overton House. They say it's full of witches and ghosts. They say you were forbidden to marry."

"People say all sorts of silly things. They're for the king, they're against the king. They're for the queen but against the nuns. We run in every direction at once. We draw and quarter our own island." Catherine opened her eyes and looked at the girl. Eleanor's face shone with sweat. "Have you ever seen a ghost at the House?"

"No. But I've searched high and low."

Catherine laughed. "The only ghosts in that house dwell in the minds of the living." She sat forward to ease the pressure from her hips. "And, yes, I was born in the convent at Mount Grace. Do you want to know who my parents were? My real blood parents? The prioress and Father John. That's right, Father John Bridle. Look at Veronica's eyes and look at his. You'll see. And William sent to the king himself for permission for us to marry."

Eleanor was staring, breathing through her mouth, and Catherine bumped her under the chin. "You'd better close that before the flies get in." The girl blushed, and Catherine patted her cheek. "Don't worry, child, I'm no witch. If I were, I'd've put a spell on the king's men to make them act like Christians."

"They drove you out, didn't they? They killed your mother?"

Catherine lifted the sides of her hood and let the air cool the hair around her temples. "The walls do have ears. Yes, that's how it was. They turned us out, and I walked an old friend of my mother's to Lynn. It was high summer and hot. And the rains would not relent. But we went, on our own feet the full way. We found her niece, and the morning after we arrived, her heart burst. I walked home again. Her name was Veronica and she was another mother to me." Catherine's stomach felt scorched and shriveled and she stopped the story there.

Eleanor clasped her hands together. "And Master William was waiting for you in the road when you returned, and he carried you to your father's house and prevailed against the king and married you, isn't that right? And then you had little Robert."

Catherine choked out, "You have told my life story, Eleanor."

"It is too beautiful and sad. It is a tale for children." Eleanor unhooked her hands and began to twist a stray tendril of her hair around her finger. "Robert was a sickly child because he was born too soon. Oh, but he looks the image of you, Madam."

Catherine regarded the girl. "That is a *non sequitur*."

"A what?"

"The one does not follow upon the other."

Eleanor gazed across a small field where some pigs grazed. "Madam, tell me about the court. When you were there."

Catherine drank from the wineskin on her saddle and let the liquid cool her insides. Then she could begin again. "It was full of music and dancing. The queen's women wore gold brocade and rubies, and her walls were covered in carpets of blue and green. She gave me a locket, traced silver, and I wore it for years. Until one of the king's men tore it from my neck. The queen's eyes were deep as still water, and she spoke with the notes of Spain in her words."

"And her daughter, Mary. The elder of the king's daughters. Will she know you?"

Catherine shrugged. "She might recall my name if the occasion is brought to her memory. We are close in age."

"The king does not love her. Nor the younger daughter."

"They say not."

"Both are called bastards."

"I have heard it said so. But they may win back his love yet."

Eleanor worried the lock of hair again. "Madam, do not think me impertinent."

"Don't be impertinent and I won't."

"Master William does not love little Robert."

Catherine's heart tipped over. Her ribs felt tight. "Who says so?"

"I don't wish to spread tales, Madam, but he's so cold sometimes. It's like winter blows into the room when he's with the poor little boy." Eleanor looked at Veronica's head, bobbing against her chest. "The little mister says it himself, even. And here we are, without him."

Catherine's throat had filled, and she could barely get words up. "No more talk."

"Forgive me, Madam," Eleanor whispered. She squeezed the baby, though Veronica hadn't wakened.

Joseph trotted up beside them, grinning. "We're almost there!"

"Yes," said Catherine, and she sat back as William rode up beside the young man.

"How do the ladies? Dust-smothered yet?"

"Well-nigh," said Catherine, waving her handkerchief. "I will be happy when my head can stop bouncing."

"Before dark, my love, you'll be drinking wine at a gentleman's table." William spurred his stallion and twisted around to speak to the men leading the pack horses. There was laughter in his voice.

Catherine closed her eyes again and listened to her blood keeping time to the pounding of the hooves that carried them forward. She must have dozed, because Eleanor was suddenly shaking her knee, saying "Madam, look!" and she opened her eyes again to the sight of buildings. They were thumping down a sludgy way. The soft road sucked at their ponies' hooves, and the animals plowed ahead. They passed a narrow side road, almost an alley, and Catherine spied a small girl in a doorway. Her shift was a rag, and the bones of her face pushed against the thin skin. The air smelt of smoke, and the baby began to cough.

"It is paradise!" said Eleanor.

Joseph plodded along nearby and he pointed. "Look at that, Lady Overton. What is it?"

"The Tower."

Eleanor gasped and clapped her hands. "That's where they kept the Boleyn woman, isn't it? Where the princes were murdered by the hunchback, isn't it?" The maid gaped at the dark walls as they passed, straining to see the buildings inside.

"It is where queens go before they are crowned and before they have their crowns removed," said Catherine.

They rode a while in silence.

"And there, look at that," said Eleanor. They had come out by the Thames, and a small boat drifted in their direction. "Is that the king's?"

"No, it's too small." Catherine sat forward. The sails fluttered, red and blue flags, and a young man, sun-reddened and hard-muscled, worked in the bow. Joseph waved, and the other man arced his cap at him. Joseph whooped and raised himself in his saddle.

"Did you see that?" said Eleanor. "It is as fine as anything I have ever seen."

The sun burned away a cloud and shot a gold streak across the water. They were nearing London Bridge, like a long skinny town of its own, stretched over the river. The shops teetered and leaned, and people gathered at the north end, in twos and threes. Catherine's throat closed completely. Once, she had wanted to be at court worse than she had ever wanted anything. But that was years ago. She'd been a girl. The spikes still speared the sky on the south bank, the shriveling heads of traitors and thieves enticing crows by the dozen. Catherine shuddered. Even that. She had wanted even that.

"Do you see? Look, are those dead men?" Now Eleanor was pointing.

"A piece of them." Catherine could not help but stare. "A reminder that our king is now the head of our church. You see how they overlook it?"

They could just see the corner of Southwark Cathedral, but William went to the right, and they were back in the dark streets of London Town again. Then left, and right again, until Catherine had lost her way. She saw the dark stretch of St Paul's behind them, but nothing else looked familiar.

Eleanor clapped her hands and sprang up and down on her saddle. "We are almost arrived. I feel it!" Her pony veered over and bumped Catherine's.

"We will all feel it if you don't sit still, Eleanor. You're like to capsize us into the mire." Catherine touched her own cheek. "We must look like a pack of beggars."

Eleanor lifted the ends of her hair and sniffed. "I stink, but you are beautiful, Madam, as always. And little Veronica is an angel."

"We all smell like old meat in summer," said Catherine. "Let's pray there's a bath and clean clothing." They turned one more time, left, through an arch into a grassy courtyard, and stopped before a grim, pale building. The windows were curtained and the flat façade was streaked with grime. The front door opened, and a large man came out, hailing them and waving. "And we had better pray quickly. We're here."

13

Catherine waited while William greeted his brother's old university friend. They slapped backs and laughed while she tried to check the snugness of her bodice without looking down. "Am I covered?" she said, and Eleanor, glancing over for barely a second, nodded brightly.

"All right, then. Be ready to hand down the baby when I ask."

"Yes, Madam. You may depend on me."

Joseph was on his feet, stretching, and here came William and Benjamin Davies. Benjamin was the taller of the two, and while William's brown hair showed glints of the Overton red under the sun, this man was black-haired, with curls almost to his shoulders. His beard was salted with stripes of white, and he didn't seem to mind showing his teeth when he smiled. It was no wonder. They were solid and straight. He put Catherine in mind of a good-tempered sheepdog. The pack horses had been brought forward, and the men pulled bits of wool from the sacks. Benjamin stretched a strand between his hands and nodded. William gestured broadly across the animals then came to help her down. Catherine's breath hitched and stuck in her throat.

"And here she is, my gentle Catherine," said William. He gave her his hand, and she slipped to the ground.

The sun tore through another cloud, and the force of the light stunned Catherine's eyes downward. Her curtsey felt more like surrender than greeting. "Sir."

"No 'sir,' please, lady." Benjamin lifted her by both hands and held out her arms. His smile beamed through the dark cloud of his beard and Catherine blinked. "She is a beauty, William! No wonder you've been keeping her to yourself up there in the wilderness. Look at you, Catherine Overton."

"I'm hidden under a blanket of muck just now. You should see how I look when you can see my face." Catherine put her fingers to her neck. It felt hot and she hoped she wasn't blushing.

Benjamin bellowed out a great laugh and Catherine could see his tongue. "She has a wit, too. William, your ship has certainly come in with this one."

"And see what she has brought with her," said William.

Catherine beckoned to Eleanor, who handed down the baby, then hopped to the ground and waited quietly behind her mistress. Catherine offered the child for view. "This is Veronica, our daughter."

Benjamin held his breath and folded back the cloth covering her face. "She is barely born."

"And already perfect." Catherine pulled back the cloth further. "Perfect as her father, and with hair flaming as any Overton."

Benjamin laughed again. "William, she has hair like your brother. She will grow up to look like Robert."

William put on a look of horror, but there was pleasure behind it. "She will certainly be more handsome."

Both men suddenly fell sober. "It was hard, how your brother went," said Benjamin. He tucked the cloth back up to the baby's chin. "He was always afflicted with a bilious humor."

William nodded. "The illness affected his reason. It almost broke our family apart. He went so far as to accuse me to the law."

"Indeed, the news reached me here. It's hard times we live in. Families are in splinters all over England. Some have gone over to Flanders." Benjamin's voice had dropped almost to a murmur. "A man must take what he can and keep his head on his shoulders." He looked directly at Catherine. "Women too."

"You know my history?" Catherine asked.

One of Benjamin's thick eyebrows lifted. "Enough."

"I was a nun."

"I've heard the tale. At least one man's version of it." Benjamin's mouth was tight with the effort not to smile. "But he is your husband now and the king's loyal subject and it behooves him to speak ill of a nun's profession."

"I wasn't a very good one."

"There's no shame in being in a convent. Now, staying in a convent is another matter these days." Benjamin looked from Catherine to William. "We won't have a flock of black birds about the place, will we?"

"No." William took Catherine by the hand and squeezed.

"Good enough." His head on one side, Benjamin swept his eyes over her, top to bottom and back up. "We'll get you in with the daughter's household, of that you can be sure. But you'd better keep out of the king's sight."

"Does he hate the sisters so much?" asked Catherine. "Even reformed ones?"

"He doesn't care one way or the other about them," said Benjamin, "as long as they don't marry and he has their lands in his pocket." His face blazed behind the beard, and he coughed. "The ones without his blessing, I mean to say. He is unmarried himself just now and he's not a man who likes his bed to stay cold." He shook his hand in the air. "Enough of that. All is well. Come inside." He put his hand on William's back.

The house was dark but rich on the inside. The rushes were plushy and fresh, and Catherine's feet sank in as she stepped over the threshold, releasing the scent of lavender and rosemary and rose petals. Sunlight slanted through the drawn curtains, gilding the tapestries along the far side of the big hall they entered. A large table sat in the room to their right, but not like the big trestle table in the gallery of Overton Hall. This one was carved dark oak with crouching lions for legs. The ceiling was painted with scenes of Jupiter and half-naked women, the god as a bull, as a swan, as a shower of gold. The rafters were set with wooden dragons and deer and leaping fish in painted green and blue and red. Catherine gaped upward until her neck seized.

"You must be starved half to death," said Benjamin. He stepped past the table and roared through a doorway. He waited for movements below before he added, "Let me show you your chambers."

They followed him up a staircase against the side wall of the first big room and down a long gallery hung with portraits. A stuffed boar threatened the air from a raised platform, and Benjamin polished its snout as they walked past. "Here." He pushed open a door and they stepped into a brightly lit bedroom. A cradle had been brought in and filled with folded bedding. "Beyond is a room for your maid, Catherine. William, that door opens into your rooms, with a closet for your man on the far side."

A full ewer sat on the dresser, and Catherine suddenly itched all over again. "I would like a rest before we eat."

"God's blood, have a whole bath if you want. There's a tub in the alcove between this and the maid's room. I'll have a girl carry you up some hot water. William?"

"I'll walk down with you. Let the women have their privacy." He kissed Catherine on the cheek and was gone.

"Thank God," said Eleanor when the door closed. "I thought I would burst." She ran through to her little room, and at the sound of urine hitting a chamberpot, Catherine clutched her own skirt and searched under the bed for another one.

She laid the baby in the cradle and squatted. The release felt good, but she was still bleeding lightly, and she called for Eleanor. "I need you to help me stand up."

The maid came back, smoothing her skirt. "Do men never need to piss? Mother of Christ, I can barely hold it when my monthlies are coming."

"Men can use trees and ditches." Catherine folded a new pad and tucked it between her legs. "I'm almost whole again." She tossed the old one into the hearth, and the embers flared. Catherine held her nose against the stench of stale blood and went to the window, pushing open the leaded pane and leaning out. A man and a boy were below in the narrow passage between the back door and the outbuildings. The boy's head was hanging and the man was yelling. He grabbed something out of the child's hand and backhanded him so hard the boy fell onto his back. The man flung the object to the stones and disappeared into the house right under Catherine's window. The boy rubbed the side of his head, then pushed himself up and wobbled off into a shed. Catherine leaned out farther to look. It was a rosary, though the little Christ had broken at the waist in his fall and his face shone silver, unaware that his legs had rolled away into a muddy crack. Maybe rosaries were allowed again now and no one had told the man. The boy might be getting his beating for nothing.

Eleanor had thrown a couple of sticks onto the fire and was stirring the offending cloth into ash. The stink had burned off and she added a thin log. "Want to bathe, Madam?"

"More than anything." Catherine stripped to wash at the basin but stood staring at her reflection in the water. "No," she said. "There is one thing I want more."

"What would that be?"

"I want Robbie." Catherine didn't care that the water was tepid. The soap smelt like roses, and she ran the cloth over her neck and arms and breasts. Eleanor held up her mistress's hair and wiped down her back and nape.

"You will need to be cautious, Madam. What Master Benjamin says, it's true?"

"You mean about the king and his appetites? God knows. I likely will look like an old married woman in his eyes. I think I am bound for the daughter anyway. Is there a basin in your room?"

"A small one. It's enough. Give me a minute and I will come dress you."

Catherine handed her the soap. "No sense letting this dry out."

Eleanor held it to her nose and closed her eyes with pleasure. "One minute." She was already pulling her apron loose as she slipped into the next room.

Catherine regarded her face in the small glass on the wall. Dark hair, curlier than she had thought it would ever be. Her skin was pale, like most women from the North, but her eyes were the same green as John Bridle's. She bit her lips and they bloomed red. From her small case she drew a box of rice powder for her chest and cheeks. A fresh shift and a straightened hood on her head, and she was ready to be seen.

Eleanor came in, tying her hair up with a clean ribbon of silk the color of twilight. "I found this in the cupboard. It is almost the Overton shade of blue. Will I be whipped for wearing it?"

"Not if it is a reformed ribbon," said Catherine. She held one raveled end to the light. "It is close enough to our color."

"I found something else." The maid ran back to her chamber and returned with a handful of lavender, the heads heavy with blossoms. "Can you make use of these?"

"Oh, thank God above," said Catherine. The flowers were still fragrant. She stripped off some petals in one quick motion and sprinkled them over her trunk. "Now let the bedbugs go bite elsewhere." She handed the remainder back to Eleanor. "There are still plenty of flowers there. Go strip them off into your clothing and your bed."

Eleanor did as she was bidden and returned with the decapitated stems, which she strewed among the rushes on the floor. She stood behind Catherine, who sat to let the little maid smooth her sleeves and the back of her hood. Eleanor's hand rested on Catherine's shoulder. "Madam?"

Catherine was enjoying the petting. "What is it?"

"You look fine."

Catherine hefted her breasts and let them fall. "I feel like a dowdy cow."

"No. I mean you look very fine. I cannot help but think on what the gentleman said. Do you want to look so well? Is it safe?"

Catherine looked in her glass again. "I will keep out of the sight of the king's men. The king himself, too, as well as I can."

"That house is full of men, I have heard. And the king himself sniffs through the ladies for his prey. Even married ladies. There is no telling, Madam, what might happen to someone who looks like you."

14

Supper was being prepared, and William sat with Benjamin at the long dining table, drinking wine. Catherine swept into the room and waited for her vision to adjust to the gloom.

"Catherine. Love," said William. "We have been speaking of you. Come, sit with us and we will map out your future."

"Our future, surely you mean." When she could pick out his dim figure, Catherine chose the seat across from her husband, pulled her spoon from her girdle bag, and wiped it on her handkerchief.

"I have dinner tools for you," said Benjamin. "I promise they're not poisoned."

Catherine cursed herself silently and set the utensil gently by the silver plate. "I thought no such thing. I am a simple woman, accustomed to my own." Her hand remained on the cool pewter handle. "William tells me that your lady was taken down by the pox. It grieves my heart to hear it. Were there no physicians in London to be had?"

"Physicians coming out our ears. No one who can stop death when it breathes on a person."

"Catherine can stop it," said William. "It was she who brought me through the pox."

"Was that you?" Benjamin looked at Catherine with new eyes. "I thought you had bewitched his soul, not his skin."

"I cared for him as well as I could," Catherine said. "The pox is a powerful enemy."

"Would that you had been here when my wife fell ill. She has lain in the Davies family tomb for over a year now. And I have seen her resting place only once in that time, though it is less than a week's ride to Conwy from here." Benjamin seemed to be speaking to himself.

Catherine moved her spoon an inch from the linen napkin, then pulled it back again. She said into the silence, "How is it that you are called Benjamin? It is not a Welsh name."

The man brightened at that and spoke directly to her. "My mother is as English as you. A conquest of my father's. His second. Or third. The man married so often his children had difficulty keeping up. I am his third son, which absolves me of all responsibility in the matter of names and ancestral properties. I am a free man, as you see." He spread his arms as though his liberty showed on his body. "I have a daughter of my own, but she keeps to her room. She is just thirteen, and has given herself up wholly to piety. I will have her down directly to sing to us if I can haul her away from her prayers long enough." He sighed. "She misses a mother, as all girls do. I think she would like us to bring back the Mother of God so that she will have a place to direct her petitions."

"Yes," said Catherine. "I understand. I would be pleased to hear her voice."

Benjamin put his elbow on the table and pointed at Catherine. "And speaking of conquests, this Elizabeth is the one you should fasten upon. The child is mostly forgotten, mostly without friends, but the king will have her provided for. He must. She's a small meteor, that girl. You can see that she's a bastard by her bad behavior. But she's the king's, no doubt about that. The hair." Benjamin touched his own head with the tip of his knife, then beckoned to a man at the door who held another platter of meat. "Bring it in." The food was laid, and the man called upon two boys who scooted in with bread and more wine. "Ah," said Benjamin. He sat back while his plate was loaded with slabs of venison and chicken. A bowl of leeks and carrots was laid, and he helped himself with a big spoon. "Give the lady some wine, lad. Then go fetch my daughter."

Catherine's stomach had shriveled, hungry as she was. "So a bastard can be discovered by her evil manners, is that it?"

Benjamin opened his mouth. Then he closed it. "I meant no offense." He cut a piece of meat. "But I believe you said yourself you were no good nun."

Catherine's guts were shifting about, and she thought she might cry. Instead, a laugh erupted from her. He was in the right. "I stand corrected. I have laid claim to my own devil, haven't I?"

"You're the greater lady for having to build a character from the ground up," said Benjamin. "And perhaps the king's bastard will do the same."

"Perhaps." Catherine rubbed the handle of her spoon. It was smooth and familiar under her fingertip.

The men fell to their food, shoveling meats and bread in together. They finished one loaf and called for another. Catherine sipped at the wine and pushed the meat around on her plate. It left a bloody trail and she set down her knife.

"Your lady has no appetite," said Benjamin, sitting back and sucking his teeth. "Are the victuals not to your taste?"

"I am weary from the road," said Catherine. She took a piece of bread and drove it through the juices. She took a bite and her stomach closed up. She could eat nothing until she spoke. "I thought the princess was at Hatfield Place. Is there nothing I can do for her?"

"That's who I've been telling you about. Hatfield House. The place has not been a palace for ages. Yes, the child wants a friendly face."

"Yes, of course. I mean, no." Catherine took another bite of bread, plain this time, and washed it down with wine. Her face was aflame, and her guts felt like sparked tinder. "I mean the older daughter. Mary. She has ladies, too, doesn't she? I might serve her better. We are almost of an age."

"Catherine—" William said, a warning note ringing at the bottom of his voice.

Benjamin raised his hand. "No, let her speak. Let me counsel you about the Lady Mary. She's possessed, out of her mind. She seems gentle as a spring rain one minute, but I know more than one woman who's been dismissed from her service with scratches on both face and soul. I should know. My wife was one of them." He drank deeply and lifted the goblet for his man. The servant sprang from a dark corner and came to the table with a jug. "And with your history, you will make no lasting friends if you go down that path. You might find yourself quite alone."

"But she must be mad with grief," said Catherine. "Her life has been a torture. It would try the patience of a saint."

"Mary Tudor is no saint and if her life is torture, I know many a felon who would change places with her. She maintains ties with Rome. The king is forced to keep a watch on her day and night. Her head is likely safe enough, at least for now, but I would not send another woman into her circle for Christ's big toe in a silver ring."

"Perhaps she needs physic," said Catherine. "Sometimes maladies of the mind can be calmed through care of the body. I have made studies of women's ailments. I could be of service to her."

"No." William pushed back his chair and stood, leaning onto the table with both palms flat. "She is a papist. You cannot serve her. You will not. You will serve the Protestant daughter."

"The bastard, you mean," Catherine murmured, picking at the meat with her knife. "The evil one."

"They are both bastards, for all that," said Benjamin. "The king recognizes them as his flesh, but not as his heirs. There is now a boy, so you'd best go where you're safest. I tell you, Mary Tudor is beyond physic, for the body or the mind. Her soul is black, and her wits have descended into that same dark pit. She has enough old nuns hovering about her. It's like a school for angels of death. She doesn't need another one."

Now Catherine stood and met her husband's eyes evenly. "Very well. I see that my course has been chosen for me. I will present myself to the daughter of the Boleyn woman and we shall see if the little bastard will have me."

"You will present yourself nowhere," said Benjamin. "I will present your husband to the master of the house. His name is Sir John Shelton. He may present you both to one of her women, who will examine you. If she approves, you may be given a trial. That's all I can promise."

"It has been a long journey to beg to nurse a brat," said Catherine.

"Indeed. But this is a brat with diapers of gold. Ah, and here is my Diana now." A tiny girl with nut-brown hair entered the room, carrying a lute. "Will you give us a song, child?"

"As you wish, Father, but my voice is not in good tune." She plucked at the instrument and adjusted the strings.

William murmured, "I mean what I say, Catherine. You are to serve the Protestant daughter. Elizabeth."

As Diana opened her mouth, Catherine nodded and smiled. She would see about that.

15

The next morning, William was up before dawn, fretting about the wool. He was gone to meet some merchants from Flanders by the time Catherine washed, fed Veronica, and pulled on her red skirt and sleeves. The make was fine, with slashings and Overton blue embroidery across the bodice, and Eleanor stroked the fabric over Catherine's back after she tightened the laces.

"You will look as high a lady as anyone at the court in this."

"It is not the court proper. The child stays at Hatfield Pl--House, and we are to go there. I think you'll find it far removed from the glories of the king."

"But she is royalty, Madam. Isn't she?"

"So they will say. But shh, Eleanor. We must hold our tongues until we see the lie of the land. I mean to have my son here if we stay. Will you bring Veronica?"

"Yes, Madam."

Downstairs, the morning meal had been laid and eaten by the men. Eleanor took the back steps to the kitchen, and Catherine sat alone in the dark, hollow dining room, picking at the loaf growing stale on the table. A man came to the side door and waited with his hands folded. He said nothing.

"Have you any ale?" asked Catherine.

"Yes, Madam." He withdrew backward, and she was alone again. When the draught was brought, Catherine took the cup and loaf and slipped after Eleanor, down toward the sound of laughter. She entered a large white-washed room, where half a dozen women surrounded a trestle table, rough-hewn from fir. An old lady was holding Veronica.

The noise ceased when Catherine appeared. "Do not stop your talk for me," she said, sitting on the nearest bench. "I will break my fast among you women, if you will have me."

"Madam, this is the kitchen," said the old woman. She handed the baby to Eleanor.

"Oh, I cry you mercy, I thought I was in the queen's bedchamber," said Catherine, breaking the loaf. She looked hard at the woman, then laughed and patted the stringy arm. "I know where I am."

"The master will whip us to shreds if he catches you among us," the woman whispered.

"Wherefore should he whip you? I have legs enough to carry me where I mean to go. My woman is here. My daughter is here. Here is where I mean to be and I will stand between you and the scourge if he do but try it."

The women all looked toward the door behind her. "You heard the lady," said Benjamin Davies. "She will bind me hand and foot and let the daws peck at me if I speak a cross word to you."

Catherine rose. The heat had come into her face again. "I do not mean to overturn your house, Benjamin. I was lonely for women's voices. That's all."

"Come, then, and I'll take you where the chatter of females never ends." He winked at Catherine, and she followed him back upstairs. William was in the main gallery, counting coins, and he rattled his purse when he saw her.

"The Overton wool is still thought the best," he said. "This will outfit you for any king's daughter. What say you to opening a drapery at home? We could make the new worsteds and sell them direct."

Catherine went to the open door and measured the weather with her face. The sun shone with a fierce expression, but the wind was cold. "It might be the best use for the old convent buildings."

"You think like a man, Catherine," said William. He jangled his purse again and stuffed into his pocket. "Is it time we rode to your country house, Benjamin?"

"I await your orders, sir," said Benjamin.

Catherine waited in the doorway for the horses to be brought around and watched William, in the yard with the pack animals, directing his men. He was in deep conference with his reeve, who had purchased a proud young Suffolk ram. The poor animal flailed and thrashed, but they tied it up to the harness of one of the horses and it settled into sullen submission. Joseph was returning with the animals to Overton House, and he whispered into the ear of a sniffling

Eleanor. Finally, the horses and men and sheep got into line and made their progress out the front gate. Catherine threw her cloak over her head against the damp breeze and ran for her pony, jumping into the saddle without assistance. William leapt up behind her. "Eleanor and the baby here behind Catherine."

Benjamin mounted his big gelding, and they jolted into movement.

Catherine trotted up beside William. "I haven't brought anything with me but the receipts that are in my head. No books or pens. What will they want me to do?"

"Just hear you talk at first, I predict. We will send home for anything you need. Benjamin knows his way around these royal people and he's sure of you."

"That counts for one," said Catherine. She waved as they parted from Joseph and his caravan, sat back and watched as the town became countryside, then deep woods. Eleanor plodded silently behind her.

They traveled all afternoon and into the night, stopping only for a meal and drink at twilight. Catherine did not think her legs could be wearier if she had walked the entire way and she closed her eyes now and then, but still she saw the pony's thick ears and the long road printed upon the backs of her lids.

"Wake up," said William, shaking her arm.

Catherine blinked. All was dark, but before her she saw a large house, like a black mound heaved up from the earth. Eleanor was at her side, holding a sleeping Veronica. Catherine asked, "Where are we?"

William grinned, and she could see his teeth. "Your future."

16

The Davies House was a heap, with overgrown hedges and dark shutters that looked moldy and warped. But the building was huge in the moonlight that had cut through the clouds, and it hunched on its foundations like a raven. A man watched their approach from the doorway, a weak taper in his hand, and when he saw Benjamin, he stepped forward. He was grizzled and gristly, and he seemed stuck in a bent-forward posture.

Catherine and William tumbled out of their saddles, stretching their cramped limbs, and Eleanor followed, gazing up at the house with big eyes.

"Master Benjamin," the man said. He bowed slightly farther from the waist. It seemed to pain him.

"Jack, you might at least say hello to our guests." Benjamin guided Catherine forward with one hand on her back. William stepped up beside them. "William Overton. You have met him before. Years back. Robert Overton's younger brother. This is Catherine, his wife."

The man bowed stiffly again.

"This is Jack Huff, Catherine. He runs my household in my absence. He was my mother's father's man before mine. How many years have you, Jack?"

"More years than a man should see." Jack shook his grey head. "The world alters too fast for my eyes. Can't hardly recognize my own face in the glass." He squinted at William. "I know you, young man. I recall you from some seasons back. You had a big laugh once. You were headed to be a priest."

William peered upward. "There was more jesting to be done in those times. With age comes a sober disposition. And different callings."

"'Tis true," said Jack. "Old Fortune sends a boy flying upward on her wheel, and when he begins to enjoy the flight, she flings him down."

"Enough philosophy," said Benjamin. "We've been on the road for hours and we want refreshment."

The interior of the house was almost as dark as the outside, and Benjamin sighed as he threw off his cloak and hat. The walls of the entryway were lined with old, cracked portraits and musty tapestries, and the staircase to the left sagged from decades of feet. Benjamin led them into a gallery where a plank table had been newly illuminated with tapers at either end. Catherine swiped her finger around the candlestick and found dust and grease thick enough to leave a print upon the metal. The place seemed like a dungeon.

"Sit, sit. We will eat and drink before we sleep." Benjamin threw himself into a wooden armchair and propped his boots on the corner of the table. Eleanor hovered, holding the baby, at the door, and Benjamin waved her in. "Come on, girl, the kitchen maids are all in their beds. There's a spot for you by the window."

Catherine nodded and Eleanor took a three-legged stool by the side table. Catherine herself slid onto a short bench next to Benjamin. William sat across from her and gazed around the room. "The last time I was here, I was with Robert. Jack's memory is good. I was still planning on the priesthood. Do you remember?"

"Do I? It was I who told you to change your mind before Cromwell took it off your shoulders with the rest of your head. A priest." Benjamin spat onto the floor. "You were no more made to be a priest than Catherine was meant for the convent."

Catherine felt her cheeks go hot yet again and was suddenly glad for the darkness.

"You see why I keep a house in London," Benjamin said. A boy entered and set out bread and wine and cheese. He put his hand against his mouth to conceal a yawn as he bowed and retreated. One of his stockings had rolled down around his ankle. "This place is only fit for the dead and the dying. And for you, little Jack." The boy stopped, blinking. "This is old Jack's grandson. Stepping into your familial shoes, are you, boy?"

"Yessir." The boy looked from Benjamin to William to the floor.

"Well, you had better make sure that you don't trip over them." The boy spotted the weary stocking and yanked it into place, but it sagged again as soon as he let go. Benjamin laughed and broke the bread. "Go to bed, little Jack.

We'll worry about your livery in the morning."

"Yessir." The boy continued backing up until he was out of sight.

Benjamin poured them all drinks, and Catherine passed a cup to Eleanor.

"The conversation is as sparkling as the furniture," said Benjamin. He emptied his cup.

"The sheepfolds are still full, though?" asked William.

"Full and plump," said Benjamin. "The whole world wants English wool. We played our hands right in that, Will. If we build our own draperies, we'll be two of the richest men on the island."

Catherine's eyes found the ceiling, painted with unicorns and Tudor roses, but they looked older than the decorations in Benjamin's London house. The air was damp and she felt she'd grow mold on her eyelashes if she didn't move soon. She glanced over her shoulder. Eleanor's head was drooped over the baby. "So this is why you keep it? For the sheep?"

"There is only one other reason," said Benjamin. "Hatfield House is within two hours' ride. And the king seems to like to pen up his children there for fattening." He drank again and wiped his mouth with the back of his hand. "Between you and your husband and me, we're going to shear them, too."

17

The sun was barely up when Catherine was on her pony once more, headed back east toward Hatfield House. Still sleepy and sore from the previous day, she dawdled behind William and Benjamin. The light had reached the skeleton tops of the trees when they rode through a garden up to a wide doorway. Two men stood sentry, noses in the air, as though to help her from her saddle, but Catherine was on the ground before they moved. William jumped down beside her, and they gazed up the red façade.

"It puts me in mind of Kimbolton. Do you remember?" William murmured.

"How could I forget?" Catherine choked down the butterflies in her throat. Queen Katherine had been there, old and sick, and she had run away from William, after he had risked reputation to follow her there. The day before she had first taken him into her. "I was still a nun," she added. A quick laugh shot from her. "I believe I knew that my old life was over before I crossed the moat." She glanced around. "No water here. No, it is not like Kimbolton, except in our minds."

"Do you want me to beg your forgiveness?" He took her arm. "I have never regretted one day, Catherine. Not one."

"Not even the day Robert was born?"

He let his eyes drift from her to the house and she could see him smile at the future he imagined. "I took you as you were. Robert is my son."

Catherine put her head on his shoulder. "And I am your wife."

"Ah. Lovebirds." A man came to the open doorway with Benjamin. He was not smiling. "Come in before you scandalize us all."

"You are John Shelton? Sir John?" William moved forward to shake his hand.

"And you are William Overton." His hand moved into William's.

A woman came out behind Shelton. She headed straight toward Catherine, already scrutinizing her. "And you are the nun?"

Catherine curtsied and rose. "Once Catherine Havens, now Catherine Overton. I was a nun at Mount Grace convent, but now I am reformed and am wife to William Overton. I hope I can be of service."

"We all hope that. Come inside and let's look you over." She retreated into the front hall, and Catherine followed. William lingered with Benjamin and Sir John, and she saw him wink as the door closed behind her. "Come in here, Catherine Overton who is no longer a nun. I am Lady Bryan, and I oversee the care of the Lady Elizabeth."

They turned right into a bright gallery. A fire burned in a large hearth, but it was halfway down the room and Catherine felt none of its heat. She pulled her cloak around her and sat in the chair indicated by the other woman. It was stiff, and she was forced to perch on the edge, propping her weight on her toes. Above her was an array of unhappy-looking portraits. Old women with prunes for mouths. Scowling men with jewels on their fingers. A dog. Two young girls, side by side, in identical frocks. Catherine could see her own breath on the air.

"Now tell me. What are you doing here?" The woman pulled another chair close to Catherine's and sat with an officious thump.

"I was called to serve the daughter of the king. Or so my husband tells me."

"What can you do?"

Catherine considered this. "I can read and write, in both Latin and English. I have practiced translation of the Holy Scripture and I can do illuminations."

"Is that all?"

"I can keep accounts if the numbers are simple enough. I am disastrous with a needle, however, I must warn you."

The woman's face softened a little. One corner of her mouth lifted. "The little one dislikes sewing. We have women to teach her embroidery already and maids to do the mending. But come. You are a physician, are you not?"

"Who says I am?"

"Your husband. He told Benjamin Davies, who told my husband. He reports that you have the skill of Galen. What say you? Is this a lie?"

Catherine took a breath and held it. Let it out while she counted five. "It is forbidden for a woman to be called a physician. I would hold it a more accurate truth to say that I have studied the properties of plants. I have some experience with surgeries. I can set a broken limb. I can pull a rotten tooth. I have midwifed live children into the world. I can stitch an open wound, if the needle is big enough and the patient is not too particular about the beauty of his cicatrice."

Now the woman laughed out loud. "What do you know of cookery?"

"I know that what goes into the mouth flavors the entire body. I have made study of the use of greens and young herbs as preventive physic as well as ornaments to the taste of a meal."

"And what would you do for a patient with particular appetites?"

Catherine sat back in the chair and dust puffed around her face, drifting into the strips of sunbeam from the long windows. "I would see to the condition of her urine. The color of her skin and eye-whites. The hardness and smoothness of her fingernails and toenails. If she seemed in otherwise good health, I would let her eat what she craved. A woman with child is very particular. If she had a yellow cast, I would add fennel to her salads. If she were thin, I would add richer meats and butter her bread. I would be sure she had good thick ale."

Lady Bryan coughed gently. She lifted herself from the seat, smoothing her skirt in the back, and went to one of the windows. She fingered back the drape, then dropped it. "Why do you suppose I was referring to a woman?"

"I would do the same for a girl. A child, even, if she were old enough to be weaned."

"Why did you suppose I meant a female?"

Catherine tried to see the other woman's expression, but she was a shadow against the glass. "I would suppose that a man would prefer a physician. A man like himself."

"The prince stays here. Did you know that?"

"Prince Edward?" Catherine's stomach twisted and her mind went windy. "I have not been called to serve the prince."

"You have been told this?"

"No. But I am not suited for it." Lady Bryan's face showed nothing, and Catherine rushed on. "I cannot lay hands upon the prince. Upon any royal male. It is a man's office." Her fingers were numb and shaking, and she searched for something to lean upon. There was nothing nearby to mask her.

"Rest easy, child. You have answered rightly. The boy stays on the other side of the house. He has women enough to tend him. And men. But I have another test for you. I have a pain myself and I would have a remedy." She sat again and motioned for Catherine to lean forward. Then she scooted the chair closer. "I suffer a woman's pains. I am in the change of life, and my breasts hurt me so that I cannot sleep at night. Tell me what I should do, lady healer of women."

"I will need to examine you. Is there a private room?"

The woman motioned for Catherine to join her in a small sitting room. "This is mine, for my meditations." There was only one small window, and Catherine put back the shutters while Lady Bryan fastened the door behind them.

"Open your bodice and come into the light." Catherine waited for the woman to loosen her clothing. She seemed to be a normal aging woman, with wrinkled, sagging breasts. "Do you notice any matter from your dugs? Any twisting of the nipple or knots in the skin?"

"No."

"May I touch you?"

"There is nothing but an old woman's hide."

Catherine kneaded and pushed, but she found no object living under the skin. "You have had no growth? Felt nothing pushing outward? No pain like a needle inside you?"

"I just ache like I've a hot devil on my chest."

Catherine nodded. "You will wet cabbage leaves in heated water until they are soft and lay them against the skin. The outer ones will do if you have older vegetables in your cellar. Let them stay for at least an hour before you retire. Then wrap your bosom in soft, warm linen and sleep facing upward."

"That is all?"

"Drink a large glass of good wine before you retire to bed. I believe it will help you."

"If it does, you will have a place with us. I will send for you." She led Catherine back to the front doorway and Catherine squinted into the cold sunlight. William was still outside, in conversation with John Shelton and Benjamin Davies. The men turned and Lady Bryan nodded. "If you hear nothing," she added softly, "do not come back here."

18

Catherine was dazed all the way back to the Davies House and could barely drag herself to the table. The men laughed and drank, but Catherine could take only a glass of wine and a bite of bread before she called Eleanor to bring Veronica to her chamber.

The maid laid the baby in the cradle and waited to help Catherine into bed. "What was it like, Madam? Did you see the princess?"

Catherine sat, laid her head back, and let Eleanor take down her hair before unlacing her bodice. "No, but the prince is there."

"No! The little prince?"

"There's not a large one, to my knowledge," said Catherine.

Eleanor began brushing Catherine's hair. "It will be like the tales of old. You will see them grow up and marry and the prince will take himself a bride." Eleanor sighed and let the bristles hang in Catherine's curls.

"You listen to too many midnight stories," said Catherine, shaking her hair loose. "I saw no one but an old woman with an aching chest. Hand me the baby before I become just like her."

Eleanor pulled off Catherine's bodice and sleeves, and Catherine climbed between the sheets in her shift. The cloth smelt musty, like dry weeds. Catherine's eyes filled against the scent and she wiped her face on the pillow.

The maid sat beside her on the bed. "It must have been thrilling, though, Madam. Was it not? To know that the prince was there? The Prince of Wales!"

"It would thrill me more deeply to know that my son was here."

"Yes, Madam." Eleanor, pouting a little, laid Veronica beside her, and Catherine fell asleep with the baby at her breast.

The pounding on the bedroom door woke Catherine with a start from a dream of Joan, walking toward her through the gorse. Joan was saying something, but the words blew away on the wind as she opened her eyes. It was morning, and William was beside her in the sheets. The knocking continued, and her husband threw back the curtains, shouting "What is it, in God's name? You'll wake Hell itself."

The door swung inward as he got up, and Benjamin walked in. "Call me a devil if you will, but I have news." He slapped William on the back. "Get your lady onto her horse, man. She's wanted."

"I can get myself up, I think," said Catherine.

"Well, do it. And bring the baby. She'll charm the whiskers off the old ladies." Benjamin hit William again as he left.

William bounded back to the bed, leaping in next to Catherine. He pulled her into his arms and nuzzled her neck. "You see? We are made. Ha, love, you thought me a simple man of dreams, did you not?" He kissed her on the mouth and pushed her backward. "And soon enough we can get started making a little brother for our Veronica."

"You." Catherine lay back and pulled his hands onto her. "I am not as maidenly as I was, even after being churched. I'm fatter."

"Churched, churched. That business is for country girls anyway. We'll have our church right here under our sheets." He pulled the blanket over her head and pulled up her shift easing his hands along her thighs. "I love you when you're like this."

Catherine lifted the cover and watched him nose her belly. "You mean when I'm unbathed and naked?"

He chuckled and crawled back up to her. "When you're warm and soft from a baby. But we have orders to get up, so up we go." He leapt from the bed again and gave her his hand.

They were at the table breaking their fast within the half-hour. Catherine was in her green bodice and skirt with the gold embroidery, and Eleanor wore a plain dress of the same hue. "They will love you," said Benjamin, snapping his fingers for more ale and bread. "And if they love you, the king will love me and your husband." A man appeared in the doorway, cap in hand, and Benjamin stood. "Eat your last, ladies. The horses are ready."

Catherine jammed a wad of bread into her mouth and brushed herself off. Eleanor grabbed half a loaf and the baby. The ponies were moving almost before they were settled onto the saddles.

The men talked quietly all the way, and Catherine watched the sun rise on her new life. She couldn't shake the image of Joan from her mind, though, and she rode in silence.

A trio of women, huddled at the door of Hatfield House, awaited their arrival. Eleanor hung back as they rode up, but at the sight of Veronica, the serving women surrounded her and pulled her forward. "Look at the hair!" one said. "She will be a poppet for the princess. The Lady Elizabeth. We will take her while you get yourself acquainted." They trotted off around the side toward the lower rooms with Eleanor still on her pony, and Catherine was left alone until Lady Bryan appeared. She waved William off without a word while Catherine dismounted and handed her reins to a groomsman.

"I slept like a baby myself last night," said Lady Bryan. "Your cure worked a wonder."

"It pleases me to hear it."

"And I have a wonder in return for you. But the other ladies must stay out of the way. Come inside." They walked into the sun-lit gallery, and at a flick of the woman's hand, two servants scurried out of sight. "Let me show you through the rooms." The woman walked briskly before Catherine, indicating bedrooms and maids' closets, a library, the dining hall. The kitchen below was a flurry of cooks and maids and Eleanor, looking bewildered, and they walked through with a brief stop to look out the window at the herb garden. The knots of green looked well-tended, but the plot was small and Catherine could already see where an expansion could be made. Lady Bryan said, "You will make good use of that" and walked on. Catherine hurried after.

By the time they reached the top of the house, with its small, dark chambers, Catherine was winded. She could not have told one room from another, and when Lady Bryan stopped, Catherine collapsed onto a stool, breathing hard.

"I have exhausted you already," said Lady Bryan.

"No, no. The exercise strengthens me." She smiled and held her hand on her stomach. "It will work me back into a better condition."

"A commendable disposition. But I have yet to show you the wonder."

The room they were in opened into another, then another, smaller chamber, and Catherine could see all the way to the corner, where, on a worn window seat, lay a gilt-edged book. The furniture was cramped but glossy, and the cover on the bed was pale silk. Catherine ran her palm over its surface. "Is this the royal chamber?"

"This entire house is a royal chamber," said Lady Bryan. "And you had best not forget it. Tell me," she said, folding her arms and plucking at her sleeve. "They say you visited our late queen, many years ago."

Catherine studied the woman. She already knew. "I saw Queen Katherine twice. Once, when I was a girl. I visited her at Greenwich, with the prioress of the convent where I was raised. There was talk that I would join her court. I saw her again at Kimbolton, when the changes came. The prioress had hopes that she would save our house. It wasn't possible."

Lady Bryan nodded. "The prioress was your mother, am I right? Your natural mother?"

"I knew it only in the moments before she died."

"I wasn't seeking a confession, Catherine." She smiled. "Confirmation, perhaps."

"I was a nun, but not for very long. Our house was dissolved and I married William Overton after we received permission. I had a son. His name is Robert. And now we have Veronica."

"Veronica. An unusual name."

"It reminds me of a woman who was once one of my caretakers."

"And now, here is the wonder I promised you."

A young woman entered from the antechamber. She was dark-haired and somber-eyed. She took Catherine's hands. "And you are to be my new companion, as long as I am allowed to have anyone at all?"

Catherine recognized her at once and bent her knee, but the young woman raised her again. "I am no queen, Catherine Overton."

"No, but you are the daughter of the king, Your Grace." Catherine got reluctantly to her feet. Her stomach flipped like a fish and her hands had gone cold. She felt that she could not meet the dark eyes, but the young woman stood silently until Catherine looked. She was not dreaming. She was face to face, not with one of Elizabeth's women, but with Mary Tudor.

19

The king's elder daughter took one of Catherine's hands and lifted her arm, twisted her right and left, and let her go. "I have heard that you are a great healer. Is there magic in you?"

"No magic. Just my eyes and my hands, which God has given me. Have you heard other news of me?" asked Catherine. Her skin was pricking. "Have you heard that I am a witch?" It had come out before she could stop her mouth.

"Have you heard that I am a madwoman?" answered Mary Tudor.

Catherine bowed her head so that the princess could not see her smile. "I have heard no such thing, Your Grace."

"Tush, you have. I know you have. I see it in your face. Come and sit here with me." Mary walked through the antechamber into the far room and set the book aside. She perched on the cushion and patted it. There was nowhere else to sit in the tiny room. "They say I am possessed of a devil and that I tear my own hair out, don't they?"

"There are likely some fools who say such things. Men often do not rein their tongues. Nor women."

"They shift with the wind." Mary leapt to her feet, not even noticing when Catherine also stumbled up, then down to her knees. The princess paced the few steps around the room, tapping her left palm with her right fist. "They are all the friends of the boy. And such a wonderful boy he is. So devout. So holy. So legitimate. So much a boy. Born to be a king. He already looks like a king, when he can stand on his own long enough to count a hundred."

"What do you mean?" asked Catherine. "Can the child not walk?"

"Oh, he can walk. He can strut like a baby monarch. Then he falls over and they take him to his bed and give out that he is at his meditations and prayers.

He will author a sermon before he is five, no doubt, and set the Christian world a-gaping at his intellect."

"Meditations? He is toddling yet."

"He will toddle into their clutches, once my father is dead, if his counselors have aught to do with it, and be married to one of their mush-mouthed daughters. They would like to see my head off first." She stroked her neck, and her eyes glittered.

"Are you in danger, Your Grace?"

Mary laughed a peal that brought Lady Bryan running from the other room. "Don't put any of your smelly old poultices on me," said Mary to the older woman. "My nerves are fine. Fine as a king's daughter's. Wouldn't you say?" Mary held out her hand, palm down. It trembled slightly. "You see? I am steady as a summer sky."

Lady Bryan was studying the princess. "My dear lady," she said, taking Mary's fingers, "do you not want to rest?"

"It is barely past midday, and you will force me back into the bed? No, Catherine Havens Overton and I will read together. I have been told that you are a great reader."

"I am not as quick as some," said Catherine, "but I will read if it would please you." She rose and took up the book. The Psalms. "The sun touches the window comfortably."

Mary Tudor put out her hand. Catherine carefully took it and let herself be led back to the seat.

Catherine said, "Where shall I begin? Close your eyes, Your Grace, and choose a starting point for me." She offered the book, and, when the book fell open, Mary placed a finger on the text. Catherine took it back, but Mary's eyes remained closed, and she put her head against the dingy leaded window while Catherine read.

> He shall cover thee with his feathers,
> and under his wings shalt thou trust:
> his truth shall be thy shield and buckler.
> Thou shalt not be afraid for the terror by night,
> nor the arrow that flieth by day;
> Nor for the pestilence that walketh in darkness;
> nor for the destruction that wasteth at noonday.

A thousand shall fall at thy side,

and ten thousand at thy right hand;

but it shall not come nigh thee.

Only with thine eyes shalt thou behold

and see the reward of the wicked.

Because thou hast made the Lord,

which is my refuge, thy habitation;

There shall no evil befall thee,

neither shall any plague come nigh thy dwelling.

For he shall give his angels charge over thee,

to keep thee in all thy ways.

They shall bear thee up in their hands,

lest thou dash thy foot against a stone.

Thou shalt tread upon the lion and adder: the young lion

and the dragon shalt thou trample under feet.

"Psalm 91," said Mary Tudor, opening her eyes.

"Yes, Your Grace. Would you like me to finish?"

"No. It is like a blade in my heart. To think that bastard is treated as my equal. The girl is a pestilence, and the boy is an arrow that flies through my day." She whirled on Lady Bryan, silent in the doorway. "Where is she? Where is the bastard?"

"In her chamber. She has not been allowed out today."

Catherine gasped. "She is in this house?"

Mary Tudor giggled, then she leaned toward Catherine and whispered, "I am only here to be their serving woman. They want me to take my meals in the gallery now, like a common member of the household. The Princess Mary is not here at all. I am a ghost!" She jumped up and pirouetted about the room. Her skirt brushed the embers in the small hearth, and Catherine jumped up and flung her arms around the whirling princess to stop her.

"Forgive me, Your Grace, but you will set yourself afire." Catherine let Mary go. "I thirst. May I send for drink?"

"Ah, I am parched as well. What shall we have?" Mary pulled herself loose, spun one more time, and skidded up to Catherine. She was flushed and her eyes held an unnatural light again.

"We will have wine," Catherine said to Lady Bryan. She walked the other woman to the door and murmured, "Have you any herbs in your still room?"

"Indeed we have."

"Have you any poppy? Or hellebore?"

Lady Bryan went to the farther door and stared down the hall. "I will inquire."

"Infuse the wine with poppy if there is any to be had. Hellebore if there is not. Small amounts. Tiny." Catherine pinched her left forefinger and thumb together.

"I am gone and back." Lady Bryan fled the room, and Catherine returned to Mary and took hold of her forearms. Her skin was cold, even inside the silk sleeves, and Catherine could feel the life thumping unevenly along her wrists.

"Have you friends, Your Grace? Surely there is someone who knows your station."

"I have nothing. I am nothing. My father would sell me to a footman if he could get him a new wife for the trade. He would like me in the tomb next to my mother. No. Not next to my mother. He would fear that we would rise together to haunt him." She snorted out a laugh, and her nose ran. Catherine offered a linen cloth, and the princess allowed her face to be wiped, as a child might. She drew a set of beads from inside her bodice and pulled them over her head, then pressed them into Catherine's hands. "You will have these. And you will hear mass with me. Put them away and show them to no one."

Catherine lifted the rosary and the small silver Christ twirled. She rolled them around her hand and secured them in her pocket. "I stood before your mother. Twice. She was every inch a queen."

"And now she is worm's meat. Rotting in the tomb." The eyes brightened and Mary Tudor giggled again. "And so is the bastard's dam. With her head under her arm like a lap dog."

"Your Grace, I would serve you. I will serve you."

"You will only if you are let to. Ah, here is our refreshment."

Lady Bryan had come in with a pitcher with a long wooden spoon in it and goblets. She had brought a fresh loaf, too, and Catherine stirred the wine, lifting the ladle to see if the herb had been crushed properly. The poppy mash floated up, and she mixed it back in. "This is good. Let it sit while we break this bread, and our hearts will be eased by it." She tore off a bite for the princess, and while Mary ate, Catherine swirled the drink around. Finally, she poured, sniffed, and tasted. "This will do for now. Drink, Your Grace."

Mary did as she was bidden, and Catherine, giving another goblet to Lady Bryan, took up one herself. She sipped, watching the princess over the edge of the silver, until Mary had emptied hers.

"I cannot stay here," Mary said, "if they will make me eat the food they give the servants. I suffer from the headache. I cannot eat fat meat. I must have white bread." She looked into the empty goblet, then up at Catherine. She smiled. "You have healed my heart, and now you must stay with me. You say you will serve me, Catherine Overton? You will not stay under the hand of the bastard?"

The light in the princess's eyes had dimmed, and she was any young woman again. Lady Bryan had backed out silently, but still Catherine whispered. "I will be at your service, Your Grace, if I am allowed."

Mary Tudor's eyes glowed again. "I will have the head taken from the shoulders of anyone who removes you."

20

"Now we will go see the Lady Elizabeth," whispered Lady Bryan. She was waiting outside Mary Tudor's door, and she continued on her way as though there had been no interruption in their perusal of the house.

Catherine followed her down the drafty hall. "Do they never meet? Does the princess stay only in those stifling rooms? It must be like a prison to her."

The woman stopped, and Catherine almost toppled over her. "The Lady Mary does not come out often. She tends to both body and soul privately. Do you hear me?"

"Yes." Catherine lowered her voice. "Is there a priest?"

"Not to be spoken of. Lady Mary is delicate and she must have dainty food. She prefers to take her meals alone. That is what we say." Lady Bryan tiptoed to the main stairs and peeked down. "Sir John believes she should eat in the gallery. He has lately been insistent. It will kill her. You are to see to her food, do you understand me? You are to oversee her health. Make certain that she eats enough. That she has physic for the headaches. Her flowers are not regular, either, and you are to see if you might not have her flowing like a regular woman." Lady Bryan took a breath, then two steps down and halted again. Stepped back up. "And, yes, she is in a sort of prison. She has been in a dungeon of the soul these ten years and more, since the Boleyn woman became the king's whore. You will teach the other one her letters and read to her as it pleases the child, so that you may have tales to tell your husband. You may see to her meals, as well."

She hurried on down the hall. Catherine could hear high-pitched wailing, a child's pitch, and she said, "Is that my Veronica? Eleanor should be tending to her."

"It is not your baby," said Lady Bryan. "Your baby doesn't throw fits and break her dishes, does she?"

"No," said Catherine. "Do you mean—?"

"Yes. It's that little red-haired Welsh horror. You will have your hands full, trust me." She opened a door and waved Catherine in. "Brace yourself."

They entered a large room, lit by banks of windows in the far wall. The hearth blazed, and the chairs were covered with velvet the color of claret. A long wool carpet, worked with Tudor roses and unicorns, covered the oak planks, and on it lay a small girl. Her legs were in the air and she beat at nothing with her fists as she screamed. Two women gazed down at her, one in an attitude of disgust and terror, the other in despair. Neither of them moved toward the child.

Catherine walked up to the trio. "What is this? Is this a royal baby?" She looked back at Lady Bryan, who was still by the open door. "You surely do not expect me to teach this."

At her words, the girl fell silent. Her hands dropped to the rug, and she opened her eyes. Seeing Catherine, she rolled to one side and pushed herself to her feet. She set her fists on her hips and stared, silent. The tears still shone on her pale lashes. Her hair was fiery in the sunlight. She kicked at a torn edge of the rug. It looked as though it had been ripped from the wall.

"This is an infant," said Catherine. "She needs a wet nurse, not a teacher. I study physic. I can teach letters or translation. I can teach reading. I can teach cookery. But this?"

The child sniffed once and swiped the back of her hand across her nose.

"No, no, that will not do," said Catherine, kneeling. "You must clean your nose upon your cloth. There are evil spirits in that discharge and you will fall ill under their influence if you don't rid yourself of them completely." She drew a cloth from her pocket and dabbed at the child's fingers. "You're as fair as a snowfall in March. You must care for a skin such as this."

The girl slapped at the cloth, and Catherine gave her a hard tap on the side of the face with her forefinger. The women behind her sucked in their breaths.

"By my troth, you will not hit your elders. Do you mark me? It is wicked. You are a king's daughter, and you will behave like one. It is common and low to strike out in temper. It is not like a lady. Nor is dragging the hangings from the wall."

The girl's eyes opened wide. She did not speak, but she allowed Catherine to touch her.

The two attendants tittered. "She has not been so tractable since we have served her."

"So this is she?" Catherine rose. "This is the little Lady Elizabeth?"

"Elizabeth," repeated the child.

"So she is," said Lady Bryan. "She is a froward thing, and she will now be the charge of Kat Champernowne, the new waiting gentlewoman, and you will meet her soon enough. My time with the child is at an end."

"You are leaving Hatfield?"

"No, but I will be overseeing the care of young Prince Edward. I will be here if you need me to help you teach this Elizabeth her lessons. I will just be on the other side of the house. I trust I have left things in order on this end."

Catherine regarded the pale girl. "Any child may be taught her lessons, if she is not stupid or spoilt. Are you stupid, Elizabeth? Are you spoilt and stinking like old meat in the sun? I will not waste my time on a child who is already rotten."

Elizabeth did not move. She shook her head slightly.

"And what is it I am called to teach you? I have a son just a few months younger than you. His name is Robert."

Elizabeth still did not move.

"And what do I teach my Robert? He must bow to his elders. He must not pull the cat's tail. He must not let his temper run off with him like a wild pony. An ill-governed temper is the doorway for the devil, do you hear me, young Elizabeth?"

Elizabeth pouted, and her hand came out as though to slap, but Catherine caught her wrist. The child squirmed and squealed, but Catherine hung on.

"It matters not a flea to me whether you are the king's daughter or my bitch's whelp. You will not strike your teachers."

Elizabeth went slack and Catherine set her back on her feet.

"Oh no, little lady, none of those games. You have legs like any girl, and you will stand upon them."

The child glared silently. Finally, she put out her hand, as though in greeting.

Catherine shook it. "That is a proper greeting. I am glad to make your acquaintance, Lady Elizabeth. My name is Catherine Overton."

"It is a miracle," said Lady Bryan.

Catherine said, "It is simple firmness. One could find it taught in a dairymaid's home." She directed her eyes onto Elizabeth. "If I had acted so when I was your age, my mother would have whipped me to kingdom come and let me go hungry along the way."

"I have no mother," said the child.

Catherine's heart shriveled with pity. "You have women about you who will love and care for you."

Lady Bryan was watching with narrowed eyes. "You will help Kat teach the girl comportment and manners. You will read to her and instruct her in her letters as needed. You will spend most of your time on her diet and on . . . other matters. Is this agreeable?"

"I will stay," said Catherine. She stood now and faced Lady Bryan. "But only if I might have something in return."

21

Catherine rode to Hatfield House every day with Eleanor and two of Benjamin's men, and for the first week they returned to Davies House every evening. William was always waiting at the door as Catherine dropped from her saddle with the same questions. "What news? Are they pleased with you?"

And Catherine's answer was always the same. "The girl seems pleased with me, but she is a child and children have moods."

The conversation varied by no more than a few words. "Good, good," William might say. Or "We are made at last." He rubbed his hands together too often, and Catherine would wait until Eleanor was safely on the ground with the baby, then she would motion for the pony to be taken away.

At the end of the seventh day, William introduced a new question. "What do you school the child in?"

Eleanor snorted, and when William scowled at her, Catherine said, "Manners. The little one has been let to run wild."

Benjamin appeared at the door that day, leaning against the jamb and crossing his arms. The weather was warmer, and he raised his face to the new sun. "Have they got you on your knees to that brat yet?"

"It is the only way to be with her at all. She is no bigger than Robert." Catherine held her hand flat beside her thigh. "She is only that high." Veronica cried, and Catherine took her. "She misbehaves because she lacks her parents." She turned a look on William.

William colored under his chin. "Come inside." He took her arm, but before they could move, a rider came careering into the courtyard. His gelding skidded to a stop, almost landing on its hindquarters. The man slid to the ground and looked from Benjamin to William and back again.

"Have I the good fortune to find William Overton of Yorkshire?"

"I am William Overton. Who are you?"

"I am sent by the constable in Havenston. He has sent a letter for you. And is this lady Catherine Overton?"

"You see me standing here," said Catherine. "I can answer for myself."

"I only wish to be relieved of my burden. This comes from your woman at Overton House." He handed letters to both William and Catherine and bowed.

"Will you go around to the kitchen and refresh yourself?" asked Benjamin.

The man nodded. "May I wait for an answer?" The horse blew froth from his nostrils and the man yanked the reins.

William nodded, already walking into the house.

"Leave your mount in the stable." Benjamin pointed the way. "And I will have victuals and drink set for you in the kitchen."

"Your servant, sir." The messenger bowed and walked the horse to the side path.

As soon as he was out of sight, Catherine, following her husband, ripped open the sealed note.

"Come to the table where the light is not so harsh," said Benjamin. "The news cannot be so dire as to keep a cup of wine from drowning it."

Catherine was already reading by the time they sat at the big table. A goblet was set at her elbow, but she ignored it.

My Dearest Catherine,

This letter comes from the pen of Hannah Hoskins but the mind of Ann Smith. Ruth has been found in the same manner of Joan. Her body was buried among the gorses west of the House. She was found by the hunting dogs of one Master Muckenfuss, who was chasing down a fox when the hounds led him to her. The constable has been called and asks questions, but we have no killer yet. He reports that the king's men will come to set matter right. Ruth's throat shows the same marks of violence. Direct me and I will follow your orders. Come home or I will come to you. There is much danger here.

Yours, etc—
Ann Smith

"Ruth is murdered," said Catherine, throwing the letter onto the table. Her chest was heavy, as though a pile of stones lay around her heart. "She was throttled in the same way as Joan."

Eleanor, sitting in a corner, yelped, "Ruth is dead?"

"Dead as Joan. She has been found in the gorse like an animal. William, what will you do?"

William had laid down his letter and pinched his lower lip between his thumb and forefinger. "This is from the constable. He has questioned everyone he knows, to no end. He asks me to return home to see to my household. I suppose the time is right if I am to begin a drapery."

"Ann asks the same of me."

"She has no right." William's voice was hot, and he grabbed up Catherine's letter. "You will not be summoned by Ann Smith." He skimmed the message and laid it down. He swallowed. "You have work here."

"I would like to bring her to me. And Robert. For their safety."

William leaned on the table to speak. "Why do you fret? Joan and Ruth were strangers to Overton House, women who came as beggars to our door. We don't know what enemies they might have made down in the village, poking their noses into other men's families."

"They were under my care and direction," said Catherine. Her eyes were on the letters, and she watched them close slowly on their own creases. She couldn't look at her husband. "They were good women who tried to teach the girls in the village. There is no harm in that. And no crime, either."

Benjamin put out his hands as though to separate the couple. "This is no place for a debate upon women's education. I have always held that a woman needs a little training to be a good mother."

Catherine raised her eyes to William. "Agrippa holds that women have capacities superior to those of men. I studied my whole girlhood away and it has not damaged me."

Benjamin drank. "Not a whit. I hope my Diana might be half the scholar that you are. You're as fine a lady as any in the land, Catherine, except when you quarrel with your husband."

"We are not quarreling," said William, sitting again. "We are deciding upon a course of action, like reasonable Christians. I do not think Ann Smith would be the prey of a killer. She is strong as an ox." He tried out half a smile.

Catherine's chest muscles softened and she took William's hand. "She's solid enough. But Hannah is old, and Teresa is fitful. She cannot care for everyone."

"Then they should go to their families, Catherine. I have said this before now."

"Listen to your man," said Benjamin. "You're young and beautiful and witty. Why waste your talents being a nursemaid?"

Catherine felt that her tongue had been touched with fire. "Is that not precisely what I am every day at my husband's request?"

Benjamin leaned forward and thumbed Catherine's goblet toward her. "Drink. Calm yourself. Your nursemaiding here will raise you up a pot of money if the child continues in her affection for you. The bastard likes you, doesn't she?"

"She does, as it happens," said Catherine. "And the ladies of the house do, too." She looked from Benjamin back to William. "And they would like to have Robert here as a playmate for Elizabeth. They have already agreed that I should bring him. They expect him. I think the timing is auspicious. And we would not want to jeopardize my position by refusing." She took a long draught of wine.

Benjamin roared. "Well played, lady. You will be a rich and famous woman yet." He sat back and linked his fingers across his flat belly. "William, your wife is as good a bargainer as any I have seen, and I think you owe her a son."

William looked again at the letter from the constable and sighed. "You have trumped me, indeed, Catherine. And since it seems I am called north, I will fetch the boy myself. Will that satisfy you?"

"I suppose it must," said Catherine, "if I cannot go myself."

"You must give me your word you will continue with Elizabeth. You must do it without complaint if we are to be preferred with the court."

Benjamin went to deliver the reply to the messenger, and Catherine pushed her letter into her pocket. The rosary was there, and she crushed the paper against it to keep the beads from rattling. "I will continue serving the king's daughter, if you require it, William," she said. Her hand was still curled around the crucifix. She told herself that it was not precisely a lie.

22

They all retired early that evening, and Catherine was still wide awake when William slid into the bed beside her. He pulled her to him, lifting her thick hair away to nuzzle her neck. His beard tickled, and she pulled him closer.

"You still want my touch, Catherine?" He moved his hands down, over her breasts and flanks.

Catherine raised her head and parted the curtain to be sure the door to Eleanor's room was closed. "I have never ceased wanting it. Not from the first time I felt your eyes on me. It sinks my spirits like stones in a pond when we disagree."

Now he stroked her arm with his thumb. "I was terrified that God would strike me with a thunderbolt for touching a nun, but there you were, with your herbs in one hand and your book in the other. I thought I had seen an angel in the flesh." He kissed her collarbone and breathed in deeply. "I have always wanted what is best for you."

"I believe that," she said, lying back on the pillow. His hand was on her thigh, and she felt herself loosen toward him. "I am still tender, William."

"You have always been tender. But are you healed?"

"I believe I can manage a way," she said, turning back the heavy covers. "Let me touch you as you touch me." She felt his skin stiffen and she ran her fingertips over the soft hair of his chest and belly. She traced the outline of each muscle as she went. "There. You see?"

But William had no more words for the moment. Catherine pulled the light sheet over them as his hands came over her. He moved above her, and she let herself fall open to the heat of him. He made a low sound, from his throat, and then she was falling into a warm place, like a pool in summer, and she closed her eyes and allowed the waves to draw her out of herself.

Afterward, they slept wound in each other's arms, and when Catherine opened her eyes again, the sun was high in the window. William flopped onto his back, snoring with his mouth open. She stretched, and her body felt lithe and young. She had dreamt nothing. She could hear Eleanor talking to Veronica in the next room. Her son would soon be with her. She smiled and shoved the curtain open.

"Madam?" said Eleanor, poking her head around the door. "Are you ready to break your fast?"

William opened his eyes. He blinked a few times, then sat up. "You women will sleep all day, will you?" He flapped the covers, and Catherine squealed, jumping out the other side. "You girls are as lazy as the day is long. I must ride today." He leapt out in nothing but his long shirt and came around to chase Catherine, but she ran into the nursery with a screaming Eleanor. They collapsed against the cradle, laughing.

"I will eat all the bread," called William.

They heard him pull on his breeches and slam the bedroom door. The two women looked at each other, and the moment's pleasure was gone. Catherine knew they were both remembering the letter. Eleanor was already dressed, and she handed the baby over for nursing. Gathering Catherine's clothing, she said, "I will lay these out in your bedchamber while you bathe."

Catherine took her time over the basin. The water was cold but clear and sweet-smelling, and she wiped her neck and belly with the soft cloth. She soaped under her arms and between her legs, and by the time she was ready to put on her shift, she tingled all over. Eleanor was brushing the green skirt, and she helped Catherine into her bodice and sleeves, then pulled her hair back and twisted it onto her head.

Catherine said, "William will bring Robert when he returns. Perhaps Ann will come and we will have part of our family again."

Eleanor pinned down a stray curl before she fitted the coif on. "I can feel your joy, at least at that," she said, tucking more of Catherine's hair under the linen. "You will leap out of your own skin, Madam."

"I may indeed. Come, let's put on our best faces. Our food is waiting for us." Catherine went with dry eyes from the room, Eleanor behind her.

Eleanor went on down to the kitchen, and Catherine joined William and

Benjamin in the gallery. The men were not talking, and she slid onto one of the wide benches across from her husband.

"Is there anything you would like to tell me before I go, Wife?" said William. He was not smiling now.

"Tell you? To ride safely and return swiftly?"

William glanced at Benjamin, who looked down at his plate. "Anything? Have you a confession to make?"

Catherine's hand stopped in the middle of reaching for a cup. "Do you play the priest now, William? What ails you?"

William lifted the rosary from the bench he sat upon and laid it beside Catherine's knife. "What is this?"

Catherine shivered. She did not touch the beads. "It is a rosary. You know as well as I do."

"Where did it come from?"

"From the church is my guess."

William glared over the board. "Do not mince words with me, Catherine. Not today. I found this on the floor of our bedchamber just now."

Catherine stared at the small Christ nailed to the wooden cross. "The king's daughter gave it to me," she whispered.

"The king's daughter? You mean Mary? Mary Tudor?"

"I do." Catherine's voice was barely audible. "She stays in the rooms upstairs."

"And is that where you spend your days?"

"No!" Now Catherine stood. "Mary's health is delicate and I am needed to prepare her meals so that she may retain her privacy. I am ordered to do it. I am called upon to examine her for signs of illness and adjust her diet." Catherine lifted the beads and closed her fingers over them. "She gave these to me in thanks. You know her religion. She considered it dear."

William stared at her fist. "And you? What did you consider it?"

"I considered it a part of my service to the household. A service I was ordered to by you. It would have been a rudeness to refuse them. And I knew you would act just as you are acting if I showed them to you."

Benjamin had sat silent all the while, and now he cleared his throat. "If the older daughter is in the house, she will not be ignored, William. She is strong-minded, I assure you. Your wife is in no position to say her nay, not if she is to stay in their service."

William blinked and sat again. "She could be arrested," he said to the air before him. "She could be charged with treason."

"For accepting a gift from the Lady Mary?" asked Benjamin. "Her stubbornness in the matter of her faith is widely known." He lifted the beads from Catherine's fingers and dropped them. "It's not such a crime these days as it once was to have them."

"But you have been carrying them?" William directed his words to Catherine. "You keep them about you?"

Catherine sat up perfectly straight, though she felt a small tug in her spine. "Did you find them upon me?"

"No." William thrust his fingers through his hair. "You are a mistress of prevarication, Catherine. Let me be direct. Do you hear mass with this king's daughter?"

"I have not heard mass with her." This was the truth, and Catherine's chest warmed as she answered. She could breathe more easily. "She is in the house, William, and I must see to the meals. I cannot ignore her. Listen to Benjamin. No one else in the house would deny her."

"But you neglected to tell me," he said miserably.

"Listen to yourself and you will know why."

"You win the day again," William said, "and I must be upon the road. But promise me this before I go: that you will put that icon away where it will not be found. Do not carry it about your person."

"That I will vow."

Reginald came to the doorway. "Jupiter is saddled, Master."

Catherine followed the men out. The stallion was pawing the gravel, and Reg took the reins from the stable boy.

William was examining the leather strap that held the right stirrup, and Catherine came up behind him. "So you forgive my hard words?" he asked.

"There is nothing to forgive," she said. "We are all wound on a rack."

He kissed her on the mouth, then wrapped his arms around her and held her tightly against him. "I will not see you in prison. I will die before I will see you in prison. I will be back before you can count one hundred. You will keep in the graces of that royal child while I am gone, Catherine? The little one, I mean?"

"If I'm able." Catherine did not meet his eyes when he let her loose.

"Then I'm gone." He took a package of cold meat and bread from the kitchen maid, and Benjamin came out, shading his eyes from the sun. William said, "Keep my wife for me, will you, man?"

"You may depend on me," said Benjamin, "though I think your wife can keep herself."

"You will be glad to have your birds again," said Catherine. "Perhaps you could bring one back with you."

"You keep birds these days?" called Benjamin. "You aim to be a regular gentleman, William. Go build us those draperies, and you can buy yourself a dozen peregrines."

"You never flew them, did you, Benjamin?" William asked, swinging himself into the saddle. Reg followed suit, leaping onto the saddle of his brown gelding.

"Never bitten by that bug yet. But bring me a falcon and we will fly them."

William looked happier, and Catherine said, "Ride swiftly now, love." She threw her husband a kiss, and the men were gone. She said to the dust they left in their wake, "Return safe with my son." Her hand went into her pocket and she clutched Mary Tudor's rosary.

23

The day brightened, and Catherine was sweating by the time she had collected her things and called for pack horses. Eleanor's eyes were red and swollen when she came up from the kitchen, but she did not weep in the presence of others. She wiped her nose on the baby's coverings and held her lip between her teeth.

"We will find out this killer, even from a distance," said Catherine. "Turn your mind to your reading in the meantime. It will ease you."

"Reading. What good will it do the likes of me?" Eleanor tucked the baby against her chest. "I am not a prodigy, Madam."

"No sullen moods, Eleanor. You have as fertile a mind as any girl, and God didn't put it in your head to go to weeds. Look, the sun smiles upon you. Smile back. Keep a good face on when you are out of your room."

"The sun is a jaundiced old man," grumbled Eleanor.

Benjamin watched the horses being loaded. "You will return here to comfortable quarters. You don't want to stay at that house by yourselves. They will lodge you in the servants' rooms."

"We are servants," Catherine reminded him, "and we are treated well enough there. Your family needn't bother itself with strangers."

"Go to, you are no strangers. I have promised your husband to stand in his place, and if anything were to befall you, it would land on my shoulders. No, you must return here, where I can keep you. I insist. I have just this morning sent for my daughter and she will cry herself to sleep if she fails to see you."

"Very well, Benjamin. We will return, but only for tonight to allow the women of Hatfield to prepare a place for us." Catherine took his hand and he flushed bright red. "Now may we go?"

"Off with you," he said, stepping back.

They rode all the way in silence, and Catherine's hand went again and again to her pocket, where the letter from Ann lay. But she said nothing to Eleanor, who brooded upon her pony's thick mane. When they arrived at Hatfield, their mood seemed to infect the air. Elizabeth was fretful and kicked her heels against her chair as Catherine read from the psalms. Then she wandered to a window, where she stared out at the fine, waning day, pulling on a strand of her red hair until it came loose in her hand.

Catherine set the book down. "Shall I read to you or not?"

Kat Champernowne was rocking in one corner, her embroidery in her lap. "Sit still, Lady, and listen to Catherine. The air is too cold yet for you to play outdoors."

"It was once 'Princess' and not 'Lady,'" said Elizabeth. She lashed out at the leg of Catherine's chair with her toe and then howled at the pain.

"You see?" said Kat, rising. "You must learn to hold your peace or evil will come and seek you out." She lifted Elizabeth onto her shoulder, where the girl sniffed and wiped her eyes.

Catherine returned the book to the shelf and, walking her fingers down the spines, landed on a copy of *City of Ladies*. "I own this," she blurted. "It is genius. She writes of women's virtues and how learning and discipline make the world go forward."

"Yes," said Kat without looking, "a work of great renown." She patted Elizabeth and kept walking in a circle. "You must read it out to us one evening when we are more settled."

"I will fetch you some dinner," said Catherine.

She had ordered a roast of venison to coax both sisters downstairs, but Mary would not leave her rooms. Elizabeth sat next to Kat, and as soon as the meal was finished, Catherine brought a special pudding with currants and almonds. "This might settle you, small lady."

Elizabeth squealed and dug her finger into the pudding. Kat gave the fine-boned hand a slap. "You will use a spoon or you will eat nothing at all." Elizabeth cut her a resentful look, but she plucked the utensil up and fell to the pudding.

Catherine slipped back down to the kitchen before Kat could order something else for Elizabeth and made up another platter of meat in savory sauce, roasted turnips and carrots, and warm bread. She filled a small jug with French claret and tiptoed up the back staircase to Mary's apartment.

Mary Tudor was alone, as she so often was, kneeling at her prayer bench. "Sit with me, will you?" she asked, rising as Catherine laid the meal.

Catherine sat, her hands folded in her lap, while the king's daughter picked at the food. Fifteen bites. It was more than Catherine had ever seen Mary Tudor put into her mouth at one sitting.

"The wine is French, is it not?"

"Yes, Your Grace. Is it to your liking?"

"You know my tastes well, Catherine Havens. Catherine Havens Overton."

"My husband has returned north this morning, but he will order you a case of it when he returns if you desire it."

"And where do you stay?"

"We have stayed with Benjamin Davies. With my husband gone we will have to beg a bed here."

"It is done," said Mary Tudor. "You need not ask. The house has plenty of rooms unused. You will not stay with Benjamin Davies. I know of him. He is widowed. You will not abide in an unmarried man's household."

"I have a baby with me, Your Grace. She fusses as any baby will. She may disturb your devotions."

"A child should be with her mother. She will stay here with you." Mary dabbed at the corners of her mouth and stood. "Come, we will have it done."

They went directly downstairs, Eleanor following along with the baby, and Catherine waited in a room off the gallery while Mary spoke with her chambermaids. Through the rear window, she could see Kat Champerowne walking, bundled under furs, in the garden with Elizabeth, who ran, stumbled, and fell. Kat bent over the wailing child, brushing her skirt until the fit passed, and they walked on.

"Shall we see the gardens?" said Mary Tudor behind her, but as Catherine opened her mouth to answer, Mary linked their arms and pulled her into the gallery. They walked out the wide front door together. The slap of fresh air made Veronica suck in her breath, and Eleanor closed the clout over her face.

"What is the child's name?" asked Mary.

"The same as yours," said Catherine. "Mary. But her second name is Veronica and we call her by that."

"Let me hold her." The king's daughter took the baby and walked on, as though the child were her own. Catherine followed, Eleanor tripping along behind.

The herbs were in a separate bed in the side garden, and Catherine lingered, running her hands over the spiked stems of the rosemary, letting the baby sniff the sharp scent on her fingers. The sage was overgrown and bent, silvered, in the cold, and Catherine squatted to pinch a few wilted stems from the stalks. The labor pleased her.

"You are a gardener, like Eve in Paradise," said Mary Tudor. She sat on a bench with her face turned up to the sun while Catherine moved among the remnants of plants, pruning yellowed leaves and old stalks in the lavender bushes and mounding the soil around the young growth of mint. Some old hips had shriveled on a rose vine at the edge of the garden, and Catherine plucked them off, sliding them into her pocket. The baby wailed, and she looked up. A young woman had appeared, and she was kneeling at Mary Tudor's feet. Her face was bent over little Veronica.

"That is my daughter," Catherine called, picking her way back across the neat rows. "You need not bother the princess, madam."

"She and I are well acquainted," said Mary Tudor.

"Eleanor has shown the baby to me," said the young woman. She was thin as a wheatstalk and just as pale. Her hair frizzed out around her cap. "I am Ursula Baynham. I work in the dairy. Are you not worried that the child will catch cold?"

"She is well padded," said Catherine, brushing her hands clean as she came across the garden. She sat next to Mary Tudor and opened the baby's blankets. "You see? Not a drop of moisture has come through. Children need a certain amount of the clean air in their bodies."

"Is it not dangerous? The air, I mean?" asked Ursula.

"Only when it bears disease," said Catherine. "And there is no malady about this house that I have smelt."

"It may be no disease, but the little lady suffers from a sudden pain in the belly," said Ursula, "and I am sent by Kat Champernowne to seek you to examine her."

"If you mean Elizabeth, I am not here as her physician," said Catherine. "I oversee her meals, that is all."

"I beg your pardon, but you are sought."

Mary Tudor rose, her lips tight. "You must go, Catherine. Eleanor and I will keep the baby."

Kat came around the corner of the stable and called, "The Lady Elizabeth—" but stopped when she saw Mary Tudor. She hurried forward and curtsied. "Elizabeth complains of her belly. We can find nothing the matter with her. Perhaps you might have a look?"

Catherine curtsied to Mary Tudor. "If I may have leave to go. I will stay if you prefer it."

Mary Tudor waved her hand. "No. Go tend to the little bastard's bellyache. God forfend that she die too soon. Or too speedily."

24

Catherine and Kat led Elizabeth, wailing, up the broad stairs to the apartment of the second royal daughter. Elizabeth threw herself onto the floor, tossing a stuffed doll one way, then the other, by its yarn hair. When Catherine knelt beside her, she rolled to her back and lay staring at the ceiling.

"I hear you are in pain, young Madam," said Catherine. "Tell me, where does it hurt you?"

"Here." Elizabeth placed her hand on her middle. "I feel that I am full of poo."

"You may very well be," said Catherine. "May I have leave to touch you?"

Elizabeth flicked her eyes toward Kat, who nodded. "Yes," the child said. "But it pains me."

"I know it does. I promise to be gentle. You tell me if I hurt you." The child lifted her hands over her head and Catherine placed her palms on the thin ribs. She pressed ever so softly. "Does that hurt you in any way?"

Elizabeth shook her head. Her hair was loose and it clung to the rushes in bright strands.

Catherine moved her hands down. Elizabeth wore heavy clothes, and she couldn't feel well enough through the layers. "May I remove your apron?" Elizabeth nodded, and Catherine unknotted the linen garment and slipped it off. The skirt and bodice the child wore were thick wool. "This clothing," she said. "Is it of your lady's choosing?"

"I hate it," said the child. "It itches me mightily and it is ugly."

"I would think it might scratch you indeed. This weave is too dense for your size. Let's put you into something else." Catherine rolled Elizabeth over and loosened her ties. "Who has trussed her up like this? I wonder that she can breathe."

"Her limbs must grow straight," said Kat, "and we do not get the clothes we once could expect from the king. I have written but I receive no response. This skirt was made from one of the maids' old frocks."

"God's wounds, no wonder the fabric is so weighty and stiff. Does the king not think of his daughters at all?"

"Shh," said Kat, shutting the door.

"Tush, let me get this girl undressed." Catherine stripped the skirt off. Elizabeth lay in her tattered, patched shift, and Catherine could now feel the small hips and protruding belly. Elizabeth cried out when she palpated her, and Catherine said, "You are indeed full of something, my lady." Catherine glanced over her shoulder at Kat. "Will you have one of the kitchen girls make up a dish of rhubarb and prune stewed with some honey and bring me some fresh lettuces to the kitchen?"

"Where will I find such things? The spring is too young yet."

"There is rhubarb growing along the south side of the house," said Catherine. "The stalks will do. The lettuces are sprouted in front of it. I expect the store room has some prunes. Apples will do if there are none."

"Of course," said Kat. She went, closing the door firmly behind her.

"And you, Elizabeth," said Catherine, raising the child to her feet, "must take some exercise to move things along inside you. I know you would prefer to lie here, but put your trust in me. Your body wants to be free of all that."

"It hurts me. I fell in the garden and scraped my knee." Elizabeth lifted her shift to show off the soft new scab. The garment had been mended all over, and one patch was coming loose.

"I know it does. But we will go outside and watch for bluebirds, and that will take your mind to a more beautiful place."

Catherine searched through the trunks until she found a lighter skirt for the child, threadbare at the hem and too short, and walked with Elizabeth around the garden. Kat walked along beside her, wringing her hands.

A young woman brought the sweet stew to them, and Catherine said, "You will eat this all up, and while you have your rest I will prepare the other for you." They sat together on the crispy grass in the high cold sun, and Elizabeth ate, complaining all the while that the fruit would not go down.

"It will go," said Catherine. "And it will push the other on out. Mind me now, or that old dress will have to go back on. And, Madam, it is a hideous thing indeed. If you eat, I will have Eleanor make you a fresh one from one of my summer skirts."

Elizabeth gulped down the rest, and Catherine walked her back to her chamber and undressed her for a nap. The girl was still sleeping when she'd finished the lettuce juice, and Catherine left it in the hands of Kat. "I have given my word to return to my house tonight, but we will be back at first light to see how she does."

Kat held Catherine's arm as they walked down. "The Lady Elizabeth is not a barnyard animal upon which you may test the properties of your plants."

"They are not my plants, and I am not the one who bound the child up like a piglet," said Catherine, freeing herself with a jerk. "And as I recall, it was you who asked me to treat her. Now if you will let me go, I will see to her condition at dawn."

Eleanor watched Catherine wide-eyed all the way back to Benjamin's house, and, over supper, Benjamin himself laughed out loud at the story. Diana Davies had arrived from London, and she joined them at table, sitting beside Catherine, who carved the mutton leg for them all. The girl yawned, her hand over her mouth.

"You should sleep, Diana," said her father. "Go on, child."

"No, please! I want to hear about the princesses. What is it like, Lady Catherine? Are the young ladies covered in gold and jewels?"

"They have barely clothes to their backs," said Catherine, lifting a slab of meat. "And what they have is not decent."

"It is impossible!" Diana lowered her spoon. "The king would not let his children go poor."

"Not all of his children do without," said Catherine, "though I only work on the distaff side of the household. I expect the young prince is outfitted just fine."

Diana sputtered and complained until her father shooed her off to bed. "You will have royal nightmares, daughter. Get you to bed or you will have bags under your eyes."

Diana kissed Catherine's cheek and bowed goodnight to her father and departed as she was instructed. Eleanor slipped out behind her.

"What did they say when you stripped the girl?" Benjamin said, once his daughter had gone.

"I didn't strip her bare. I simply took off the thick wooly thing they'd stuck her in. Poor child, it's a wonder she could stand up at all."

Benjamin cleaned his teeth with a wooden pick. "So you have come over to the side of the Protestant bastard at last, have you?"

Catherine emptied her wine goblet and set it hard onto the board. "I am on no one's side. I order food for the two daughters. The little one was ailing with an obvious constipation and I did what I could do to ease her. She's a child. That's all. Her religion is not my concern."

"There are some who would let Elizabeth Tudor choke on her own shite and laugh all the while. There are some who would stuff a footstool for the Lady Mary with Elizabeth's guts."

"Don't be vulgar. Anyone with a thread of humanity would have given the child a physic. It's nothing more than her mother would have done." Catherine's teeth caught her tongue. "Her lady-in-waiting, I mean to say."

"Indeed." Benjamin's eyes narrowed. "The Boleyn woman couldn't ease her own pain. And someone must find her daughter a husband before she gets much older. God help the child."

"God works through human hands," said Catherine. "As does Satan. And a husband? Honestly, Benjamin. The girl is not yet five."

Benjamin scratched at the beard on his cheeks and yawned. "I have nothing to say to the methods of heaven and hell, but I know a girl who needs to be spoken for when I see one. Now Mary Tudor is different. That young woman is too mad for a husband. Did you say your prayers to the Virgin as you made the child drink your potion?"

Catherine pushed back. "What makes you say that?"

Benjamin leaned his chair onto two legs and regarded Catherine at a sharp angle. "Your husband has enough on his hands trying to be lord of his manor. Poor man, made an heir when he was raised to be a priest. He knows little of women, less of women like you."

"Do not speak of my husband."

"Then I speak of the younger brother of my old university acquaintance." Benjamin belched quietly and patted his stomach. "He struggles, Catherine. Trying to fill his brother's boots without becoming a lickspittle to the king. You are quicker than he is. I hope you are not too Papist as well. The first will make William Overton a better man. The second will make him a widower."

Catherine looked around for the serving staff, but she was quite alone with Benjamin. "I have to be up before the sun," she said, standing. "I will retire."

"You needn't go so quickly," said Benjamin, examining her over his goblet. "You are no servant, down with the sun." He stood and moved to offer his arm.

Catherine made herself smile. "In this house, that may be true. At Hatfield, I am a servant indeed. It is time Eleanor was in bed. I must fetch her." She rose but he did not move away.

He breathed deeply. "You do not smell of incense. You smell of roses." His face was close to hers and his presence made her guts flutter. "You must not do anything that stinks of treason. Your husband will not be able to withstand it. Nor will you, despite your wits."

Catherine backed away. "You need not worry on that account. The Lady Mary is the king's daughter as well as the Lady Elizabeth, and I will care for them as instructed."

"A politic answer, Catherine, as usual. If your husband were as skillful a navigator of rough waters as you, he would be an Earl by now."

"Goodnight, Benjamin." Catherine curtsied slightly, her eyes on the floor. "Please don't feel you need to rise in the morning to see us off. We will go very early."

"Goodnight, Lady Catherine. But I will see you off. I would never forgive myself if I were not there to set you onto your steed."

25

Catherine lay awake most of the night, listening to the beams and rafters of the house creak in the wind. The baby gave a thin wail, and she rose silently, lifted the child from the cradle, and, sliding back between the sheets, fed her until the baby dropped back into sleep. The moon was high and its broad face drew Catherine to the window. The narrow back courtyard was empty, and she leaned her forehead against the glass until she felt the cold in her bones and returned to bed. Still she could not sleep. She thought she heard soft footsteps in the hall outside her door and sat up, sweating. The steps seemed to stop. A hand on the latch. Catherine stared through a crack in the curtains across the dark. Held her breath. She thought she had locked herself in, but keys were surely downstairs for anyone who knew how to get them. The latch seemed to click once, but the door did not open. A slight shushing faded down the hall, and Catherine was left to thrash the night away, alone with her thoughts, then with her dreams of Mary Tudor, who seemed to be speaking in her ear, though Catherine could not understand the words.

"Madam?" It was Eleanor, standing in her nightgown by the bedside. Dawn was just fingering the eastern sky. "Is Veronica well?"

Catherine rubbed her eyes, but they were still hot and itchy. She lifted the cover. Her daughter was curled against her side, breathing quietly. "She's fine. It was too cold to leave her in her cradle."

Eleanor plopped herself onto the bed, and petted Veronica's curls. "Babies do best by their mothers' sides."

"Did you hear anything last night?" Catherine scratched at her scalp, trying to waken.

"I slept like a stone. I dreamt that we were on a ship, and a storm rolled in from the far sea. The waves rocked us and rocked us, and Veronica laughed. I wasn't afraid."

Catherine smiled. "You're more anchored than some these days, Eleanor. I feel that I have not slept thirty minutes, though I seem to have done so." She crawled from the bed and splashed her face with stale water from the ewer. "We must leave this house."

"Forever?"

"For now. We will stay at Hatfield tonight."

"Will they have us? So soon?"

Someone rapped on the door, and Diana Davies called, "Catherine? Are you awake?"

Catherine nodded, and Eleanor opened up for her. The girl was dressed, waiting until Catherine motioned to her. She slipped inside and spotted the baby in the bed. "She is just tiny. May I hold her, please?"

"Do you know how?" asked Catherine. Diana shook her head, and Catherine demonstrated, lifting the baby with one hand behind her head. "You see? Like this so that her neck does not give way. Her bones are not fully formed yet."

The girl allowed Catherine to transfer the infant into her hands, and pulled the small body up against her own. "They are like small flowers," she said. "I won't crush her, will I?"

"I believe she will let you know straight away if you squeeze too tightly," said Catherine.

Diana backed up until her shins found the seat of the rocking chair, and she lowered herself into it. Veronica continued to sleep, and the girl relaxed the baby onto her lap. "You do not believe in swaddling?"

"I do not see that it does infant or mother well. There are books that say babies grow as well with their arms and legs free. Better, even."

Diana nodded, solemn. She took the baby's left foot in her hand and the tiny pink toes curled against her finger. "Your husband has gone to get your son?"

"So he says." Catherine peeled off her damp nightdress and washed her breasts and under her arms. She could feel Diana staring at her woman's body and pinched her side. "You see what two children will do to your waistline." She dried with a bath sheet and pulled on a fresh shift. Eleanor helped her with her corset, and she lifted her breasts to settle them into place. "It will do wonders for your bosom, though, at least for a few months."

Diana giggled and Eleanor helped Catherine with her sleeves. She brushed out her hair and fixed it at the back of her head before situating a fresh coif. Diana watched the whole process, her hand in her own hair as Eleanor worked Catherine's, and finally said, "There is no one to show me what to do."

"Get you a husband," said Eleanor. "He'll show you."

Catherine elbowed her in the ribs and Eleanor yelped.

"He will show you to a big belly, for sure," said Catherine, rising from the dressing table, "but do you know any man who can show a woman what to do once she gets it?"

"The belly?" asked Eleanor. "No, Madam, you win the wager there. Most of the men I know flee when they see a woman in full sail coming their way."

Diana's face was white, with blooms of red on the cheeks.

Catherine put her hand on the girl's arm. "Have we shocked you? Forgive us. We are from the wild north, and I am bred from women who did not hold their tongues."

"But I want to hear how women talk. My father will not let me converse with our servants, and I have no aunt or cousin near me. I feel a prisoner here. I talk more to the dog and my lute-master than to any other person. And he is ancient and decayed."

"The dog?" asked Eleanor.

"No." Diana laughed. "My lute-master. He has whiskers like an old cat."

"Then you must clip them," said Catherine, powdering her cheeks. "Here, let me do you up." She dabbed Diana's skin. Then she loosened the girl's hair and rebound it so that it showed off her smooth forehead better. "Bite your lips and they will be redder. There. You are ready for court."

"Tell me about the convent," said Diana. She put her fingertips gently against her chin, skimming the powder. "Tell me what the women did there. Were you great scholars? Did you keep lovers under your beds?" She was breathing hard, and the red spots in her face were even brighter.

"Oh, yes, we kept the men for a month or so each, and when we tired of them, we whipped them down the road with our beads. We liked to keep them tied upside down by the legs like chickens." Catherine sat back and smiled. "You don't believe that, do you? In all soberness, we were scholars, as much as we were able. We prayed for the villagers and taught the small children. Some embroidered and sang, those who could. I was a tragic seamstress. I made books and tended the sick. I kept a great garden." Veronica began to squirm, and Catherine took her. "And I kept not even one lover under the gooseberry bushes."

Diana whispered, "It sounds to me like heaven, but my father would beat me for saying so."

"Then do not say so," said Catherine, "at least not out loud. But you must study your letters and your music because you can never tell when you will need them." A bell sounded downstairs, and they all stood. "Eleanor and I must go break our fast."

Diana held Catherine back by the hand, her face strained and earnest. "You will not leave me, will you? Alone with my father? He is a good man and kind to me. But please tell me you will stay and teach me all about the communities of women."

Catherine opened her mouth, but the bell rang again, and her name was called from below. "I must not betray your father's trust, but if you can get his permission, you may come with us. Only with his blessing, though, do you mark me? I will not be called a child-snatcher as well as a witch."

26

The road seemed shorter this day. Benjamin Davies had lifted Catherine into her saddle, requiring her promise to visit before he would let go of her waist, and Catherine set her pony at a trot as they turned from his house. Men were to follow with her belongings, and before she and Eleanor were fully on the road, with Benjamin's horse master at their side, Catherine could see the small caravan behind them. The day shone fine and blue again, and a smiling Kat Champernowne met them at Hatfield's door. "The child is bright again and playful. Come in, come in. She will want to see you." The woman hurried up the broad stairs, and Catherine, throwing her reins to the stable boy, followed. Elizabeth was on the floor of her bedroom, rolling a small terrier onto its back. She stood when they entered, and Catherine curtsied to her.

"How do you this morning, Lady Elizabeth?"

"I am well, Catherine Overton." The child patted her stomach. "I have my full health again, and I thank you for your pains."

"Listen to the girl," said Kat. "She is her father's daughter." There was no trace of irony in her expression.

"Yes," Catherine said. "Every inch." She almost expected the child to offer her a coin.

Elizabeth crossed her arms like a grown woman and said, "You have a daughter, like me?"

"Not just like you, Lady. My daughter is a little baby. But she has red hair, like yours. Would you like to meet her? She is downstairs in the kitchen with my woman."

"Bring her," demanded Elizabeth. She punched her palm with her right forefinger. "I want a girl baby."

"You do not like boy babies?" asked Catherine. She felt a hand on her shoulder.

"We will fetch the infant for you, Elizabeth," said Kat.

"My brother the prince is a boy baby," Elizabeth said. "He is my father's best child."

"Yes, Lady," said Kat, ushering Catherine into the hall. She shut the door behind them. "Do not excite her."

They descended to the kitchen in silence. Eleanor was at the table, and Ursula Baynham was tickling Veronica with a feather to make her smile. Eleanor's small traveling box sat in a corner, beside Ursula's milk bucket, with Catherine's cases around it.

"Where is my large trunk," asked Catherine, "the one with my books in it?"

Eleanor said, "By my troth, I told the men that this was not all, but they would not stay. They said this was all they were told to fetch, and then they were gone."

Catherine toppled the cases onto the floor and shoved them apart. The trunk was not there. "God's Mother, I will slay someone if they have lost my books along the way. Have they gone?"

"I fear so, Madam," said Eleanor. "I saw them ride off as Ursula brought the cream."

Kat went to the door. "I will send a man to Davies House to see after your trunk. What does it look like?"

"Brown, ordinary," said Catherine. "It has my initials stenciled on the top: CH."

"Not CO?" She halloed, snapped her fingers, and beckoned at a passing stringy-bearded man who came slouching up to the door, pulling the cap from his head.

"I had it when I married," said Catherine. "It contains all of my notes and records."

"I see. Hutchinson, you will ride to Davies House and get Catherine Overton's trunk. It is brown and has the initials CH stenciled upon it. Take a light wagon to haul it back."

The man dipped and departed, one eye twitching as he cast his gaze over the women.

"Is the baby clean and dry?" asked Catherine.

"She is, Madam," said Eleanor.

"I will feed her before we go upstairs," said Catherine, untying her bodice.

Kat took a step backward. "You nurse her yourself? Your woman doesn't do that?"

"My woman has not given birth," said Catherine. She cut a look at Eleanor, who blushed hotly. "She is not even married. Yet." She took the baby and opened her shift.

Kat raised an eyebrow. "There is a young man? Go to, girl, it is nothing to be ashamed of."

"He is in Yorkshire, seeing to the new draperies. His master will be there soon," said Eleanor.

"Yes," said Kat. "Better that he continue there since you are unmarried. We will have no breath of scandal in this household. It's danger enough that—"

"That what?" asked Catherine.

"Nothing. I meant nothing at all."

"That I came out of a convent?" Catherine's chest tightened and she swallowed hard to keep the temperature of her voice down. "Is that your nothing?"

"You say you are reformed. You are married to an Overton. You have a name for learning and for teaching the young and for sober judgment. That is all I need to know about your past, and your conscience is your own and the king's. Your present circumstances, however, are my concern. Better that your woman's suitor is absent. Better that you stay here. You cannot sleep under the roof of an umarried man without your husband." Kat was talking very quickly.

"Benjamin Davies has a daughter. Diana. She is as solitary as the goddess she is named for."

"A pity for the girl. Yes, I know of her. He neglects her domestic education and training. She will be in trouble before she reaches sixteen if he does not watch her more closely."

"He knows nothing of raising a female, that's all, though he believes he does. I am fond of her, and she needs a woman's hand," said Catherine. "Perhaps she could come here and help with the children. It would be a steadying task for her. If I am to see to the Lady Elizabeth's diet properly, I could use another pair of hands in the garden."

Kat's face cracked, almost into a smile. "I see how you managed to accumulate a school in Yorkshire."

"Who has said I have a school?"

"You think we are so far out in the country that we do not hear the news? There has been talk of the little school for girls in Yorkshire, indeed there has."

Catherine's heart wobbled. "What do they say?"

Kat shrugged. "That you have gone from the convent to the hearth with your circle of women. There is word that some of your women have run off." Kat's face contracted. "You are better off using your skills where they are needed. The nuns of old England will need to conform to the new world. They should return to their families."

Catherine's face was hot. "The women of my household guide the local girls in gardening and cookery. They teach some lettering and embroidery. If they choose to leave Overton House and go elsewhere, we do not hold them where they do not want to be. Many of these women do not have families to take them in, and their dowries have been eaten up by the church."

Kat's right eyebrow arched. "You do not say by the king."

"I do not blame the king for what he has not done. He has enough to answer for on his own." She swallowed past a hard spot in her throat. "As do we all."

Kat studied Catherine for a long moment. "Let me see this Diana and I will take the matter to Lady Bryan to decide."

Catherine shifted Veronica to the other breast, and the baby cried out. "Hush, child."

Kat plopped onto a bench and put her chin in her hand until the baby was fed. "She is a hearty girl. With hair like a Tudor. There is no need to hide her in the scullery." She fondled the fine curls. "Does your son look like his sister?"

"Not much," said Catherine. "He looks the image of me, as black haired as he can be."

"Green-eyed, as well?"

"Yes, but with streaks of gold."

"You must want him by your side." Kat did not look at Catherine now, but played with Veronica's chubby fingers.

"Every minute."

Kat looked up at Catherine. "What woman would not want her children near her?"

My husband promises to fetch him here.

"Fathers often promise more than they deliver," said Kat, softly now. "Come, let us take this doll up to the princess."

"Very well. Eleanor, will you gather me some onions from the cellar? And did someone kill me a bird this morning?"

"Yes, Madam."

"Pluck it and put it on to boil, and cut plenty of the onions into the broth."

"Very well."

"See if there are apples. Old ones will do."

"It's done, Madam."

Catherine went back upstairs with Kat. "Does Mary Tudor never come down to visit with her sister and brother?" she asked, without looking directly at the other woman.

"Now and then. They take the air in the garden together sometimes." Kat stopped on the landing. "Why do you ask?"

"No particular reason," said Catherine. "We are almost of an age, and I think she must be lonely."

"She is a scholar and an excellent musician," said Kat. "She is our king's elder daughter and we treat her with the respect accorded her. She sometimes deigns to visit her sister but do not make the mistake of thinking that there is much love toward Elizabeth in her."

"Her days have been much troubled. It must be hard for her to look on the face of Anne Boleyn's daughter."

The stiff shoulders sagged and Kat whispered, "The whole world is troubled. Mary Tudor must always be welcomed in this house, but she is rigid and fanatical. She would put the Pope's foot on our necks thinking it would push aside the king's. About that she is wrong." The woman whisked her skirts around her and hurried down the hall, but at Elizabeth's door she stopped again, one hand on the latch. "Mary Tudor is a bastard," she whispered. "Her mother tore our island in two with her stubbornness. The Spanish mother's reputation rides before the daughter's, and its mount is lame. If you will be in her company, tread carefully, Catherine. Remember, in this house, the king of England rules. On this whole island, the king rules. Whatever he may choose to do."

27

The stable man Hutchinson was back by mid-afternoon, hovering at the back door until one of the maids let him in and called for Kat Champernowne and Catherine.

"Where is my chest?" asked Catherine. The horse, though lathered with sweat, was completely unburdened.

"Master Davies says he doesn't know nothin' about no trunk but what ye took when ye went. Not my place to be sayin' otherwise. Back I come, trunkless."

"You didn't see it along the road?" asked Kat.

"If I'd've seed it, I'd've brung it along. Saw nothin'. I come home. The horse'll be wantin' a rub-down, Madam. Don't want 'im tight'nin' up."

"No, no, of course. Go on."

"Wait," said Catherine. "Is there a light pony I might beg? I know the chest and I will ride myself to get it. Have you got a fresh cob?" She took Kat's hands. "I must have that chest or know what has become of it. It is my life's work."

"Life's work," said Kat, recovering her fingers. "A woman's life work should be the care of her children."

"If that is the case, then I should pack up my daughter and my woman and go back to Yorkshire." Catherine kept her eyes on Kat's, and the other woman finally lowered her gaze.

"Harness up Little Nick. He's been in the stall all week and wants the exercise. Hutchinson, you ride with her." Kat shook Catherine's hand quickly. "Don't ever ask me to play cards against you, Catherine Overton."

They rode like bandits, Hutchinson barely able to keep up with Catherine as she whipped the pony along. Benjamin's manservant was at the door when they clattered up to the front door, a question on his face. The stable man leapt to the graveled circle and sullenly held both bridles.

"What are you doing back here, man?" the servant said, but the stable man simply raised his hand at Catherine.

"Ask the angry madam."

"One of my chests has been left behind and I mean to have it," said Catherine. "You men seem unable to locate it. It is only as big as that pony." She pointed at Little Nick, who nipped at Hutchinson's shoulder, gaining himself a slap on the muzzle.

Benjamin Davies appeared at the door, his thumbs hooked in the waistband of his breeches. "Have my songs to the skies drawn you back to me, Lady Catherine?"

"Stop playing the courtier, Benjamin," said Catherine. "It doesn't become you. Your men have lost my best goods."

Benjamin backed into the doorway just far enough to let her pass. "Then we will have them beaten and you will walk over their carcasses to find what belongs to you." He bowed after she went by and followed her inside, closing the door behind him.

Catherine trotted up the stairs to the chamber she had used and flung open the door. There sat the trunk, in the middle of the floor. The clasp seemed unmolested, but she unlocked it anyway and began throwing out skirts and sleeves and gloves without seeing how they fell. A soft fist knocked at the door. Diana, already in her nightdress and cap, peeked in. "Lady Catherine, I am glad to see you. I have been thinking of our conversation." She gathered up a handful of the discarded clothing.

"I am not returned, Diana, just getting the rest of my things." The chest was now half-empty, and Catherine lifted out the lightest of the books. "I will ride back this night."

The girl withdrew to the threshold, still clutching the skirts. Her heel scraped the floorboard, back and forth. "You're leaving me."

Catherine pulled Diana inside by one shoulder. "I must. William is gone and people have already noticed me here, under your father's roof. I cannot risk my name by staying another night."

"Have you told Father that you are leaving again?"

"Not yet." Catherine swept aside the brushes and combs and counted the volumes. Two were missing. "A horse is waiting for me in the courtyard. He cannot imagine that I mean to stay."

Diana began to weep silently, swiping the back of her hand across her cheeks.

Catherine searched under the bed, behind the wall-hangings, and finally knelt to the drawer at the bottom of the large press. Under a stack of bed linens lay the missing volumes, and Catherine lifted them out. One was the old copy of Margery Kempe's visions that she had taken from the convent. The other was her own *For Women in Travail*, which she always kept under the more common recipes for diet and healing. She took the clothes from Diana, arranged them back on top of the books, slammed the lid, and turned the key. She pulled the chest around to the candle and examined the clasp. In the light, she could see the scratches. "You may come with me, if your father will permit it. I have assurances that you can be given a trial."

"What could I do at Hatfield House? I know nothing useful."

"What you don't know, you can learn. You have hands. You can work in the garden with me. Do you know how to read and write?"

"I can read some. I can sign my name."

"A woman needs a great deal more. I can teach you to write. You can learn herbals. But you must have his word."

"I will go beg it of him." Diana's eyes were liquid with excitement, and Catherine took her hand.

"Steady now. Convince him soberly."

"I fly," said Diana, and she was gone.

Before the girl's footsteps had faded down the stairs, Benjamin Davies came to the door from the other direction. "I hear our house is too poor for you." He hadn't moved into the room, but Catherine backed a few steps away. He continued to stand where he was.

"Not too poor," Catherine said. "I'm much in your debt, and your hospitality has been impeccable. But William is gone and the women at Hatfield House know it. The way is tedious, anyway, and they worry what people will say of the Lady Elizabeth's household. They cannot have a woman in their company who is not in their care or the care of her husband." Catherine shrugged. "William will eat his heart out with grief if he returns to find I have marred his hopes with a misstep. They were unmistakable in their warning. It has nothing to do with you, Benjamin."

He stepped into the room and did a quick survey. His eyes stopped on the chest. "So you have found your lost lamb?"

"Yes. And its missing limbs, too. I will have to polish the clasp to remove the scratches, though."

Benjamin's fair skin flushed. "I confess it. A stupid stratagem to make you return." He scuffed the rushes with his toe. "Can you forgive me?"

"Benjamin. These are a young man's tricks. You are too old to play the pining lover. Now, I do believe I have all of my belongings. Diana seeks you with a request, and then I must go."

"Will you not eat even a meal?"

"No. I go."

"Well, those prissy little bitches certainly know how to frighten you, don't they?" He now came fully into the room and closed the door behind him. Catherine felt the window seat at the backs of her knees and sank onto it.

"The king's daughter suffers from the memory of her mother," said Catherine. "It hangs over the whole place like a pestilence."

"One you have not the skills to cure?" Benjamin strolled to the window on the other side of the dressing table. He drew back the curtain and looked down, but there was nothing to see in the dusk that was settling over the yard, and he dropped the drapery again. "And I am a particularly infected part of this pestilence?"

"You're a man—"

"Indeed. My daughter has already told me you would like to pack her along with you. Make her one of your brood."

"She's been invited." Catherine rose now, and Benjamin faced her. "Diana is coming into her womanhood, Benjamin. I would see to her reading and writing. I would have her by my side to learn healing."

"This is the very vein your husband warned me of," said Benjamin. "He's told me of this coven you run in Yorkshire."

"William would not say anything so foolish! He knows perfectly well that I maintain worthy women for the improvement of the minds and skills of girls. There is nothing of the devil about it." Catherine's voice had gone tense and she put her hand on her chest to cool her tone. "Only a simpleton confuses education with witchcraft."

Benjamin took a step closer. "Do you call your husband a simpleton?"

"No, no, no such thing. You have misunderstood him. And me. He knows what I do. He has a full mind these days, with the bad harvests and wages so high."

"And a son who is not his own?" Benjamin now positioned himself right in front of Catherine. He smelt of golden hay and ale.

She breathed in, breathed out. Held her breath altogether. Then, "What did he say to you?"

"Men share their deepest fears," said Benjamin, "but I think he has judged you harshly." He edged forward, and Catherine stepped backward. She was in a corner. "I have tried to tell him that you would tempt any man, but he tears his soul to shreds with the thought of that Adam."

Catherine could not get a breath now at all. "He was armed. We were being dissolved. William was in the gaol. I had no protector." Her throat closed up and her voice was almost a whisper. "I was a nun. He had no right and I had no weapon. I never lied to William. Or to any man." She thought her knees would give way, and she leaned backward to find a wall.

"I don't judge you, Catherine," said Benjamin. He was too close, but her back was against the wall. "Your husband doesn't understand a woman like you. You require someone with more experience."

"I require no one," said Catherine. He seemed to come forward an inch more, and she said, "Do not. Let me pass."

Benjamin stepped away, bumping against the table.

Catherine slid around him. "You're supposed to be William's friend, not his betrayer."

"Forgive me." He raised both hands. "I know your husband, but I have never called him my companion. I can tell you he's no match for you. But I'm no brute. Will you show me mercy if I tell you that Diana will go with you? That I trust her to your care?"

Catherine was brushing down her sleeves and skirt. "I suppose I must show you the charity I would show any person." She narrowed her eyes at him. "Not that you have deserved it."

"I'll only ask this: that I be allowed to visit her. Will a father be given that favor?"

"Of course. If you keep your hands to yourself."

Benjamin nodded. "Consider me scolded. I will send her to you. And I will order a wagon for your chest. If you will forgive me." He bowed his head as though for a benediction.

"I forgive you. Now you must give me leave to go." Catherine waited until she heard his boots clopping down the big stairs then she bent and held her knees to stop them from shaking.

28

Diana was on her pony already, a small case on her lap. "I am set to ride."

"Now? Tonight?" Catherine directed her chest to be tied down in the small wagon, and the stable boy, yawning with the back of his hand against his mouth, nodded wearily. She looked back at the high façade of Davies House, but no one appeared. "Have you bid your father farewell?"

Diana picked at the ribbon around her case. "He said he could not bear to watch me go. He means for me to learn. He wishes me well. He will send my things along later."

"Indeed." The dark house put them in shade. All was still, but Catherine shuddered. Diana was watching her, and she maneuvered the movement into a reaction to the weather. "The night is turning too cold for me and I have forgot my heavy cloak." Hutchinson came plodding around the corner with the cob, now pulling a wagon that bore the trunk. "We will be there before the rooster opens his throat."

The moon had lifted like a pale eyebrow on the face of the dark sky when they trotted into the courtyard of Hatfield House, and Catherine was dozing in her saddle. Eleanor came running from the house, squealing when she spotted Diana, and woke them all up. Kat Champernowne came behind, her hands knotted around her girdle.

"You have brought her!" said Eleanor, jerking at Diana's boot before they were completely stopped.

"You have brought her," repeated Kat without smiling. "I did not expect so speedy a delivery."

Diana stepped down and stared at the red wall of Hatfield House. One finger of torch, held by a manservant who came out after Kat, made the surface of the stone flame. Catherine put her hand on the girl's shoulder. "Ask and ye shall receive," she said to Kat.

"You are more wit than I can bear," said Kat drily. "Bring the child in. We have settled you and your woman on the first floor. There is a chamber attached that we can make up for your pupil. Hutchinson, take that trunk directly to Lady Catherine's closet, will you? I hope we hear no more about it."

Diana and Catherine trudged upstairs. After Catherine nursed a hungry Veronica, she tried to sleep, but it was no use. Her head was too full and soon the house was too noisy. They all finally got up to put their things away. Eleanor undid their hair, then Diana took down Eleanor's and brushed it out. Diana had brought several cakes of rose-scented soap, and they bathed with the fire burning hot, the green-smelling wood mixing with the smell of petals as they dressed for the morning.

"What will we do now?" asked Diana, climbing onto Catherine's large bed and tucking her bare feet up under her skirt. "Will we wait on the king's daughters?" Her voice was tight and excited, and Catherine laid the baby in her cradle and sat next to the younger woman.

"The king's daughters are not sisterly, though they are sisters," said Catherine. She lifted a damp strand of Diana's hair and smoothed it up, under her coif. "Mary stays in her rooms most of the time, and when she walks in the garden, she prefers to be alone. The waiting gentlewoman keeps watch over Elizabeth much of the day and will call you if you are needed. Lady Bryan has been moved to the apartments of the little prince. I have only seen him once and that from a distance. We are not to tend on him. You must not push yourself into the matter, Diana. Indirection is the most direct way forward."

Diana fell silent, disappointment etching the skin between her brows. Catherine touched the spot and pushed. "No frowning, Your Majesty. It will wrinkle you before you are old."

Diana giggled, and, the tension snapped. Eleanor sat at their feet. "It will be just like home, Madam. We will teach the other women and each other. Ursula Baynham is lovely. You will meet her, Diana. She works in the dairy, but she has the best stories."

"Shh, nothing of home," whispered Catherine, placing her finger on Eleanor's lips. "They have heard of our little gathering, and I think Kat does not approve. It may be why we are here."

"Wild dogs will not drag a word from me," Eleanor vowed.

"And now to the kitchen." Catherine flapped the cover, and the other two went running down the back stairs. Catherine followed more slowly, wondering if she had acted wisely.

They quickly developed an easy routine. Catherine worked the herb garden into an intricate pattern for savories and medicinals and began seedlings, Eleanor and Diana setting the young plants with her. Spring blew in a few warm days, and Catherine showed Diana and Ursula how to fix lettuces and young onions for purging salads and how to choose the best rhubarb stalks and radishes for spring cathartics. Veronica squirmed on her blanket in the greening grass, reaching for the sun, and when Elizabeth escaped to the outdoors, she would run around the baby, stopping to play with her outstretched fingers.

The three women continued to share their suite of rooms, and within a couple of weeks, Catherine had Diana and Eleanor practicing their writing at the side table while she oversaw the royal daughters' meals down in the kitchen. While she selected the vegetables for Elizabeth's fussy digestion and shook the oil and vinegar for Mary's salads, Diana and Eleanor read out loud to each other. They spent their afternoons in the laundry or the garden. After Diana's soap cakes dwindled, Catherine taught them to make more, and set them to the removal of stains from fabric with verjuice or heated urine. In the evenings, Catherine sat at the table beside them, correcting their letters.

"Why do we waste our time with rhetoric?" whined Diana one night. She had been unable to write a summary of a passage from Christine de Pizan which Catherine had laid before her, and she shoved the paper aside. The evening was warm, and she flung open the back door. There was no wind, and the scent of damp grass spiced the air. Diana leaned on the doorjamb. "We are women. I should be helping with the laundry. No one cares what we think."

Catherine had been rubbing a liniment into her hands, which ached from weeding and transplanting. One of the scullery girls had cut her arm on the frayed edge of a bucket, running a sliver of wood clear to the bone, and Catherine had spent an hour seeking fresh wort to make her a poultice. The wound had been hot and angry, and Catherine worried that it would fester if she'd overlooked some bit trapped under the skin.

She snapped at Diana, "God cares if you can think. Where will women be if they allow men to argue for them? Who will stand between you and your judgment at the final day? Will you look for a husband to plead your case for you? Trust me. He will not. Nor will any other man. And paper is expensive. You will not waste it."

"You are almost a Jesuit," grumbled Diana. She returned to the table, leaned back, and scrubbed at her eyes with her fists. "And does this Christine write of nothing but war?"

"Shh," said Catherine, rising to close the door. "No talk of orders. We are simply women who improve our God-given talents, as the parable instructs. We take no vows. We wear no habits. And this Christine is thought to be wise indeed, even for an Italian lady."

"We will make ourselves so learned that we won't get any husbands." Diana whined. She sniffed at her armpits. "It is so warm tonight that I stink of myself."

Eleanor grinned at that. "I know some men who like a woman with a tongue in her head and a bit of smell on her skin. They aren't all tyrants."

Catherine sat. The anger had drained from her. "You miss him," she said to Eleanor.

Diana looked from one to the other. "Who? You two have been keeping secrets. Who is he?"

"Joseph Adwolfe," said Eleanor. She closed her eyes and smiled. "He likes to hear me talk. He says he wants a woman who stands on her hind legs."

"And so he says, even though he likes them well enough when you're on your back, as well."

"Madam!" Eleanor blushed deeply.

Catherine lightly slapped her on the arm. "I think you will still speak your mind. And do your will too."

Diana leaned forward. "You have had him? And still unbetrothed? How do you dare? What if you should get a child from him?"

"There are methods for preventing such things, aren't there, Madam?"

Catherine took Eleanor's hands. "You must keep mum about these matters, Eleanor. I tell you truth. And no method is beyond accident. The later remedies are dangerous. Of this I am sure."

"What are you talking about?" asked Diana. "You two know things that I don't. Tell me. I want to know."

"You speak too loud," Catherine said. "What is it we can tell you?"

"I can ask anything?"

"Anything. I may not have answers for you."

Diana took a breath. "What is it like to be with a man?"

Catherine and Eleanor looked at each other and burst out laughing. "It depends upon the man," said Catherine.

"With the right man," said Eleanor, "it is like a fire that warms without consuming. It burns from within but leaves you cool and refreshed. Like fire and water together. Like a wild summer storm with a winter pool at its center."

Catherine said, "You are a poet."

"Is it that way for you?" Diana said to Catherine.

Catherine sat back and folded her hands.

"You don't have to tell anything, Madam," said Eleanor. "Some stories are meant to be private."

"No. I will tell you. The difference between a man and a man can be the distance between nightmare and dream." She put her palm on the tabletop. "The day they closed our convent, I was surprised by one of the king's men. He pushed me under a table much like this one. He was a beast, and his breath felt like the mouth of Hell upon me. They say that a woman must have her pleasure to conceive, but it is not so."

"Madam," said Diana in a horrified whisper. "Veronica is—?"

"No, Veronica is my husband's daughter."

"Does he know? Your husband?" asked Diana.

"I did not lie to him. It was his free choice. Of course, men often regret their choices and seek a place to set their grief."

"He blames you?" asked Diana.

"Men have their moods," said Catherine. "They will call us fickle and say our monthlies make us creatures of a moment, but men are more changeable than any woman with her flowers. They are like children aching and wailing for a shiny toy, and when they get it, they want to throw it down and break it." After a moment, she added, "Bless them."

Diana and Eleanor sat silent, and Catherine finally wiped her hands on her skirt. "Enough of this confessional, ladies. You ask for tales to distract me from your instruction. Back to your letters now. We will speak more of women's problems at another time."

Eleanor and Diana bent to their papers. Catherine watched them for a moment. It would work this time, she thought, and no one would harm them.

Overton House was another life, and she found she could barely bring the image of its flat, cold face to mind. She checked the baby, then went to the pantry to seek turnips, but she had barely pulled the cloth from the root baskets when Eleanor called her name.

"What is it now?" she asked. Eleanor pointed out the window, where a woman slouched in a heavy hood.

When Catherine flung open the back door, Ann Smith said simply, "Hello."

Catherine grabbed her and hugged her until she groaned.

"You'll crush the breath from me! Let go and I will show you a secret treasure."

Catherine backed up, wiping her eyes. Ann pulled the child from behind her by the hand. It was Catherine's son, Robert.

29

"Robbie, let me feel how tall you are." Catherine was on her knees, squeezing the boy's wrists and ribs. "You have grown a mile toward the sky." She pushed Robert to arm's length and examined him up and down, then pulled him toward her again, kissing his face and stroking his soft, dark hair. "Thank God you are here, child. I have dreamt of you every night."

"Mother, you will break me into pieces," cried Robert. Catherine sat back on her haunches and gazed at him. He put his small hand against her wet face and said, "Have you got a treat for me? Auntie Ann said you would have something for me."

"Oh, she did, did she?" Catherine swung the boy onto her hip. "Let's see if we can find a tart for you."

"An apple tart!"

"I will have the very thing made for you this minute. How would that be? With fresh milk?"

The boy clapped his hands, and Catherine laughed. She searched the shadows of the yard beyond Ann. "And where is William?"

"Not with us," said Ann. "We should step inside, out of this air. It's bad for my breathing." She placed her palm over the scar on her throat.

"Yes, yes," said Catherine, ushering her into the kitchen. Eleanor was waiting with her hands out, and Diana had stood. "Girls, my son is here. Robbie, you know Eleanor."

She set him on the table, and the boy bowed like a miniature courtier, sweeping his small hat to his side.

"And this is Diana Davies, my new friend. Diana, make the acquaintance of my son, Robert Overton."

Diana put out her hand and the boy bowed again, kissing her fingers. "I am pleased to know you, Mistress Davies," he said.

Diana asked, "How old is he?"

"How old are you, Robert?" asked Catherine, and he solemnly held up three fingers.

Diana took back her hand. "A prodigy! You have been training this one for the court since he was a baby."

"He seems born for it." Catherine set him on the floor. "Now, what do we have here to make an apple tart?"

"I will see to that," said Eleanor. "How do you remember me, Robert?"

"You are my mother's lady's maid," the boy said. "Will you fix me a sweet?"

She tapped him on the nose. "You men all think alike. Come with me to the cellar, Robert, and you may choose the fruits you like best."

Catherine nodded, handing her a taper, and the boy trotted along with Eleanor. Diana scooted after them.

Ann sat and Catherine brought out a jug of claret with two goblets. "William has elected to stay at Benjamin's, I suppose?"

"William is still in Yorkshire," said Ann. She drank. "He has business with the constable these days."

"Tell it. Don't leave anything out." Catherine opened her bodice and gathered the baby up.

"She has sprouted like a little weed. You must be a cow."

"She is as good a child as I have ever seen. And the king's daughter adores her like a favorite doll."

"King's daughter, eh? No 'little bastard' these days?"

"Shh. The others may hear you. God's blood, my heart goes out to her despite myself, Ann. The poor thing is ignored by her father and shunned by most of the court. No one comes to see her. Her sister despises her, I think, though I hardly blame her for it. They both bear a world of hurt."

"Does she remember her days of glory? The small one, I mean?"

"She's quick as a bolt of lightning, mark me. She feels her fall."

"Mm. That's what they said about her mother, too. Fast."

"Still, the child's condition grieves me. As does the princess's. The Lady Mary." Catherine turned the baby to the other breast. "But what is the news from Overton House? Has William sent you alone to bring Robert? All that way?"

"I brought a man from the village with me, but he turned back when we caught sight of the house and I came up alone. Hannah and Teresa have gone missing. Ruth was found. You got my letter?"

Catherine nodded.

"The disappearances cause murmuring among the tenants. People in the village are saying that Overton House is bewitched, that the women are practicing dark arts and that demons are killing them. Killing us, I should say."

"I hope that Father John has come to tell them how silly they are. Witches, indeed." Catherine spat on the floor. "We are supposed to be sensible these days. We are supposed to have freed ourselves of superstition. What are they saying, that Teresa rode on a broomstick and made potions out of dead frogs? Hannah is no more a witch than Robert's pony is."

"You may scoff, but the constable has been at the House. He speaks to William privately and won't look me in the eye."

"Coward."

"Margaret has not been quiet in all this either. I heard her taking William to task for allowing them to stay. Blaming you for bringing sin to them all. She has been slinking around like a cat with mustaches of cream."

"But she was more smiling of late. At the churching—"

"That tune has changed since your departure. Margaret bears herself as the lady of Overton House and says right out loud that you will never return to Yorkshire."

Catherine's throat narrowed as she pictured William's sister. "And what does my husband say to this?"

Ann's eyes shifted away. She picked up her goblet, but it was empty and she set it down again. She went to the window and, making a hood of her hands, looked through the glass. Then she sat again heavily. "Your husband says very little to anything."

"But he must have been concerned for your safety. And Robert's. To send you away."

Ann turned, chewing the inside of her cheek, and studied her goblet. She poured herself another drink. "Robert's pony bucked last week, and his boot was caught in the stirrup. I barely made it out the door as he came by. I got him free, but his head was covered with welts the size of boulders."

"How did that happen? He is not supposed to have stirrups at all."

"You tell me. I caught the pony myself. And listen to this—when I get the boy loose, I look up and who is standing at the door of the stable, calm as a frog in a pond? Geoffrey White, your husband's master of horse. And what does he say? Not a word, as I sit here."

Catherine could not breathe without opening her mouth. It could not be. The stirrups must have been an error in judgment. "Did he explain himself?"

"Not one word, as I say, and not a hand to help. He saw that I had Robert, and he went back in. But I swear those stirrups were a man's size. A boy's foot would have slipped through at the slightest push."

"And so William sent him with you?"

The chewing began again. "And so I brought him away. To you. For his safety. You're his mother, Catherine, and he ought to be with you."

Catherine gasped. "You took him without William's leave?"

Ann shrugged. "I brought the boy to his mother because he was injured and no one was overseeing his welfare."

"Who knows you are here?" Catherine jumped up and closed the shutters. Diana and Eleanor opened the door just then, and Robert followed them in. The younger women emptied their aprons into a bowl.

"Who will make the coffin?" asked Diana.

Catherine latched the door behind them. "Eleanor, can you do it? You have the skill with pastry and I have some business with Ann upstairs. Show Diana how to break the fat into the flour."

"Yes, Madam, of course. Shall we keep Robert here to oversee his sweetie?"

"Will you stay and not run off?" Catherine tousled the boy's hair, but she was feeling for the injuries. He seemed healed well enough.

"Yes, Mother." He climbed onto a stool and folded his hands. "I will be the best boy in Christendom."

"Keep the shutters closed and the door locked," said Catherine. Diana and Eleanor looked at each other, but Catherine didn't answer the questions on their faces. "I have reason," she said simply.

Ann followed Catherine up to the school room where Elizabeth took her music lessons in the mornings. They could hear the strings of a lute being plucked out, then a twang, then a sharp rap, then a cry. It was too late for the music master. "It must be Kat. She is the little one's favorite gentlewoman,"

Catherine said. She listened at the door. "We can wait out here." They sat in the hallway while the music went on, and by the time the door opened, Ann's head had fallen back against the wall and she was breathing lightly through her mouth.

"Wake up." Catherine nudged her. Kat Champernowne came out with Elizabeth in hand. The child stared at Ann, who was rubbing her eyes.

"Who is this?" Kat asked. She extended her hand but her eyes were hard with suspicion.

"Ann Smith. From Mount Grace, then Overton House. She is a respectable widow and she has been my dearest friend since I was a girl. She was a lay sister at the convent after her husband died. She has brought my son to me."

"Elizabeth will be delighted to have another playmate," said Kat. "Will you not?" Elizabeth regarded Ann warily, and the lady went on. "The boy is younger than she is?"

"He is just three."

"Good. And keep in mind that she already has one boy who will command her. She doesn't need another." Kat turned her gaze on Ann. "You have been on the roads. We will find you a room. How long will you stay with us?"

Catherine stepped forward. "She may stay in my room. Ann and I have been bedmates many a night. Ann is strong and she would be a good hand for me."

"I thought Diana Davies was your second set of hands."

Ann showed her muscled arms without embarrassment. "I am a skilled laundress, and I am not too proud to do it. I can make excellent soap. I can also kill a chicken or duck with one hand."

"Well. We could make use of a laundress who earns her keep." Kat looked at Catherine, then at Ann. "What is it? What is the secret?"

Now Catherine gnawed at her lip. She moved close to Kat and spoke in a murmur. "Ann has brought my son away without the express permission of my husband." Kat's face went ashy, and Catherine quickly added, "William was gone to fetch him anyway, but four women of Overton House are missing and two have been found murdered on the grounds and he has much to occupy his mind."

"The child was not safe," said Ann. She stood straight under Kat's scrutiny. "I felt it was my duty to God to protect him when his father was distracted. I brought him to his mother."

"Will we have the law at our door, is that what you tell me?"

"No," Catherine said. "I will have charge of Robert, and if his father comes, I will keep the boy or let him go as my husband requires. Ann will bring us no trouble."

"But you would like to keep her hidden away in the laundry."

"Not hidden." Catherine ran through a catalog of euphemisms in her mind. "Busy. We would like to keep her busy."

One of Lady Champernowne's eyebrows went up. "They say idleness is a sin in women. Get her to the laundry at first light, and if anyone asks me about her, I will send them to you."

"I will bring no troubles to this house," said Catherine.

"You had better not," said Kat. She had not taken her eyes off Ann. "Or you will be sorry indeed."

30

No one came for two full weeks, and in that time Ann accustomed herself to the pace of the household while Catherine went up and down stairs, directing the choice of fresh salad greens and young vegetables in the kitchen or sitting with the ladies up in their chambers. Elizabeth, preferring to play in the garden, grew fussy over her letters. Catherine diverted her by bringing in Robert to work alongside her, but the boy, shy in the company of the king's daughter, would not speak to her, and she forced him into her cast-off garments until he cried. Then she dried his tears with her own skirt and Catherine relented and let her take him outside to sit in the sun and watch the birds and roll Veronica about in the grass to make her laugh.

Mary Tudor's menses were late, and Catherine sat at the table five evenings in a row, stirring draughts of primrose and wort to bring on her flowers without making the young woman even thinner. The receipt was her own, and Catherine did not breathe easily until the morning that Mary called her upstairs to say that she was a regular woman again.

Diana was skilled with her needle, and she sat with Elizabeth in the late afternoons, showing her how to sew fancy stitches, while Eleanor stayed in the kitchen to make bread, Catherine sniffing the brown grains for freshness. Eleanor wanted to use the softer white flour, but Catherine refused. "The child suffers from an anxious stomach and the darker grain will clean her insides."

"But this is what ploughmen eat," complained Eleanor. She threw down a handful in disgust.

"And ploughmen seldom complain of their guts," said Catherine. "And take those greens off the fire. You will spoil them."

"I have never heard of so much raw food for a princess. We feed her as though she were a hare."

"It is not raw. Vegetables that grow above ground are creatures of the air and cooking them over much kills their spirits. Then they do the body no good. They are delicate in nature. Earthy vegetables can endure it. They are like trolls and enjoy the darkness and heat. Those that grow toward the clouds must be treated with an angel's hand."

"Where do you get these ideas?" asked Eleanor. She tasted the greens and smiled. "They taste like spring."

"You see? You haven't destroyed their virtues. And you must call her 'lady,' not 'princess.'"

And so it went. Catherine told herself that William would understand, that Robert and Ann would be woven into the fabric of Hatfield House without a dropped stitch, that when William finally came south they would have a grand meal to celebrate his return.

It had been precisely a fortnight when Catherine, coming down from Mary's chambers with her empty dinner things, heard a rapping on the great front door. She froze on the landing to listen. Lady Bryan was speaking to someone. A man. Catherine ran on her toes down the hall and descended by the back stairs.

"Where is Ann?" Catherine whispered, coming into the kitchen.

"In the laundry," said Eleanor, pulling a dark loaf from the oven and turning it for inspection to the light from the hearth. "Where else?"

"Run and tell her to lie low," said Catherine. "Like the wind now, go."

"I am gone," said Eleanor, plopping the bread down just as the bell rang to summon Catherine.

She removed her dirty apron and pulled on a clean one. She checked her hood for neatness and went up the back way. She saw them before they saw her and she put on her most innocent face. "You need me, Madam?"

Kat Champernowne was now with the man. He had the bearing of a constable, and he held his cap in his hand. "Have you a boy here by the name of Robert Overton?"

"I have. Of course I have. He is my son and my husband sent him from our home in Yorkshire to abide with me here. Would you like to see him?"

The constable looked at Kat, who had raised her eyebrows and pursed her lips. She said nothing.

"I am here to rescue a stolen child." He opened a crumpled letter and squinted at it. "It says here that the boy is taken by force from his home and must be returned."

"The boy is away from home, I grant you," said Catherine, "but I am his mother, and he is here because I am. He is only three years old. I shall send for him and you may see." She started away, but the constable raised a hand to stop her.

"You have a letter from your husband?"

"I have several letters from my husband. Which one would you like to see?"

"The one that says he's sending the boy to you."

"Why would he send me such a letter? He went north to fetch the boy. We agreed between us to the action before his departure. There was no need for a letter. He has sent the boy."

Kat went to the stairs and called Eleanor up. "Get little Robert and bring him here, will you? Who's got him?"

"He's downstairs. I'll fetch him, Madam." Eleanor curtsied deeply and disappeared again.

They waited in silence until Eleanor returned, holding Robert by the hand. When he saw Catherine, the boy ran to her and she lifted him onto her hip. "Robbie, this gentleman would like to meet you. Can you say hello? Be polite, Son." She set him down again, and he bowed with a little flourish of his hand.

The man squatted. "I am the constable, boy. Can you say who is your family here?"

Robert took Catherine's hand. "This is my mother, who serves the Lady Elizabeth, who is the king's daughter." He pouted a little and added, "She has made me put on her gown." He took Kat's finger with his other. "And this is Madam Champernowne, who switches us when we misbehave."

Kat laughed, and the constable stood. "Where is your father, boy?"

"My father is on our estate in Yorkshire, overseeing his tenants and my Aunt Margaret. We have a constable, too, and he has a much larger nose than you have."

The constable coughed and examined his letter again.

"May I see the order?" asked Catherine. "Perhaps I can solve the mystery for you."

He frowned but handed over the paper, chewing on the nail of his forefinger while Catherine read. It was signed by Margaret Overton and charged that

Robert Overton had been taken without his father's consent. Her chest loosened. She almost laughed. "This is from my sister-in-law," said Catherine. "She has misunderstood her brother's intent in the matter." She handed the letter back. "It is not an uncommon occurrence. She often suffers from such disorders of reason."

"Well," said the constable, peering into the message. He looked up at Catherine. His lower eyelids twitched and stiffened. "I see no cause to take your son."

"I will send to Overton House myself, to ensure that my husband knows Robert has arrived safely here. If there is trouble, I will let you know."

"Well," he said again, shifting his weight from one foot to the other. "If you will swear it."

"Upon my mother's virtue," said Catherine, her hand on her breast.

The constable bowed and scraped his boots and backed out, his cap going on and coming off again three times.

Kat closed the door behind him. "I have heard tales of your mother, Catherine."

"I didn't swear that she was virtuous," said Catherine. She smiled. "He's gone, is he not?"

Kat smiled too, but with only half of her mouth. "For now."

"And before he thinks to return, I must send to Overton House in truth. There is no good reason for this letter to have come from Margaret instead of my husband."

31

Catherine wrote the letter that afternoon, down in the laundry. She sat at the narrow board table while Ann rinsed Elizabeth's narrow shifts, sweeping back her sweaty hair with one forearm. "Go on, read it out," Ann said, hanging another small garment over a wooden bar. She stepped back and looked at her work. "A king's child and she wears cloth that is almost ready to dissolve. It shames me to think he is England."

"My Dearest Husband William," Catherine began.

"Oh, I see. You aim for irony," said Ann, pulling a cap from the pile of clothing and shaking it out. "Look at this. It disgusts me. The seams will give way any minute."

"We don't know that William is to blame for any of the business at home."

"All right. William is a saint." Ann softly slapped the surface of the wash water to test its temperature, then dunked a handful of caps and scrubbed them together.

"It goes like this. 'I have received a message from Margaret inquiring as to Robert's safe arrival at Hatfield House. He is here and he thrives in the company of young Lady Elizabeth and the other children. Veronica grows by the day and looks more like you every time she opens her eyes. My position is satisfactory to me, and I hope that you will find yourself welcomed at the court the next time you come south. Send me word of your health. Your most loving wife, etc. etc.' How is that?"

"No question of the missing women?"

"I think perhaps it is wiser if I seem to have forgotten them. He may believe that I am so busy here that it has slipped my female mind."

"Or he will think that I am here with you and that you mean to distract him."

Catherine folded the letter. "He may be convinced you are missing like the others. There was no mention of your name in Margaret's letter. If she suspected you, she surely would have had the men of Yorkshire up in arms to haul you back."

"Or she is a simpleton. How else will he think Robert got here?" Ann put her hands on her hips and sighed at the huge basket of wrinkled linen. "This labor has made me strong as an ox. They had better be armed mightily if they mean to lay hands upon me."

"Do you want me to solicit for a different task?"

"No. It pleases me. The work clears my mind and hardens my hands. It makes my soul feel stronger." She transferred the caps to a rinse tub and swished them about.

"I will have Eleanor run this to a messenger today."

"Did you call me, Madam?" Eleanor was in the doorway, and after Catherine sealed the letter with wax, the maid tucked it into her pocket and promised to return before dinner. Rocking the baby, Catherine walked to a window and watched the young woman hurry away toward the main road and thought how straight and firmly Eleanor walked. She could pass for lower gentry, and now she could read some. Soon she would be able to write a passable letter herself. She might marry a merchant and bring him no shame. Or she might encourage that Joseph to better himself along with her. He might learn accounts or enough letters to manage an inn. Catherine smiled to herself. She glanced at the courtyard. She blinked. As though she had conjured him, there he was, Joseph Adwolfe, riding in on a lathered gelding, sliding to the ground, walking around the corner of the house. He handed his reins to one of the stable boys. Catherine rubbed her eyes, but Joseph was no ghost. He pulled off his hat to slick back his hair before heading toward the front door.

The knocking had started before Catherine reached the top of the stairs, and Kat was directing the door to be opened. Kat stepped backward at the sight of the grubby young man. "And who are you?" Catherine heard her ask.

"Madam, I am William Overton's stable man, and I crave a word with Catherine Overton."

"You may find Catherine in the kitchen overseeing her duties there. Or she will be in the garden."

"I am here," Catherine said, stepping up behind the other woman. "Joseph, it will be more convenient for me speak to you in the kitchen. Meet me there."

"Pardon me, Madam, but I have news that the lady of the house may want to hear." Joseph stood his ground, not quite inside, but not out in the yard either. "I will deliver myself of my message here."

"Very well," said Kat, crossing her arms. "Deliver it then."

"Your husband lies ill, Madam," Joseph said to Catherine. "He suffers from an ailment that will not relent. He cannot keep food on his stomach and his color is wrong. His sister tends him but he has sent me to gather you. He says she has not the skill to mend the sick and he fears for his life. His man stays beside him but he has no knowledge of illnesses."

Catherine's heart tightened like a fist. "I have just this minute sent to him to see how he does. Eleanor has taken the letter. What are his symptoms, Joseph? Have you laid eyes upon him? Has he sores?"

"I bade him farewell at his bedside four days ago. I have rid almost without ceasing but for sleep and victual. He was hot and red in the face. He is much withered. But I saw no sign of sores. He seemed thin and excitable. He clutched me by the hand and told me to come direct to you."

"And you have come to us with the disease upon you?" asked Kat. She was waving her hands in front of her face as though it would ward off whatever he carried. "You will infect the entire household. The king's children are here. Get out."

Joseph backed away at this. "I have a strong constitution, Madam, and I have ridden four days straight without sign of fever. My hunger is good and I am strong in my limbs." He flexed his arms for her. He stared directly into her eyes. "I have no signs of sickness anywhere. You may examine me if you like."

"Catherine will meet you downstairs," Kat said. She whirled around and glared. "You must go."

"It seems so," Catherine said.

Joseph knocked a slab of mud from his boot and Kat glowered at it as though he had shat on the shrubs. "And you will return north to tell your master that his wife returns."

"Might I eat first? Have a drink?"

"Have it, then go." Kat lifted her arm.

Joseph jogged around the corner of the house, headed toward the kitchen.

Catherine asked, "May I take some stores from the garden?"

"Take what you need. Ann can do your duties in your absence?"

"Some of them. Let Diana aid her to manage Elizabeth's diet. The girl is coming along quickly."

"What of the children?"

"I'm their mother. They should go with me."

Kat's forehead glistened with sweat, and she pulled a handkerchief from her pocket and dabbed at herself, then scrutinized the cloth as though a fever might be crawling among the fibers. "We can find a wet nurse."

"No." Catherine crossed her arms. "I have no confidence in them."

Kat wiped the cloth over her eyebrows and examined it again. "I know someone who has extra horses available, but you will have to be the one to petition him."

"You mean Benjamin Davies."

Kat shrugged. "He has an entire stable at his disposal. We need to keep our household intact."

"You seemed to want me clear of that man," said Catherine. Kat was still smearing her skin with the cloth and studying its surface. She was not looking up. "I will speak to Diana," Catherine finally said. "And now I should go see to Joseph's victuals."

Kat folded the handkerchief once, then twice. She pinched the edges flat and inserted the soggy mess into her pocket. Her eyes were bright with fear and anger. "I do not like your being beholden to that man. He doesn't have a woman and you are too beautiful. But I see no other path before us. You must go and no one must know why."

32

"You cannot go now," announced Kat the next morning. Eleanor peeked out from the maid's quarters when she heard the familiar voice and quickly withdrew. Kat had driven Joseph off at first light, and Eleanor looked as though she had no wish to answer any questions about where he had spent the night.

"Why?" Catherine had been making out a list of Mary Tudor's preferred foods and paused her writing. "Is Elizabeth ill? Mary?"

"No, but they both may be down in their beds before the week is out. We all may be. The king is coming."

"Here?" Catherine dropped the quill. "When?"

"In three days, and the house must be in perfect order. The Lady Mary must attend him. She must behave and she must hold her tongue. They must both be fed well, and the king must see who oversees his younger daughter's diet. They must not look sallow or thin."

"That is enough must to make wine, but I fear it will be sour," said Catherine. "Three days? My husband may be upon his death bed. I cannot stay."

Kat crossed her arms. "You will remain here until the king has gone. We need every hand." She looked at Catherine and finally sat. "I wish I could let you go. I know what it is to love a man, but is his sister not with him?"

"She is a fool, God forgive me," said Catherine.

"And you are not. Stay and the reward will be great. That should heal him quickly enough."

Catherine considered it. If she lost her place, he would be sick at heart, perhaps to death. "I will stay, but I fly the moment the king leaves."

"I will set your things upon the pack horses myself," said Kat.

"But three days?" said Catherine. "Mary and Elizabeth are neither one of them hearty. We must get a calf fresh killed. And all the geese and ducks that are fat." She glanced down at the list and handed it to Eleanor, who'd stepped into view. "You will oversee the bread. Can you do it?"

"May I use the white flour?"

"Use both. They will complain after if we seem to serve them finer when the king is here and rightly so. The father should see what his daughters eat. But we should have finer for the head of the table." Catherine turned suddenly to Kat and pitched her voice to a more submissive tone. "Unless you think otherwise, of course."

Kat sniffed. "The king will hardly see what color of bread he puts in his mouth, as long as there is meat, and we give him tarts and puddings afterward. And plenty of wine."

"Mary will not eat more on account of his coming," said Catherine.

"She must eat. She cannot appear sickly."

Catherine removed some of the garments she had packed. "She is fastidious, but perhaps I can entice her with her favorites. There is good French claret still and I will make her a meal to celebrate her mother's memory. She will eat for that."

Kat came forward in a rush as though she meant to slap Catherine, but she stopped, quivering all over, just short of a collision. "Are you a simpleton? Speak of her mother? Now? Mary will work herself into a consumption over it."

"No," said Catherine. "I am sure it will please and calm her. She is slim, but her skin is clear. If she is happy, she will look healthier and will act the part of a king's daughter."

Kat's eyebrow went up. "How can you know this?"

Catherine stared back. "Mary is tightly strung, but like a lute she can sing if played rightly. Let the spirit of her mother be called out of her for a bit and her natural love of her father will be the next tune."

Kat thought this over. "We can try it." She waved four fingers at the chests. "Put these things up for now and get busy."

Catherine nodded. "Eleanor, get you down to the kitchen and have some of the fatter hens killed." Eleanor twisted herself past Kat and fled the room. "I will see to salads. Ann can help with the tarts. There is rhubarb and new strawberry."

"Come on then," said Kat, pulling Catherine by the elbow. "The king will eat the whole house down."

The sky had turned dark with storm when Catherine found Ann in the laundry. Eleanor skipped behind her, holding onto Robert, and when Catherine told Ann she was staying, the maid clapped the boy's hands inside her own.

"We will see his majesty!" Eleanor said. Her voice was breathy and ragged and she seemed to have forgotten that Joseph was gone.

"'We' will likely not," said Ann, "unless you spy him as he goes past a stairwell. Eleanor, quiet yourself. The king doesn't bother himself with maids and laundresses."

"He lacks a wife just now," Eleanor said, smirking. "Perhaps you can snag him, Ann."

"Oh, yes, that is exactly what I had in mind," said Ann. She showed her hands, red and puffed from hot water. "I'm sure I will be invited to lay these upon the royal willy."

"Ann, shh!" said Catherine. She checked the door, but they were alone.

"Who is Willy?" asked Robert.

"You see what your mouth does?" Catherine swung the boy up to the table. "He is a make-believe playmate. You have real ones."

"I have a Willy, too!" cried Robert.

Eleanor burst out laughing and Catherine cut a look at her. "Just wait until you have a child. You will see what I teach him."

Eleanor flushed, but then she grinned. "The king is coming here!"

"I know, I know," said Catherine. "You see to the vegetable stores. I am going to get the girls to gather fruits for the tarts. Ann, you might see to the soft flour for the coffins."

By the time Catherine had directed the other maids in the butchering and roasting, the clouds had opened, and the rain came down hard as arrow tips. Catherine left the children in the kitchen with the other women and, pulling her apron over her head, waded out to the strawberry beds. She plucked buckets full, then pulled out her knife and slashed the young rhubarb stalks. By the time her arms were full, she was drenched to the skin, and she ran back to the kitchen, where she dripped by the fire.

"Don't forget Elizabeth's meals for today," she said. She stripped off the wet layers. Robert had been summoned upstairs to play with Elizabeth through the foul weather, and Catherine turned her back to the fire until she was warm and dry again. A rumble of thunder shook the windowpanes and the children's squeals echoed down the stairs. She couldn't stop the warmth of relief that she wasn't on the road from spreading through her limbs. "Elizabeth sounds well enough," said Catherine, tilting her head to listen. "That should please her father."

"Are you not at all excited?" asked Eleanor. "To see the king?"

Catherine and Ann exchanged a look. "He will be grand, no doubt," said Catherine. "He has been little enough of a friend to women."

"But he is the king," said Eleanor. "He owes nothing to anyone but God."

"There was a time in this land when that was supposed to mean that he cared for his subjects as the children of God. All of his subjects," said Ann.

"I don't believe a king cares for anyone but himself," said Catherine. "I don't believe such a king as you describe ever existed. A king is a man like other men, except this one can cast his women on the dungheap when he is weary of them."

"He is anointed by God, Madam," said Eleanor. "Everyone knows that. And the queen must obey him, as other wives obey their husbands. It is natural as we are daughters of Eve."

Catherine was tired and her tongue hurried on. "He is anointed by men in large hats, and queens have sat their thrones by themselves. But in England, the price of queens has fallen. There is a cheap market for them since our Lady was thrown into the dirt." Ann had brought her a dry skirt, and Catherine pulled it on and tied up her bodice. "Agrippa contends that women were the last creation of God, made flesh from flesh, and that a woman is the pinnacle of creation."

Eleanor gasped. "Do you mean we should—?"

Ann put a warning hand on Catherine's arm. "There's no going back. For any of us."

"I mean nothing," said Catherine. "Don't listen to me. Except for this. The Lady Mary's mother was once queen of this island, and her mother was queen of Castile. Queen. She had a husband and still she ruled. God did not frown upon it. The king of England did. That is all."

Eleanor sat with a thump on the bench at the long table. She stared at nothing. "So the king is not sent to us by God to be our head? Are we not bound to obey him?"

The warning hand squeezed, and Ann's brows bent into a dark look. She shook her head, and Catherine knew she was worried for Eleanor's discretion, alight as she was with anticipation. Catherine stroked her maid's head and murmured, "Forgive me. I talk too much. We will speak more, but not today. I am worried about William. He may be in need of me and we are forced to stay. I do not mean to sound bitter."

"He has Margaret," Eleanor said, looking up. Her voice had loosened with relief. "She will take care of him until you can go."

"Let's hope so," said Catherine. Eleanor chose a bowl and trotted off to get flour, and Catherine watched until the maid was out of hearing. "I shouldn't speak of our old life. To her or anyone else."

Ann said in a low voice, "You had better not. Not now." She began to hull the berries. "Best for us to turn our minds to work."

Eleanor returned and began on the pastry, flinging flour with such fury that she powdered herself to the waist with the stuff. Ann gathered the stems into her apron, and, ducking her head against the wind and rain, went out to dump them in the slop pail. When the door closed behind her, Eleanor let her fingers drift through the soft pile. Her face was suddenly a map of worry wrinkles, etched in flour.

"Tell me a story, Madam. Not about England or our king. Nor of the church. No, you needn't speak to me of the church. You may say a fairy tale if you like. A legend from long ago, if you will have it so." She was almost whispering now. "But tell me, if you will, a little story about these queens."

33

For three days, the house was in a fever of cooking and cleaning, everyone shouting and running through their tasks. Barrels of ale and wine came by wagon. The bedding was hung from the windows for airing, and Hatfield began to resemble a fairground. The maids sang loudly as they beat the tapestries out on the grass. The stables were rearranged, and the men brought carriages and wagons and animals in and out as they decided where they would lodge the royal procession, while the dogs ran about their feet, barking and growling at each other. Kat's voice was seized by a hysteria that lifted all her words by their tails.

Catherine knew he had arrived before the call came ringing down the stairs. She heard the horses gallop into the courtyard, and Kat's tone shifted to a deeper, more formal note. Different dogs appeared outside the kitchen windows, and the Hatfield hounds came lunging up in defense, pulling the intruders down into dusty snarlings. One huge hairy thing sauntered triumphantly to the back door and snuffed wetly at the threshold, then pranced to a window and leapt up to stare in, its tongue lolling against the sill. It left a long smear and Catherine shooed it off by snapping a towel. Men were laughing out front, Kat and Lady Bryan both barking crisp orders somewhere inside the house. Eleanor was panting and clapping her hands, almost jumping. Ann disappeared into the laundry. Veronica began to wail from her pallet in the corner, and Robert squatted beside his little sister, patting her forehead.

"You have to go up, Madam," said Eleanor. "I'll keep the children. Kat'll burst wide open if you don't appear."

Catherine smoothed her hair and her skirt. She checked her nails. She examined the reflection of her teeth in a spoon. Her chest was tight, as though her ribs were shrinking. Maybe they would ignore her.

"Catherine!" came the summons again down the stairs. "Upstairs! Now!"

Catherine breathed into her palm to check her breath. She pinched her cheeks.

"Go, Madam. Go!"

"I'm going." But Catherine's feet dragged on the stone steps, and her heart fluttered like a trapped sparrow. She entered the hall and Kat Champernowne grabbed her by one shoulder.

"Get in line," she whispered fiercely, pointing to a row of servants. "There. Get at the end. Beside her tutors."

Catherine positioned herself. She thought the man beside her was the music master, thought by some to be a genius, but he was greasy and fetid. She placed herself as far from him as she could, and he did not look at her but peered at the spray of light spilling from the open front door. A few old oak leaves blew in, weaving themselves into ruffles along the edges of the fresh rushes. Kat bent to pick them up, but they crumbled in her hand. Elizabeth stood, bouncing on her toes, at the top of the main staircase, and she suddenly cried out and ran down, holding her skirts in one delicate hand. The doorway darkened and Catherine smelt something rotting. Like a bad tooth. Like something dead. The stench stiffened her nostrils and bile filled her throat. Elizabeth fell to her knee in an elaborate curtsey. The king walked in.

Henry VIII was huge, and Catherine backed a step as she bent toward the floor, but she studied the man out of the corner of her eye. His gold hair, shot through with white, blazed around his big head. He seemed swollen, exuding light, and he lifted Elizabeth into his arms. He looked her over, one side, then the other, and set her on her feet again. "Let me hear what you have learned."

Elizabeth began to recite, her voice tense and flute-like. "O be joyful in the Lord all ye lands: serve the Lord with gladness, and come before his presence with a song—"

Psalm 100. From the king's own Bible. An inspired choice, thought Catherine.

The child hesitated. The king narrowed his eyes.

Kat gripped Elizabeth's shoulder until she started again, running it through to the end without stopping. Then the lady smiled. King Henry looked at her, and she curtsied again, saying "Elizabeth is a very forward child, Your Majesty."

"So she seems." The king walked down the line of servants, who had all fallen to their knees. The smell of death hung so strong that Catherine held her breath and kept her face low. Kat was introducing each member of the household as he came, grunting, down the line. She'd made one poor young woman, who cleaned the floors and grates, join them because she was pretty, and the king lifted the girl by one arm, looked her over, and set her back where she had been. He was drawing nearer, stopping to greet the reading master, then the music master. Then the king of England was before her.

Kat was saying, "And this is Catherine Overton, of Overton House in Yorkshire. She has knowledge of diet and herbals and oversees the Lady Elizabeth's and the Lady Mary's meals."

"Is she lame?" said the king.

Catherine shot straight up at this and looked at Henry VIII. He was too fat, with small crimson lines threading his sunburnt skin. His pale eyes shone from deep inside fleshy pouches. He stank of sweat and pus and horse hair. He was staring at Catherine.

"You can stand?"

"Yes, Your Majesty."

"What else can you do?"

"I can cook and I study the properties of herbs for the preservation of good health, especially in women. I can teach the primary elements of reading and writing."

The king leaned closer, and Catherine gulped shallow breaths. The stench he emitted was putrefying and her nose bone felt like it was melting. He seemed to be staring down at her breasts.

"You have a husband?"

"William Overton is my loving husband. We have a son and a daughter." Catherine was trying to steady her breath to keep her chest still but she could barely get enough air.

"Overton. From Yorkshire." The king scowled and looked back at Kat. "This one's the nun, isn't she?"

"Formerly," said Catherine. The corners of her mouth ached. "And I thank you for your intervention in the matter of my marriage."

The king gave a thin smile, then he laughed out loud. "You got the man who got your land, didn't you? A cunning move. Why did I do it? Give you permission?"

Catherine's knees were rattling, and she pressed them together. "I was with child, Your Majesty," she said softly. "Master William took responsibility for me and our son in his letter. We thank you for your kind generosity to our family."

"Maybe I should make them all get married, if anyone will take them," said Henry to no one in particular. "Nothing I hate more than old spinsters. They're barely women at all. They're barely people."

Kat murmured, "Yes, Your Majesty."

Catherine was silent, and Henry went on. "Your father is the priest, am I right? Your mother was a prioress." He leaned back and bellowed out another great laugh, his hands braced against his belly as though to keep it from splitting. He wiped his eyes and they glittered from their spongy pockets at Catherine. "You see? The pope is no more than a man and his houses no better than any other. You are proof of my argument. You were made to hold up a man, not a habit."

Catherine's cheeks were hot with misery and shame, and the other servants were staring, but she mustered a "Yes, Your Majesty, and I thank you for your kindness."

Henry looked Catherine up and down, then glanced back at Elizabeth, who waited for him in a halo of sunlight by the front door. "She has grown. You do well, Catherine Overton." He slipped a small ring from his least finger and put it into her palm. She dropped again and lowered her head.

"Thank you, Your Majesty. You are most generous."

"I am!" he replied, turning to the assembled line and raising his arms. "You hear? I am generous and forgiving, and I am starving. Let us see what victuals the mistress of the kitchen can summon to our table." He walked back to Elizabeth and, lifting her, beckoned to someone. A dozen men rushed in and the king handed his daughter to Kat before all the men went up the stairs, followed by the pale lady-in-waiting, clasping a straining Elizabeth to her side. "Now where is my son?" Henry shouted as they reached the first landing.

The music master gave her a ferrety, self-satisfied look. "Let's hope you can cook as well as you claim, or he'll have all our heads on pikes."

34

"He carries an infection somewhere upon him like the plague itself," said Catherine, back down in the kitchen. She collapsed onto a bench, gasping.

Eleanor had scrambled onto the seat, and now she slumped, chin in hand. "Is he not grand?" A slight whine thinned her voice.

"He's big," said Catherine, wiping out her nose with a cloth dipped in sage water. "So is his smell."

Ann came through the other door, her arms full of stacked napkins. "I thought I heard your voice. Eleanor, run these up to the table, will you?"

The maid skipped over and took them with a lop-sided grin on her face.

"No gawking," said Catherine. "Even if you see him. You curtsey, you speak if you're spoken to. Only if you're spoken to. Do not ask questions. And do not stare. If you cannot get away quickly, you bend your head and keep it bent. Fix your eyes on your toes. Back away if you find yourself in his presence."

Eleanor's face sagged a little. "Yes, Madam."

Guilt stabbed her under the heart, and Catherine said, "I tell you this for your own good. If you make a favorable impression, perhaps you will find yourself even closer to the court. You want them to think of you as a superior servant, not an impertinent one."

Eleanor's eyes lit up again. "Yes, Madam. I will be there and back without a misstep."

Three of the other kitchen maids were waiting for orders, and Eleanor lingered to hear their instructions. Catherine tasted the leek soup and nodded. "This first, with the salad greens. Be sure there is vinegar upon the table. Take plenty of bread and leave it upon the sideboard for the serving men. Take the carrots and onions next and cover them to keep them hot until they are served.

Then take the roast beef and the chickens. Be sure the stuffing is still steaming. Stand in the corners, outside the gallery door, and do not belch nor fart. Do not talk, not to the guests nor to each other. Is that all clear? When they finish with the meats, the men will stack the used things near the door. You bring them down and then you will take up the tarts and more wine. Do not be seen except briefly. You enter the room, you leave the goods or remove the bones. You depart without a word. You are invisible. You are silent. Do you hear?"

The three young women bobbed their heads.

"If any of the candles on the sideboards should burn down or blow out, you may relight it from one of the tapers you will have beside you. But do not go to the table and do not drop even a button of wax. Keep your sleeves and skirts well clear. If the men are at the sideboard, you do not enter unless you are summoned. Do you hear?"

The heads went up and down again.

"All right then. Off you go." Catherine shooed them all out. "Eleanor, you stand by and be sure the service is smooth."

"Yes, Madam." She gave the younger maids a firm look and followed at their heels.

Ann watched her go. "She is very eager. She wants to please you as much as she wants to see the king."

Catherine leaned back on the table and took a mug of wine. "She has wits. You have heard how her reading improves. Diana's presence brings her along, as well, and she will soon be writing as beautifully as any clerk."

"Where is Diana?" Ann looked suddenly alarmed. "We have no task for her."

"No need," said Catherine, drinking. "She has been invited to table."

"Ah, well. And you are not."

"I'm just as happy here," said Catherine. She spooned leeks onto a couple of plates and set them before Ann. One of the smaller chickens and a dark loaf of bread completed their meal, and she sat to cut the bread while Ann poured wine for them both. "He likes to laugh about my parents. Next it will be William he pokes his fun at. I wonder he does not divorce us."

Ann chewed on a thumbnail. "You are going back to Overton House for certain? With the children?"

"William's sick." Catherine tore a leg from the hen and laid it on her plate.

"Come with me and he'll have nothing to say to it."

"I don't care what he says." Ann checked the stairs and sat again to her food. "I tell you, Catherine, it's not safe. Someone fastened that stirrup to your son's pony. Someone who knows he's your son."

Catherine did not respond and Ann rushed on. "I don't like saying it outright, but you cannot act like a blind woman. You think it's coincidence that your women disappear one by one? That your son is almost killed? You could be next."

"His own wife? His own son? William has always been devoted to family."

"Robert's as good a boy as I know, but William can count. He can see, too. And the boy doesn't look like him."

"No. He looks like me." Catherine's voice crumbled and the words were barely audible.

"Yes," said Ann, taking the other chicken leg. "Exactly."

"I have to go. Margaret will have me before a court of law if I fail to return."

The young women returned for the vegetables. Catherine checked their tenderness and color and approved them for the table. Eleanor showed the younger maids how to fill the serving dishes and the four of them were gone again.

"William is the reason I'm here." Catherine looked at the ceiling. "I hope Diana has enough sense to show herself a pleasant presence at the table."

"Not too pleasant, I pray," said Ann, swigging from her cup. "The king will want to marry her before he departs."

Catherine shuddered at the image of the slim girl trapped under the heaving bulk of Henry VIII. "God's cross, how could any woman bear it?"

Ann shrugged with one shoulder and poured herself another drink. "He is a king, Catherine. Need I say more?"

"Diana is a practical girl. And she likes her learning." Catherine could hear the tremor of insistence in her voice. "She does."

"So did the Boleyn woman." Ann thought a moment, wiping butter over her bread. "We have us another school then." She nodded toward the door. "Those three younger ones may come to you for instruction in intellectual matters as well as manners."

"Perhaps." Ann was smirking, and Catherine added, "They may not be geniuses, but they could learn to read accounts and sign their names. It would do them good."

"More good than reading Cicero," agreed Ann. She'd plucked a volume from the windowsill and plopped it onto the table. "You will not subject them to this, will you?"

"We have different ideas about reading." Catherine fished in her pocket and drew out the ring. She tossed it onto the boards and it rattled toward Ann. "What think you of that?"

"Where did this come from?" Ann lifted it with her middle finger and let it slide down. The garnet at its center glowed, and the gold foil glittered. The red stone was surrounded by small pearls.

"The little finger of Henry VIII," said Catherine. She lifted it from her friend's hand. "Looks like a drop of blood, doesn't it? And I fawned like any merchant's wife to get it. Thanked him for his generosity."

"We say what we must to keep our heads on our necks."

"I once despised such opinions. But that was when I was sure of truth's strength." Catherine threw the ring down again. "I will sell it for some paper and ink. For our school, as you call it. For books."

"It troubles me," said Ann. She listened for a moment to the shreds of laughter that twisted down the stairs from the gallery. "To have women gathered together for study. After what has happened at Overton House. I do not believe that Ruth and Hannah left on their own. Not for a second." She snapped her fingers.

Catherine went to the door and checked the stairs again. She and Ann were alone. "Are the children still sleeping?"

Ann stuck her head into the side room that led to the laundry. "Like two angels," she said. "Thank God that Robbie is not old enough to care more if he sees a king than if he sees a speckled pup."

"Would that he might stay in that frame of mind," said Catherine. She sighed and sat at the table. She started to speak, but the four maids came trotting down the stairs and into the kitchen for the meats. Eleanor loaded up the platters and expertly herded the three younger ones out again.

Catherine waited until their footsteps could no longer be heard on the steps. "The events may be unrelated. At home, I mean."

"Do you believe that? Honestly?"

Catherine searched her mind to see if the idea would hold. All she could imagine were her two friends, lying in the dirt somewhere, prey for wild animals. "Not in earnest." Catherine spun the ring in the light. "When the king goes, I will be on the road home. I will leave this with you to sell as you see fit. William may have uncovered some lunatic. I think the villain must be someone who resented the convents."

"What about Robert?"

Kat Champernowne came down, and Catherine's chest froze up again. "His Majesty summons you," said the lady. Then she whisked off up the stairs.

"Put linen wads in your nose if you are called up," said Catherine to Ann. She ripped a corner of a clean rag and stuffed her own nostrils. "The man smells like rot. He must be filled with maggots."

"I mean not to be called at all," said Ann.

Catherine climbed the stone steps as slowly as she could, her skirt twisted in one sweating hand. She wiped the other against her side as she passed the three maids and Eleanor, who were standing at attention just outside the door to the gallery. Eleanor's eyes glowed almost feverishly and she whispered, "The king is in there!" She pointed frantically at the door. "He is there and I have laid eyes upon him!"

"Yes, Eleanor." Catherine touched her maid with a damp palm, took a deep breath, and entered the gallery.

The table was a shambles of gnawed bones and wads of glistening, chewed gristle. Three dogs crouched near the king's chair, growling and snapping over the scraps that had been tossed to the floor. Henry stripped the flesh from a breast in one rip, pulling sideways with his teeth and spitting the skin away. His plate was heaped with meat and bread, and his face pulsed with the effort of eating. He sat back and chewed, washing the mouthful down with a swig of wine. He spied Catherine as he set down the goblet. "Come, woman. Don't stand in the shadows like a ghost. Step forward and show yourself."

Catherine approached the table and curtsied. She was standing behind Elizabeth, who had nibbled at a sliver of chicken. A few remnants of salad and carrots were strewn in the grease. The child bent her head in its velvet cap backward and smiled up. "Lady Catherine. Have you made my supper for me?"

Catherine moved so that she was beside the king's daughter and curtsied again. When she raised her eyes, she met the gaze of Mary Tudor, who sat across the table from her sister. The older Tudor daughter was in dark green, and her hair was fixed severely under a black cap stitched with pearls. She nodded almost imperceptibly at Catherine. Diana Davies sat beside Mary, her face pale and bright with terrified excitement. Catherine dipped her chin, then turned to Elizabeth. "I have overseen your food, my young Lady. I trust you have eaten your fill?"

"I have." Elizabeth took Catherine's hand and spoke to the king. "Lady Catherine keeps me strong, Father, so that I excel in my lessons."

"Are you satisfied with her, then?" It was not clear if the king was addressing his daughter or Kat. His piggy eyes were on Catherine. Her chest felt exposed and cold.

"She pleases me," said Elizabeth. "Her baby is my doll, and she teaches me to make my letters beautiful so that I may write to you."

"You have a writing master for that, Daughter," said the king. "And I pay him handsomely for it."

"Yes, Father, and I thank you, but Catherine sits with me of an evening, and she lets me sleep if my eyes are heavy."

"She does, does she?" The king was still watching Catherine. "How will you learn your letters if you are sleeping?"

"Lady Catherine says that my mind is awake when I sleep, like my soul, Father, and that it needs to rest." said Elizabeth.

"And what part of Lady Catherine is awake during these times of sleep?" asked the king. "Do you sleep with parts of yourself alert?"

Catherine opened her mouth to reply, but her tongue was dry. She closed her eyes, thought, *Mother be with me*, and said, "My soul is always wakeful, Your Majesty, and it meditates night and day upon the welfare of my husband and the children who are in my care."

"Shall I show you my writing?" said Elizabeth at her side.

Henry wiped his beard and threw the cloth to the floor. "Another time, child." He leaned back and his stomach lurched until he belched. "Do my daughters always eat this black stuff?" He lifted a chunk of the dark bread and ground it with his fingers. A damp wad remained in his palm and he flung it down. The dogs landed on it as one.

Catherine felt as though lightning was rippling across her collarbones. The king was staring at her. She said, "The young ladies have delicate stomachs. The grains improve them." The words were fluttering birds in her mouth. "Their bodies must work to be strong."

The king looked at Mary. Looked at Elizabeth. "This is nun's food?"

Catherine's guts twisted and flipped. She was afraid she might lose control of her water.

Mary broke a crust and spread butter on it. "This food has made my skin shine, Father. Catherine is mistress of her kitchen and she knows what she is about." She nipped the edge of the bread.

"Hmph," said the king. "Has the mistress of the kitchen any puddings to follow the meat?"

"Yes, Your Majesty." Catherine curtsied quickly. "May I have leave to attend the younger maids in the kitchen? They are young yet and green in their duties."

"Go, go," said the king, waving his hand. He had already shifted his attention to the dancing master before she left the room.

Catherine snapped her fingers at the four young women as she hurried out. The tarts were still warm, thanks to Ann, and Catherine put a jug of sweet cream into the hand of the smallest maid as they lined up. "Hand in the pastry first. Then the cream. Replace the wine. Clear the bones from the sideboard if the men do not."

"Are you not coming back up, Madam?" said the first. "The king seemed much interested to speak with you."

"I will stay here until called."

They went in a dutiful line, and Catherine sat, putting her head on her arms.

"Is it over?" Ann slid onto the bench across from her.

"Almost." Catherine raised her eyes. "The man eats like a hog and stares like a fat hound with a cornered rabbit. Christ, you can hear the swish of the axe in his voice."

"Smells like death. Eats like a hog. Sounds like an executioner. It does not increase my faith in his church."

"Nor mine. But if the reformers are not liars, the Pope is no different. Nor the cardinals in Rome." Catherine picked up the garnet ring that Ann had left on the table and turned it. "And yet, the girl is sweet as a rose in June. With a mind as sharp as the thorns."

Ann shook her head, confused. "Which one?"

"Elizabeth. They are as different as night and noon. Mary sits still as a dark star in the sky, and when she speaks, the air changes. Elizabeth is all chatter and sunshine."

"Ah, the little bastard. You once said you would never serve anyone but Katherine of Aragon's child."

"I know," mused Catherine, though when she tried to call up the feelings of resentment she had once felt toward Anne Boleyn's daughter, she could not find them anywhere inside her.

"So which one will you give your loyalties to now?" Ann drank deeply and regarded Catherine over the cup.

"Mary, of course. She just now saved my skin. But Elizabeth when she needs me. No, Mary." Catherine wiped back her hair, dripping from the heat of the fire. Something smoldered in her chest as well and she could not get cool again. "I do not know."

35

The king wanted to go by the time the sun was well up and Catherine counted the minutes. She had been awake since the middle of the night, directing the victuals for the king's men to break their fast and making sure the ale was fresh and sweet. The maids had been baking since midnight, and Catherine had put her head down for a couple of hours in the laundry room, but when she smelt burning meat, she'd awakened to find the girls fussing over a scorched joint of pork.

"Never mind," said Catherine as the maids began to squabble at the mess, each blaming another for failing to watch the fire. "Find something else. Get the hams from the cellar." She stabbed the smoking, black thing with a long fork and opened the back door, only to be assaulted by the strange dogs. One snapped at the meat and caught Catherine's thumb. "God damn you," she blurted, losing her grip on the handle. Three animals went at the downed meat and each other, and Catherine backed away, hoping one of them would swallow the tines in its fury.

Her hand swelled and, back in the kitchen, Catherine clapped a quick poultice of fresh lard and dried thyme leaves on the wound. "Mark me if this doesn't leave a scar," she muttered.

Ann came in, rubbing her eyes. "Are you baiting bears out there?"

"You are a rare comedienne," said Catherine. "You see what those devils have done to me to get at a charred chunk of pig?" She held up the thumb and Ann whistled. The blood trickled from under the bandage.

"God's foot," she said. "You could have lost the hand. Next time throw it from a window."

"I will throw a butcher knife next time. Now let's get this food upstairs

162

before the royal stomach growls."

Catherine started loading up the platters with her uninjured hand and the maids followed suit. The baby woke and cried, and Ann went to tend her.

"Say a sweet good-bye to the royal arse as you see it depart," she whispered as Catherine went by, laden with fruit and ale and still holding the clout tightly wound around her thumb.

By the time the king and his men were finally mounted, Catherine was in the garden, watching from a distance as Henry bade his children farewell. Lady Bryan held the prince, and Catherine strained to see the boy's face, but he was swaddled too deeply. Elizabeth clung to her father's neck and he gave her a few thumps on the back before he set her on the ground and pointed his fat finger in her face. He was presenting her with some admonition or other, and Catherine was glad she couldn't hear it. Mary hung back, standing straight as a pin with her hands folded neatly in front of her. She exchanged words with King Henry briefly and curtsied low, but she did not move to embrace him, nor did he seem to seek it.

Elizabeth stood with her hand in Kat's as the horses stampeded off. She did not cry. When Mary, after they were gone, turned on her small heel and walked inside, her little sister followed without looking back.

Catherine took a loaf of fresh warm bread and a bowl of fried apples with a jug of weak wine up to Mary's apartment, but no one answered, so she went down to Elizabeth's room, knocked softly on the door, and swung it open. Elizabeth was sitting in her small rocker, with her simple embroidery in her lap, but she was not working. Kat sat on the bed. Mary was in a wooden armchair by the window, holding the edge of the curtain.

"I have brought the ladies somewhat to break their fast." Catherine set the food on a dresser, tucking the bandaged thumb into her palm.

The child set the needlework aside. The apples were spiced with cinnamon, and she lifted one to examine its color before she set it on her tongue. "Come and taste, Sister. These are like candy."

"Better for your bowels than candy," said Catherine, and Mary rose, tempted by the food, and sat with Elizabeth.

"I will cut this for you," said Mary Tudor, taking a knife to the apples. "You want smaller bites for your size." She fixed the apples, covered a slice of bread with butter, and handed the plate to Elizabeth. They could have been a young

mother and daughter, and Catherine was astonished.

She watched for a while as the sisters ate their food in silent concord. Then Mary rose and said she would retire to her own chamber. When she was gone, Catherine said to Kat, "My husband may be lying in need of me. And there is the matter of the women missing from our household."

"Yes. You will leave your children here, then?"

Catherine thought for a few seconds. The Tudor sisters had never been as tender with each other as she had just seen them. It was a temptation. But she had no idea how long she would be gone. And her son was safer at her side. "Robert has been away from me enough. He and Veronica will travel with me."

"You have spoken with Master Davies?"

"I thought you might intervene there for me."

"I've no doubt he will provide you with his best equipment." Kat shook her head. "The very best. If it suits you, I will send word to him."

Catherine went at once to pack her cases again. Eleanor brought Robert, and the boy jumped onto his mother's bed to watch while the maid busied herself in the next room.

"Will we go to see my father now?" Robert asked.

Her son was picking at the hem of his shirt, and one leg swung back and forth.

"Why, yes. We will go together."

The boy put his thumb into his mouth and Catherine removed it. He popped it in again.

"That will make your teeth crooked, Robbie. You are too old for such tricks. You must behave like a boy of your station."

Robert slowly let the thumb slip from between his lips but his eyes glistened with tears. Catherine knelt beside the bed and took his hands in hers. "Do you not wish to go home?" The boy's face flushed, and the tears spilled down his cheeks. "Mother—" he began, then he tumbled from the bed. It was too late. The wet spot was large and the child crumpled onto the floor. "I will do as you command, Mother."

"Robert, come here." Catherine held her son until he grew cold. "You must get out of these things and put on something clean." She pulled off the urine-soaked garments and washed the boy at her basin. She held the soap to his nose. "Doesn't that smell like the garden?" Robert smiled and allowed himself to be clothed in fresh linen. Catherine stripped the bed and called Eleanor to take the soiled covers down to Ann. The maid did not ask questions though the scent made the entire room acrid. When she was alone again with her son, Catherine set him in a chair and sat on the floor before him. "Now tell me. Do you want to stay here? I must go, but you need not. Ann could stay to take care of you. She would relish it."

Robert put his arms around Catherine's neck. "I want you to stay with me."

Catherine drew back. "Your father lies ill in his bed. He needs me."

"I need you." Robert buried his face in Catherine's shoulder. "Stay here with me."

"And what of your father, Robert? Would you have me leave him alone when he is sick? I would not do so if you were ill."

"No, Mother."

"Then what would you have me do?"

Robert sat back again, folding his chubby hands in his lap. He stared at his thumb but did not raise it. "You must go home to Father. And I must stay here with Auntie Ann."

Catherine roughed up Robert's hair. "I would not leave you for my pleasure. It breaks me to part from you."

"It will please the Lady Elizabeth to have me stay."

Catherine laughed at this. "No doubt, boy. Will you tell me your reason? Unpack your heart to your mother, Robert, so that I may go with a free conscience."

He swung his legs again, and Catherine finally stilled them with her hands. "Tell me," she repeated.

"My father does not love me," the boy said at last. "I fear his looks."

Catherine's heart shriveled. She would not tell the boy that his impressions were mistaken, though she longed to. Instead, she nodded. "Then you will stay here with Ann and you will pray for me and for your little sister until I return." She thought about adding William to the list and decided against.

"That I will do," said Robert without smiling. He put out his hand, and she shook it.

By the time Catherine had finished packing her things, and unpacking Robert's, the day was far gone. Ann was feeding the children, and she was sitting with Kat and Diana at supper when they heard the horses in the front courtyard.

"Who is that at this hour?" said Kat, throwing down her napkin and going to the window. "Beshrew me, it's Benjamin Davies."

"Benjamin himself?" asked Catherine. Her stomach bounced.

"The very man," said Kat, as he banged at the door, "in the flesh." She motioned one of the men to answer and went back to her seat. "Let him wait."

Catherine said, "You sent to his home?"

"Of course. For horses and men to ride with you. I didn't ask if he was there." The man returned to announce the arrival of Benjamin Davies and a messenger. "I suppose we should go and meet our trouble."

But the messenger had followed the man servant inside. "I come from Overton House with news for Lady Catherine Overton," he said to the room.

"I am Catherine Overton and you may give your news to me." She held out her hand.

"I am to deliver myself in words," the messenger said. "Privately."

"You see no one here but the private household," snapped Kat. "Say what you have come to say, man."

"Very well." He sniffed and directed his nose at Catherine. "I am told to inform you that your husband means to file a writ of divorcement against you and no longer will consider you as his lawful wife."

36

Benjamin Davies was pacing in the front hallway, and he slapped his leg when he saw the women come racing out after the departing messenger. "I thought you were sending me to the doghouses for my pains," he said, but they rushed past him.

"Who has sent this message?" Catherine demanded, but the young man kept walking. He nodded at Benjamin as he passed by and went out the door. "Who? I insist that you tell me," Catherine shouted. "He is gone. Like that. And what am I to do?"

Benjamin said, "What has happened?"

Kat came forward and took the man by the hand. "We were in the middle of dining and in comes this wretch to say that Catherine's husband means to divorce her. Have you heard of such an outrage?"

"I have not. Who was he, Catherine?"

She was still standing at the door and she pushed it closed. "I have never seen his face before." She put her forehead against the wood and whispered, "It cannot be true." She turned but the room seemed too large and bright and she leaned back against the door to steady herself.

Diana Davies came running downstairs, and Benjamin said, "There's my daughter." He grabbed Diana in a big hug and she grinned.

"Come and eat," said Kat, guiding Diana away from Catherine.

Benjamin said, "Lead on to the victuals, girl, before your father shrinks to nothing. Tell me about your grand audience with the king."

Diana took her father by the hand, prattling about the royal clothing and the mounds of food. Kat threw Catherine a look behind their backs and she followed, arranging her face for the girl. The men had begun to remove the dishes, and Benjamin shouted at them to stop and let him have a bite.

Kat nodded and the food was swiftly returned to the table, the maids peering with wide eyes around the side door, thinking the king had surely reversed his course. Benjamin sat down and looked into a goblet. "This one's clean enough. Pour me a glass, Daughter." He had Diana's own cup, and she giggled as she served the wine and watched him drink. "My God, you've grown a foot, girl. What do they feed you? Gold nuggets?"

"I eat fine meat and drink good wine. Catherine insists I get my exercise in the garden every day. I am studying herbs and diet, Father. My writing improves as well. You would have been proud to hear the way I carried on conversation with the king's daughter. She is rather froward, though, and frowns at everything."

"Herbs? Writing? So you make my daughter a scholar of weeds?" Benjamin raised his cup to Catherine. "A great taxing of female wits." He winked at his daughter and drank.

"Diana has an excellent mind," said Catherine soberly. She went to the door, where Eleanor was hiding, and sent her downstairs for the puddings. "She has capacities for much learning."

"You will make a Margaret More of her, no doubt," said Benjamin, "and then she will bore all the men to death." He smiled at Diana but his eyes returned again and again to Catherine. "So you sat next to the elder daughter, did you?"

"I did, Father." Diana's voice was suddenly very soft and her eyes were distant with remembering.

Benjamin's right eye twitched and he sank his teeth into his lower lip. "Well." He considered for a few silent moments, and Catherine almost spoke up for Mary Tudor, but he suddenly slapped his thigh again. "Lady Catherine, you can tell me her whole course of study on the road to Overton House."

"What?" Catherine gasped.

Kat Champernowne's voice was ice. "You mean to go with her?"

"Why else would I have come?" asked Benjamin. He tore himself a chunk of bread. "Have you no butter in this house?"

"I meant to travel with a few servants only," said Catherine. Bells were clanging somewhere under her heart, and she put her hand on her ribs. "How can you leave your houses untended?"

"Ah, the houses. You have come to me with a timely request, Catherine.

My brother Lewis means to visit from Conwy, and I would like a reason to be gone." He wiped his beard. "The man is a pedant and a whoremonger who fancies himself a philosopher. I would like to be gone before I am forced to endure another schoolteacher's lecture on goodness while he pinches my maidservants' backsides."

"Listen to Catherine," said Kat. "It is not proper. You will not accompany her. Not alone. No."

"Ladies, if you did not want me to come, why did you call on me? Did you think to appropriate my property and my people without my oversight?"

Kat's head reared back at this. Her nostrils flared and she looked like an angry mare. "I supposed you a gentleman who would not let a lady venture by foot alone onto the road to her . . . her sick husband." She glanced at Catherine.

"And so I would not. I mean to make sure she gets there myself. Stop worrying your head about appearances, woman. She will have her maid and whatever other girls she wants about her, and my men will be with us. I assure you there will be no appearance of impropriety. Do you want her to get there in one piece or don't you? God's foot, she's got a baby in arms." He turned to Catherine. "Where is the little one?"

"My friend Ann has her below."

"She goes with you?"

"Yes. The baby, I mean. My son will stay here."

"Your son? He is here?"

Catherine gulped. "Ah. Yes. He has arrived from the north. He wishes to remain here. He is weary of travel, I think, and has fallen in love with Elizabeth."

"The boy may stay with us," said Kat Champernowne. She was still scowling at Benjamin.

"It is decided then," said Benjamin. "Things being as they are, I will take you home."

"Things being as they are, I think Catherine should go unaccompanied," said Kat.

"You have a choice. You could have provided Catherine with horses and servants yourself. And now she will need a lawyer."

"Why does she need a lawyer?" asked Diana, and Kat scowled.

Benjamin said, "I leave the decision to Lady Catherine. Ah, here's the sweets." The serving men set down two rhubarb tarts, and Benjamin fell to, scooping out enormous bites. "Eat, girl," he said to Diana.

Catherine watched him for a few moments before she said, "I will accept Benjamin as my traveling companion."

37

Benjamin slept in a bedroom downstairs from the women, and in the morning he was awake at dawn, calling down the hallway for Catherine. She was already awake, though Ann was still asleep beside her. The dream had visited her again, but this time the man had worn a hooded cloak, and she could not see his face. Her bitten thumb throbbed, and she cursed the king under her breath. Catherine heard Benjamin well enough, but she buried her face in her pillow to block out his voice. Ann turned over and sighed irritably.

"Madam?" It was Eleanor, tugging at the edge of the bedclothes. She had Veronica in the crook of her arm. "Ann?"

Catherine threw back the sheet, and sat up. "Climb in here." She took Veronica and Eleanor bounced over her, settling in while Catherine nursed the baby. Benjamin bellowed again, and Catherine gritted her teeth. "I could chop his tongue out with a cleaver. These men, always eager to be on their horses before the sun has its chin over the horizon."

Eleanor smiled. "I think he is eager to see Master Overton."

"And you? What are you so eager for?"

Eleanor shrugged, and Catherine nudged her. "Go to, you're not so innocent as all that."

Eleanor suddenly became very interested in the state of her nails. "I suppose not. But I am full gone twenty years old, Madam. I'm not for all markets anymore." She smirked, one eyebrow going up. "I think I will die if I don't see Joseph soon. You know how it is when a man loves you? It's like he wants to eat you up and you feel all sweet inside."

"Impertinent wretch." Catherine slapped Eleanor's hand lightly and the girl rolled over, giggling to herself. Catherine switched the baby to the other breast.

"But, yes, I know how it is. I could teach you a thing or two about it."

"About what?" Eleanor was serious, and she sat up.

Catherine just shook her head. She didn't want to kill the girl's spirits, not this early in the morning, but Ann said, "She could teach you not to take the word of any man as the gospel of your life."

"Ann," said Catherine.

"I only tell the truth," said Ann. "Divorce you? How does he dare to think it?"

"We know only that a message came," said Catherine. "We have no letter from William's hand."

"Divorce?" repeated Eleanor. She shook Ann's arm. "What divorce?"

"Nothing," said Catherine. "We must go home and set our house right."

Benjamin hammered on the door. "Are you getting out of the bed before the leaves fall or will I have to break in and drag you to the horses?"

"I will tell you more later," said Catherine. "Time to get dressed." She called, "We're coming."

They were quickly in their clothes, and Catherine rebound her thumb with fresh linen, pulling the edges of the bite together to knit them. Ann brought Robert into the dining gallery, still rubbing his eyes, while they were breaking their fast, and the boy sat on Catherine's knee, leaning against her chest. She stroked his hair while she ate her bread. "You will be a good boy while I am away?"

"I swear it, Mother." The boy studied Benjamin. "Will you be good, too, sir?"

"Ha!" Benjamin pushed back from the table. "That boy has his mother's wit." He wagged his finger at Robert. "Mind your mistresses while we are away." He gave the boy a swift pat on the head and went out, humming a sad tune.

Catherine kissed Robert's hair. "Ann will give me a report of you, be sure of it. And she is fierce in her love for you."

"Auntie Ann will whip me if I misbehave."

"I will at that." Ann came in, wiping her hands on a towel. "Now come, Robert, and let your mother eat her fill." She sat at the end of the long dark table, and the boy hopped from his mother's lap and ran to Ann.

Catherine finished her ale. She could see men loading her cases onto the pack horses, and Eleanor was already outside, almost bouncing on the balls of her feet. Kat Champernowne was directing them all, and she ignored Benjamin Davies when he came by her to check his saddle.

"It's time to say good-bye, little son," said Catherine. She swallowed and wiped her eyes. "Come here and kiss me and let me remember the feel of your arms."

Robert met her halfway and hugged her tightly about the neck. Catherine's eyes met Ann's over the small boy's shoulder, but Catherine couldn't decipher her expression. She held her son, feeling the narrow ribs and hips, putting her nose into his soft black hair.

"Now. I will go see how the sun hangs over our home and come back and you will be almost as tall as I am when I see you again. You will eat, hear me?"

They walked outside, hand in hand, and Robert shifted his grasp from Catherine's to Ann's. Eleanor brought the baby, and Robert gave his small sister a formal peck on the cheek.

Elizabeth was with her writing master and could not come down, but Kat shook Catherine's hand. "The girl needs you here to keep her strong. She looks hale, but I fear her condition is unsteady." She spoke low, her eyes on Benjamin.

"I will return before the summer is high in the sky," said Catherine.

"Keep an eye on that man," said Kat. "He certainly keeps an eye on you."

"Give my regards to Reg, if you should happen to see him," said Ann. She was fussing with Robert's shoe ties and did not look at Catherine.

"That I will. Any words in particular?"

"Just my greetings," said Ann. She glanced up and her cheeks were burning with a light Catherine had never seen on her face before.

"Consider it done," said Catherine. She hugged her friend, then Diana, and arranged herself in the saddle. Benjamin threw himself onto his horse and signaled his man, who jolted forward. Catherine turned to see Robert, waving until she was out the front gate. Hatfield House flamed in the morning light, and Catherine watched until it was only a flicker through the trees.

The weather was fine, a green wind blowing the scent of bluebells and daffodils through the countryside, and the clouds tumbling as though nudged along by the finger of God. Catherine closed her eyes until a rut threw her forward. "Mother of God, that almost snapped my neck. I'll be a pile of broken sticks by the time we get there."

Eleanor was stroking Veronica's head. "I hope he remembers me."

"Joseph? He's not that dull, is he?"

"What if he has found another maid?" Eleanor murmured.

"If he has, then he wasn't for you. He has only been gone a few days. Did you not get a moment with him before he went?"

"Barely a second," Eleanor said sullenly. Then her mouth twisted. "Perhaps more than a second. But those kitchen maids were like midges in summer. I almost slapped them."

"He will be there. And if he's not, you'll find another."

Eleanor pushed herself to sitting. "But I'm not—" Her face flushed and she covered her mouth with her hand.

"A virgin?" asked Catherine. "Tush, girl, what you have done, others have done before you. There are ways to mask it if need be."

"Is that what you meant to tell me?"

"In part." Catherine leaned forward. Benjamin was riding behind them, and she could hear him, humming to himself. "I have made a study of women's travails. It is one of the subjects we were making receipts for at home. But my women are gone, disappeared. You are a woman I could trust, Eleanor, if you would want to learn what I know."

"You were a nun! A woman of God! How can you talk so?"

"The men have too many Gods these days for a wise woman to commit herself to any one of them. I say what I think, but not in the wide world where anyone can hear. There are methods to make you a maid again, if that is what you want. If you want Joseph, you must require that he take you as you are."

"As Master William took you."

"Yes. And my condition was worse than yours." Catherine glanced over her shoulder.

"Joseph was not exactly my first," Eleanor said, "but he thinks he was. I tried to act as though I didn't know where anything went. Is that evil?"

"He likely paid no attention," said Catherine. "You tell him nothing to the contrary unless your conscience demands it. Is the other man nearby?"

"He is always nearby." Eleanor pulled the baby tight against her chest and rocked her from side to side.

"You needn't tell me. I'm not your confessor. All I advise is that you protect yourself from shame and poverty. No one will pick up a woman who believes herself that she is fallen."

Eleanor said nothing for a while. Catherine dozed, and in her dreams Mary Tudor stood in the doorway of Overton House, beckoning. In her fingers was twined a rosary, and Catherine was reaching for it when Eleanor blurted out, "But your station is higher than mine."

Catherine blinked and yawned. She was coming back from a long way away, but Mary Tudor was gone and she was sitting on a pony again, her haunches getting sore. "What's that you say? My station?" She stretched and looked at her maid's troubled face. "Fut, Eleanor, I was a bastard child of a nun and a priest. Where does that put me?"

"I know, Madam. But I have thought on this. Your mother was from a landholding family. Your husband holds those lands now and has a title to go with them. I think on the king's daughters. They are called bastards, too, but they have serving people and chambers of their own."

The countryside became wooded, and Benjamin rode closer. He called to the men to slow down, and one of them rode beside the women. Benjamin's leather boot flexed in his stirrup, and Catherine eased up close to Eleanor to say, "That horse has people to bring him his hay and water, as well, but you would not call his station high, would you?"

Eleanor laughed, and Catherine tapped her knee. "I speak in earnest, Eleanor. The king's daughters have barely clothes for their backs. I have heard Kat Champernowne begging Lady Bryan to have the king send things for the girls as well as the prince. Mark me, a bastard's place in the world is as unsure as the wheels on a cart. Any small stone can break it." She sat back, biting her lip to stop herself from going on. She couldn't be sure that William had cast her off. He wouldn't. Surely he wouldn't.

Eleanor considered. "When you lived in the convent, it was better? You had a place?"

"I suppose we did," said Catherine. "There was a place for unwanted girls. We could learn to read. I was sought for and I used my mind as well as my hands."

"And you do not do that now?" The girl's brown eyes were intelligent as well as curious.

"Yes, I do. For now, I do. I would that you might do the same."

"Oh, Madam. You want the world to be a paradise."

"At least, perhaps, a garden." They passed out of the woods into a clearing, and the sun glared across a wide, cut field of nettles and daisies. But at the far end she saw a mower, ruthlessly sweeping them down with the long arcs of his gleaming scythe.

38

The trip north took the small group five days. The women grew tired of talking, and the hours rolled forward. The men slumped in their saddles, even Benjamin, who had taken to riding with his fingers hooked in his beard and a dark look on his face. Catherine watched the road slide past and wondered what she would find in Yorkshire. Men had every advantage, she thought. They would have women give up their callings and their maidenheads to their husbands, but the husbands would reserve the right to set them aside. "As though we could restore ourselves to maids and sell ourselves off again," she muttered, chewing her lip. She meditated on the unfairness of it, and whenever they stopped, Catherine ordered wine, hoping to flush the day's bitterness from her heart. Benjamin always chose the far end of the table when they dined, then retired with a bow to a back room. Catherine and Eleanor, too worn down from the bouncing gossip, washed their feet and hands and faces and fell into bed, the baby often sleeping between them.

Catherine did not dream again until the night before they were to arrive back home. She lay next to Eleanor, who was on her back, arms and legs flung out. Their clothes, hanging nearby, smelt of sweat and earth, and Catherine was caught in a fitful, hot sleep. She seemed to see William, covered with smallpox, but when she pulled back the sheet to examine him, he had the face of Robert, his dead brother. Catherine opened her eyes in the dark. The baby stirred, in a cradle this night, and Catherine took her to the window, where a gibbous moon hung, great-bellied, in the sky.

Someone moved downstairs, and Catherine could hear men's voices. She tiptoed to the door and listened. Benjamin was talking to someone, maybe the innkeeper, about the horses. The other man said something about "the women," and Benjamin's voice lowered. Catherine could no longer understand him. Soon, goodnights were exchanged and a light came up the stairs. Catherine held her breath, but Benjamin clomped on by and she heard him enter another room and close the door. Her heart suddenly felt hollow and swollen, and Catherine laid her forehead against the wood until the pounding in her chest slowed.

They jangled through Havenston the next day with the sun still high above them, and the men urged the horses forward. Catherine could see the light of anticipation in Eleanor's eyes. Her own guts were dancing a little, and she peered through the trees, in full leaf now, for the square grey towers of the House. Eleanor squealed as they came into view, and Catherine felt nauseous, though whether from excitement or dread she couldn't determine.

The small herb garden was visible from the front drive, and Catherine could see that it had overgrown itself into a wilderness of weeds. She wondered if there were any vegetables in the house. Her husband's sister had never favored anything green and detested the idea of food that had been in the ground. But Catherine had little time for wonder. William was standing in the front door when they rode up, and he stared at Benjamin, who jumped off his horse and approached to shake his hand. William was thin as a quill, and when he recoiled slightly at Benjamin, he wavered, grabbing at the corner of the entryway to hold himself upright. His breeches hung around his hips, his hose were loose on his legs, and he had left his shirt hanging out. He looked greasy and worn out, as though he had been cutting hay or moving stones. Catherine leapt from the pony before it had fully stopped and ran to him, but Benjamin was between them, and she had to push him aside.

"William." Catherine pulled him into her arms, but she could feel his muscles stiffen at her touch. Even through the thick doublet, she could almost count his ribs under her fingers. His cheek was hot. His arms came around her, though, and he finally sagged against her.

"I am not well, Catherine. I am glad to see you."

"Are you, then? Am I welcome here?" She pushed his hair from his forehead. He was perspiring slightly, and the old smallpox scars glowed white. "We will have you back to your old self in no time."

"If anyone can do it, your woman can," called Benjamin, but William did not answer him, just staggered back indoors. Catherine followed, beckoning behind her for Eleanor to take Veronica around to the side. Reginald Goodall stepped forward and took his master's right arm. Catherine supported the left and together they kept William upright.

"Why have you brought him along?" said William when they were on the stairs. He leaned on Catherine's shoulder as they went. Halfway up, he pitched forward and crawled the rest of the way.

Catherine followed, horrified at his decay. At the landing, she helped him stand again. "It was not my choice. He provided the ponies, and the night before we were to go, he appeared. The Hatfield horses and servants were not made available."

William stopped. "The night before? You slept under the same roof with him?"

"He slept on a different floor. I did not see him again until I stepped into the saddle."

"And you did not tell him you would go alone."

"Would you have wanted me to ride five days alone?" He didn't answer, and she added, "Come, let's get you into bed. You're on fire."

He fell against the wall, shrugging off both Catherine and Reg. He began pulling himself along the hallway. "Let me do it myself."

"Very well." Catherine walked beside him, and when they achieved the chamber door, Margaret came out of her bedroom.

"I see you have brought a suitor with you," she said, crossing her arms. "My brother did not expect to see his wife arrive accompanied by an unmarried man."

"What is wrong with this house?" Catherine said. She could taste the heat in her voice. "I did not bring Benjamin Davies. He gave us the use of his ponies and his men. He rode alongside for fear of highwaymen and to see William. He is not my suitor. I wouldn't even know him if William had not introduced us. Is this not the case?"

Margaret slid her hand around William's arm. "If you say so, Catherine."

William flung his sister away. "She speaks the truth, Margaret. I am at fault, and you should mind your tongue. I have a fever upon me. What ails you?"

"I will not stay to be insulted in my father's house," said Margaret. "I suppose you have dragged the children along the road, as well?"

Catherine said, "I brought Veronica rather than leave her to a wet nurse.

Eleanor has taken her around to the kitchen."

"You have Robert?" William asked.

Catherine hesitated, then said, "He has stayed at Hatfield House." A breeze blew through her words, as easy as the truth. "I was surprised that you sent him, but he has settled in nicely. He plays with Elizabeth, and if he misses a day, she asks for him." William began to speak, but he bit his lip, and Catherine rushed on. "The boy will surely have a place with her as she grows up. He is happy that you sent him."

William glanced at Margaret, whose face was patched with red, and said, "I am content if he has found a home. It would be better if he were at court."

"If I were at court, he would be. But he prospers where he is. I think he will be at court soon enough."

"And you? How do you do, Catherine?"

"The work is not onerous. The child eats well, and I have enough women around me to be my gossips."

"Who? What women? Who are they?"

"Eleanor, of course. Diana Davies, who has come to work at the house. Kat Champernowne, who seems to have become the chief lady. The three young kitchen maids."

"No one else?"

He was waiting for her to mention Ann, but Catherine maintained their charade, as though they could both pretend that Robert had made his way to Hatfield alone. Perhaps he thought Margaret had sent the boy. She would not take the chance of a misstep. "They are enough."

"Enough, indeed. Don't think of starting another school, Catherine." William fumbled with the latch and stumbled into their large chamber, where he dropped onto the bed. Catherine knelt and removed his boots while Reg poked the fire back into life, and after she unfastened his doublet, he curled under the sheets. "You know what your school brought us. We need no more of that."

Catherine sat on the edge of the bed and adjusted the covers. "What news of the women? Have they been found?"

"Speak to the constable. He has all the news. I cannot be bothered with it any longer." He closed his eyes, and Catherine laid her hand on his forehead.

"I will make a tisane for you." She rose and stepped into the hall, shutting the door behind her. Margaret was standing there, as though she'd been waiting.

Catherine said, "Have you just watched him get sicker all this time?"

"Oh, and where have you been? Down with the royalty, entertaining your gentleman? Are you going to lay another bastard at my brother's charge?"

Catherine's hand came out before she could stop herself, and she slapped Margaret hard across the mouth. The other woman went to her knees, screaming. "Stop your blubbering," Catherine said. "Your brother is trying to sleep. Will you ever be a bitch, Margaret, even as he lies burning up with fever? You sent that message, didn't you? Confess it."

The door opened behind them, and William glared out. "You two are at each other's throats already?"

Margaret put her head down on the rushes and whimpered. "She attacked me, Brother. You wife acts like the no-name that she is."

Catherine's bitten thumb throbbed from the impact, and she clenched her fists to stop herself from repeating the blow. "Get up, Margaret, and shut your mouth." She turned to William. "I am going to make you physic. You may see to your sister if you like, but I assure you she is as provoking as any woman I know." She stomped back toward the stairs, and she could hear Margaret whining. The house felt cold. Behind her, Margaret said, loudly, "She struck me, Brother. She means to bring us all down. I've told you."

At the front door, Benjamin Davies was busy cleaning his nails with a small knife. He flicked something from one finger into the courtyard and watched Catherine descend. She said, "Come inside if you're coming. You'll let mice in."

Benjamin walked inside and pushed the door shut. "I think the vermin are already here."

"You heard all that, I suppose?" Catherine put her complaining hand against her cool cheek. "Christ, I have as bad a temper as Elizabeth."

Benjamin checked the stairs for eavesdroppers. "I have known your husband for more than fifteen years and I have never seen him act like this, even as a boy."

"I have known his sister since our convent days, and she has always been a sniveling bitch," said Catherine. "But it doesn't excuse me."

Benjamin laughed softly. "She does seem to have had some practice." His face went sober. "I will go if you wish it, Catherine. This minute."

"No. But you will have to behave yourself."

Benjamin bowed. "You have my word. I was very bad. You are quite a temptress, though, Lady Catherine."

"Don't blame me for your behavior," said Catherine, "or I will be forced to rename you Adam."

"A hit," said Benjamin, touching his chest. Then he looked up the stairs. "It is no wonder he worries over you. I suspect the sister in this divorce business, but by the blood of Christ he shames himself. I will stay if you allow it, but I reserve the right as a man to correct your husband if he does not mend his ways."

39

Eleanor was in the kitchen, playing with the baby, when Catherine came in and slammed her hand on the table. "That cow. That lazy, conniving cow."

"Who, Madam?"

"No one," said Catherine through her teeth. "Everyone. Margaret. That puddle of muck. That pit of rotten bones. That sack of toad-guts."

Eleanor said, "Madam, I have never heard you curse anyone."

"I am not cursing her. I am painting her portrait." Catherine shook her head and dragged her hood off. "The woman will drive me to a . . . to a . . . I can't say what. She means to bring William to a divorcement of me, despite him. Despite me. Of that I am sure."

"And then what will you do?"

Benjamin Davies had followed her. He strolled in and threw a leg over the bench at the table. "You will let your houseguests dry up and blow away. Have you got a cup of ale, girl?"

Eleanor got a quick nod from Catherine and disappeared into the pantry. She brought out a jug of ale and set it before Benjamin. "I will take the baby out, Madam."

"Gather some green onions and mint from the far garden if there are any to be had," said Catherine. "And see if the radishes are ready. And the lettuces, if they are not too woody or drowned in weeds."

"Yes, Madam." Eleanor gathered up Veronica and fled through the back door.

"You've frightened her," said Catherine. "You heard my speech, Benjamin. I'm sorry." She checked to see that her coif was in place. "I was horrid."

Benjamin drank and wiped his beard with the back of his hand. "My daughter can learn more than pots and potions from you, Lady." He belched and grinned. "'Conniving cow,' eh, Catherine?" He chuckled. "Toad guts?"

Catherine's face went hot and she ducked into the pantry, furious with herself. Her stores had been swept away and the shelves lay empty but for a few wrinkled carrots and a half-dozen dusty bottles of wine. "God's foot, what have they been eating?" Catherine muttered, gathering the wilted vegetables for the pigs.

"What, indeed?" Benjamin stood nearby, cup in hand. "I was hoping for a bite of something, but I think I can wait."

Reg came in from the back stairs. "You may be waiting a long time, sir. The meals have become rather unpredictable lately." He bowed to Catherine. "How do you, Lady? And how does Ann Smith?"

So he knew. "She sends you her greetings," said Catherine.

"I am glad to hear it. Now I must return to my place." He bowed again and turned to go.

"Good man," said Benjamin. "Now what will we eat?"

"Must you follow me about? Go to, Benjamin, you cling like a plague. Can you not see that the household is in disarray? I have work to do." She tried to push past him, but he wouldn't give way.

"Why? So that he can let his sister convince him to divorce you? You would put his house in order before he puts you on the road?"

"I was speaking in heat," said Catherine. "To my maid. It was not for your ears."

Still he did not move. "I am at your service, Catherine. We can ride south as easily as we rode north."

"Stop it." Catherine put her hand on his chest. "Now. I am not jesting, Benjamin."

"Neither am I." He took her hand. For the blink of an eye, she relaxed, then she stiffened, pulling away.

"Stop. Now." She shoved him, hard.

"What's this?" It was Margaret, behind Benjamin.

"It's nothing," said Benjamin. "Catherine's just taking care of her guest. Aren't you?" He held out the cup.

"She's supposed to be taking care of her husband," Margaret said frostily. Her maid Constance appeared like a wide apparition, slipping from behind her mistress and waddling toward the pantry.

"Someone needs to," said Catherine. "You certainly haven't been doing it. Have you thrown away every herb on the property?" Her voice stuck in her throat and she shouted to get it out. "Do you two have nothing better to do than haunt me? Mother of God, you hover like a couple of hungry kites. Now step aside, both of you, and let me work."

Margaret moved in closer. "This household is under my command, and we can do fine without you." She looked down her nose at Benjamin. "What are you staring at?"

"Ladies, ladies. You shouldn't quarrel like this. It wrinkles you." Benjamin smiled at Margaret, and she simpered.

One hand went into her hair, twisting a curl. "I'm not one for distempers," she said. "I've ever been a woman who prefers quiet."

"I've known you to talk loudly enough," said Catherine. She rolled up her sleeves and wiped the table clean. "You're only quiet when someone requires sober judgment."

"You hear how she upbraids me! It is like living with a harpy for a sister." Margaret put her face into her hands and her shoulders heaved. "Connie! I need you." The maid emerged from the pantry. Constance had grown to look even more like Margaret, though the roll she carried about her middle made her grotesque in the tight bodice. She had something in her hand, which she shoved into a pocket.

"I haven't seen to the stabling of my horse," said Benjamin. "I will leave you women to yourselves. What time will we dine?"

"You men," Margaret teased. She gave Benjamin a dainty whack on the chest. "Do you think only of your appetites?"

"What else is there?" He opened the back door and Eleanor ducked in under his arm. Then he went out whistling.

"I found radishes and onions," said Eleanor. "Some strawberries still good. The greens are as stiff as boards and they've got bugs. There's still mint growing along the south edge of the house." Eleanor emptied her large apron, and Catherine began sorting. "Will this cure a fever, Madam?"

"It will make him stronger. The fever may have to run its own course. These maladies are like the sun, sometimes, Eleanor, breathing hot for a while, then cooling in their age."

Eleanor gathered the strawberries into a bowl and poured water over them. "And they return like the August heat, then?"

Catherine trimmed the onions and put the mint to soak. "Sometimes. A man's life is very like the turning of the year, and once a man is burned, the heat can lie dormant in him, deep underground in his body."

"What is this? A lesson?" asked Margaret.

"It is conversation," said Catherine. "Something you practice too little." She set the mint aside and helped Eleanor hull the berries. "We will slice these and flavor them with tarragon, if I can find some. Let me take this mint up."

"He will refuse you," said Margaret, "after the way you have treated me. And I have treated you as a sister. Con and I have taken the best care of him we can. He knows to trust us."

Catherine poured the infusion into a pitcher. "He knows better than that. And so do you. If he refuses me, he will die."

40

William was sleeping when Catherine tiptoed into the chamber. Reg retired with a nod and she poured a drink before setting the pitcher away from his thrashing arms. "Wake up. This will cool you." She shook his shoulder, and William opened his eyes. They were fiery pits in his swollen face.

"Is that you? Catherine?"

"You see me here. Sit up. Come, let me help." She held his head while he swallowed, then let him fall back onto the pillows. "Now go back to sleep."

"I am a wicked husband."

"No, you're a sick husband. Don't tax your mind. It will keep the fever burning in your head."

"I have done you wrong. A grave wrong."

"We all do wrong, William. You may correct anything you have started. Rest now and I will come back before supper. Do you think you can eat?"

He shook his head, leaving damp streaks on the linen, and she covered him. She drew the draperies, glancing out to see Benjamin in the yard below, running one hand down his stallion's back leg. He did not look up, and she finished darkening the room before she went out. Margaret was right outside the door, and she reeled backward when Catherine opened it.

"Have you turned servant, Margaret?" Catherine whispered. "Listening at keyholes should be your maid's trick."

"My office is to care for my brother." She crossed her arms.

"It will heal him mightily to know that you're sniffing at his door."

Margaret's tone smoothed into conciliation. "He is still feverish?"

Catherine nodded. "Let him sleep. I need to go out."

"What about supper?"

"I will set Eleanor and the kitchen girls on it. Marry, Margaret, where is all of the food?" She headed for the stairs, and the other woman followed.

"There is meat and there is wine. What have you given my brother? Will it improve him?"

"I pray so." Catherine stopped at the front door and checked her purse. Only a penny. There was ready money in William's chest in the gallery, and she grabbed a handful of coins.

"Where are you going?"

"I will return shortly."

"Is Benjamin going with you? Is he going to get you a place with the king? Have they made you take the oath of succession? You need to put a leash on your need to roam before it puts a halter around your neck."

Catherine snapped, "Do you dare to speak that way to me?"

She started out the door, and Margaret called, "William was my brother before he was your husband. This house was my home before you ever saw it." But Catherine kept walking.

She was halfway to the village when she heard the rider behind her. She stepped over to the verge, head down and napkin over her nose. The horse stopped beside her, though, and when the dust settled, she uncovered her face. Of course it was Benjamin. "Do you never take no for an answer?"

"Not when I see a lady in distress," he said, leaping down and bowing. "I wish I had lived in the times of the knights errant. The damsels wanted their gallants in the old stories. But now the weather has shifted and we men are all in the way." He cocked his head at her and motioned at the saddle. "Will you ride?"

Catherine stepped backward and almost lost her balance in the weeds. "I am going to the constable. I will not be seen in the village sitting behind you."

"How does it look for you to walk in coated with dirt? I will walk like a manservant beside you, if you please, and you shall ride in upon my Caesar like the lady of the manor that you are." He did his silly bow again, and Catherine snorted out a laugh before she could stop herself. Then he added, "But why are you going to the constable? Do you think he will intervene in this divorce business?"

"He may not have heard about it. I will not mention it to him." Catherine tightened her lips. She did not move toward the horse, which was clopping with one great hoof at the road bed and stirring up the dust again. "But I must know about my women. William is too ill to pursue the matter. Margaret is too . . . too--"

"Foolish? Shrewish?"

"Don't say that. She is William's sister."

"Oho, the family loyalty rears its head. Get on the horse, Catherine, like the angel you are, and I will walk down here on the earth in my mortal manhood. Come on, I won't bite your ankle." He held out his hand. The day was growing hot, and her legs were tired. The road lay before her like a long pale scar and she no longer wanted to walk. She sighed and let him help her onto the stallion. Caesar gave her a white-eyed look over his shoulder and tensed as though he would bolt, but Benjamin jerked his reins and he settled into a resentful walk. Catherine searched behind her for Overton House, whose highest windows barely showed above the trees. They were surely too far away for anyone to see them.

41

"Your husband's birds are neglected badly," Benjamin said as they walked along. "They look as though they have sat behind bars for weeks. He will never make a gentleman with frowzy falcons."

"You do not keep birds at all," observed Catherine.

"No, but if I did keep them, I would keep the feathers on them. If it weren't for that Joseph, they'd be bald as any plucked chicken. They need good feed and exercise."

"William is ill," said Catherine. She did not look down at the man but she could see him frown from the corner of her eye. They strolled into the sorry little village with its lines of sagging cottages. Plague had carried off half the population years back, and the empty dwellings were falling back into the shapes of fallen trees and brush piles. Mounds of moldy thatch lay against sprawling, unpruned rose bushes. Catherine had always thought Mount Grace small and poor, but compared to Havenston, it was a paradise of tidiness and business.

"So this is your ancestral town," said Benjamin. "Named for your family, am I right?"

"My mother's family," Catherine said. She unhooked her leg from the pommel and as she slid off the saddle, Benjamin caught her and lowered her to the ground. His hands only slid a little way up her bodice, and he let go before she had to shake him off. She regarded the high road, her hand at her brow for shade. "I have wanted to improve the place, but it gets sadder and sadder. It wants a guiding hand. It needs hewing and shaping, like a hedge of greenery."

"There is perhaps an opportunity before you," said Benjamin, when they came up to the constable's house. "May I have leave to relax at the public house while you carry out your investigations?"

"You don't need my leave. You may do what you like." Catherine pointed up the road. "It is just there. Sign of the Rose and Thistle."

"I know where it is," he said.

"How?"

"You talk as though I'm a stranger here. Catherine, I knew Robert Overton from university. I knew about your convent and all you women long before you knew about me."

Catherine blushed and she put her hands over her cheeks. She was a fool, supposing herself in command of Overton. Once it had been Havenston House, a smaller and darker dwelling. But that was before her birth. Its long history hung over the village like an angry old ghost. No one woman could lay it to rest. Certainly not a nun. Whether that nun was a Havens or an Overton.

Benjamin said, "You don't need to be ashamed. Other women are not ashamed. You were in the convent. Now you are out."

"I am not other women and you know nothing of my feelings."

"Of that I have no doubt." He tipped the front of his hat at her and led the horse down the dusty road, leaving Catherine alone to knock on the constable's door.

The man opened before Catherine had rapped twice, and she almost struck him on the face. Peter Grubb had a nose like a rooster's, and he leaned forward into the world, as though a strong wind were always at his back. Now his blue eyes widened. "Are you home then, Lady Overton?"

"It seems so," said Catherine. She drew back to avoid collision with the nose.

"Bad doings up at the House." Grubb made room for Catherine to enter, and she squeezed around his forward posture. The constable's house was one of the largest in the village, and the walls were hung with tapestries that might have at one time been beautiful but were spotty with mildew and moth holes. Catherine's convent had owned better ones, and Robert Overton's men had kicked them aside in disgust. The king's men. Grubb's windows were cloudy and the front room stank. Mistress Grubb met them by the stairs and silently held out a hand to Catherine. She only came to Catherine's shoulder, and the coif didn't completely disguise her scalp through her thin curls. She said, "What have you done to your hand, child?"

Catherine held up the bandaged thumb. "A royal dog."

"So you have met the king?" said Mistress Grubb.

"And his animals, as well. Is there any word about Teresa and Hannah?" Catherine followed Peter, who followed his wife, into a small front room. It was dark and hot from a murmuring fire, which sent tendrils of smoke slithering both up the hearth and into the air. Catherine wanted to tend the chimney, but Mistress Grubb went on through a far door and Peter motioned for Catherine to take a wooden armchair. Neither of them seemed to take note of the dimness.

"Gone," said the constable. "I figure clean gone. No remains but a few strips of cloth a mower found in a hedge along the Durham Road." Grubb opened a wooden box on a table in the corner and drew out a scrap of blue wool. "Is this something you know?"

Catherine went to the sooty window to see the piece better. "It's too small. This could have come from anything. But what about Joan and Ruth?"

Peter Grubb folded the fabric back into the box and scratched the white stubble on his chin. "Them two were from up north, weren't they?"

"Years ago. What does that have to do with anything?"

Mistress Grubb came in with cheese and bread and a pitcher of ale. "I figure there's people here don't want northerners in the village. Not northerners teaching girls to live above their means. They won't be able to get them husbands. They're fighters up there, making like they aren't part of this island." The constable worried his chin whiskers again. "Some say you shouldn't harbor Scotswomen in your house."

Catherine said, "They think these murders are my fault? I have not even been here."

"Fault or no, they were in your house." Peter Grubb dropped into a cushioned chair, which bloomed dust around him. He chopped off a piece of bread and stuffed it into his mouth. "They was murdered sure as England belongs to King Henry, and not by your hand, Lady Overton. I figure there's some wishing I would sweep the whole matter into the back garden and be done with it. But I don't care if they was havin' supper with Old Nick under the moon, I won't have women throttled to death on my watch."

"There's others that do care," said Mistress Grubb at the doorway. She settled her haunches onto a stool across from her husband. "We've got shed of the Pope. There's those who'd say we don't need to be spinster-ridden. Upsets the order of things. Pour me a draught, Peter. I'm not saying that I agree."

The constable did as he was told, for his wife and for Catherine. "Killing turns the whole world upside down," he muttered.

"You won't find any agreement about that in this village," said his wife. "Folks don't care that they're dead."

"I figure that's not altogether true, Mistress Grubb. The women whose daughters were learning to read and write never complained. Not one. They embroidered. They learned herbals."

Mistress Grubb's curls bobbed in her fury. "You hear any of them asking you to send them more teachers? You hear that?"

Catherine couldn't breathe. "Perhaps if I were to speak to them—"

Mistress Grubb heaved herself to her feet and huffed with the effort. "You should leave well enough alone, Lady Overton, pardon my saying so. I don't blame you, you know I don't. I was ever the friend of you and your sisters. But there's no improving this village." She shook her head and let her gaze drift to the ceiling.

"Constable Grubb," said Catherine. "Have you any idea who did this?"

"No," he said. "More's the shame on my head."

"Well, I will let you be for now," said Catherine. "But I mean to speak to the people of Havenston."

"I figure I'm not the man to stop you," said Peter Grubb. Mistress Grubb said nothing.

The couple let Catherine find her own way to their door. The sun had shrunk to a white dot high in the sky, and Catherine hurried to the Hill cottage, where Ruth had spent her last morning. She knocked, and though she thought she heard scuffling inside, no one answered. The window was open, but no one responded to Catherine's call except a small striped cat. It leapt onto the oak sill and arched its back. Catherine gave the animal a pat and moved on.

Joan had been just around the corner and through a tall hedge, teaching the MacIntosh girls their letters. Catherine was sweating but the cottage was only a few paces on, and a child skipped across the front garden and pushed through the gate as she approached. The girl had left the door open, and Catherine called a hallo as she stepped inside. The dwelling was low-beamed and blackened by fire, and the dirt floor had not been swept. A pot bubbled on the small hearth, and a pile of cloth lay on a plank table.

"Mistress MacIntosh? Are you here?" Catherine came a few more steps into the room and called again.

After a few seconds, a narrow door squeaked open. It was clearly a space for wood and cooking tools, but a whole woman stepped out. It was the girls' mother, shrunken and scared, staring out from a collapsed face. She appeared to be toothless, though her hair, sprouting from around the edges of her filthy coif, was as dark as it had ever been.

"What in the world are you doing in there?" asked Catherine. "Are you in some danger?"

"Not 'til you arrived. Madam. I supposed you meant to stand there until you seen me, so here I am. And now you must go. 'Twill go bad for me for you to be seen here, rich as you are."

"Has someone hurt you? I am trying to find out what happened to Joan." Catherine took a step forward, and the woman backed away with light steps, ready to run.

"You sent her here to ruin my daughters. We were trying to live right and you sent that woman here to put my children out of their heads. I know now. I know how the world should go. This is England and I will be an Englishwoman."

"Who has put this into your mind?"

"Who has put me right, is what you should say. Don't need to say, got a right to my thoughts like any other Christian. Now I have work to do, if it please you. Madam." She stepped around Catherine and opened the door wider. "Have my young ones to feed."

In the light, Catherine could see how thin the woman was. "Was Joan here the day she went missing?"

"Don't know. Can't remember. Oughtta sent her away sooner." The woman gazed into a spidery corner, by the little door.

"Will you not help me find out who killed her?"

"Naebody done it. Naebody atall. That girl gone and got herself killed and I just thank my God she didn't get me killed along with her." She trained a dim look on Catherine. "Now you must go back to your castle and your husband, Madam, and leave the likes of me to raise my bairns—my children—according to God's and the English king's will."

The woman clutched the handle of the open door until Catherine ducked her head and went out. The door slammed behind her, and the heavy latch dropped into place.

42

Catherine stood alone in the high road. Havenston was closed up tight and quiet as an old graveyard, the doors locked in their frames as far as she could see. The sign for the Rose and Thistle creaked a little in a soft wind. A bee swirled past her head, and she swatted it away. Did someone laugh behind a nearby shutter? She turned and looked back the way she had come, but the constable's comfortable beam and plaster house was closed as fast as the others.

"What bedevils you people?" she cried out to no one. "Women have died and you hide like frightened children." She wiped the sweat from her face and could feel the life galloping inside her wrists. Her thumb throbbed with anger and yellow spots bloomed and faded before her eyes. The coins she had meant to give to the MacIntosh girls jangled in her pocket.

The door of the inn opened and Benjamin Davies came out, shading his face. "I thought I heard your voice, Catherine." He screwed down his eyebrows into a mock scowl and bowed. "Let me fetch our steed."

"I will walk," Catherine said, but as soon as she spun on her heel she could hear him running toward her. She braced herself for the tug on her elbow and let him turn her.

"What do you mean, bellowing in the road like a fishwife? Let me get Caesar and get you home before the constable sets the watch upon you. You think William needs to be redeeming his wife from the gaol?"

"Oh and what are you now, my savior?" It came out too loud, and she saw a shutter flap open a little nearby. "Show your face, will you?" she yelled at the blank cottage front, but nothing else moved. "Why would he redeem me, to divorce me in private? I don't know that he would set foot outside the house to redeem me from the devil."

"I am your kindly friend, lady," said Benjamin. "And your voice will be heard all the way to your home."

"I cry you mercy, I took you for the gallant who has followed me halfway across England." She shook him off and pointed at a cottage. "And you are in there. I can hear you. I can see you!" She stomped away. "Toads and chickens. A village of sheep. You all act as though the Scottish king has invaded us already."

Benjamin called after her, "No. Do not walk alone. I will not allow it."

She kept walking. He ran off and before she reached the hedge that marked the Havenston boundary he had caught up on Caesar and ambled along beside her, his hand down. She did not look up. He rode on ahead and leapt to the ground, blocking her path, and she lowered her face.

"Will you continue the stubbornest woman in Christendom?" he asked. He was in her way and she stopped, staring at the toes of his boots.

"The women who put their trust in me have been slaughtered like animals," Catherine said, "and not a soul cares. They will rot wherever they lie, and the worms will love them more than their fellow Christians. So hold your tongue on the subject of religion. I see few signs of it here."

She glanced up. He was looking over her head, back at Havenston. "The men at the inn were laughing about it. Their wives are afraid."

"Of their husbands?"

Benjamin lifted his shoulder. "Of the world. They have been visited by the watch. Some have been called in to the constable. They say he has sent for soldiers and that they are on their way. The last time they were called, it was to make them swear Henry as the head of the church and Elizabeth as his heir. Then came the prince and now Elizabeth is a bastard. The Latin is out, then the Latin is in. They cannot tell the difference, Catherine. They want to keep their heads on."

"So did Ruth and Joan. And so did Hannah and Teresa. God help us all because we surely cannot help ourselves." She slapped at his boot, but he sat fast and she could not stop the tears from running down her face.

"Get on the horse, I beg you. It shames me to have you walk." She walked on, and he called, "I will help you find out what has become of your women if you will ride."

At that she stopped and faced him. "Do not perjure yourself, Benjamin. This is not a joke."

He showed her his palm. "God may damn me if I am not your right hand."

"You wager your soul?"

"You heard the words."

"All right. Put me on the horse." She returned and offered her foot. He hoisted her easily into the saddle.

By the time they trudged into the courtyard of Overton House, Catherine's breasts ached and her head was heavy. She checked the high windows as they rounded the corner into the back yard. The curtain at her chamber fell, and she slid down before Benjamin could touch her.

"I must see how William does."

Benjamin looked up, but the house showed nothing now. "Are you one of those women?"

"What women?"

"Those who are afraid of their husbands."

"Go to. William is gentle as a lamb, but he is sick and the fever puts him out of his senses."

"So he has disavowed this divorce business?"

"I haven't spoken of it. And I won't unless he does. The constable said nothing of it either. It's a fantasy."

"As you wish. And so the messenger was a spirit. However it stands, William seems much changed." Benjamin pulled the reins over Caesar's head and led him to Joseph, who waited at the stable door.

Catherine went in through the kitchen. Eleanor sat at the board table, with Veronica in her arms. "Madam, your sister has been in a fit," the maid said.

"Margaret? She is always in a fit over something or other." Catherine took the baby and loosened her bodice. "The people in the village are all bewitched by terror. They will not a one of them speak to me of Hannah and Ruth."

Eleanor leaned forward and whispered, "No, I mean a screaming demon is in her. Margaret. She has been up and down stairs crying you down. That nasty maid of hers, too. I wonder that the walls have stayed up."

"Over what?"

"She says you have poisoned her brother so that you could ride away with his friend. She has sent down to the constable."

"The woman makes herself look a lunatic. Has my husband waked?"

"I don't know. I stayed down here with the baby."

"Did Margaret ask you anything of me?"

Eleanor nodded. "She asked me if you stayed in your bedchamber at Hatfield. If Master Benjamin came to visit. If he ever stayed the night."

Catherine stretched her neck right and left. "That horse has wrenched my backbones all out of place. I suppose she thinks Benjamin has been stored under my bed like a chamber pot?"

"I told her you were as proper as could be. That Madam Champernowne would have it no other way. There's rumors enough around Elizabeth is what I told her."

"What do you know of rumors?" Catherine put Veronica to the other breast.

"I will bet she knows plenty," said Margaret at the door, "and while you have been off riding with your suitor, your husband has been wrestling with Death himself." The red-haired Constance crossed her arms behind Margaret.

"I will take him another draught," said Catherine, rising and passing the baby to Eleanor.

"You will taste that draught yourself before you pour it down my brother's throat," said Margaret. "You have poisoned him into an unnatural sleep enough for one day."

"Margaret, charm your tongue and get you upstairs," said Catherine. "I've no more poisoned William than you have read three words this twelvemonth. You haven't the sense to know sleep from an epilepsy, and you ought to keep your ignorance to yourself. A lack of reason is a worse infection than the pox."

"You may cover your felonies with glib speech, but I will have the constable to hear of this."

"I have been at the constable's house this day, Margaret, and you have piled yet another stone upon the monument of your reputation for silliness. Do you see any constable? He seems not to have rushed in obedience to your summons."

Catherine went to work mashing fresh lettuce leaves. The drink upstairs would be stale if William hadn't finished it. When she was done, Catherine pushed past Margaret, sloshing a little on her.

William was sitting in an armchair by the hearth, though the room was stuffy and hot. Reg squatted on a stool in the corner, whacking a rag over the surface of a boot. Catherine checked the pitcher by the bedside. The drink sat, a film upon its surface, where she had left it. "This smells spoilt," she said. "I have brought you a new one."

William slouched, not looking at her. She thought he might be sleeping, and she touched his shoulder.

"Where have you been?" he asked

"In the village. I went to speak to the constable and to the women whose children Joan and Ruth taught."

"Who was with you?"

"No one, until Benjamin caught up to me and loaned me the use of Caesar. Insisted upon it. I did not ask him. I did not invite him."

"And so my wife was riding through the village on the arm of Benjamin Davies?"

"You're in a fever, William. No such thing. I rode and he walked. We parted company at Peter Grubb's house. He accompanied me back home. Nothing passed between us beyond what is warranted by honest Christian friendship."

"And did you bring back the bodies to lie in our kitchen and stink?"

"William, drink this. Your heat is conjuring Beelzebub in your mind. You need to cool down and rest."

"I saw you ride in with him."

"If you saw indeed, then you saw me ride in, with him walking at my side. If you saw what Margaret has reported that you might have seen, then you are letting her eyes see for you. Benjamin walked by the horse's side. That is all." She held out a drink and he regarded it warily. "Your sister has been making you hotter with the flames of her accusations, William, and it's no wonder you haven't improved in her care. Her reason is thin, and it blows this way and that with every puff of an idea. Drink. Here, I will drink first." Catherine swallowed a large gulp while he watched. "See? Now drink."

He took the goblet and looked into it. Then he drank the cup empty.

"Now come to bed." She pulled him out of the chair, and when Reg had slipped out the side door and William was settled, she lay next to him. "Do you recall those days of your smallpox?"

The tight cords of his arm relaxed. He squeezed her hand and smiled. "You cured me."

"So you have always said. But I wonder if such a malady can live deep in the body and waken now and then to cause you harm."

"Like a viper?"

"Something like." She rolled to her side and stroked his damp hair. "But I see no signs on your skin. It is probably just a fever and will pass if we keep you down. Your birds must miss their master."

"Very like. But it is you I fear will fly away from me. Don't leave me again, Catherine. I need you here." His voice grew thick. "I cannot live alone in my mind when you are away." She started to ask him what he meant, but William was gone back into a fitful sleep.

43

"Madam, your ladies were all good women, were they not?" Eleanor was bouncing Veronica on her knee while Catherine leafed through her receipt book, searching for remedies for fever that she had forgotten.

"Yes, of course." She closed the book. A pain hammered the space between her eyebrows, and she rubbed at the spot with her forefinger. "Who says they weren't?"

"No one." The baby screwed up her face, ready to cry, and Eleanor passed her to Catherine.

"Come into the garden. I need to think." Catherine pulled on a hood and threw a wrap around her shoulders. The sun was high but hoarding its heat today and the pale young leaves on the trees shivered in the wind. The three younger kitchen maids were weeding the salad greens. The radishes and onions were spearing the soil, but the dock had been allowed to spread under the ground and it threatened to choke them off. Catherine got on her knees. "It might do," she said.

"What, Madam?" Eleanor squatted by the first row of strawberry plants and pulled a sprout of wild daisy. She tucked the straw back under the runners and flung the weed aside.

"Or willow bark, if I could lay my hands on it. Could Joseph ride down to Mount Grace and fetch me some?" She spied the limp plant in the grass and lifted it. "Daisy." She smelt of the leaves. "They might give some relief, but they're not mature. In full flower would be better." She pocketed the weed and called to the other maids to bring the dock leaves when their baskets were full. "Come walk here with me while the air is fresh." They strolled along the grass verge for a minute, and when they were far from the house, Catherine said, "Has someone been talking of them?"

Eleanor was fiddling with the baby's cap. "Who, Madam?"

"The women who lived here."

Eleanor shook her head. "No more than usual. There is gossip, you know. The younger girls hear the talk in the village."

"Then why did you ask if they were good?"

The maids caught up to them with the dock and Catherine inspected it. "This is good. Take it to the kitchen and wash it well. Put the bigger leaves to soak in salted water." They went off together, swinging their baskets.

Eleanor watched them go. "It's just that you cared for them and taught them so well. And now all you have is me. And those girls." She waved at the retreating forms. "They don't have much interest in learning to read or write. Margaret has told them they must not."

Catherine eyed Eleanor. "Flattery usually oils the way for a prickly request. What is it?"

"Nothing." Eleanor shifted a clod of dirt with her toe.

"A confession? Have you done something?"

"It's not a thing I have done. Not alone, anyway. And I will not have the reputation for holiness that your scholars had and you will cast me off." The baby whimpered, and Eleanor gave her to her mother.

Catherine laughed. "Eleanor, I saw you through the window upstairs with your shift up around your ears. God's blood, I am not going to turn you out, I thought I had made that clear. But others feel differently about such things, and I advise you to be cautious. At least go indoors if you have to lift your skirts."

"I have," Eleanor said miserably. "And much good it has done me." She was looking at Veronica, who was smiling now in Catherine's arms.

They walked toward the house, Catherine stopping now and then to turn a leaf or pull a weed. At the door, she put her hand out to stop Eleanor opening up for her. "Are you with child, then?"

Eleanor's face bloomed red, and she peered through the window beside the door. The maids were chattering amongst themselves as they sorted the dock on the table. "They look so happy. It's because they are young and pretty and know nothing."

"This way." Catherine led the younger woman around to the front courtyard, and they took a turn on the graveled walk. "Now tell me, but keep your voice low."

Eleanor rubbed her palms down her skirt, then scrubbed them together and rubbed the skirt again. "I fear me so, Madam. What have I done?"

"As you say, you've not done it alone. Have you spoken to Joseph of this?"

"I am afraid."

Catherine halted. "I cry you mercy, of what? Does the young man care for you or doesn't he? He works for this house, and he will not be getting my maid with child without answering for it."

Now Eleanor laughed but the sound was syncopated with crying. She began to hiccup, and Catherine said, "Hold your breath," while she counted slowly to ten.

Eleanor exhaled with a low note. "Will you speak to him for me?"

Catherine set off on her circular route again. "Marry, that I will not. You must be a woman and say your mind. You're no girl, and he has used you like a wife. How will your life go if you let a man get up inside you, then shake to speak of it to his face? No, I won't have you some wilting rose afraid to show her face to the cold wind of trouble." Catherine laid Veronica in the grass and leaned on the broad edge of a stone pedestal. The vase that had sat upon it was empty. She would need to plant something in it. "But before you speak to him, you must tell me how far along you are." She pressed her hands on Eleanor's narrow waist. "You don't show any swelling at all."

"I have missed my flowers once. And I sick up at the sight of fat meat."

"So hardly at all. Maybe not at all." Catherine released Eleanor. Counted backward, staring up at the sky. "God's foot, Eleanor, you must have gone to it when he came to fetch us home. Did you bring him up those back stairs?"

The maid tightened the bow of her apron. "We had been apart some time, Madam."

A cloven-tailed kite sailed overhead and dived knife-straight into the far field. "Do you want this child? If child there is?"

"Want? What difference what I want if God has delivered it to me?"

Another kite came into view, circling the area where the first had come down. After two circuits, the second landed, too. Catherine breathed deeply, but she smelt nothing. She shivered and plucked Veronica from the grass. "Tush, God didn't deliver it. You went in search of it. We can try to unseat it before it's settled, if you want. If you have only gone past the moon once, there is yet no soul."

Eleanor pursed her mouth in thought. "How long before the soul enters?"

Catherine headed back to the house when the third bird came into view. "They say you will feel the child leap when its soul comes to it from heaven."

Eleanor's mouth dropped open and she put her hand on her stomach. "How does it get in?"

Catherine put her finger under Eleanor's chin and pushed. "Through there, if you're not careful. Now, do you mean to bear this child?"

"Let me think."

"Think before you speak to Joseph. Words are children, too, though they are conceived in your mind, and you cannot take them back into you once you have loosed them into the world."

"Might we marry?"

"Do you love the man?"

"My body does."

"What of your mind?"

"I cannot use my wits at all when I am with him. And my soul seems to fly out of me and cling to him."

"That is lust, Eleanor, not love. It's a tasty feeling, but it won't nourish a marriage. What do you talk of when you're not abed together?"

Eleanor cocked her head. "Horses. He is mad for horses. I talk to him of my dreams. My fears."

"And what does he say to them? Will he put them on a horse and ride them away?"

"No, Madam. He says I must learn to read and write so that I may keep his accounts when he has an inn. He will make a fine trade of it and buy me a white cob to ride."

"He will make a gentlewoman of you, then?"

"He says so."

"Joseph sounds like a good young man. He thinks of your talents. But what are these fears you speak of?"

"I don't know. Perhaps that I am dull for learning and that he will see it. Madam, I want to be like Ruth and Joan were. How firm they walked when they would go off down to the village. I would watch them as far as I could see. I used to imagine I was one of their charges, improving my reading and writing."

They were at the back door, and Catherine said, "You are improving in those very skills. Now go tell Joseph that I need him to ride to Mount Grace for that willow bark. And study whether you will have him for a husband or no. Remember, you will vow to be his for life. That's a long time."

"Longer for some of us than others, Madam," said Eleanor.

"True, Eleanor. True," said Catherine. She kept her eye on her maid until the younger woman disappeared into the stable, then she walked back to the front of the house. Another kite had joined the first three, and they all circled over the far field. She must check on William's falcons. She inhaled deeply again. Those birds didn't come in such numbers for nothing. But the wind brought her only the scent of the gorse and the broken stems in the garden. She plodded back to the kitchen and opened the door onto the chatter of the younger girls.

44

The infusion of dock made William's eyes water when he brought it to his lips. "Can you do nothing to disguise the flavor?" He sat up in bed, held his nose, and drank it down, then coughed until Catherine thought he would retch. "Good God Almighty, if that doesn't kill everything inside me, I don't know what will. It tastes as though it came out of the arse hole of a dragon."

"It does not attack fever," said Catherine. She took the cup from him and set it out in the hall. "It is a good tonic, though, and the leaves are bright. Stuffed with physic." She sat back down and put her wrist against his forehead. "How do you feel?"

"Stuffed with physic," he said, falling back onto the pillows. "Where is our daughter?"

"Down in the kitchen with the maids. She grows like a dock herself."

"She will be tall like you," said William. He closed his eyes. "And red-headed as my brother was. I hope she has a better temper than he had."

William almost never spoke of his dead older brother. "Robert was ever fiery in his opinions," said Catherine simply.

"Hot as hell, you might say. I still wonder sometimes that he actually accused me of theft. And here I lie in his bed." William opened his eyes. "If Robert had not had a fever much like this, he would have been Master of Overton House and I would have been hanged for a felon and a traitor against the king."

"And I along with you, perhaps." Catherine pushed back her husband's hair and stretched out next to him. "Let's not talk of the past. The convent is closed and your brother lies in his tomb. I am no longer a nun and you are no longer a younger brother. God has mysterious ways."

"As did your mother." He slid his arm under her and held her against him.

She could feel the heat of his breast and hear his heart banging like a panicked animal in the cage of his ribs. "Who would have thought a prioress so quick to poison someone?"

Catherine pushed her face into his neck and murmured, "Who indeed." She didn't like to remember what all her mother had done as prioress.

"And what ever became of her books of venoms?"

"I couldn't say." It wasn't precisely a lie, and Catherine felt the shame come over her like a dark veil, but William was too ill to notice.

"Well. I must train myself not to judge if I am to die of a fever and meet God."

"Don't talk that way. You must ask God for the gift of forgiveness. It will ease your mind and your body may follow the way to health."

"I will try."

They lay quietly for a while, Catherine listening to the bird cries outside. The light through the window was buttery. "Tell me," she asked quietly, "who do you judge?"

William laughed, a short, bitter sound. "Have you time for a list? My brother. My sisters, both the dead one and the live one. Myself." He lay silent a few seconds. "No more. Let me sleep."

"I'll return before dark." Catherine slid from the bed and pulled the blankets to his chin before she left the room. She went straight to the front door for fresh air. Three more kites were circling over the far field, and two of them landed before Catherine fetched her wrap and a hood and a stick and started walking. A few sparrows harried the larger birds, hoping for a scrap, and a couple of ravens knocked them aside and sparred with the kites. None of William's falcons were in the fray, and Catherine reminded herself to make sure they were safe at home and fed before she retired for the night.

She smelt it before she saw it. All of the birds lifted into the sky as Catherine walked over the grassy swathe, the sparrows skittering off on a plane of wind, but the prey was in the gorse that surrounded the field, and the kites landed heavily in the branches of the nearby oaks, hunkering down and waiting. One stayed on the ground, and Catherine beat at it until it backed away, hissing and waving its huge wings. The sun glowered down on the prickly bushes, and Catherine was sweating as she pushed through, searching. The thorns punished her skirt and sleeves, and she thought she heard a voice far off, calling her name, but she pressed on until her hands were bleeding. Some of the bushes lay already bent and shorn. Someone had passed this way before her. But it hadn't been easy. Catherine stopped to breathe. The call came again on the breeze. From the house. She didn't turn but shoved on until the stench forced her to cover her mouth and nose with her apron.

The kites darkened the sky, surrounding her now, but Catherine didn't need them. She stepped into a small clearing, disguised by broken branches. The flowers and leaves had wilted, however, and they made a sad shrine over the shallow grave. The heavy woven blanket that had covered it had blown into a mouldy heap and stank of rot and dung.

Catherine stepped backward when she saw the bodies and fell into the outraged and dismembered gorse. The sticks clung to her arms and hips and dug in their thorns, and she had to fight her way to her feet again. Her hands tore, but she didn't see them. She saw only the dead women, half-covered with dirt and leaves. The kites had scratched much of the sorry covering away. The shredded clothing had not flown far, and Catherine freed a scrap of embroidered wool from a thorn. Bits of linen fluttered among the yellow flowers. She held up the cloth to the sun. It was a piece of Ruth's skirt.

Catherine sat on the damp ground and wailed. Even from here, she could see arches of pale rib shining through the torn breasts, one delicate, decayed hand lying upon the yielding earth. She started to lift away a stem, but the wood seemed heavy as stone, and she could not make her fingers remove it. A long twist of dark hair, loosed from its scalp, lay in a muddy trench, and Catherine pulled it out, her stomach lifting and heaving, and wound it into her handkerchief. She stumbled out by the rough path. It seemed hours since she had entered the gorse patch, and she collapsed at the edge of the grass field and vomited.

"Catherine?"

A warm hand touched the back of her neck, and Catherine opened her eyes. A pair of brown boots. The grass, sparkling and innocent under her thighs. "I'm all right," she whispered.

"You're not." Benjamin pulled her to her feet. She was still weak, and she wobbled. "Let us help you back."

"Us?" Catherine shaded her eyes and Reginald Goodall came into view. Joseph was wringing his hands beside the other men. "Reg." She stumbled to him and caught his arm. "Where is Veronica?"

"Eleanor has her, Madam. She was sleeping like a lamb." William's servant looked into Catherine's face. "Lady, you are white as any ghost."

Joseph shifted from one foot to the other. He was chewing on his lower lip.

"Ghost. Yes. You all are witnesses." The bile threatened Catherine's throat again, and she swallowed the urge. "Benjamin, I will need you to ride and fetch the constable. This evening. Two women lie in that gorse patch, shrouded in dirt. It is a murder, and he must remove them before the kites devour them completely."

Reg covered his face with his hand, and Benjamin tracked Catherine's footsteps until he saw. "Do you think I would lie?" Catherine called. Her skin stung all over. She wanted to slap someone.

Benjamin came back, quieter than she had ever heard him. His face was ashy and he wiped his beard. "I needed to know what to tell the constable."

"I will ride with you, sir," said Joseph.

"No," said Catherine. "You must go to Mount Grace and fetch me the bark of the white willows, the ones that grow along the lane south of our old convent."

Benjamin was looking back at the spot where the dead women lay. "I will move more quickly alone anyway. You go get the lady's physic, son. Go on, run ahead."

"Tell my father he must return with you," Catherine added. "There must be a burial."

"Lady Catherine, this grieves me to the soul," said Reg. He was gazing back at the dark house.

Joseph bowed quickly and yanked his cap onto his head. "I will be back before you know I am gone." He sprinted over the field, but as he turned away, the young man was gnawing his lip again and meeting the eyes of no one.

45

"Where have you been?" Margaret was stationed at the front door. "The ways are pure dirt. I cannot be expected to go in search of you."

"No one expects you to search for me," said Catherine.

"I have seen to supper," said Margaret. "Connie and I. She is still in the kitchen. The other girls were busy with the baby. Reginald, your master will want you."

Catherine tramped around to the back door and threw off her hood inside the door. The girl Connie was stirring something at the hearth, and Eleanor sat at the table with the baby, and she laid Veronica in her mother's arms. Catherine's hands trembled and her eyes itched, but she could not bring tears. The air seemed to glitter with menace. Her skin felt too thin to protect her muscles. She was cold. "They are in the gorse. Our women. The kites have been at them."

Eleanor gasped. Connie stopped stirring.

"How could any man do such a thing?" said Catherine. "We are creatures of God and we are worse than animals to our own kind."

Eleanor stared into her cup. "Were they throttled like the others?"

"How could anyone know? There is not enough left to tell."

"To tell what?" Margaret had come down. She seemed to be tying her hands into knots.

"What killed the women of this house. They lie in the east gorse, torn to ribbons." Catherine swallowed her ale. "Let's get this stew upstairs."

"Connie and I have et already," said Margaret, "but she'll serve you right here. No sense in dirtying the hall."

Connie brought wooden bowls of brown gruel and set them beforeCatherine and Eleanor. "There's bread, too, Madam. I'll fetch it."

Eleanor took the loaf and broke it, and Catherine dipped a chunk of it into the bowl. "What is this?"

"Rabbit that one of the tenants brought."

Catherine bit in. Her jaw spasmed at the taste, but she worked it down. "What have you flavored it with?" She spoke through clenched teeth to check the urge to vomit.

"The green things in the garden."

Eleanor nibbled at the bread. "I've got no appetite." She drank off her cup of ale. "I will take the baby upstairs."

"May Benjamin ride swiftly," said Catherine. "Change her clout before you lay her down, Eleanor."

Margaret made a show of straightening her fancy little headpiece as Eleanor passed by. She rearranged her expression and Connie took the remainder of the stew out, headed toward the stables. "Benjamin again?" asked Margaret. "Why is it always Benjamin? Have you not had enough men for one woman, Catherine? How many have you had?"

"Is this what you fed me for? To fatten me up to be slaughtered by your insults?"

"Stop it." William limped into the kitchen, with Reg behind him. "For once, Sister, shut up, will you?" He put his arm around Catherine. "I feel better. I wondered if you could give me another of that horrid drink."

"I see how my efforts are rewarded," said Margaret. She went out, taking the loaf with her.

Catherine said, "I must prepare the drink fresh. Sit you here and talk to me of your dreams."

He sat, eyeing the kitchen as though he had never seen such a room, and Catherine called down to the laundry for a maid. "Bring me some fresh dock from the garden," she ordered the yawning girl who answered. "And herb-of-the-Cross. Be sure it is in flower."

"Yes, Madam."

"Your sister did prepare supper for us," said Catherine. She forced herself to eat another sour mouthful then nudged the bowl to the center of the table.

"I want no food," said William. "I've tasted her suppers enough."

They sat in silence until the girl returned with the plants, and Catherine began

211

tearing the tough center veins out and laying the tender parts flat in a pot of water. She stoked the flames and set the pot high over them so that the water would not boil too ferociously. "Do your feet hurt you?"

"My soles are on fire." William propped one of his slippers on the bench, and Catherine pulled it off to examine the thick skin. It was still scarred from the bleeding her father had given him during his smallpox, and she pressed her thumb against the white line. The flesh was ridged and hard, as though a shard of stone were lodged there.

Catherine shook her head. "This will never disappear. Bleeding does nothing but weaken the sick further. I wonder that anyone does it. And with a knife, God help us."

"When they hurt, I know there is a storm coming, so I am useful as a weathervane now," said William. He grinned at Catherine and looked like himself again.

"You," she said. She ruffled his hair and turned back to her hearth. She could not smile, and she could not tell him what she had found.

"You work like a servant," said William.

"Like a woman with tasks," said Catherine. "I do not like sitting still. I will flay my fingertips to shreds if I'm forced to be idle too long."

"That you will. It looks as if you already have. What happened?"

"The king's dogs gave me a nip," said Catherine. "But it is almost healed." She held out the hand to show the pink scar.

"God has given you too much heat in the blood for a woman. How long does it take to make the drink?"

"Some small while. I will add honey to this one to make it go down more easily." She put her wrist on his forehead. It was almost icy. "Do you feel a chill?"

"Yes, now. It comes on me suddenly. It feels better than burning, though."

Catherine sat across from him and looked at his eyes. The whites were yellow, and his cheeks were sallow. He said, "You have been out walking."

"Yes. Over the field into the gorse. There were kites."

He nodded. "I watched you from Reg's room."

Catherine got up and checked the dock. The water had begun to simmer, and she stirred the leaves. Their scent was like hot iron on grass, and her eyes teared. She could not hold it back.

"Catherine?"

"Sir—," said Reg.

"No, I will tell it." Catherine wiped the spoon and laid it on the hearth. "I found Ruth and Hannah."

A sound came from William's mouth, but he choked it down. "How long?"

"Since they were laid there?" She put her palms over her eyes. "A month, maybe more. What day did they go missing first?"

"It was the beginning of May. The mornings were still cold."

"And afternoons warm. It is hard to know for certain. They had been covered."

"You took the cover off yourself? With your own hands? Catherine, look at me."

She blinked and let her eyes be seen. "No, a storm likely blew it. The smell brought the birds. The birds brought me." She took the handkerchief out of her pocket and opened it. "This is all I touched."

William stared at the skein of damp hair and again the sound erupted from his throat. "I am ill again," he whispered. "I will go back to bed." He rose and, leaning on Reg's arm, staggered from the kitchen.

46

It was full dark by the time Peter Grubb the constable came up from the field. He had with him two watchmen, who carried the long, sorry bundle between them. The constable signaled for the other men to wait in the yard, and he knocked rapidly at the still room door, though he had looked through the window and had seen Catherine standing in the candle light. When she opened up, the death smell from outside blew over the vervain that was scattered over the table, killing its sweetness.

"Where is Master William?" Grubb hovered on the threshold, cap in hand.

"In bed," said Catherine. "And where is the man who fetched you here?"

"Don't know. Not my concern. My concern's what to do with a couple of women rotted into a heap. Got to have them buried somehow. Somewhere. Need to have the Master direct me."

"Come inside. I'll see if I can get him up. Follow me."

"What's all this?" He indicated the table.

"Herb-of-the-Cross. William needs it to take the yellow from his eyes. I am preparing a tisane for him."

"Is this some Popish remedy?" The constable lifted a stem. Tossed it back with the others as though it burned him.

"I have not seen the plant attend either mass or chapel," said Catherine evenly. "They say it is the herb that was placed in Our Lord's side when he was speared by the Romans."

"Hmph. And he died anyway, seems like." The constable was peering into pots and shelves, lifting the utensils and putting them to his nose.

Catherine snatched a spoon from him and returned it to its hook. "And he rose again on the third day."

"Smells like a witch's brew in here." Grubb was now spying into shadowed corners, as though he would find a murderer crouching in one of them, bloody knife in hand.

"It smells like a still room," said Catherine. Weariness gave her temper free rein. "Have you never been in one before now?"

"I figure I should keep to my study like any other man."

"Then you had best prepare yourself for a shock above stairs. William is in what is known as a bedchamber." She lit a taper at the hearth and led him up to the second floor. "Wait here. He will not want to be caught unprepared."

The constable's eyelid flickered. "Don't take too long. I'll need to have your testimonies separate."

"For Christ's sake," sputtered Catherine. "I'm the one who found the women. Would I have sent for you if I were trying to hide them from you? Wait outside the door if you are so worried."

"Don't know for sure who found them. Not my concern. I figure my concern's to get to the truth here. Not wanting to hear the same story come at me from every direction."

It made sense enough and she beckoned for him to follow her. "I will only be a moment." Catherine slipped into the bedchamber and found William propped up, awake, against the pillows. An empty cup sat beside him on a table, still giving off the scent of dock, and Catherine moved it away as she sat on the edge of the mattress. "Peter Grubb is here. He wants to speak with you."

"I heard him. The man's got a voice like thunder. And he is almost as articulate in his speech. Well, send him in."

The door opened and the constable was with them. "Heard the invitation. Need to get this business done. Madam, if you will leave us."

William nodded slightly. Reg stood by without speaking.

"As you wish," she said.

Catherine wandered down the hall to the far window, where she could see the watchmen in the gloomy moonlight. They'd set the bundle on the flagstones and were in conversation with Geoffrey White, William's master of horse, who stood with his arms folded tight against his chest. One of the watchmen was pointing in the direction of the field and nodding. Then he pointed at the house. Geoffrey White unfolded his arms and wiped his face with his palm. The watchman took off his cap and scratched his head. Said something to his companion. Geoffrey raised his shoulders. The other watchman shook his head and made a chopping motion with one hand, to which the first responded by mimicking a strangling. Geoffrey wrapped his arms around himself again. All three then cast their eyes on the damp bundle and seemed to stop talking altogether. Geoffrey turned on his heel and walked back toward the stable. The other two watched him go, and the first one nodded sagely at some scrap of wisdom from the other.

Catherine was sweating, and her belly cramped. She turned away from the view below, and the hallway wobbled before her. Overtired. She needed sleep.

The chamber door opened and the constable emerged. "Thanks for that, sir. I will tell the lady."

"Tell the lady what?" called Catherine.

"Oh, there you are. I thought women kept their ears to keyholes when men were conversing."

She'd had enough of the man. "And where did you hear that? At a keyhole?"

"Your man says we're to have them buried in the family graveyard. We'll have to put 'em in together though. He says to call on your father to say the prayers."

"It's already been done." Catherine led the way down stairs, the constable on her heels. She called Geoffrey from the back door of the kitchen. "Have you seen to William's birds?" she asked.

"I'm gone to it just now, Madam." He did not look at her. "Glad to have an order 'round here at last that begs to be followed." He bowed slightly and backed away, then trotted toward the stables.

47

Catherine sat at the still room table and, pulling the candle stick closer, began sorting the vervain. A pain wormed through her, and she pressed her forehead with the back of her hand.

Peter Grubb coughed and shifted his feet. Finally he sat across from her and said, "I figure I will take your testimony."

"Ask your questions. I have to prepare this before the leaves spoil, so you will have to ask while I work."

"Ladies usually cry. Your women lie murdered out in the yard. Murdered in a most horrible fashion. And your eyes are yet dry. I have a wife who laughs when she delights, weeps when she sorrows. I don't see her managing her household affairs when the dead are rotting in her garden."

"Your wife is an uncomplicated soul. I am happy for her. If she has women to do her tasks for her, I am even happier."

"And your situation is complicated then? You want to tell me what gets in the way of your tears? You clogged with guilt, woman? You know something you shouldn't? Seen something you can't get clear of?" He took the leaf from her hand and ripped it down the middle with his teeth. He spit the remains onto the floor.

Catherine chose another and examined it, front and back, before laying it into the basin at her elbow. "You measure all women by your wife. That is perhaps an error. Not all who weep are grieving. Not all who keep their own counsels have secrets. Those women were dear to me. They were not my women. They were their own and God's. Someone has taken their lives and the lives of two before them. My grief lodges here." Catherine touched her own breast. "If I weep, I will do it alone, I thank you. I work because there is work to be done. My task is to rid my husband of a fever, and if you will stop ruining my herbs I might succeed at it. Your task is to find someone who will strangle innocent women with his bare hands."

"His? You know it to be a man?"

"I know it to be death by strangling. There were marks on the necks of Joan and Ruth. Teresa and Hannah were found buried in a similar way. It points to the same villain. Two of them at once? It could not have been a woman. At least not a woman alone."

Margaret came down the stairs, calling for Catherine. When she entered the room and saw Peter Grubb, she froze. "What, another suitor for my brother's wife? Are you having a private conversation under my brother's roof? Or perhaps you are asking her about her movements with one Benjamin Davies down in the village?"

"I am taking the mistress's testimony," said the constable. He took the measure of Margaret with his eyes and stood. "I figure I will need yours as well, Lady."

"Mine?" Margaret's fingertips fluttered to her throat. "I told Catherine not to keep those women here. I told her they were unreformed. I thank God they have been taken without someone burning down the House around our ears. I told Catherine they would bring us all before a court for treason." Her voice had gone high and breathy, as though a cloud were in her throat.

"You told her all that, did you?" The constable moved a step closer to Margaret. "Sounds to me as though you had some knowledge of these women's heresies yourself."

Margaret backed up, keeping the distance between them. "I certainly did. They wore their beads inside their dresses. They kept relics and icons." She pointed over the constable's shoulder at Catherine. "She knows. She tutored them. Ask her."

"He has already asked me his questions. Now let me ask you, Margaret. How came you by such knowledge?" Catherine rose. "You make up your stories as your tongue rides along. You know of nothing those women did or what they wore. You wouldn't know a relic from an old bone if John the Baptist himself sprang full-formed from it and twisted your nose."

Margaret smirked. "Is that how you concealed them? In the charnel house? Well, that is certainly where they will dwell now, to all eternity, so you should be content."

"You weasel-hearted acorn-brain." Catherine felt the rage in her arm and she raised it, but at the constable's glance, she picked up another leaf. "You haven't got the sense God gave a new-hatched pullet, Margaret, and you never have had."

The constable looked from one woman to the other. "You sisters need to work out your differences." He shook his head and muttered, "Women's tempers. I figure that to be the death of men. I will have these bodies laid in a tomb until your priest arrives and we will bury them as he sees fit. But we will speak of this further, you two and I." He went out to the watchmen, shaking his head.

"Now you may see what your great learning has brought upon us," said Margaret. "Four dead and the law at our very doors. It is no great wonder my brother lies ill. He has not been well since he laid eyes upon you. You should let me make him his drink."

"He has had a sad spell of sickness. It is common enough among mortal men. But I see nothing from your hand that heals him."

"I am a simple woman caring for a family. How can I fight against your power?"

"What power? Margaret, your brain is filled with girls' fancies."

"You know what power. Others know it too. They say you have the devil in your fingers and his imps dance in your eyes. If the constable has not heard it yet, I expect that he will before this is over."

48

Father John and Joseph arrived together the next morning, grey-faced with exhaustion. The priest tumbled from his gelding at the kitchen door without speaking to the young groomsman, who caught up the reins and plodded both horses on to the stable. Catherine had heard them ride up and ran out to meet him.

"The constable has been here," said Catherine. "The man suspects the whole house, and I am sure he will be back here before the sun is high."

Father John came in, easing himself onto the kitchen bench, and Catherine slid a goblet of ale and a loaf of bread between his elbows. The old priest fell to the food without speaking, and when Joseph came to the open door, Catherine raised her arm toward the table, and he took a seat across from the older man. Catherine brought more drink, and Joseph emptied the willow bark from a leather bag onto the far end of the table.

"Did I hear a horse?" Eleanor came in from the laundry, carrying the baby in one arm. When she saw Joseph, she raised her hands for an embrace, but Catherine shook her head slightly and Eleanor bent to the bark instead, as though she had meant to inspect its quality. "I am glad you're here, Father," she said.

The priest paused over a chunk of bread. "It's a sorry reason for my presence, girl."

"Yes, Father," muttered Eleanor.

"This is fine, Joseph," said Catherine, turning over the willow.

"Your husband does not improve?" said Father John.

"The fever comes and goes. One minute he is better. The next he is down in the bed," said Catherine. "It mystifies me that a fever can work so on a body."

"Perhaps bleeding would issue forth the demon," said Father John.

"Let me try this first," said Catherine. There was noise outside, and they all looked to the window. The constable was handing his reins to Geoffrey, and the watchmen were dismounting. "Speak of the devil."

"I'll be off now, Madam, if the willow is acceptable," said Joseph.

"Off? Where?" asked Catherine.

"I have chores. The stables need cleaning." He was chewing his lip again.

"All right. Stay close in case the constable wants a word with you."

"Yes, Madam." Joseph pulled on his cap. His eyes met Eleanor's for a second, and he gave her a half-wink before he disappeared out the door into the house. It would take him either to the front door or around the servants' stairs to the lower door on the other side of the house. Father John seemed not to notice that he had gone the wrong way out, but Eleanor watched the doorway for several seconds after he was no longer in it.

"Eleanor," said Catherine, "will you set this to a soak? Heat the water just to simmer and weight these so that they stay under."The constable let himself in, knocking as he opened the door. "The priest is here. Good. There is work for you, sad work indeed. I figure this is the worst job a man of God would have to see."

"God sends us the tasks that need doing," said Father John, stretching. "Where are the bodies?"

"In the tomb," said Catherine. "Let me get William and we will have the funeral." She hurried upstairs and into the bedchamber, shaking her husband awake. But William would not come down. He pulled the linens up to his chin, pleading. "I have a great heaviness of the head. I cannot rise." Reginald came silently to the door that led down to his sleeping chamber. He looked at William for a few seconds, then disappeared from where he had come.

"Father is here," Catherine said. "I have fresh willow bark, and I am making you tea. You might have another draught of dock in the meantime."

"No. I cannot. Let Margaret attend," William said, rolling away from Catherine and putting his face into the pillow. "She is desperate to prove herself the mistress of this house. See how she likes watching her dead flopped onto a shelf to soften."

"They are not her dead," said Catherine, bristling a little, but William groaned and pulled the linen over his head, and she went out without him to put Hannah and Ruth to their rest.

49

The funeral was a dismal ritual, the bodies wrapped tightly and stuffed together into a plank box cobbled together from scraps. Catherine had packed sweet marjoram around the shrouds, but Father John Bridle leaned away from the coffin as he spoke. Margaret was at the front beside Catherine, and halfway through the first prayer, she began to drum her fingers lightly against her thigh as though she could speed up the priest. Benjamin was on the other side of her, and Catherine, on the verge of her sight, could see him casting irritated glances at the beating hands.

The maids stood with Reg Goodall behind Catherine and Margaret. Eleanor whimpered softly, and one of the younger girls wailed once and went suddenly quiet, as though someone had elbowed her ribs. The men were behind the maids, unchanged from their work clothes, and the sweet musk of horse and iron and manured earth stirred up with the profound and sickening tang of human decay that wafted from the front. The constable and two watchmen stood in the back, and Catherine knew they were taking measure of the mourners.

Father John cut the ceremony short, and when he finished he crossed himself quickly, then beckoned to the manservants to carry the dead to the family tomb. The maids and Catherine followed, but Margaret excused herself.

"This tires us all. Let me take the baby, Sister." She held out her hands for Veronica.

Catherine studied Margaret. "You want to hold her?"

"Yes. I am weary and I want comfort." Her voice grew silky. "Please, Sister. Let me be mother to the child in this time. You will feel the grief on you too and you need to rest. This is no time for us to contend. We argue too readily. We always have."

Catherine handed the sleeping baby to Margaret. Perhaps death had warmed her heart a little. Margaret put her face against the soft tuft of red hair and went up the stairs without looking back.

Peter Grubb stepped between Catherine and the three maids.

"I figure I need to speak to these young ones," he said.

The women's faces were pallid and twitchy with terror, like a trio of trapped rabbits, and Catherine couldn't tell whether they were more afraid of the constable or of the dead women.

"Yes," she said. She thrust her finger toward them. "You speak the truth, upon your souls, do you hear me?"

"Yes, Madam," they chorused.

"Take them into the front gallery," said Catherine. "And keep your voices low. William is sleeping and the whole family needs calm."

"I will attend them," said Benjamin, "with your permission, Catherine." The constable glowered at him, but Benjamin went on. "I wish to take my own record of the inquiry."

"I figure I can keep notes for myself," sniffed the constable.

"Very well. I will keep them for this family then," said Benjamin.

"It pleases me," said Catherine. "Peter, Benjamin will go with you."

Catherine returned to the kitchen to wait and found Reginald seated at the table, a cup between his palms.

"Should you not be upstairs with your master?" asked Catherine.

William's man refilled his cup from an ale pitcher. "Master's not wanting much service."

"No." Catherine sat across from Reginald. "What ails him?" she asked softly.

"He doesn't confide in me, Madam. He's eaten up by his sickness."

"He doesn't mend under my care. I have wondered if there is some unseen malady. Some trouble in his soul. Has he said aught to you, Reginald? Anything?"

The man shook his head. "Not to me. Master says almost nothing to me since we returned to this place. I wish he did."

"And you are well? No fever or sweats?"

"My mind is as clear as summer, and I have been at his side every day."

"Curious," said Catherine.

"Indeed." He looked her boldly in the face. "The whole house has gone curious, if you ask me. I feel a cold spirit blowing through it." He bit his lip. "May I have leave to go up?"

"Yes, of course, Reginald."

He set the cup with a pile of dirtied pots before he left. Outside, Geoffrey and Joseph passed by on their return to the stable, wiping their hands on their breeches and keeping a distance beyond speech between them as they went. Catherine went out when she saw her father come by.

Joseph brought out the priest's pony gelding, and Catherine asked, "Must you hurry off?" Joseph tightened the belly-band and slipped the bit between the bored old thing's yellow teeth. Father John swung himself into the saddle. He'd grown portly in the last few years, and his toes nearly touched the ground.

"If you need me, send for me, Daughter. There's bad doings here, and you might be better off down in Mount Grace with me. You come if you need a roof. Your husband has not lifted the first board toward making those draperies, and the convent buildings stand empty. It needs a master's eye on the work. Or a mistress's. People have already begun to scavenge for stones, and your man Benjamin won't like to know his investment stands open to thieves. Come on, now, and see to your land. It's yours as much as his. More."

"I must stay here for now, Father. I've not felt myself today. I don't want to ride."

"As you wish. But I will sleep better inside my own four walls." He clucked at the pony, which sighed and ambled forward. "I keep a bed for you, Daughter. For you and the little ones if you need them."

When Father John disappeared around the corner, Catherine hurried back to the house, preferring the door into the kitchen to the wide front entrance. Catherine wanted solitude now, a mug of strong ale and her thoughts.

But Margaret was in the pantry, and she brought out a glass, a mate to one that sat, filled with wine, on the table. Veronica was sleeping in Margaret's arm, and she poured the second glass. "Come drink with me. The baby is settled and William is sleeping."

"You prepared this for me?" Catherine lifted the closest glass and drank. It was old claret and she let the musty scent bloom in her mouth. "Thank you, Margaret. It is most welcome."

"Our minds are too full." Margaret took up her wine and offered a toast into the air between them. "Drink, Catherine. We may be all we have left."

"God above, I hope not," said Catherine. "Does he honestly mean to cast me off?"

Margaret drank again. "He spoke of it, and I sent you word, but in his illness I fear my brother thinks of little but his own comfort."

They finished without any more talk, and when the glasses were empty, Margaret stood. "I will take her upstairs. I feel a heaviness on me."

"Thanks, Margaret. I mean that."

Catherine gave herself a few minutes, before she tended on William, to walk out alone, around the garden to the east side of the house. But the gorse now had a tarnished look, and Catherine turned away from it. Her vision wobbled and she almost fell. Her head felt fluid and swollen.

She staggered back to the house, through the front door and down the corner stairs. She was trying not to vomit until she could be alone. William would have to wait. He was surely still asleep anyway.

But William was not sleeping. The kitchen was in disarray, and Catherine could hear that someone was in the still room. "Margaret?" Catherine called. But it was William, kneeling on the disemboweled floor. Catherine's books lay around him, and he was hunched over one, turning pages. He flung it aside and pulled out another from the hole.

Catherine asked, "What do you think you will find there?"

He whipped around. "You have a whole witch's library here."

"You're ill. You don't know what you're saying." Catherine knelt beside him and gathered the volumes into a stack. He was sweating and she could feel the heat of him. He breathed heavily. "I'm feeling unwell myself, and you should be in bed resting. You're weak and your mind is wandering. You know I keep a library. I always have."

"Why do you keep it under the floor? It's what you did in the convent, when you thought they might be found." William grabbed Catherine's elbow and her head went around. She dropped a volume. It was her mother's book of venoms. She turned it over, but he saw. "That one. You told me you had no such collection."

Catherine shook her head and tucked the poisons among the others. "It means little to me. I forget that it exists. It might be useful for vermin."

"Mice? Rats?"

"Something like that. It was at the bottom." Catherine sat on the pavers and looked at her husband. His eyes were bright. Too bright. And his skin shone with his fever. Or was it her? "William. Let me help you."

"You cannot. Or you will not. It was right here on the top. "

"You're strong. Your heart wants to live." She ran her hand into his hair, but he pulled back, sitting hard against the stone wall.

"Give me the poisons."

"Why?" Catherine pulled the books closer to her skirt, out of his reach, but her grasp felt drained and her thumb ached. "What do you mean to kill? Has there not been enough death already?"

"Give it to me." He snatched the volume from her, dragged himself to his feet, and searched the books that sat on a shelf over the table. "And what is this?" He had the *City of Ladies* in his hand.

"A gift from Father." Her voice fluttered and she laid her warm palm against her throat. "For the birth of Veronica. You may ask him." Catherine piled up the other books and waited.

"Well." He threw the book back where it had been and, taking the book of venoms with him, left her.

Catherine placed the other books on a high shelf, behind the jars of dried herbs. When she stepped into the kitchen, William was standing at the hearth, searching through the cooking herbs. "Tell me your thoughts," she said. "They're fiery, and they heat your brain. William, I am ill myself, I tell you."

William pulled out a dried sheaf of sage. "What here will bring a man to God? Swiftly and without mark. I would have no marks."

"William, what is this madness?" Catherine took the flattened stem. "This herb will poison only a melancholy. It may help clear breathing. Will I make you a tea of it?"

"I will not be cured." He opened a jar and sniffed at the mint. The next was rosehips and he threw a handful away. Then he began to weep. "I am becoming a woman," he said. "Next I will be a child. Perhaps I will melt away entire and the world will be newer."

Catherine snapped. "Stop talking like that. I didn't marry a whining child and I don't mean to watch you become one now." She gathered a few of the scattered rosehips. "You know how long it took my women to gather these?"

"Your women. You will always have your women, will you not?"

"What would you have? A troop of chirping boys to cook your food and keep the garden? You think the chickens will bring their own eggs to the house? Your hose will mend themselves? What is wrong with you, William? Be a man, even if you are a sick one."

"A man. What is a man, Catherine? A creature of God? A stick on two legs, crawling toward the throne hoping for a crumb from the king? Blood of Christ, I had rather be one of my hounds barking at the moon than a man in this country."

"When have you come to talk so, Husband? I recall a time when you knew how to manage your king and your conscience without doing violence to either."

"That was when I had an elder brother. I had no name then and could afford to be brash. Now I carry my father's name on my shoulders. This house. You. And now the children. That boy."

Catherine sucked in her breath. "Is it Robert? Is that who you mean to murder? Your son?"

"My son. Or another's. There is no way to know, is there, Catherine? And he laughs behind my back over it. Says he sees his eyes in the boy's face. Says it puts him in mind of you."

Catherine's stomach went cold. "How can you know that? You have never spoken to the man."

"People talk. Benjamin knows. There is no pretending anymore. That Grubb will bring him here. Him and all his riding mates. They will know. They will ridicule me."

"And you will murder an innocent child for talk? It sickens me, William. It is no wonder your body rebels against your mind. It is unnatural and evil, even to think. It is a sin."

"You don't understand. And what is the wages of sin, anyway?" he said. "Tell me where to find a poison."

"I will not. You cannot wring it from me."

"You are my wife. You are bound to tell me what you know."

"I am a child of God before I am your wife and you will not stand between my soul and my judgment in the end. No, when you behave like a proper head, then I will obey you. When you act like a puppet on the finger of Satan, I have a head of my own that does me fine."

"Where is my daughter?"

"Our daughter? Our daughter is with your sister. She took her upstairs after the funeral."

"And you let her? You who have never let the child out of your arms?"

"Stop it, William. Stop. Margaret is her aunt. You're feeding the demon in you."

Eleanor came up from the laundry, looked from Catherine to William, and backed out again. "Pardon me, Madam."

"Stop there, girl," said William. "I want to know where your mistress keeps her venoms."

Eleanor stared wide-eyed at Catherine. "My lady keeps nothing such. I don't know what you're talking about. There is a trap for rats in the laundry. It has some moldy cheese in it. That's all I know."

"Lying little bitch," said William. The maid backed away. "You will tell me or you will live to regret it."

"I know nothing." Eleanor fled out the door, and William went after her, shoving Catherine as he went. She stumbled and he grabbed her flailing arm, steadying her. They were staring into each other's eyes, and William held her so tight she could feel his ribs against her, the unsteady clamor of his heart.

"Follow me at your peril," he said, setting her away from him as though she were a doll. Then he ran out after the maid, slamming the door behind him.

50

Catherine was on William's heels, and her calls brought Joseph, running from
the stable, and Reg, coming around from the front. Eleanor dashed past Joseph
and he wavered at William's approach, putting out his hands, then turning his
head to look for Eleanor.

"Out of my way, boy," said William.

"What's the girl done?" said Geoffrey White. Joseph ducked away at his
appearance, and the master of horse, arms crossed, arrested William's advance.
"That child never hurt a bedbug. Why do you chase after her?"

"Stand aside." William's hand went to his hip. Catherine skidded to a halt
and Reg, panting, stopped beside her. William and Geoffrey were within striking
distance of each other but neither moved. A kite screamed from the top of a
distant tree, and one of William's neglected falcons gave a feeble answer. "Stand
aside," William repeated.

Geoffrey shook his head. "I will yield when William Overton acts the man's
part. Eleanor is Joseph's woman and you'll not touch a hair of her head. You'll
not put that blade into me, neither, so take your hand from your side. Sir." He
held his ground.

William took a step backward, almost treading on Catherine's toes. "I'll not
have the women of my house defy me." William saw Reg and turned back to
Geoffrey. "Nor the men neither. You are no longer master of my horses. Get
out."

"You overstep yourself," Geoffrey said. He didn't sound like a servant of the
house. "There will be an answer to this."

"You presume too far, White. Out, you lickspittle. Now. Before I take that
tongue from your head." William pulled out his sword. His right hand shook.

Geoffrey pushed the blade aside with a snort. "You haven't the stones to scratch my thumbnail, William Overton. I don't give a fig for you or your position. I know what I know. Keep your distance from those youngsters or you will hear from me."

Catherine stepped between them, and Geoffrey backed off a step.

"What does this mean?" asked Catherine. "Since when do you call your master by his Christian name? What is it that you know?"

"I call him by name since he has become neither a Christian nor a man." He was staring over Catherine toward William with eyes dull as a fallow field.

"Explain yourself."

"Let him explain it." Geoffrey White nodded toward William, then walked into the stable. He emerged again before Catherine could move or speak, a satchel on his shoulder and a cloak upon his arm. "You will find me in the village if you seek me. You know where my mother and wife bide. Mayhap I will speak with the priest and calm my soul. Mayhap the constable will give me greater peace. They say soldiers are coming toward us. They might make me better masters."

He stalked off down the wide gravel drive, and William slowly sheathed his weapon again. A shadow crossed a window, and Catherine glanced up. Benjamin was watching, and he stepped out of sight as she raised her hand to shade her face.

William swung his head toward the house. He moved like a man with soft bones. "Who do you signal?"

"No one." Catherine wrapped her skirts in her sweating fists and walked fast, trying to settle her head. William dropped back and she was first at the kitchen door. Benjamin opened it before she laid her hand upon the latch. "What did you see?" she asked.

"I saw a man lose his position. Two men, I would say."

William was coming. Reg walked dutifully behind him.

"Say nothing to him," Catherine whispered. "He is defeated and sick. Do not shame him further." She went straight to her still room and let herself fall onto the floor. The pavers were cold and she laid her forehead on them, but she could hear the men in the other room.

"So it was you," called William. "My wife gives you hand messages now? You stare after her?"

"I might look out a window when I hear shouting as well as any man," said Benjamin. "You say what comes into your mind these days, William, and your mind is fevered. You begin to remind me of your brother. You should learn to hold your words until you are yourself."

"I am myself. Has my wife not told you that I carry a fire in my head as my reward for sins?"

"I never thought of burning as a wage," said Benjamin.

"I'm sure you have that from your scripture," said William. "You are at it night and day no doubt."

Catherine pulled herself up on the wooden shelves and joined them. "Stop it. Both of you." She crossed to the pantry, found a bottle of wine, and brought it to the table. "We are bound by grief and we snap at each other like cats in a bag. William, this is your brother's old companion. I am your wife who loves you. Poor Eleanor has probably lost half her hair in terror. Now sit down and drink. The weather has sapped my strength."

"The day is fine," said Benjamin.

Catherine opened the wine. "Perhaps it is the weather in my head."

William sat and Benjamin took the seat across from him. Reg leaned against the wall in a corner. Catherine poured and when all of the men had settled their hands around their cups, they watched each other. Something moved out in the yard, and Eleanor came creeping out of the stable, Joseph behind her. The girl was weeping, and Joseph was wiping her face.

"Is the constable finished with the maids?" Catherine asked Benjamin.

"He is. They are likely hiding in a closet somewhere, he frightened them so badly. Talked of hanging until they could say nothing at all. I sent him off. I should have sent him with two blackened eyes, but as I am in your house, I thought it beyond my authority. The man will return, as he suspects the murderer is in the house. I will ask your permission to give him a drubbing then."

"I must to bed," said William. He was pasty, making his red-rimmed eyes look even sicker. "Reg, help me."

"I will make the willow bark tea for us both," said Catherine. The light came through the window directly onto his skin, and though the scars showed, she could see no other symptom of disease but the pallor. "Let me look at your eyes, William."

He sat quietly as she stretched the lids and peered into the soft flesh. She tilted his head one way, then the other, feeling his neck, but there was no sign of the sweat. No plague. No coughing or blood. "The tea is the last hope I have to cure you," she said.

"Bring your maid to help you. I will be in my chamber." He slid the goblet away and Reg, blank-faced, offered his arm.

"I have never seen such a thing," said Benjamin, watching the empty space where William had been. "What do you think the malady is?"

"I don't know," said Catherine, "but it may not be an illness of the body."

"What other kind is there? You're not turning theologian on me, are you, Catherine?"

She could see Joseph and Eleanor in front of the stable. Eleanor was shaking her head, and Joseph was pointing toward the kitchen. "Not exactly. Perhaps. I will tell you this. The head governs the body as a king governs his kingdom."

"Then we are all dead men for sure." Benjamin swigged at an empty goblet, and Catherine refilled it. "Damned, too."

"That's true whether we are ill or not. Mortal, I mean. If the body is sick enough, whether from an ingrown malady or an outside infection, it will destroy the ability of the head to reason. Dying men rave and confess sins they have thought they could conceal. It is like a king who can no longer control his subjects when they rebel or rise against him."

"I have seen it."

"Just so. If the head is diseased, the body fails. The process may be longer, but the body will die if the reason is infected." She put her hands on her temples. "I may suffer from it myself."

"I will send for a physician, Catherine. I cannot stand to see you sick." He pushed back from the table, but she stopped him with a raised hand.

"What I need is sleep without dreams."

Benjamin nodded and sat again. "But how does a man's reason become infected? You mean William has been listening to wrong-headed ideas?"

"No. I mean he has a weight on his imagination. Or his memory."

"So you are a theologian after all. You think he needs a priest. You've got one in your family, Catherine. Call him and let the man confess."

"It is something more than that. William has never failed to confess his failings, and the priest has been here. No, Benjamin, it's something more. He is beyond weary and into the grip of something more. I just don't know what it is."

"Then perhaps the man you should call is your constable."

51

William was awake, sitting in the chair by the window, when Catherine came in with the tea. He dropped the edge of the drape but did not turn. "Did you make peace with Eleanor?"

"She's outside being comforted by Joseph," Catherine said. She set the tea by his hand and took a bowl for herself. "Drink that. You gave her a fright, but she knows we are all treading through a nettle-patch of late."

"Prickly indeed," he said. He emptied the bowl. "That tastes like your other concoctions. Like damp shit and moldy leaves." He grinned at her with half his mouth. "But I'm sure it's good for me."

"I suffer it with you, Husband. For better and for worse." Catherine drank hers off and shuddered. "It does taste like a witch's spit."

He wiped his lip and studied his fingers. "I'm a brute and a villain and I don't deserve you. Have I spread my illness to you?"

She pulled up a stool and sat across from him, taking his hand in hers. She pressed his wrist and palm, feeling for the life force. It was warm and strong, and she let her hand drift up to his elbow. "Perhaps we need to be next to each other. Where is Reg?"

"I sent him away."

She pulled him to his feet and, backward, over to the bed. They fell together onto the cover, and she loosened his shirttails from the breeches.

"Is this not a sin during the day?" he asked, leaning back to let her drag the garment over his head.

"Let God look all He likes," said Catherine. "He can cover the sun if we embarrass Him." She loosened the ties of her bodice and slid the dress down to her waist. "Touch me."

William's hands on her shoulders and back were damp and searing, and Catherine gasped at their heat, pressing herself against him. She had almost forgotten the feel of him, and she ran her fingers into his hair and kissed him full on the mouth. He moaned and rolled her onto her back, grasping at her skirts to get her legs free. She wriggled and stretched herself completely onto the bed, opening herself to him, laying her head back onto the pillow. The heat was in her now, and she lifted herself toward him, wanting to feel him on her belly and between her thighs.

He moved against her, still working her underskirts out of the way, and Catherine looked into his eyes. She thought she would see desire there, and love, but when William's gaze fell onto hers, his face went white again, and he dropped his head onto her shoulder and lay still. His whole body collapsed onto her.

"William," Catherine said softly. She pressed his hipbones hard with her palms, but he lay still and she breathed through her mouth, trying to settle her blood. Stars sparked in her head and she had to pull herself back into herself, like walking in from a summer storm. She stroked his back. His breath came in heaves and spurts and she thought he might be crying again. "William," she repeated.

He rolled away, fastening his breeches and tucking in his shirt. He sat on the edge of the bed, his elbows on his knees. "Forgive me. I'm no longer a man."

"It will come," she said. "In time." The room was darkening to its regular color again, and she rolled to the opposite edge of the mattress and stood to fix her clothing. William hadn't stood, and she came around to kneel at his feet. "Do you want to tell me what it is?"

He put his hand on her cheek. "More than anything," he said. "Now let me sleep."

52

Catherine wandered back down to the kitchen, craving a drink of wine alone in the still room. Her head was alight with pain, as though a handful of sparkling shards had been scattered inside her. She found an open bottle of claret and, sitting on the pavers, poured a glass. It was good, and the ache in her thoughts dulled. She drank another. She was alone. She could do as she pleased. She struggled to her feet and skimmed her hand along the top shelf until she touched her books. They were safe enough. Where was Eleanor? She felt dizzy. Catherine dropped her head into her hands and felt the room tilt. Maybe her maid and Joseph had taken one of the cobs and escaped. And who would blame them? The house was silent above her, but she could feel the weight of its stones, pushing down upon her like grave dirt. If he would divorce her, then so be it. She would take her books, her clothing, and her table. She would set up house with the children and her father.

The room was still turning, and Catherine, finding the bottle empty, curled up on the pavers and cried. The other maids would go, one by one, or be taken, and theirs would be a ghost house in a hostile, suspicious village. And she had thought to create a city of ladies. What a fool. The fool of the Fates.

"Catherine, what are you doing in there?"

It was Benjamin. Catherine had forgotten he was down here. But he hadn't been in the kitchen. Catherine wiped her eyes on her skirt, but before she could stand, he was kneeling beside her.

"What has he done?"

"William? He's done nothing. He doesn't know his own mind. His body is sick because his heart is sick. None of us can escape ourselves." Catherine curled her feet up under her and sat against the rear wall. Her mind was sodden with the wine, and she let her head flop backward. She was hot. She wondered briefly if she was going to die. Then she laughed. They were all going to die. "I cannot find my way to the truth, and my mind is tying itself into knots."

Benjamin lowered himself to the floor and leaned against the opposite wall. "Shall I say it?"

"Do you ever refrain from saying what you think?"

"You believe that William killed your women."

"Shh! My God, someone will hear you." Catherine slouched forward and put her hand over his mouth, but she wobbled and lost her balance.

He caught her by the wrists and held her up. "You don't disagree with me, I notice."

His grip was firm and he guided her toward him. The stars in Catherine's head had all gone out, and she was in the dark. All she could sense was the heat of the man, the closeness of him. He smelt of grass and grain, a clean animal. She could somehow see his eyes, the same clear blue that the sun cast across snow. "Don't say it," she whispered.

Benjamin eased Catherine backward, onto the floor, and she allowed herself to fall and be held there beneath him. He kicked the door shut behind them, and Catherine felt him hard upon her. He worked his hands into her bodice, and her breath got hooked in her throat. She was a caught in a wave, pulling her away from herself again, and then he was pulling away her skirts. His hands not so very different from William's, but his body taller, heavier, and his mouth on her neck and breasts harder. The stars sparked behind her eyes again, and her body lit up, heat deep in her belly, her knees weakened and open. He was on top of her, parting her legs, then inside her, and she held onto him, pushing herself against him until the warmth overtook her, and the breath came rushing, free, from her. The stars disappeared into a cloud of fire that licked itself to the ends of her body. She lay back beneath him and let herself burn.

When Catherine finally opened her eyes again, Benjamin was sleeping beside her. The room was dim, but she could now see the outline of the door, his boot still propped against it. The shelves revealed their edges over her, like a line of steps walking up the wall toward the black ceiling. The air was thick and beating in her ear. Someone far away was calling her name.

Catherine fixed her clothing in the dark. She drove her toe into Benjamin's shin, and when he complained, she squatted and whispered, "Wake up. Be quiet." Catherine scrambled to her feet, patting down her clothes, and put her ear against the door. The person was not in the kitchen, and Catherine tumbled Benjamin's leg away and cracked the door. She heard no one in the kitchen, but a chicken was cooking somewhere. She stepped through, closed the door on the man, and checked her skirt and apron. Her hair must be a nest of tangles. She pulled it down and combed it quickly with her fingers, then wound it again on the back of her head and secured it with a long pin and the rumpled coif. Through the kitchen window, she could see Eleanor's back, bent over the far rows in the vegetable garden. One of other kitchen maids was on her knees nearby, and the other two were headed back to the house.

"Catherine!"

It was Margaret, but her tone had a new, plaintive note. Almost like a friend seeking a friend. She was still upstairs. Catherine hurried up to the front door, arranging her face into a normal expression, and met her sister-in-law coming down with the baby. Margaret handed over the infant. "I would say she's hungry. How does our William?"

Catherine's ears went hot at his name. She busied herself with Veronica to avoid looking at Margaret. "He is unwell. I have given him a dose of willow bark tea, and if that does not improve him, I am at a loss."

"But you are a genius," said Benjamin behind her. "I think there is no ailment of the body that you cannot cure."

Catherine's throat closed and she thought she would choke. Her legs began to shake and she felt the stain of shame on her face. Margaret would surely see, but when Catherine looked up, Margaret was smiling at Benjamin. Simpering. "No," Catherine blurted, and Margaret readjusted her gaze onto Catherine.

"Oh, I agree with Master Davies," Margaret said. "You have done all you can for my dear brother."

Catherine spun around, and Benjamin reared back as though she had offered to strike him. His eyes were wide and he threw up his hands. "I meant it as no insult, Lady."

"Of course not." Margaret swayed around Catherine and snagged her arm on Benjamin's. "You know how to divert a woman, don't you, Benjamin? Shall we make a circuit around the gardens while Catherine oversees our dinner? It would lift my spirits after this miserable day. Catherine. Sister. You look as though you'd watched the night away."

Benjamin looked at the hand that had suddenly appeared inside his elbow as though it were some strange breed of small rodent. "Very well, Margaret."

They went through the front door together, and Catherine ran back to the kitchen, Veronica in one arm. She laid the baby on the pavers and vomited into a bucket.

53

The three maids tiptoed into the kitchen, followed by a scolding Eleanor. "That man can't hang you without evidence," she was saying, but she stopped when she saw Catherine on her knees. "Madam, have you caught the master's sickness?" She caught up Catherine's hair and tied it out of the way.

Catherine sat back on her haunches and wiped her mouth with the back of her hand. Eleanor dipped a towel into a basin of water and Catherine accepted it gratefully. "It's nothing, Eleanor, just the day's demons in my head. God's bones, I need something to drink." The wine had worn off, and her eyes felt swollen and pebbly. She wondered if she smelt of a man. She wanted to run the cloth between her legs. She wanted to run the clock backward a few hours.

The baby cried, and one of the maids took her up. "There, there, little one. You're safe enough."

"Would that we all were," muttered another. "We will be blamed for those murders one way or another."

Catherine dragged herself up to the table. The three maids before her were her women now, and she barely knew their names. The slender, fair one cradling her daughter was Agnes, of that she was sure. Yes. Agnes Cartwright. The murmuring one was called Helen. She could recall that because no young woman bore less of a resemblance to that legendary beauty than this upright slab of muscle and wiry hair who stood before her, broad-shouldered and frowning. What was the name of the third one?

"Maddie, will you give me a hand here with the joint?" Eleanor was removing the meat from the fire, and the unnamed maid jumped to assist her.

Maddie, yes. Maddie Sawyer. Not a one of them had ever seen the inside of a convent. Catherine tried to imagine the three girls at their books, but for the moment she could not paint the picture in her mind. "The constable must ask his questions, Helen," Catherine said. "You may be sure that Master Davies was there on your behalf." His name was a coal on her tongue.

"That he was," said Agnes, suddenly animated. "He sent that constable on the run. I thought he might lift him bodily and throw him through the front door."

Helen was moved to giggle at this, though coming from her horsey bulk, the girlish sound was slightly grotesque. "I'd've liked to seen that." She held out her arms. "Let me hold her, Agnes."

But Agnes wasn't listening anymore. She was pulling back the blanket on Veronica. Catherine's beautiful, delicate daughter. "Madam," the young woman said, "the baby doesn't look well."

54

Dinner was laid on the table, and Catherine sat with Benjamin and Margaret. William had come down to take the head spot. Margaret had made the salad with her own hands, but it sat wilting on its platter. No one was eating. Catherine was bent over Veronica, examining her eyelids and tongue and the moist, warm creases of her arms and legs. The baby did not cry, but lay limp and breathing in shallow gasps.

"What's ails her?" said William. He clenched the carved arms of his chair, the chair that had once belonged to the Mount Grace convent, and it passed through Catherine's mind that her mother had used to clasp them in the same fashion when she was ready to deliver a pronouncement. Or a punishment.

"I have said it a dozen times already," snapped Catherine. "I don't know." Her chest constricted with guilt the moment the words were said. It wasn't William's fault. And she could not look at Benjamin at all, though she could feel the warmth of his gaze. He would look pitying. Or smug. He might wink. It would be unbearable. "I see no signs of fever or plague. The skin is clear. I can't tell what it is." The baby lay listless upon her arm, one small hand reaching at nothing. Her eyes opened and closed, seeming to see her mother then to drift toward the painted constellations that lit up the timbered ceiling. "Did she sleep well in your bed?"

"Like a cherub from heaven," said Margaret. She was sitting beside Benjamin, and when he set down his wine goblet, she placed her hand on his. "She never stirred." Margaret sat back and watched Catherine. Then she scooted forward and served the limp greens to each of them. "We must eat. You and William must regain your strength." She took up for her knife, but instead of spearing her meat, began to polish the blade with her napkin. "I am no physician, Catherine. I only watched her." Margaret placed the utensil neatly by her plate and dabbed the corners of her eyes. "Poor mite. Perhaps she senses the mood of the house. I only meant to relieve you of a burden. To give you some time for your meditations."

Catherine's guts shriveled now with shame. "I know, Margaret. You three should eat. Let me take her downstairs and see what I can do."

"Eat first," said Margaret. "I worked myself like a servant over it."

Catherine shoved a few bites of the salad into her mouth, but even the oil had no flavor. She forced it down with wine. "Thanks, Sister."

"I will come with you," said Margaret when Catherine rose from the table.

William took his sister's hand and held it. "No. Stay here with us. We need a woman's talk at table."

Margaret twitched her fingers gently, but her brother held on. "I will stay if you require it. Will it lift your spirits for me to stay, Benjamin?"

"Your conversation always amuses me," he said evenly.

Catherine gathered up the baby's clouts and went to the kitchen. The maids jumped to their feet at her entrance, their faces tight with fear. She passed through to the laundry, saying "Stay here, girls." She pushed the heavy door shut and bolted it.

Catherine laid her daughter on the flags and uncovered her completely. The body was smooth and clear. She lifted the curled legs to check for scours or sores, but the child was clean from top to bottom. There was only one thing she could think to do. Turning the baby onto her stomach, Catherine reached down the tiny throat with her least finger until the baby retched. Curds of milk, some dark, watery fluid. Veronica wailed and vomited, and Catherine cleaned out her mouth with a corner of the blanket, and cradled her close. She whimpered for a while, then nestled against her mother and closed her eyes. Catherine rocked her in one arm and stirred the murky pool on the floor. Lifted her finger and squinted. Sniffed. Sour and acid. The child was sleeping soundly now, her breathing regular and deep. Could be nothing more than a bellyache. Could be.

Catherine knelt and knotted her fingers together, trying to pray, but nothing came except her own soft breath, hot on her knuckles, hot as any sin. She said, "Don't punish her for me," but she heard nothing in reply. Her knees ached on the hard stones, and she lay on her back, under the table. No one ever cleaned this room but Ann Smith, and in her absence the beams that crossed beneath the table had grown furry with dust. The table was from the old convent, and in it was still concealed the altarpiece. Only Ann and Catherine knew it was there. She lay now under the fragmented face of the Virgin. One of the painted eyes was clearly visible, the wood having dried and shrunk some, and streaks of pink and red showed her skin. The Child was beginning to show behind the planks Catherine's mother had had nailed across Him, but it was the Mother of God whom Catherine sought.

"Don't make her suffer because of my sin," Catherine whispered. "Lady, make your namesake well and strong again. I will go back to Hatfield and lay me down at the feet of Mary Tudor if you will intervene for me. I swear it. The crime was mine. Mine alone."

She lay still for a few moments, listening to the house snap and creak as it settled into the moors for another night. She wondered that the place didn't crumple into a heap of stones in its own cellars, a tomb for them all. The eye of the Virgin caught a reflected light from somewhere and glittered for a second, then went dark again. There was no sound. The child wailed softly, and Catherine slid out and rearranged the blankets so that she could hold Veronica in the crook of her elbow. Night came over the room like a curtain being slowly drawn, and Catherine lay watching the dark while the child slept, coal-hot, beside her.

55

Catherine woke with a gasp from a dream of gardens and death. The leaves of the plants had been broad and bright, and when she folded them back, babies' faces emerged from the flowers' centers. Then the man was there, saying it again, "Lady, there's been a body found," and then he held out the covered head. Catherine was lying in the same position under the great table, and her daughter was awake. When Veronica saw Catherine's face, she reached out both hands and opened her pink mouth. Catherine slid out and rearranged her skirts on the floor. She was stiff and cold, and her stomach was roiling, but she took up the child and gave her a breast. "Thank God," she said to the sweet, yeasty-smelling wisps of hair on her daughter's crown. The baby suckled, but weakly, and Catherine laid the backs of her fingers on the pale cheeks but felt no heat. She lay on her side and watched the sun brighten in the window.

The feathered sound of whispering flew to her from the kitchen, and Catherine wiped up the dried vomit with a towel, tying her bodice closed before she stood and unbolted the door. "Lady Catherine," said Benjamin, but he did not enter the laundry, nor did he comment on yesterday's dirty clothing or Catherine's uncombed hair. His eyes were fixed somewhere in the vicinity of her chin. "You will want to know that the constable has returned, and he has a troop of men with him. He says that soldiers have arrived in the village to examine this house."

The trio of maids twittered behind him. They retreated to the kitchen, nestled down around the hearth, one stirring a pot of something vile-smelling, and waited.

Catherine came forward. "So early? Why does he come again to disturb us?" She rubbed her eyes with one hand, but they still felt gritty and swollen.

Her stomach threatened to heave.

"How does little Veronica this morning?" asked Benjamin.

Catherine felt the anger drain from her heart. "Better. She eats and has slept the night." She looked past him to the maids. "What in Christ's name are you cooking over there? It smells like the armpit of Mephistopheles."

Agnes said, "We are boiling stockings, Madam." She peered into the pot. "The laundry door was bolted."

"So it was." Catherine held her nose. "You should wash them more often."

Agnes stirred solemnly. "Yes, Madam."

"Where is Eleanor?"

"Here, Madam." Eleanor came in from the pantry, her face puffy and white. She had clearly slept there instead of up in her own warm bed. "I'm here."

Benjamin coughed. "Your husband and sister are already in the dining gallery."

It was not a command, but Catherine went upstairs before Benjamin, who ushered her by with his arm. Eleanor trailed silently after them. Margaret and William were sitting at table, and Peter Grubb stood nearby. The front door was open. A dozen men milled around the front courtyard, kicking the gravel and comparing their swords.

Catherine stomped into the room. "What do you mean by this? Have you not disrupted this household enough?" Veronica cried out at the cold breeze, a lusty howl, and Catherine said, "You see? You even frighten the baby."

The constable studied Catherine, up and down. He swung his head like a yoked ox and gave Margaret and William the same look. "I figure you want to know who killed your womenfolk, and the only way for me to find out is to ask questions."

Something outside fell and shattered. A clay urn, Catherine thought. "You have to arrest us as felons? With hired men? My daughter is ill and we have buried two women. We are tired and sick and sad. Can you not leave us in peace for one entire day?"

"Well, now. I wonder that you, who have been knocking down my door demanding some justice, are suddenly so eager that I get sufficient leisure. I figure that you're happy enough to have me sniffing at the doors of good people in the village as long as your own stink don't seep out."

William was watching the exchange. His hand was over Margaret's again, the fingers white at the nails where he gripped his sister's neat little paw. She was nibbling very daintily at her lower lip and staring at Benjamin.

Benjamin stood within touching distance of Catherine's arm. She thought the nap of his coat was brushing her sleeve, but she didn't look. Something was thumping in her neck, and the air had gone stale and dusty, though the breath of morning blew freely through the open door. It seemed to carry the shadow of some putrid mass from very far away. The whirr of doves seeking the sky pleated the soft fabric of waking insect sounds. One of the falcons screamed. "William," said Catherine. "Veronica seems somewhat better. I am going to take her upstairs and leave you to manage this situation."

"Are you well enough, man?" said Benjamin. He stepped around Catherine, his hand tracing her waist for a moment, and went to the table.

William's hand came away from Margaret's. "I'm as well as any man here." His face was patchy, though, and the hand trembled when it moved.

"Then I figure we can begin," said the constable. He blew a whistle, and three men came inside. The one in the lead was no watchman. It was the soldier, Adam Hastings, the very one from that day in the convent, and he gave the room a proprietary scan as he entered.

Catherine's throat closed completely and something clanged in her ears. Was he looking for the boy? She squeezed Veronica and the baby squealed.

"Don't throttle the tyke," said Adam. He was studying her face.

Maybe he didn't recognize her. "You should begin your interrogations with those who speak against this house," she snapped at Peter Grubb. "They are probably right under your nose. Come with me, Eleanor."

Upstairs, Catherine fell across her bed. Veronica bounced once and burbled, a happy sound, but then fell to twisting her head as though trying to escape some pain she couldn't locate. Catherine wrapped her in a fresh blanket and, stripping off her own clothes, lay beside her. "Get some rest, Eleanor. You look as though Satan's wife has painted your face for you." Eleanor stumbled to her chamber, but though she lay exhausted in the softness of the feather mattress, Catherine did not sleep. The room again seemed to turn and she closed her eyes. She could hear voices. A door slammed, and Margaret shrieked. Men were arguing, but Catherine couldn't untangle their words.

"Madam, what is it?" Eleanor came trotting in, tying her apron. "What is happening?"

"I don't know." Catherine blinked, pushed herself from the bed, pulled on her shift, and went to the door, but even with her ear pressed to the keyhole, she couldn't make sense of the noise. "Get your shoes on, quickly now."

Eleanor scooted off, and Catherine drew on a clean skirt, but she needed Eleanor to fasten it, and she drove her fingers into her hair. The woman in her glass looked wild, black curls all over her shoulders and eyes still inflamed at the rims. "I look like a hag," she said to her image. She pulled down her lower lids. She had slept badly. That was all.

Margaret screamed again, from downstairs this time, and Eleanor returned, holding the shoes. "Let me do that, Madam," she insisted, taking the mass of Catherine's hair and taming it to pins and a coif.

Catherine splashed her face with cold water and pinched her cheeks. She allowed herself a swish of powder, and, turning, dabbed Eleanor's nose as well. "We had better look like ladies. It sounds like my sister has turned fury."

Eleanor gathered up the baby, and Catherine, taking a deep breath, opened the door.

56

The long hallway was dark and empty. Margaret's chamber door was open, and a dust-embroidered shaft of light fell across the weave of rushes on the floor. Catherine leaned over the stairs, listening. Eleanor whispered, "What do you hear, Madam?"

"Shh."

Margaret was below, talking, her voice high and tight. Catherine couldn't see anyone without descending and showing herself.

"You will not question my maid," Margaret said. She was closer, her words clear, and Catherine pushed Eleanor back and pressed herself against the wall. Margaret flounced past the staircase without looking up.

William followed. "You must submit," he said clearly.

Catherine ventured a peek. Margaret had whirled around, and her face was a storm cloud. "You will not tell me what I must do. I must hold my position, Brother, or the entire household will fall to pieces. I am an Overton and I will act like an Overton, even if you do not."

"Margaret, tame your tongue. Someone will hear you."

"I don't care if Beelzebub himself hears me," she shrilled. "I will not have my personal servants interrogated like common thieves."

The constable's voice rumbled from behind William. Catherine couldn't see him but he was unmistakable. "You figure your people to be more holy than ordinary serving folk? I would say they've got nothing to hide, if that be the case."

"Get that man away from me," said Margaret. She snatched up her skirts in one hand and pitched herself through the front door.

Catherine hid herself again to listen. "You see that you have bedeviled

249

my sister into a state," her husband said. "She is a high-strung woman and her moods must be kept in check. She needs quiet and calm."

The constable's voice sounded closer. He was probably standing right at the foot of the stairs. "Quiet and calm is what them dead women are feeling right about now. Quiet and calm 'til the end of time. You want me to stand around cap in hand until some others go finding quiet and calm so that your lady sister there can keep her steady humors? I figure the people will have me stocked if I proceeded in my calling in such a way."

"Can you find no one else? Do you not have suspicious characters down in the village?"

"I figure we got as many suspicious men as the next town, but that skids about the point, sir. Them women was found on your land, on Overton land."

"Any man and his dog can walk through our fields. Christ's nails, that counts for nothing?"

"And any of your servants might have seen such a man and his dog going for their walk, 'specially if he's dragging a dead woman or two. No, sir, I can't leave off. Must have a word with the servants of the house. I've talked to the kitchen maids. Figure I need to talk to them all."

William sighed, and Benjamin spoke from somewhere out of sight. Catherine could not help but look.

"I sat by while he talked to the maids, William. I could do the same with the others."

"No, there are too many. Our house will be out of order for days." William was staring at the closed front door.

"Let the man go about his business," Benjamin urged. "It will be over and done. Perhaps someone did see something."

William turned around and Catherine shrank back. "You are all against me. Very well, take your informations. Be quick about it, and don't disturb my sister, do you hear? And keep those rogues of yours out. All of them."

"I figure I might begin with your lady wife and the other household maids. She has a personal servant, does she not?"

"She does, but she was the caretaker of these women," said William. "It was she who demanded that we find them. And two of them disappeared while she was away. Our daughter is ill. I won't have my daughter's health imperiled."

Silence for a few seconds. "I will begin with the dairy and the stables, then. Them that runs the outbuildings might be more likely to see suspicious movement."

"No," said William. "Start in the house. Have done here first. I need to direct my master of horse about a lame mare of mine just now."

"Who is lame?" asked Benjamin.

"The little one. The one Catherine used to ride sometimes. You may speak to the stable men later."

"You say you need to speak with your master of horse?" The constable wore half a grin.

"I said so. How many times do you need to hear it?"

Peter Grubb stretched one eyebrow upward. "Don't know. What I do know is that your master of horse is in the village with his wife. Been there all the morning."

All was silent again. Catherine risked a glance. William yanked open the front door and surveyed the front courtyard. His silhouette in the light was bent and thin. She would have taken him for an old beggar, come to the house for a morsel or a drink before he went on his solitary, endless pilgrimage.

"Question whoever you want," William said. Then he stepped outside, stooping a little under the sun's sudden glare, and pulled the door closed behind him.

Benjamin said, "You had better make sure you find your murderer, man, or you will answer to me."

57

The house fell quiet, and Catherine slipped down a couple of steps and peered left and right. No constable or Benjamin. No soldiers. No husband. Not even a chamber maid to be seen. No voices. A door boomed closed somewhere in the back of the house, and Catherine ran back up. "Come with me. I want to see what's happening." She trotted to her chamber door, and, Eleanor on her heels, hurried to the window. She stood back far enough not to be viewable from below, but there was no one in the stable yard. Eleanor took hold of the drape on the other side, and Catherine checked her maid's hand.

"Don't. They'll see you. Like this." Catherine skimmed her hand along the edge of the heavy fabric, easing it back enough to gaze down. The leaded panes were cloudy with grime, and for once Catherine was grateful. The constable thumped along in his bent way. Benjamin walked at his side, speaking and pounding his gloves into his palm. The constable ignored him, not stopping until he came to the stable door. Joseph met them, and Eleanor gasped. Catherine touched her elbow. "You know it was not him."

The three men stood close together, Joseph with his arms folded tight against himself. He was shaking his head. The constable pointed in the direction of the woods where Joan had been found, then the gorse patches, and Joseph raised his hand as though warding off a blow. Benjamin touched the constable's shoulder, but the man shook him off and marched past Joseph into the building. The other two men followed.

"Now," whispered Catherine. She cracked the window on her side, and Eleanor mimicked her. "Now step back."

They didn't have long to wait. William came out of the stable, holding one hand against his head, with Margaret. Benjamin and the constable came behind,

252

and Benjamin pulled on the constable's arm, saying "Stop. Good God, he has told you what he knows."

"I figure I will stop when the truth is told," said the constable. "Master Overton, I beg you, don't walk away or I will have to place some of the household under arrest."

"Who do you mean to arrest?" asked William, turning to face him. "Geoffrey isn't under my protection anymore. You know where he is yourself. If you have questions about him, go to his house and ask them."

Margaret bunched her fists against her hips. "You waste your time here and interrupt our household's workings. My sister-in-law brought these women here, and if there is anyone you need to speak to, it is she."

"The Lady Catherine was unchurched yet of her daughter when the first woman disappeared. Is that right?"

Margaret waved her hand to dismiss him. "They were her women and they brought shame and suspicion to our house. Who their enemies were she knows best."

"That's enough, Margaret," said Benjamin. He left the constable's side and took Margaret's elbow. "Come along inside."

Margaret submitted waftily, smiling up as she collapsed against him, and her eyes flicked up to Catherine's window. The two women upstairs stepped back quickly. They exchanged a silent look. Eleanor opened her mouth and Catherine shook her head. She waited a few seconds, then whispered, "Go to your room and take up some embroidery."

Veronica had been quiet all this time, and Catherine laid her gently on the sheets. The baby was pale, and she had shat her clouts in a stinking, dark mess. Catherine cleaned the small bottom and legs and wrapped her in fresh linen. She took the dirty linen to the light and studied it. She frowned and, wrapping the edges to the middle, placed it in on the sill behind the drape and pulled the window shut.

By the time the knock came on the door, Catherine was sitting in the rocker beside the cradle, humming to herself and nursing her child. William hesitated, his hand on the latch. "The constable would like a word with you before he goes."

"I have told him everything I know," said Catherine.

"So I have reminded him."

Margaret slipped in behind her brother. "I can hold the baby for you." She was already in the room with her arms out. "I have already told the man that the village is where he will find his killer. But he does not listen to reason. Go, Sister, and have done with him." She plucked Veronica from Catherine's arms.

The constable was talking to Benjamin by the front door. William led Catherine down the wide front stairs and delivered her up, but he wavered, grasping the banister to steady himself, as they reached the bottom.

"William, you should lie down," said Catherine. "I can answer questions myself." She directed her words to Peter Grubb. "My husband is suffering from a lingering malady and should not be weighted with this matter just now."

William coughed. "I should likely be in isolation."

The constable's eyes flared slightly at this. "You got plague in this house?"

"Go to bed, Husband," Catherine said, and William made his slow way back up. They watched until he was gone. "Now, what more can I tell you?"

"You can tell me why your husband's master of horse is fled of a sudden and all the groomsmen and stable lads got bridles on their tongues. There's something they know, and I'll be damned if I won't know it too."

"Wait," said Catherine. "I must fetch my maid. She and one of the groomsmen are sweethearts." She ran back upstairs to her chamber, expecting to find Margaret rocking the baby, but the chair was empty. She walked through, calling, "Eleanor!"

The maid came out with her embroidery dangling from one hand. "Is he gone?"

"No. I need you downstairs. Where is Margaret?"

"I heard someone go out. I thought it was you."

The constable squinted at Eleanor as she came down the stairs. "You the groomsman's lady?"

Eleanor curtsied with downcast eyes. "I am no lady, sir, but Joseph Adwolfe and I are friends."

"Friends, eh? I figure you are, girl, yes, I suppose you are. So tell me. What do the groomsmen know of these killings? They got the ladies' money and valuables stashed amongst themselves out someplace on the property? Which one of 'em done it, eh? I figure it's got to be one that has strong arms. That isn't your lad. He's a long stick of a boy yet. But I figure he knows which of them is strong-armed. That right, girl?"

Eleanor was shaking all over, and she thrust her hands into her pockets. "I don't . . . no one said a thing . . . .Geoffrey keeps his own counsel, sir. I don't know what he told you."

The constable leaned into her and his face was tight. "But your man does know, don't he? And this Geoffrey is an angry man, I'm figuring. That right?"

Eleanor's eyelids dropped and Catherine pushed her forward again. "Just say what you know," said Catherine. "Tell the truth."

"Joseph's always said Geoff's a good man. They do as they're told. We're not owners, sir, and we don't have a choice." Eleanor gulped and her knees buckled, but she recovered herself.

"No choice? You got no choice in the matter of breaking a woman's neck?"

Now Eleanor buried her face in her hands and sobbed. "I don't know a thing about women's necks."

"Enough," said Benjamin. He had been leaning against the wall by the stairs, and he moved forward into the constable's space, one hand out between the man and the maid. "She's answered your questions. You're torturing the poor girl. Let her be. She's been with her mistress through this entire business."

"Poor girls often know more than they say," said Peter Grubb. "Dainty features can hide gross minds. But I reckon you can go on now, girl. Stay out of the stables for now, though, you hear?"

"Yes, sir." Eleanor curtsied again. "May I go, Madam?" she asked Catherine.

"I will go with you," said Catherine. She put her arm around the smaller woman's shoulders and steered her around. Margaret was standing at the top of the stairs, holding Veronica.

"What is happening down there?" she demanded. "Peter Grubb, are you browbeating our house servants still?"

"I figure I'm done in the house for now," said the constable, bowing. "I will be riding back home for now and asking my questions there. If I have leave to depart, Lady."

Margaret pushed at the air with one neat hand. "Go, go on. Get out of here. Come back when you have a reason to be here."

"Ladies. Sir." The constable bowed twice and backed to the front door. Benjamin opened it for him, and he made his way out backward, as though he were leaving the royal presence. But as soon as the sunshine found him, he turned in the gravel on one heel and hurried to his servant, who was holding his horse in the front courtyard. The other men had vanished.

Benjamin closed the door, and behind it a twist of fresh green air swirled through the entryway. Catherine and Eleanor exhaled. "I said nothing, Madam," said Eleanor. "Does he know that the master and Geoffrey quarreled?"

"I'm sure he's had plenty of conversation with Geoffrey about all kinds of things," said Catherine. She wondered where the other men had gone. Whether Adam Hastings was leading them.

Benjamin was frowning. "That man's going to be back. And you had better be prepared for him to take some one of you with him."

"Will he take Joseph away, do you think, Madam?" piped Eleanor as they went upstairs. "You must speak for him, you cannot let him be locked up."

"We will watch from the window," said Catherine. "I will go for him myself if they try to take Joseph."

Margaret said, "This baby is still unwell," and offered the small bundle. The baby was pale and limp in her aunt's arms.

Catherine's belly seized up. "What's wrong with her?"

"She hasn't cried," said Margaret.

Catherine laid Veronica on the rushes and pulled off the clouts. She rubbed the chubby arms and legs, chafing the skin until the child squealed. Eleanor was bending at her side and Margaret did not move. The baby began to heave, and Catherine flipped her onto her stomach and patted her back until she retched onto the open cloth. The vomit looked sinister, dark and clotted, and Veronica shrilled in agony as the stuff came up. There was no time for privacy this time. Catherine drove her little finger down the tiny throat until her daughter emptied her stomach.

"Madam! You will choke her!" Eleanor knelt beside her.

Margaret said, "Don't throttle the poor child!"

"I'm not throttling her," said Catherine. "I'm getting whatever is making her sick out of her." The baby threw up again, and Catherine gathered a bit of the stuff between her fingers and mashed it flat.

"What is going on here?" Benjamin had come up and he was on his knees next to Catherine. "What are you doing?"

"She is white as death. She is not breathing as she should. She needs to be emptied."

"Should I send for a physician?" Benjamin put his hand on Catherine's arm, and his touch was hot. "I will ride right now if you say yea."

The baby shat loudly, wetly, and cried. Catherine pulled off the rest of the filthy clout and laid it aside. "These are precisely her symptoms from yesterday. She recovered quickly after her body evacuated itself." Catherine picked up the naked baby and held her to her breast. She pressed her lips to the top of Veronica's head. It was salty and damp. "Good. She sweats. It will clear her skin." Catherine let her eyes slide over to Benjamin's. He was very close to her. "I will see to Veronica if you will see to the groomsmen and stable boys. Make sure they're ready for Grubb next time."

Benjamin bowed. "As you order."

She heard his boots clatter down the stone stairs and out the front door. "Well, you have made a conquest there," said Margaret acidly. "I am glad my brother isn't here to witness this."

Catherine's heart rose into her throat and she had no reply. "Come with me, Eleanor." She started for her chamber, then turned. "Eleanor, would you gather up that mass and bring it? I would like to examine it."

Eleanor scooped up the rushes and linens and came trotting along. Margaret called after her, "You must behave like an Overton, Catherine. Stand your ground. Will you hear me?"

Catherine kept walking. Walking like a Havens, she said to herself. Not an Overton.

58

Catherine wiped Veronica's mouth out with water on a soft cloth, and she gagged and cried.

"O, baby, O little love," said Eleanor, watching at her mistress's elbow.

Catherine cleaned the small body of its waste and her daughter's eyes drifted closed.

"Will she be all right?" asked Eleanor.

Catherine laid her hand softly on the Veronica's chest, feeling the rhythm of the rise and fall. "She is breathing normally. Let her recover some and we will see if she eats." She crawled into bed and settled Veronica next to her. "Come in with us."

Eleanor eased herself onto the other side of the mattress and stroked the baby's head. They lay there together, listening to the tiny sounds the baby made between them. Now and then Catherine moved her hand over the child, from chest to belly to forehead, back to chest. Eleanor's eyes closed, and the light lost its grip on the high edge of the wall and began to slip downward. The baby squirmed and opened her eyes, and Catherine scooted into a sitting position. Veronica suckled a little and fell asleep again. Eleanor woke suddenly, sitting up as though she had been caught neglecting her post. "What o'clock is it?"

"Early yet. You slept for perhaps an hour. Veronica has taken some milk."

Eleanor pulled back the blanket and peered at the little white face. "That's a good sign."   "Very good. Where did you put those clouts? The ones from out by the stairs?"

"Here, Madam." Eleanor rolled from the bed and laid them out on the small table by the window.

Catherine joined her and pulled back the curtain. The vomit was dry now, and its evil green hue had paled to grey. "This isn't natural. I have never seen milk curdle to such a color." She raised the clout and sniffed. "It smells like nothing." She laid it down again and regarded the evidence before her. "I have never seen such a thing come out of a child that's not yet weaned. It's strange. Passing strange." She put her hand on her own stomach. "Perhaps it is something in the ale I have drunk. Perhaps the wine has gone off."

A clattering of hooves raised their eyes to the window. The constable had ridden in with a half-dozen men, and they all threw themselves from their saddles and marched forward like soldiers. Joseph met them at the stable door, and Catherine leaned out the open window to hear. She didn't care if they saw her this time. Joseph was raising his hands, saying no, no, and the constable ordered his men to the house. "Spread out and be at all the doors," he said, and Joseph was flung back and held at sword's point when he tried to run for the kitchen.

Eleanor screamed, and a couple of the men looked up, shading their eyes. Catherine pushed her maid back. "Stay here. Come for me at once if Veronica struggles for air or vomits again."

"Where will you be?" Eleanor's eyes were bright with tears, and she wiped her face fiercely with the back of her hand, trying to be brave.

"I will not leave the house without informing you." Catherine ran for the door, and, stopping as she went through, added, "Bolt this behind me."

The men were already in the main hall and the dining gallery, their swords drawn. The servants had disappeared with alarming efficiency, and no one kept the intruders from the interior doors. Catherine came flying down the main stairs and found Benjamin, leaning against the newel post.

"Did you not even try to stop them?" Catherine cried. "Why didn't you stop them?"

Benjamin recoiled from the heat of her anger. "I opened the door," he said simply, but his voice sounded hollow and stunned. "I was having a glass in the gallery and I saw them ride up. No one came to meet them, so I did the service. And they drew on me. Here, in Overton House. Three of them. They are seeking to make arrests."

"You are to be arrested?" Catherine said hotly. "On what charge? You are a guest here."

"Not me," Benjamin said slowly. "Not me." He finally looked full on her.

He was serious indeed.

"Then who?" asked Catherine. "It is not one of our people. Surely not."

Something shrieked like a hare in a falcon's talons, and they both looked up. Peter Grubb appeared at the head of the stairs. He must have taken the back way. He had known which chambers he sought. William was at his side, stooping and pallid, but the cry had not come from his mouth. They came down together and the constable bowed, a little stiffly, to Catherine.

"I must take your husband with me, Madam."

"This is not possible," whispered Catherine. "William?"

"No shackles, you see, Lady," said Grubb. "We will treat him as his station demands. But his man has been talking, and I need the master to answer for him."

"I will go, Catherine," said William. "Let me have this settled. I will not be hunted down." He embraced her swiftly. His body felt like a bag of loose twigs.

"I must come," said Catherine. Two more of the watchmen came out behind Margaret. Her eyes drifted over the group below her, then she straightened. The men followed her down, past Catherine and Benjamin. There was no cry from her now. She was slow as a court lady.

"What do you mean, taking him?" Margaret demanded.

"I've got a man in the village," repeated Peter Grubb. "I figure I need to get 'em together before the stories go racing ever which way. You got aught to say about him, Madam?"

"I have nothing to say to you or any of yours," Margaret said through her teeth. Her hair fell in yellow waves from under her coif, and she tucked it up. Her bodice was loose and one of her sleeves was unlaced. "I will come too." The girl Connie hovered behind her.

"You cannot go into the street like that," said Catherine. "You must cover your hair and fix your dress."

"Get the lady a hood and a cape," said the constable. "No one cares for fashion where we're going today."

Catherine started up the stairs, but Benjamin hooked her elbow. "I will ride with them. You stay here and keep your house calm."

Catherine dared to look into his eyes. He was right. It was the sensible course of action. "Let me get her something to cover herself."

"Run," he said.

Catherine gathered her skirts and bounded upstairs, down the hall, into Margaret's chamber. She grabbed a couple of hoods and capes, snatching up some gloves that lay discarded on a table, and came running back down as the constable was opening the door.

"Here." She thrust the bundle at her sister-in-law. "This will do for the hair."

Margaret twisted her fair hair into a knot and fixed it with its own ends. She threw on a hood, crookedly, and whipped on a cloak. She looked like a dignified scarecrow. She threw the other things at the thick-waisted maid. "Connie, get yourself together."

Benjamin bowed low to Catherine. "I will fly back when there is news." He let his eyes run up her front, and her cheeks were burning by the time his gaze met hers. "I will do what I can to help your husband with this mess. I promise it." He took her hand and she let him have it long enough for a formal touch of the lips upon her knuckles.

Catherine's legs went heavy as brass, but her mind lifted, light and feathery. Half in hell, half striving for heaven. "Benjamin—"

He pulled on his gloves. "I know," he said, misunderstanding. He did not look at her but hesitated at the open door. "I will do what I can."

59

Eleanor was jiggling the baby to keep her quiet when Catherine came back up, asking "Has anyone been here? Any of the watchmen?"

"Not a one, Madam. I heard them go by, and I heard Lady Margaret, then all was still. What is it? Have they taken my Joseph?"

"No. They took William, and Benjamin has followed. Margaret went with them. Stay here. Keep the door shut and locked in case they return." She pulled at the blanket. "How is Veronica?"

"She sleeps like the angel she is." Eleanor showed the baby's pink face. Her lashes lay on her cheeks like brushstrokes. A thin rind of white crust had dried around her perfectly arched nostrils, but it was not fresh.

"Does she breathe like a normal infant?"

"As regular as a clock." She bounced Veronica a few more times. "You will not let them arrest Joseph?"

"They haven't taken him, I say. I will return shortly. Call out if you need me."

"But Madam—"

"No arguments. I will be with you in a few minutes."

Eleanor, nodding, flitted off down the little hall to her sleeping room. Catherine opened the heavy door and slipped out. She listened for a few beats, but the house servants were still in hiding. Not even a chamber maid with a pot to be seen. She ran on her toes down the hall to William's open rooms. If she was discovered, she wanted to be alone.

William's brother Robert had had these rooms before he died, and they were still lush with the family furnishings. The house maids kept the clothes brushed and folded. The bed had two feather mattresses, and Catherine yanked

262

the curtains aside and put her hand on the spread, thinking she would need a small ladder to climb into the thing. The chests contained nothing of note, no books or writing paper or secret letters. Catherine squatted next to a small cabinet and bethought herself. What did she think she would find in here? She picked at the lavender stems strewing the floor and felt a twinge of guilt in her gut. Benjamin was doing something useful, down in the village, trying to help find the truth. Catherine was stealing about the house, looking for God knew what. She sat, gazing around the sweet-smelling room.

"Madam? Can I be of service?"

Catherine's heart skidded and she looked up to see Reg Goodall, holding out a hand to help her to her feet. She said, "Why are you here?"

"I live here," he said simply. Then he sat on a nearby stool and folded his hands into the space between his knees and studied his knuckles. "Is there something I could assist you in finding?"

Suddenly unable to endure her shame, Catherine swept the herbs back into place under her feet and sat on the floor. "What's happening, Reg? What do you know?"

The man shook his long head. "Not enough to make an accusation." He unhooked his fingers and flicked them at the bed. "You seem to have pushed some of the girls' fresh rushes underneath where they do no one any good."

"What?" Catherine had accidentally shoved a few stems under the bed in kneeling to search the lower drawers. "Will you order me?" But Reg cast his eyes away, and as Catherine dragged the stems out again, her hand touched a linen bag. It came out with the rushes. Catherine gnawed her lip, looking at it. It was nothing. It probably contained dried rose petals. Reg said nothing.

"I am damned for a nosy hag anyway," Catherine muttered to herself. She pulled the drawstring open. A smaller pouch fell out, tied at the neck with string. It was damp, and dried leaves clung to it. Catherine's feet and hands went cold, and she fumbled at the knot. It was fast, and she tucked it back into the larger bag. "What do you know of this?"

"I saw Master William place it there. That is all." He stood and stumbled into the side room without ceremony, pulling the door closed behind him.

Catherine ran down the hall and pounded on her chamber door until Eleanor opened it, trembling and white-faced. "What is it, Madam? What?"

Catherine pushed her backward into the room. Eleanor was panting with fear. "Are the watchmen going to take us, too? I have done nothing, Madam, nothing." Her voice thinned to a trickle of sound and soon she was moaning.

"Eleanor, look at this. Tell me what you think this is. Use your judgment. What you have learned."

"What?" The girl stopped shaking. She still had the sleeping Veronica in her arms, and she wiped her eyes on the corner of the blanket. "What is it you have found?"

Catherine went to her dressing table and, moving the ewer aside, shook out a clean napkin and spread it, smoothing the corners. "Hand me your knife," she said, and Eleanor dug in her pocket and laid the instrument into her mistress's palm. Catherine pulled out the small pouch and ripped through its neck. She dumped the contents onto the white cloth, then the drier bits from the larger pouch, and picked through them with the sharp tip. A few shriveled berries lay, blackened, in the mass.

Eleanor bent over her shoulder with interest. "What is that? It looks like something little Robert's Thomasina threw up."

"If that cat had eaten this, she would need to throw it up." Catherine lifted a small, wilted leaf on the blade and held it to the light. It was almost unrecognizable. Almost. "That is nightshade, by my soul. And I wager the berries are mashed in here as well." She put her nose close to the sodden pouch and inhaled. "Sweet heart of Mary, this is poison through and through." She gingerly laid her tongue on the surface of the linen bag. Sweet. "This has been dipped in honey."

Eleanor stepped backward, clutching the baby to her chest. "Where was it?"

Catherine sat back, trying to make sense of it. "Under William's bed in the big chamber. It's most irregular. If he meant to poison himself, why not do it and be done with the business?" Catherine rubbed the leaves between her fingers and spoke, more to herself than to her maid. "It's sweet. Very sweet." Catherine looked over at the sleeping baby. "Oh my God," she whispered.

60

"We must find your Joseph," said Catherine. "Now." She folded the linen into a flat package and returned it to her pocket. She dragged the drape back farther and scanned the stable yard below but she saw no one. "Reg!" she called, running into the hall. "Reg, I say!"

"Joseph will not be taken." There was a tinge of the brag in Eleanor's voice, and her chin went up a little.

"He'd do well to learn better than that," said Catherine, but at Eleanor's dropped head, she added, "because even brave men find themselves on the block these days."

"I know where he is," said Eleanor.

"Lead on," said Catherine, taking Veronica from her arms. Reg was in the hall, and he followed the women.

The stable was fresh with the scent of new hay and horse sweat, and a clean breeze gusted from front door to back, but there was not a groomsman in sight. The horses were out at pasture for the day, but someone should have been cleaning the boxes or oiling harness. Catherine called out a hallo, but it echoed away with the cry of a swallow as it swooped a dark spiral and flew outside.

"He's not here," she said.

Eleanor crept through the main corridor to a small room at the back of the building. Catherine followed her through the door, which stood slightly ajar, the rope loop unlatched from its wooden knob. Bridles and bits and long strands of leather harness were shelved and hung on all the walls, almost concealing a narrow, steep set of steps at the far end. Eleanor climbed up and poked her head into the loft. All Catherine could see of her were her worn boots and her skirt's hem. After a few seconds, Eleanor went all the way up and Catherine waited.

Before Catherine could count fifty, a pair of brown shoes stepped down, followed by a pair of dirt-streaked hose and dark breeches. Joseph bent to show his face. "Please come up, Madam, if you would like."

"I have rather a burden here," Catherine said, showing the baby.

"Bring her on, if you please." He went up again, and Reg, behind Catherine, said, "I will wait here and keep the watch."

Catherine peered up and saw Eleanor staring down.

"I'll take her, Madam. Just come this way a little." Eleanor knelt for Veronica, and Catherine climbed. The passage reminded her of the narrow steps to the room over the church porch in her old convent, and she suddenly felt peaceful. A corner of the loft had become Joseph's private spot, and he had fashioned himself a rough bench against the wall where he could gaze through a high window over the west fields. He kept a cup and plate nearby, and a set of polished tools. From here, the fields seemed endless and gently fruitful, great swathes of green and gold, punctuated with knots of sheep in their pastures. Catherine thought of the draperies that William had meant to put into service down at Mount Grace, and her throat thickened with sorrow. Eleanor and Joseph sat knee against knee on the crude bench, Veronica on Eleanor's lap. "By my troth, you look like the holy family." Catherine coughed a bitter, short laugh. "We had better hide you indeed, or some soldier will put you to the sword for a pair of icons."

Joseph squinted up at her. "There's goings on around here that aren't holy, Madam. Not at all. I s'pose I come here to get away from it and find some kind of truth." He opened his hands and revealed his calloused palms. "Eleanor tells me that you're gentle, Madam, and that you don't set your foot on the heads of the lower sorts. That you have loved her like a sister and that you don't always speak as ladies speak. You don't always speak in accord with the king of this land."

"My breeding is no better than yours," Catherine said, "though my mother claimed a good birthright. So here I am, caught between heaven and hell, like every other mortal." She pulled out a three-legged stool and perched on it. Eleanor was stroking Veronica's head and the baby was grinning up at her in thoughtless delight. Eleanor leaned her head briefly against Joseph's shoulder, and he patted the side of her hood. Any doubts Catherine had of the man fled in a moment.

"We don't all have a village named for us, though, do we, Madam?"

Catherine smiled, but Joseph was sober-faced, waiting for her to answer.

"The prioress made sure I had learning and some measure of freedom. If we had not had the convent, she could not have done so." Catherine shrugged. "But she died a shameful death and her memory is stained among those who knew her. So what I learned in the end is that anyone can learn and anyone can sin. Priest or prioress. Or king. And I will be a bastard in some people's eyes no matter how fine my dress." She pinched a corner of her embroidered sleeve. "Or how many villages bear my family's name."

He regarded her with a wary eye. "Some do speak of calling the village Overton."

Catherine nodded. "Joseph, did the constable stop you because of Geoffrey?"

The young man sat back. "Maybe."

"What is he saying?"

Eleanor nudged Joseph. "Go on. You're in too far to back out. Tell it, so that the finger doesn't get pointed at you."

"Me?" Joseph leapt to his feet, showing his palms again. "You think I could do such a deed with these hands? I can work a piece of wood or leather, but I have never killed anything bigger than a partridge."

"You talk of killing?" Catherine asked. "I have not accused you."

Joseph sat again with a sigh. Dust burst around him and he waited until it settled. "I didn't see. But I heard. I heard them talking. Up here, you can hear anything from down below. And not a soul can see. I come here to whittle. To think. They didn't know I was here. I never saw anything. But I heard plenty. And I have held my peace as long as my conscience will allow it."

"Tell me," said Catherine. "Tell it all before we go to the constable."

61

When the small party rode around Peter Grubb's house to the courtyard behind it, Benjamin's Caesar whinnied from the stable. Joseph jumped down from his gelding and handed his reins over to the wide-eyed stable boy. Reg was on the ground already, putting out a hand for Catherine. He helped her to the ground expertly, his touch on her waist neither too light nor too familiar. Eleanor jumped from her fat cob without assistance.

"We've had more folks here the last couple days than in the last year," said the boy. "Don't think I've had so many horses to feed in my life." He led the new horses to the boxes next to Caesar's.

The constable's manservant had opened the door by the time they walked up, brushing the dust from their clothes. "Lady Overton," he said evenly. He bowed minimally and stood aside.

Benjamin stood in the cramped entryway. He was not smiling. "What are you doing here? What do you do with the child in this place?"

"We couldn't very well leave her with the kitchen maids," said Catherine, pulling off her gloves and handing them to the servant. "We had no idea when we'd be back. Where is he?"

"Down at the inn," said Peter Grubb, coming from the sitting room, "though I figure I have the authority to imprison man or maid, whatever the station." He crossed his arms with satisfaction. "Master Benjamin here was telling me that I should disregard the counsel of a horse man. The horse master says he's under a compulsion. Lady Margaret keeps saying your name, Lady Overton, and here you are, like a conjured thing. What have you got to tell me?"

The entryway was airless, and the smell of wax and sweat and wool was making Catherine nauseous. "Give me some room to breathe," she said, pushing past the constable to the larger room. She stopped in the middle of the musty rug. The rest of the company crowded in behind her. "I must speak to Benjamin alone."

"I figure anything you got to say can be said before me," said Peter Grubb. "Or it will be said before the Justice."

"What Justice? There's no court in session," said Catherine. She clutched the package in her pocket.

"Justice Sillon is coming from Mount Grace. He ought to be here on the morrow. He knows of these Overtons and what they get in to. He'll hear the evidence." He grinned, a triumphant gleam in his eye. "I think you know the man."

"He dismissed the charges against William before," said Catherine, but her heart was knocking in her chest and her hand was cramping around the bundle in her pocket. "I will say nothing until I have seen Master Davies alone. I am not under arrest, and I am free to talk with my houseguest if I please."

"Not in our home, you aren't." Mistress Grubb had come in the other door and had planted herself, arms under the shelf of her bosom, behind Catherine.

"Very well. Am I to be detained?"

"Not yet," said Peter Grubb.

"Eleanor, stay here with Joseph."

Eleanor hugged the baby to her chest. "Of course, Madam."

"Master Davies?" Catherine offered Benjamin her elbow, and he stepped over to claim her arm.

They walked down the middle of the high road side by side. She looked neither right nor left, unwilling to meet the looks from windows and doors as they passed. Her boots raised a storm of dust as they went, silent for a hundred yards or more.

"It pleases me to be the one you turn to in need," Benjamin said.

"Don't. Don't speak of it," said Catherine. No one came out of doors. Havenston, indeed. She wondered if anyone knew who her mother had been. If anyone cared. "Where is William?"

"Grubb let him go on his honor." They walked on, Benjamin keeping to Catherine's pace. "What news?" he asked at last. "Something has happened."

"Geoffrey claims to have a story, doesn't he?"

"Mm, he does," said Benjamin. They were nearing the inn, and he cocked his head in its direction. "There's talk. Be ready if anyone sees us."

A figure moved across a downstairs window, but the sun spangled against the leaded panes, and Catherine couldn't see who it was.

Benjamin said, "Geoff's gone back to his mother's house, but he acts like a dead man already. Your Grubb wouldn't rack him, would he?"

"Rack him? This isn't London, Benjamin."

The man shrugged. "Or whatever threats your constable has to hand."

"What has he said?"

"Geoff White? That William wanted the women dead. That he was paid to do it."

Catherine felt the words like a blow to the chest. She staggered backward a step and Benjamin caught her wrist. She was dizzy and the sun came down on her head with a vicious heat. "He says that William gave him money? To kill?"

"He said that instructions were left for him when William was too ill to come down. Your constable made him prove he could read enough for this to be true. He can read. He said the messages were sealed with the Overton mark."

Catherine's throat was as parched as a roll of old linen, and she fought to swallow a wad of bile. The sky was scarred with cloud, and she put her hand over her eyes so that she wouldn't see it. "Where are the men?"

Benjamin looked away. "Which men?"

They'd reached the far village gate, and Catherine put her hand on the squat stone pillar to steady herself. A sleek weasel burrowed into the underbrush, and she saw the tip of its tail disappear. She thought she might vomit. "You know which men. The king's men. Cromwell's men." Silence for a few seconds. "Adam Hastings."

"Come, let's walk back," said Benjamin. "You need some shady place to sit and something to drink. You're pale as vellum."

"Wait." The road before them was empty, the light thick and shifting with motes.

"You need to be out of the heat. You need your strength, Catherine."

"And what does Margaret say to this charge? She has been in the house the whole time."

Benjamin contemplated the road. "Margaret is all smooth cream and sugar, blinking like a newborn kitten." He wiped the sweat from his forehead. "You know, I think she means to have me marry her."

"If you do, you will have to become an Overton."

"God's blood, I can think of lesser reasons than that to refuse her." He took Catherine's arm for the return. "The men you ask about are quartered at the inn. Geoffrey's been among them. Don't provoke them and they'll go. There's no reason for them to stay."

Catherine was shaking, but she had to ask. "Who will be arrested?"

"Maybe no one. It depends on what the charges are. No one will care about dead women if they are proved to have been witches. Or Roman."

"So the suspicion falls upon me next."

"Not for murder. It's clear that you were at Hatfield when the last two were killed." Benjamin pulled on her arm. "But you are better off if you don't appear to be hiding anything."

"I will hide from no one. But Benjamin, I want to say—"

"Don't. Whatever it is. Don't. Not now. Let's go back."

"Wait," Catherine said, drawing back. "I have something to show you before we return."

62

The light was fallen deep into the west by the time Benjamin and Catherine returned. Catherine did not lift her eyes to the inn, though she could feel the men at the windows. He was in there. She knew it. She tugged her hood closer to her cheeks and walked on.

Eleanor and Joseph were waiting for them in Peter Grubb's yard, and the young pair seemed to sag under the dismal leftovers of the sun. Reg was leaning against the doorframe of the stable, looking out at nothing. Catherine took Eleanor aside. "I have told Benjamin all. You get your man and go home."

Eleanor bobbed her head. "Yes, Madam." She started away, then turned. "We will all be a family."

"All of you?"

Eleanor nodded, and Catherine said, "That, at least, is decided."

Eleanor whispered, "But my father will not be asked to give me away."

"No? Why not?" Catherine asked, but when she saw Eleanor's eyes, she knew. "He is your father in blood?"

Shame streaked Eleanor's cheeks. "Yes. I could not bear to have him at my wedding."

So that was it. "God, what men will do, thinking no one sees." Catherine put her head back to smell the clean air. "No. He will not be there," she said. "I will strike him if he shows his face."

The night was already coming down like a heavy curtain, the stars punching through the fabric of the darkening sky. Joseph gathered the horses, and Eleanor said, "Shall I take Veronica?"

"I'll keep her. Come back in the morning." The sky had blackened at its eastern edge, and Catherine had to squint to see her maid as she rode off. She was still watching and listening to the silence when Benjamin touched her arm. The baby squirmed, stinking in her dirty clouts, and Catherine stretched out her arms to let the child kick. "I need to clean her."

"You will want to sup, Catherine. Let's go inside." Benjamin pushed open the door with his arm and met Peter Grubb in the narrow front hall. "The lady needs food," he said, "and a place to bathe her child."

"Well, come on, then. Mistress Grubb! Get these folks some supper." The constable led them back into his sitting room and flung his arm toward a side room. "There's water on the side board."

Catherine took the child into the bedchamber and wiped her down as best she could. She had only one fresh clout, and she folded the soiled one into a tight square and, slipping past the men, delivered it to Mistress Grubb in the kitchen.

"Poor mite," said Mistress Grubb. "You sit there, Madam, and rest yourself." Her voice was softer than it had been, and Catherine sank gratefully onto a stool. Eleanor must have spoken to her. She gave the baby a breast and the constable's wife cast a smile over her shoulder. "There's a good girl." Catherine couldn't determine which one of them she meant.

Benjamin was standing at the window when the women joined them in the front room. Peter Grubb waited while his wife laid bread and cheese on the table. "Got wine for the lady?" he asked, and she clucked at him.

"Of course, Husband," said Mistress Grubb. "I'm not a fool." She fetched both ale and wine. Catherine let the constable pour her a goblet and drank deeply.

"Where does William stay for the night?" Catherine asked. The house seemed too small to hold many beds.

"Don't know. Haven't seen 'im. You may stay here. The hour is too late for a woman to ride and the inn is dirty."

Benjamin was already standing, wiping his mouth. "You stay here. Upstairs. I will return on the morrow."

"Where is Margaret?" asked Catherine.

"Already taken to her bed. In the back. You wanting to share with her?"

"I wouldn't wake her if you have another bed," said Catherine.

Benjamin was pulling on his cloak and was through the door before Peter Grubb could get out from behind the table.

Catherine retired early and lay on the thin mattress, watching a moth beat itself against a crack in the door, trying to get at the candles downstairs. Veronica keened in her sleep, and Catherine gathered her closer. No sound from the village beyond the half-closed shutters. No light from the knife-edge of moon that tilted its blade at her. The Grubbs were talking somewhere below, but Catherine couldn't make out the words, and she finally threw off the cover and made her way to the window.

The night was clear, but she could see no movement in the high road, and if there was brawling at the inn, she surely could have heard it. A door opened below, and Catherine stepped away from the sill, but it was only Grubb, tromping to the bushes to take a leisurely piss. He sighed, and Catherine crawled back into bed. She wished she had asked Eleanor to stay with her.

She must have slept, because she opened her eyes to a pale early sun. The door opened, and Catherine sat up, scrubbing her face. Mistress Grubb poked her head inside. "There's men, here, Madam. Feed the baby, then you let me take her."

Catherine could hear Peter Grubb talking to another man, but Mistress Grubb kept her attention on Catherine, helping her dress before she disappeared down the back steps to the kitchen with Veronica. Catherine descended alone.

Peter Grubb was in conversation with Kit Sillon, but before Catherine could speak, John Bridle came scurrying in, throwing off a cloak. "Daughter," he said. "What are you doing here?"

"Father, I might ask the same of you."

"You think the priest doesn't know when the Justice is called to his daughter's village?"

Kit Sillon acted as though he'd been interrupted at his mug of ale. "Where's that Overton woman?"

"Here," ventured Catherine, raising her hand.

"Not you. The other one."

"Not awake yet," said Grubb.

"And this horse man?"

"At his mother's."

"Get them down here, will you? Or do we have to go find them? And have you got a clerk who can write more than his name?"

"They's more room in a public place," said Grubb. He went to the front door and stared out at the high road. "The innkeeper acts as my clerk. He can write a fair enough hand."

"Let's go, then," said John Bridle. He already had Catherine by the arm. He pulled her outside, and Grubb followed. They were at the gate before Sillon emerged, fumbling with his cloak and cursing under his breath.

The road to the inn seemed endless, but in the large front room, Benjamin Davies sat at a worn table with Geoffrey White. He rose when he saw Catherine.

"That's not William Overton," said Sillon.

"Benjamin Davies." Benjamin bowed with a slight flourish. Geoffrey didn't look up from his cup.

"What good are you? And where's William Overton?" asked Kit Sillon.

The innkeeper stuck his head into the room, and ducked out again.

"He's out," said Benjamin. "This is his master of horse. Geoffrey White."

"All right then," the Justice said. "Geoffrey White. Where's that damned clerk?"

The innkeeper scuttled back in, a pot of ink and a quill in his hands. He'd taken off the apron, and his breeches flapped, unbuttoned, at the front. "Here, Your Honor Sir. Right here."

Sillon cast a long look up and down the man. "Does anyone in this place own a clean sheet of paper?"

"Yes, yes, Sir, Your Honor, I keep some paper right here." The ink sloshed as the innkeeper slid it onto the table and ran to a cupboard for paper. Returning, he discovered the state of his breeches, and stood, quill in one hand and paper in the other, unable to decide how to proceed. Finally, he walked to the table as though the garment was meant to hang loose and flung himself onto a stool.

Kit Sillon sighed and turned his attention to Geoffrey White. "You. You have admitted to the murders committed at Overton Hall these last months. Is that the case?"

Geoffrey looked around. "I said was ordered to it. I didn't care about those women one way or 'tother. They were nothing to me. But I needed my position. That's all."

How dare you?" cried Catherine. "What have you said about your master? Hasn't he always treated you fairly? And him sick in his bed these weeks?"

"I knew William Overton," added Benjamin. "And you will say this before my face?"

"Yours or any other man's face," said Geoffrey, impassive.

The innkeeper trimmed his pen, and as he dipped the point into the ink, Margaret swished in from behind him, twitching her skirt around her ankles.

"Or woman's," Geoffrey said.

Kit Sillon coughed. "You say that this man, William Overton, your master and a man with no stain upon his reputation, ordered you to murder four women of his house with your bare hands and paid you to perform it."

"Just say the simple truth, man," said Peter Grubb. "Say it like you said it before."

Geoffrey gulped and now he wiped his brow. "The lady's right. Master Overton is a good master. A fair man. But he said the women from the convents were talked of. He said once that he wished his wife would leave that life behind and be a lady like other ladies. He said he had a hard enough time being a gentleman. Filling his dead brother's boots, like."

Peter Grubb scowled. "This doesn't sound quite the same as what you told me yesterday."

"No, I say the same," insisted Geoffrey. "I say the man was a fair master. Then the package came. The first one was left in my room. A message and a coin."

The constable raised his hand and came forward a step. "Wait right there. This isn't at all what you said before. You said the woman brought the package."

"What woman?" asked Catherine, but the horse master rushed on.

"Yes," White said. "The second time. The master had fell ill in his bed. She put it in my hand when she took her mare out. Said I would know where it come from."

"Who?" Catherine asked again.

"Be calm, Madam," said the Justice. "Let your man finish his story."

Catherine was shaking, and she plopped onto a stool, gripping her skirt to hold her knees still.

"Now, sir. Go on. What did these messages say?"

"They were simple. 'Get rid of the women. Make sure no one finds them.'"

"Were the women named?"

"Yes. Both times."

"You knew the script?"

Geoffrey scratched his chin at this. "Looked like a gentleman's writing to me. Wouldn't swear to it."

"William would write no such message," said Catherine. "Good God above, will my husband be hanged on the word of a man who cannot recognize his hand? Geoffrey, you never heard him say that he wanted you to do a murder. You didn't hear that from his mouth. Say you did not."

Geoffrey jutted his chin. "Not in so many words. He said enough about them women, though. About them bringing the king's soldiers down on us if we wasn't careful. About his wife being more nun than lady. He said it." Geoffrey suddenly directed his words to Margaret. "You know. You know he did. You told me he did."

The front door opened and Joseph Adwolfe stood there, with Eleanor behind him.

"You'll second me, won't you, Joseph?" asked Geoffrey. "You saw the packages. You heard the man speak."

Joseph scanned the room. "I would rather speak with the master present. I might have heard voices in the stable, but I would like to say so to the man's face."

Geoffrey's color was high, and his hand went to his side where his dagger would have been, but he had no sidearm and he clenched his fists.

"A man says idle things," said Joseph. "No one made you kill anyone. No man, anyway. Where is Master William?"

"And Lady Margaret," interrupted Kit Sillon. "We need to hear from you now. What say you?"

Catherine's hand tingled, and she drove it into her pocket. Benjamin placed his fingers on her arm.

Margaret said, "Don't speak to me of secret messages and packages. What do I know of packages?" She turned to Catherine. "William was almost upon his knees begging you to leave off your Papist ways, but you would have your nunnery right under our very noses. I have worked myself to a nub trying to be your loving kinswoman. But having those women in the house. Calling each other 'Sister' and studying and translating and setting yourselves up as physicians and teachers rather than getting them husbands as our king requires." She lifted her chin. "Some might call it treason."

Catherine sprang to her feet. "I have the king's own warrant for my marriage."

Margaret's face hardened. "My brother only married you to give you a father for your bastard. You lay with a strange man and passed your sin off onto the Overton house. You are no Overton. You are a whore and the bastard child of a whore. And your son is a bastard too. He is not an Overton and William knows it."

The room went as silent as a sky before storm. A shrill wind cut through it, and Catherine covered her ears. It whistled, then it screamed, and then she realized that it was her own voice. She whipped around and pointed at Geoffrey. "My son! My little boy! You, you are the one who put him in those stirrups! Did she tell you to murder my child? My little Robert?"

Peter Grubb blinked. Kit Sillon wrote something down, then he beckoned to the constable, whispered something in his ear, and sent him out.

The panic came up in Catherine's throat like a sickness and she grabbed at her pocket. She flung the pouch into the open space. "This package you say you got from my husband. Did it look anything like that?"

63

The linen pouch of poison landed on the table in front of Peter Grubb. Kit Sillon put out his hand and the constable laid it into his palm. The Justice turned the package over. Squeezed it. "This has been in the water, Lady Overton?"

"No," said Catherine.

"How came it to be dampened? And what is its significance?"

"Smell of it," said Catherine, and she waited while the Justice put it to his nose. His face pruned for a moment and he held the thing at arm's length. "You will perceive," Catherine continued, "that the pouch contains elements that are repellent to the nose. If you will open it carefully, you will find a small pap of noisome plants. The child fell ill and I could discover no cause. After the constable seized upon my husband, I found this under his bed. The fabric has been sweetened, but the contents are noxious."

The Justice hefted the pouch gently, as though it were a plaything. "But the daughter has not been part of the question here, has she?"

"No. But she is an heir. Undeniably."

"And you believe your husband wanted to kill his heir?" Sillon set the bag on the table and spun it with one finger. "And what of your son? You say that the boy is a bastard?"

"She said no such thing," said Benjamin, "but Margaret certainly said it."

"The packages for me looked nothing like that," Geoff said quietly.

"Why poison the girl?" Sillon set down the pouch and wiped his fingers on his napkin.

Benjamin said, "Where is William? Bring him and all will come clear. Joseph, you run down the road and look for your master."

Joseph looked to the constable, and Peter Grubb looked to the Justice. "Go,

279

boy," said Kit Sillon with a wave of one hand. "Find him."

Joseph scooted out the door, and Peter Grubb lifted the pouch with two fingers. "Perhaps the mother wanted to be free of the child. A child can be a trial to a woman's patience." He didn't look at Catherine.

"Forgive me for speaking out of turn," said Eleanor, rising to her feet. "But that is the worst of slander. My mistress loves her daughter more tenderly than ever mother loved child. She nurses the baby at her own breast. She would no more give her poison than she would take it herself. I saw. I saw the baby fall ill. I saw my mistress fall ill. I'm wondering what is making the master stay down. I'm wondering if his sickness is not in his conscience."

"You hold your tongue around your betters," said Grubb. "You will not give evidence. You are a servant."

Eleanor set her teeth upon her lower lip and sat.

Kit Sillon opened the pouch with a slice of his hand knife. He stirred the contents with one finger. "She seems to have given her evidence already, Grubb, and you seem to think questioning of servants to be allowable when it goes toward your interests." He lifted one hand toward Geoffrey White without looking up. "I don't see how Lady Catherine Overton can be both keeper of the royal daughters at Hatfield and killer of her women here. Which is it?"

"She has books of venoms," said Grubb.

"Mm," said Sillon. "Perhaps she has."

John Bridle cleared his throat. "She inherited them from her mother. The convent had need for poisons." Everyone was looking at him. "For mice and such."

"Mm," said Sillon again. "Rodents. I see. And how did you know of these volumes, Grubb?"

The constable's thick nostrils flared a little and he stammered out "Lady Overton told me. The other Lady Overton. Margaret."

Kit Sillon looked up. "Margaret Overton, you can read. Is that correct?"

Margaret almost snorted. "Of course I can read. We are not savages here."

"It's the other lady who keeps the books," said Peter Grubb. "She has pages and pages of receipts for poison."

"Is this true?" Kit Sillon had a dab of dried leaves on the tip of his forefinger, and he held it to the light. His eyes met Catherine's. "Well?"

"I have books. They are in my still room. They are not kept under lock and key. They were my mother's before they were mine, as my father has just said. They offer receipts, but they also describe signs and reliefs. I know how to use them. Whoever made that package did not. The substance made the child ill. It did not kill her, thank God. Only someone who was unused to working with noxious elements would be so careless. Or perhaps the stronger elements had been used elsewhere already. Eleanor is correct to say that my husband's symptoms have been mysterious. I was the last to fall ill, but I was only sick in the stomach for some few hours."

"That is a slander," said Margaret. "How dare you accuse your husband of so base an act as killing?"

"I accused no one of killing. I spoke of incompetence," said Catherine.

"All right, ladies," said Sillon. His gaze shifted to Grubb. "And how do you know so much of what is in these books?"

The man shook his head wildly. "I don't know how I know. Where is that William Overton?"

"That is a piece of information you should already have." Kit Sillon sighed and closed up the little package. No one spoke and he said, "Geoffrey White, have you any evidence aside from the word of a messenger woman that William Overton ordered you to commit these murders?"

Geoffrey said, "She gave me her word."

"And you in fact did the deed?"

"Under orders, as I have said. And it has cost me my position and my home. My own wife and mother have turned their faces from me."

"Orders by messenger." Sillon looked up. "   And who was she? Is she still alive?"

Geoffrey White snorted. "Alive and standing before you, sir. She's right there." He pointed at Margaret Overton.

"I?" said Margaret. "If I delivered any messages to you, White, I assure you I did not break my brother's seal and read them."

Kit Sillon ordered one of the watchmen with a crook of his arm, who took hold of the master of horse. "Geoffrey White, it seems you are guilty of four murders. Constable Grubb, go find William Overton, will you?"

The front door swung open and everyone looked toward the light, but it wasn't William. Instead, Joseph stood before them. "Come, sirs, if you please. Pray, come. There's killing going on outdoors." Joseph put out his hand as

Catherine ran to the door. "Let the men go without you. I beg you, Madam."

Benjamin and Geoffrey White were already running down the high road, and Peter Grubb waddled off behind them. Kit Sillon walked as far as the gate and watched, one hand clapped against his forehead. John Bridle waited beside him.

"Let me go," Catherine said.

Eleanor was at her other side. "Joseph says no. Stay here."

"Joseph doesn't command me." Catherine yanked herself loose and ran out, past the Justice and her father. She could see them already. Two men facing off at the end of the road. She knew William's stance even at this distance.

A small crowd had gathered, and Catherine came up behind a trio of women. One of them glanced back and stepped aside to let her through.

Someone said, "Who claims I am the father of her son?" and Catherine shoved between two more women to see. The speaker was Adam Hastings. He was dark-haired, like Catherine, still wiry and boyish. He swung his hips forward and massaged the pommel of his sword. He grinned at William. Hastings was surrounded by men in bright shirts and soft breeches. Catherine got close enough to her husband to smell the rancid sweat on him. She couldn't see Benjamin or Geoffrey.

"Overton, my man, you look like Belial's breakfast," Hastings said.

William did not move. "Leave this place, Hastings. Turn and go and don't say a word more. Not one."

Catherine's skin felt licked with flame. She stared hard at Adam Hastings, but his gaze washed over her with barely a flicker of recognition. He still smirked at William and now he massaged his codpiece thoughtfully. "You'll have to show me. Who's the lady I have favored?"

With that, William was at him. Catherine grabbed for his cloak and Benjamin flashed by her side, but William was too fast. Adam Hastings saw him coming. Before he could maneuver his sword forward, though, William was on him and had run his own blade into his gut up to the hilt.

"You will shut your damned mouth now," William said, backing off. He stumbled a step and lost his footing, catching himself with one hand on the ground.

But Hastings had not fallen, and as William righted himself, Adam, still standing in astonishment and as yet unaware of the wound's depth, moved his sword out and forward. When he drew back, William, caught on the blade, moved with him in a horrific dance. Catherine screamed, and then the two men were facing each other, attached by the sword for a moment, before Adam staggered backward, pulling his weapon free as he fell.

"I have killed you, then," said William. He sat, hard, and put his hand over the stain that was spreading over his shirt. "That's enough." Dark blood leaked through his fingers. He turned. He saw Catherine first but his eyes went beyond her, and she turned, too, to see Kit Sillon behind her. "And now," said William, "you may arrest me for your murderer and let the others go."

He wavered, his eyes closing, and Catherine helped him down to the gravel, laying her face on his chest. "William," she whispered, "what have you done?"

"I have tried to be your husband and my father's son," said William. "I have failed at both. I cannot even bring myself to death without making a botch of it."

"Did you order my women murdered? Did you make the poison yourself? In that pouch?"

"You found it?" His hand drifted to his forehead, then fell into the dirt. "Oh, Catherine, I know nothing of poisons. That's woman's work. But she would have regretted it. I took it away to save her. Forgive me. Forgive her." His vision wavered, then settled on her eyes again. "I spoke harsh words. I am responsible for my house. Give us your forgiveness, Wife."

Hands were pulling at Catherine, and she heard something shrieking like a wind-storm, but when she was lifted, the sunlight was bright across the road. Benjamin and Father John were holding her up, and her husband lay beneath her. "Get the woman away," Kit Sillon was saying from beyond her somewhere.

"No, no, let me tend to him," she shouted, but Father John said, "Catherine, there is nothing you can do."

The way was cluttered with people, and Benjamin drew his sword at them as he dragged Catherine along. "Get back, all of you," he shouted, "or I will make dog's meat of you."

The crowd backed off, muttering and glowering. Someone said "murderer," and someone else hissed.

"Get back, I say," Benjamin repeated, and they retreated, but only far enough to stay his hand.

Eleanor came running from the inn to Catherine and held her arm. "What has happened? Madam?"

The light was white in her eyes, and Catherine heard her own voice from a long distance away. It said, "He's dead. He's killed."

"Who?" asked Joseph.

"William," said the priest. "Come, bring her in from the sun."

Catherine was full of blinding clouds, and a wind whistled through her head. "I must see to him. I must tend him."

John Bridle eased her through the door and onto a stool. "He is beyond all that, now, Daughter. Drink this."

She looked at the mug of ale in his hand but did not take it. "Margaret," Catherine said. "Where is she?"

64

"Margaret Overton is not here," said the innkeeper. He'd searched both building and grounds, and now waited in the front room for instructions.

Kit Sillon shook his head and spat on the floor. "Grubb, can't you keep your eye on any of your charges? Christ on a donkey, man, what's wrong with you?" The Justice pulled back the curtain and dropped it again. "Benjamin Davies is bringing the bodies."

Catherine started for the door, but Sillon snagged her elbow. "Don't. Let them be taken to your home before you."

She could see the two forms being laid on the grass by Havenston men. Benjamin stood between them.

"You will not bring the soldier to Overton House," said Catherine. "He can be taken to the church." One of the men outdoors covered Adam Hastings' face with a handkerchief. She turned away. "You can throw him on a dungheap for all I care."

The priest went out, spoke to Benjamin, and pointed southward, toward the little church. Two men took up the limp remains of Hastings and carried him out. Two others followed Benjamin with the body of William Overton. They turned north at the gate and met Joseph, who'd come from the constable's house. He was leading the ladies' horses, and behind him was Eleanor with the baby in her arms. Geoffrey White, shackled and led by two watchmen, was with them.

Catherine could not stop herself from going out. "Where is she, Geoffrey?"

"Don't ask me. I say nothing more after today. Got my head in a noose now for speaking to her ever."

"She gave the order, didn't she? Say it, Geoffrey."

But Geoffrey White shook his head, and the watchmen led him toward the constable's house. He did not look back.

Benjamin was leading Caesar through Grubb's front gate and he passed the little group without raising his head. He watched his feet walk toward the inn and stopped just before her. He finally looked up. "Let me take you home, Catherine."

"What home?" Catherine asked. The road was still full of people. "What home is there?"

"Your home," said Benjamin.

She let him lift her onto her saddle. The ride to Overton House was silent, and the place seemed cold and dark. Catherine gave her reins to Joseph in the courtyard and threw off her riding cloak in the front hall. Eleanor was already there, holding out the baby.

"She's all pink in the face again, Madam. Veronica. She's pretty as an angel and hungry as a pup."

Catherine stumbled up to her chamber, loosened her bodice, and put Veronica to her breast. The baby nuzzled against her skin and Catherine began to weep. Eleanor slid onto the stool by the hearth and waited.

"You see, she eats as she should," said Catherine, wiping her nose. The baby's face stared up at her. "Child, child," she said, and the tears came again. Veronica put her small hand up and touched her mother's wet face.

"Madam?" asked Eleanor gently. "What will happen now?"

"I don't know." She offered the other breast to Veronica, and when the baby was finished suckling, Catherine handed her over to Eleanor. "I suppose I had better go find out."

Father John had ridden behind them, and he sat with Benjamin in the long gallery, a bottle between them. Reg hovered at the side door, and Catherine waved him in.

"You have found your way back," she said.

"As my master could not," said Reg. "Will you send me off now?"

John Bridle and Benjamin sat unmoving.

"You will stay," said Catherine, "if you choose."

Reginald bowed from the waist. "I am yours, Madam." Then he slipped backward through the doorway.

The two men at the table raised their glasses. "Sit with us, Catherine," said John Bridle, "as it seems we have already helped ourselves to your stores."

She sat and took a glass of wine. It tasted like dark flowers, like night, and she drank deeply. "What is left, Father? Benjamin, have you two been planning your great empire of wool-making in the old convent buildings? Will you be kings of the woolens?" It was unaccountably funny, and she laughed, but the sound was a little mad, and she swallowed it.

"We will have the new draperies in Mount Grace," said Father John. His face was flushed. He was maybe drunk. "The plans are already made. I will oversee the work." Catherine looked from her father to Benjamin. "What has been decided here?"

"Nothing new," said Benjamin. "The land is yours, Catherine. The house is yours. The leases will be yours. You can oversee the work yourself if you want."

"Margaret will claim that the house is hers." Catherine pushed her glass forward and Benjamin filled it again. She drank, studying the men over the rim. Father John was scrutinizing the beams across the ceiling. Benjamin began cleaning his nails with the tip of his hand knife. Catherine slapped the glass down onto the table, and its base cracked. "Margaret has been the hand working all of these puppets, and she will not be held to account for it."

Benjamin said, "You will be wanted back at Hatfield House."

"You have seen to managing my departure, have you?"

He poured. "No. You may manage yourself." He tried to pour himself another glass and found the bottle empty. He called for another, and soft soles in the next room scuffled away.

Catherine felt the storm in her belly clear off. The late sun was falling in broken pieces through the windows, and casting the specters of leaves and limbs over the table. "It's no wonder that he was unable to heal," she said to the shadows. "He was sick in body and soul. He must have known. Surely after he found the pouch."

"She is monstrous," said Father John.

"But with William gone, there is no one to give proofs against her," said Catherine.

Father John said, "When she is found, Sillon will make her talk."

But Margaret Overton was not found, not that day or the next or the next. She did not appear for the small funeral that laid William beside his brother and his father in the family tomb. She did not appear when Geoffrey White was sentenced to hanging. She did not appear at the hasty marriage of Eleanor and

Joseph.

The morning after the wedding, the couple followed Catherine on a walk through the fields and stables that surrounded Overton House. They ended at the falcon houses, and Catherine put her hand on the latch. "We will free them now." The birds hunched inside, sullen and frayed, neglect sitting like dust on their feathers.

"No, Madam," said Joseph, staying her hand. "If I may, I will tend them. Your father will be my guide."

Catherine hesitated. "Very well, then." She regarded the bedraggled birds. "Perhaps something can be brought back to health here."

"And what will we call ourselves?" asked Joseph. "Will we still be Overton House? After all of this business?"

"For now," said Catherine, "though Havens House might do as well."

Joseph and Eleanor exchanged a quick glance. "So we will be Havens House over Havenston then?" asked Eleanor.

"We'll see," said Catherine. "There is no telling what the future will bring in this country."

65

The road back to Hatfield House was stormy the first day, the clouds lying low-bellied over them most of the way. Agnes was carrying Veronica strapped to her chest, and when the rain came late in the afternoon, the little party of riders stopped at an inn. Benjamin ordered food while Catherine stretched her bones and nursed the baby. Agnes trailed after her, and they sat at a window in their cramped room upstairs, waiting for the call to dine. Catherine had brought her Christine de Pizan, and she read a little out loud. "She says here that a wife must put aside 'womanly timidity' and strengthen her heart with 'manly courage.'"

"It's a hard charge in this world, Madam," said Agnes.

"Indeed." The rain swept over the fields like grey curtains, and sparrows swooped in, under the eaves. Two of them began sparring in the air, wings beating each other as they vied for dominance. "They are just like us," Catherine murmured.

"Mm?" Agnes had slumped on her low stool.

"The birds. Someone must always be king."

The girl leaned forward dutifully to look, but the loser had already settled for a lower place. "At least they leave off before they kill each other," Catherine said.

The summons came, and the women joined the men downstairs. The roast beef was fine, and the ale was strong, but Catherine had little appetite and stirred her food around the trencher with a hunk of bread. The storm came in force, and she went to bed early, lying on the straw mattress listening to the slapping of the rain against the thatch. Agnes, sleeping on a cot on the other side of the room, began snoring softly late in the night. Toward daybreak, the sky cleared and a wedge of moon sat heavy outside the window. In the gloom Catherine could see the rafters over her head, but they looked like nothing so much as the frame of a scaffold.

She rode the next day and the next in a cloudy daze, though the July sun was high and fierce, and the fields steamed a bold green. Benjamin rode before her without speaking, and Agnes carried the baby covered to protect her skin. Reginald Goodall rode with Benjamin, as naturally as if they had always been together.

The news of Margaret Overton's disappearance had preceded them to Hatfield House, and Lady Shelton stood in the front door with a tight mouth when they rode up. Sir John pushed past her to greet Benjamin, who handed his reins over, helped Catherine to the ground, and walked inside, head inclined to speak privately.

Ann Smith was holding little Robert Overton by the hand, but he broke free when he saw his mother and ran. She squatted to gather him into her arms. "Are you home then, Mother?" he said against her neck. "I have prayed for you every night."

"As I have for you, Robbie."

Ann watched Reg dismount and stand by Benjamin's horse, one hand out. His eyes slid over. He winked. A blush streaked up Ann's face, and she smiled. Then she stepped over to Agnes, unstrapped the baby, and gazed into the small face. Catherine set down her son and curtsied. "Lady Shelton."

"Rise up, Catherine Havens Overton." Catherine had expected a harsh tone, but Lady Shelton's voice was velvet. "You are now a great lady with a great estate. Let me see the baby."

Ann turned back the blanket, and Lady Shelton clucked. "She's grown. And look at that hair." She fingered the curly red fluff. "The Lady Elizabeth will be delighted to have her doll again."

"And I will be glad to serve her," said Catherine.

They passed into the house. A lady's maid took Catherine's traveling cloak and hood and hesitated a moment, listening. "Go," said Lady Shelton, and the girl trotted off. "News travels fast enough these days," she said, watching. "We needn't give it wings to help it along."

"So you have heard." Catherine glanced into the gallery, where Benjamin stood in close conversation with Sir John.

They saw her and came quickly forward. "Master Davies will ride on to his own house," said Sir John.

Benjamin stepped forward and bowed. "If you need my services, Lady Overton, I will come at a word from you."

Before she could answer, Lady Shelton said, "Ah, here is Kat. She is to be the Lady Elizabeth's governess."

Kate Champernowne came sweeping down the big stairs and held Catherine by the shoulders to embrace her without mashing Veronica. Catherine tried to curtsey, but the other woman held her up. "Your room is ready. Marry, your skirt is more dirt than wool."

"Sodden through," said Catherine. "We rode into a storm and I never felt I could get the clouds out of me."

"You have been through a tempest in truth," said Lady Shelton. "But we will clean you up. Come." They steered her up the stairs, and she barely had time for one backward look. Benjamin was already walking out the front door. Reg followed close behind him.

The men had brought Catherine's bags and cases to the room already, and the ewer was filled with fresh water. Kat and Ann unpacked the clothes while Catherine bathed. "Ah, God, I'm filthy," she said, laying the baby in the cradle and untying her sleeves. A clean basin had never looked better, and she splashed her face.

"She will not be hanged then? Like the servant?" asked Kat, sitting beside Catherine.

"I doubt it."

"Where in the world can she be?"

"She took her maid and two man servants." Catherine rubbed her sweating hairline. "There are many places a woman can hide if she wants to disappear badly enough." She wiped her face hard.

Agnes ducked in and shut the door. "Let me undress you, Madam," she said, but Catherine waved her off. "I will tend to myself tonight." Agnes nodded and disappeared into her own small quarters.

Catherine untied the bodice and let the heavy skirt drop to the floor. She stepped out of it and toed it aside so that she could wipe her neck and arms clean. When the water was brown, she hung the towel on the edge of the ewer.

"And who will govern your properties in his absence?" asked Kat.

Catherine said, "My father. And I have left Eleanor and Joseph. They're married."

"Then all is well. A murderer is found out, and you are back with us, Lady Overton. Or Lady Havens, perhaps. You will begin again to people your city of ladies."

"And Margaret Overton lurks somewhere," Ann said, folding the skirt yet again. No one had an answer for that.

Ann gathered up the sleeves and bodice for a brushing down in the laundry, and when they were alone, Kat said, "There is another who would like to greet you before you sleep."

"I had hoped so." Catherine swiftly pulled a fresh skirt and bodice from her chest, and Kat tied up the back for her. She checked her hood for neatness, and went to the other chamber alone.

The door opened at her first knock, and the maid stepped back to let her into the dark room. Mary Tudor was kneeling at her small prayer bench, the beads unconcealed in her hand.

"Lady Mary," said Catherine, curtseying low.

"Catherine. How pleased I am to see you return safe. I have heard much of your business in the North. You are now a widow."

Catherine chanced a look up. "It has been a dark night of the soul, Your Grace."

Mary hovered over her. "But you have prevailed, I see, against heavy odds and come again into the daytime. And you will now be the only Lady of your house. Do you wager, Lady Catherine Havens Overton?"

Catherine said, "I have always put my faith in my own senses and in God." She mused a few seconds. "It has always seemed to me good to gamble on truth."

Mary took Catherine's hands in her own and drew her up. The jeweled rings pressed into Catherine's fingers, making her heart gallop with pain, but she did not pull away.

"We are something alike, Catherine Havens. This island of England will be honest again, mark me. We will bring it back to the true God. You will be grand now, and you will stand by my side. You have a great house, but with me, you are home."

"My Lady, I have sworn my loyalty to you."

The sun broke against the trees in the west, and a yellow shaft shot into the room. The king's elder daughter smiled. "I vow that I will bring the truth back to the people of England. I will turn them from these false men. A woman will bring us again to our glory. It is my dream." The gold fretting in her heavy hood seemed to catch fire in the bloody light, and the dark eyes of Mary Tudor glittered and sparked.

About the Author

Sarah Kennedy is a professor of English at Mary Baldwin College in Staunton, Virginia and the author of seven books of poems. She holds a PhD in Renaissance Literature and an MFA in Creative Writing. Sarah has received grants from both the National Endowment for the Arts and the Virginia Commission for the Arts and is currently a contributing editor for Shenandoah. Visit Sarah's website at http://sarahkennedybooks.com